BEWARE THE CLAW!

By TODD GOLDMAN

TO MY ONE AND ONLY HERO:
MY DAUGHTER ELLE, WHO LIKE THE
HOUND HEROES, IS ALSO HOUSEBROKEN.

- TODD

Library of Congress Cataloging-in-Publication Data Available

ISBN: 978-1-338-64847-8 (hardcover)
ISBN: 978-1-338-64846-1 (paperback)

10 9 8 7 6 5 4 3 2 1   21 22 23 24 25

Printed in China   62

First edition, January 2021
Edited by Kristin Earhart and Michael Petranek
Lettering by Jessie Gang
Book design by Veronica Mang

THE HOUNDS

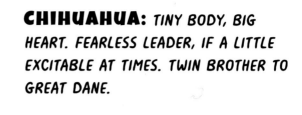

CHIHUAHUA: *TINY BODY, BIG HEART. FEARLESS LEADER, IF A LITTLE EXCITABLE AT TIMES. TWIN BROTHER TO GREAT DANE.*

GREAT DANE: *LOYAL AND KIND. EMOTIONAL AND A BIT OF A WORRYWART. TWIN BROTHER TO CHIHUAHUA.*

POODLE: *ACTIVE AND STRONG, SHE'D RATHER BE MUDDY AND MUCKY THAN PRIM AND PROPER.*

PUG: *THE BRAINS OF THE GANG. QUIET, BUT NOT SHY. SHE'S ALWAYS READY FOR ADVENTURE.*

SHEEPDOG: *LIGHTHEARTED, CAREFREE, AND ALWAYS READY TO PLAY PLAY PLAY!*

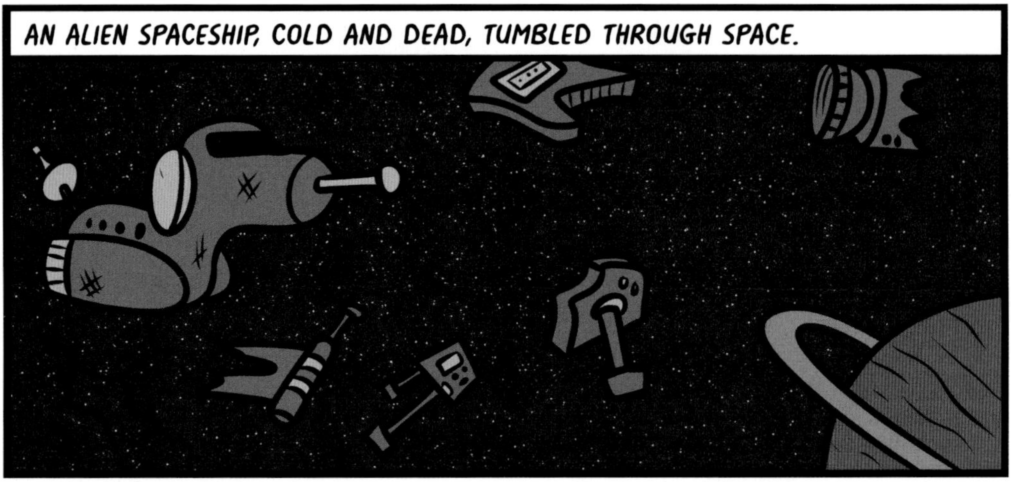
AN ALIEN SPACESHIP, COLD AND DEAD, TUMBLED THROUGH SPACE.

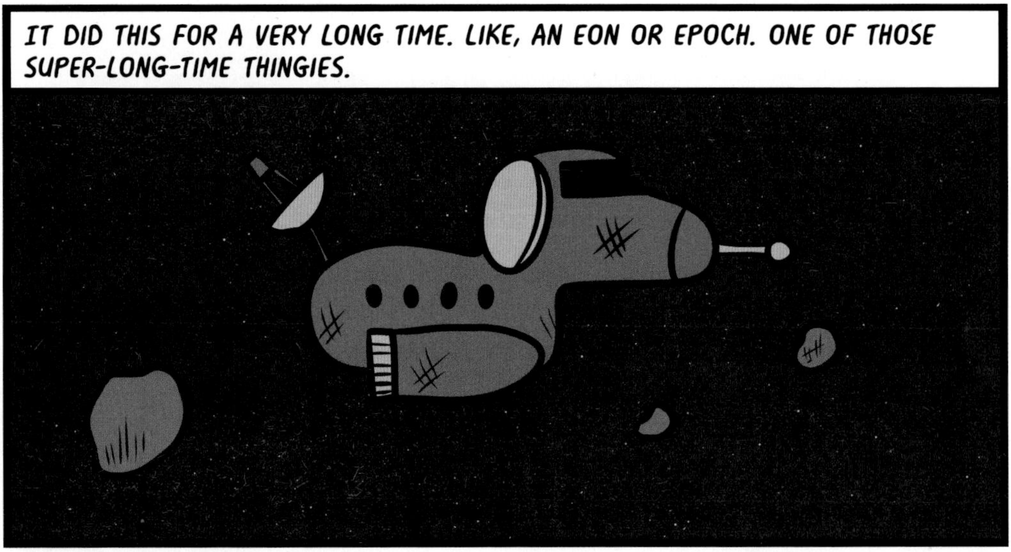
IT DID THIS FOR A VERY LONG TIME. LIKE, AN EON OR EPOCH. ONE OF THOSE SUPER-LONG-TIME THINGIES.

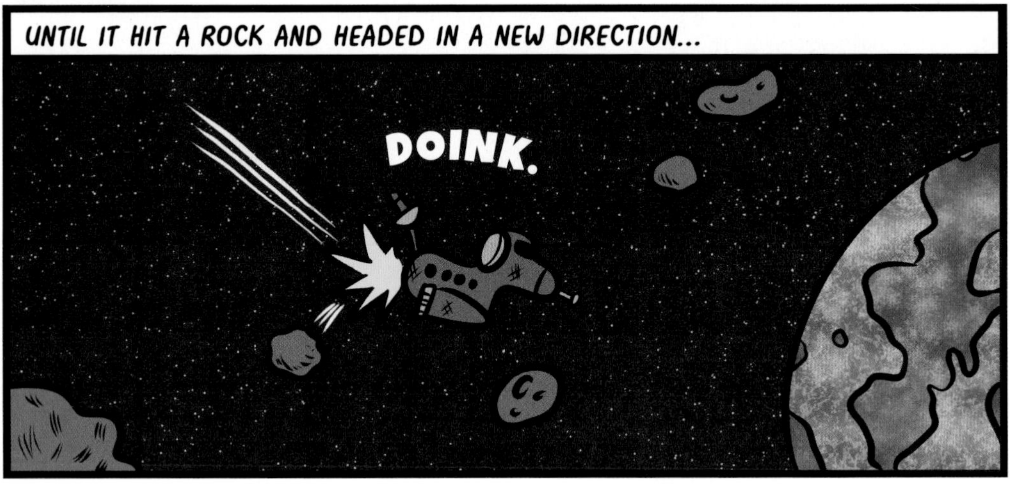
UNTIL IT HIT A ROCK AND HEADED IN A NEW DIRECTION...
DOINK.

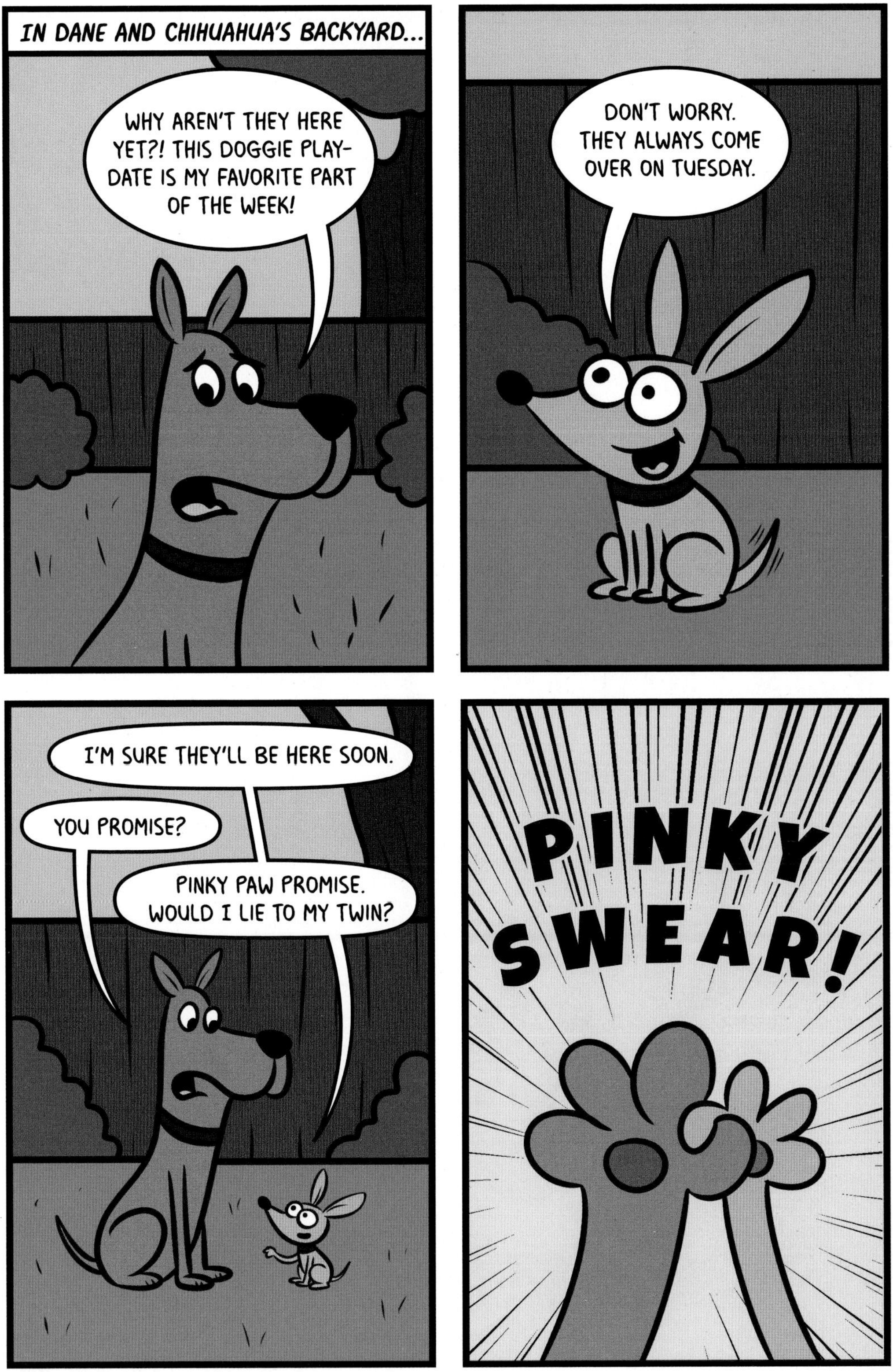
IN DANE AND CHIHUAHUA'S BACKYARD...
WHY AREN'T THEY HERE YET?! THIS DOGGIE PLAY-DATE IS MY FAVORITE PART OF THE WEEK!
DON'T WORRY. THEY ALWAYS COME OVER ON TUESDAY.
I'M SURE THEY'LL BE HERE SOON.
YOU PROMISE?
PINKY PAW PROMISE. WOULD I LIE TO MY TWIN?
PINKY SWEAR!

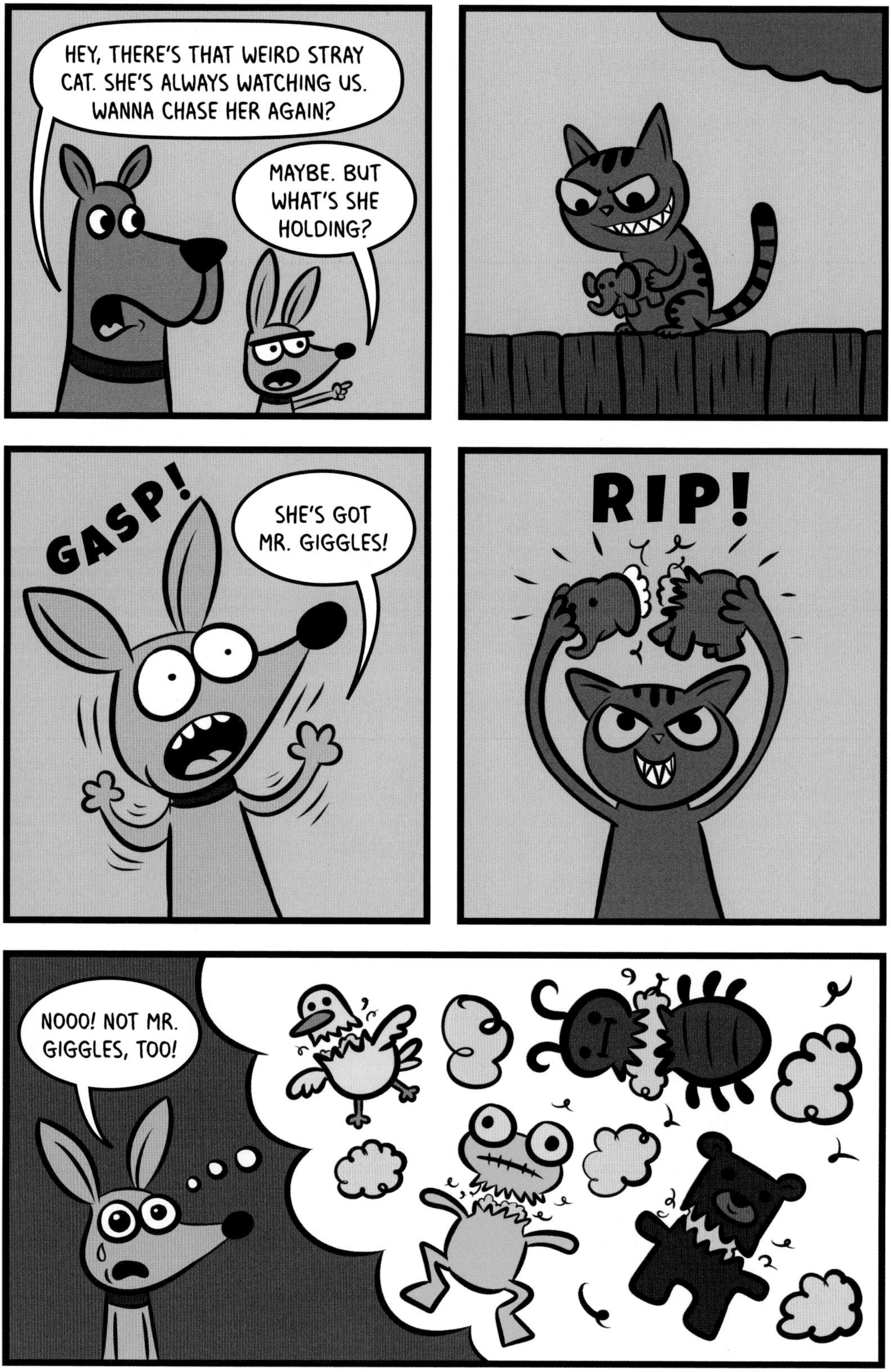
HEY, THERE'S THAT WEIRD STRAY CAT. SHE'S ALWAYS WATCHING US. WANNA CHASE HER AGAIN?
MAYBE. BUT WHAT'S SHE HOLDING?
GASP!
SHE'S GOT MR. GIGGLES!
RIP!
NOOO! NOT MR. GIGGLES, TOO!

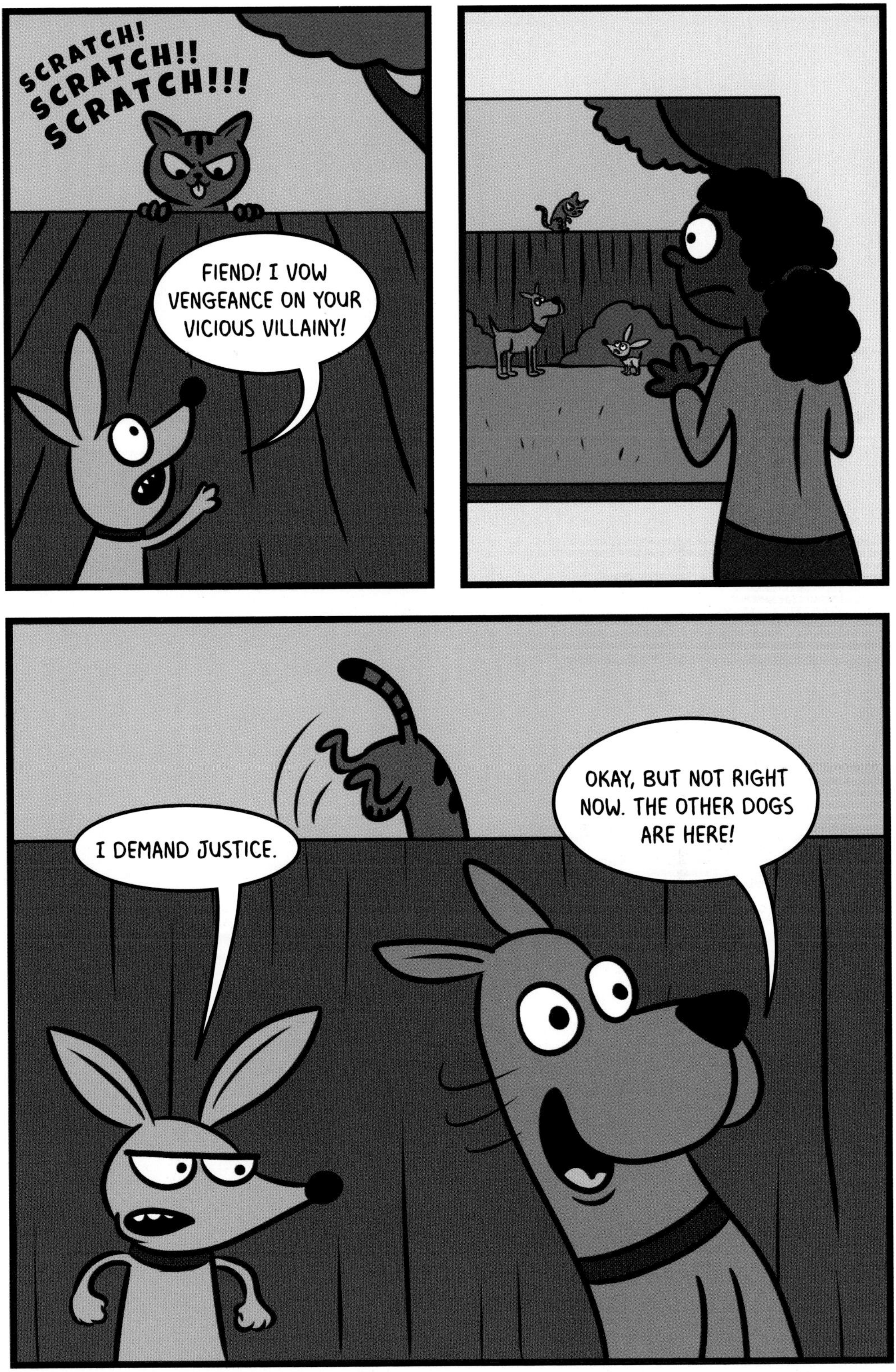
SCRATCH!
SCRATCH!!
SCRATCH!!!
FIEND! I VOW VENGEANCE ON YOUR VICIOUS VILLAINY!
I DEMAND JUSTICE.
OKAY, BUT NOT RIGHT NOW. THE OTHER DOGS ARE HERE!

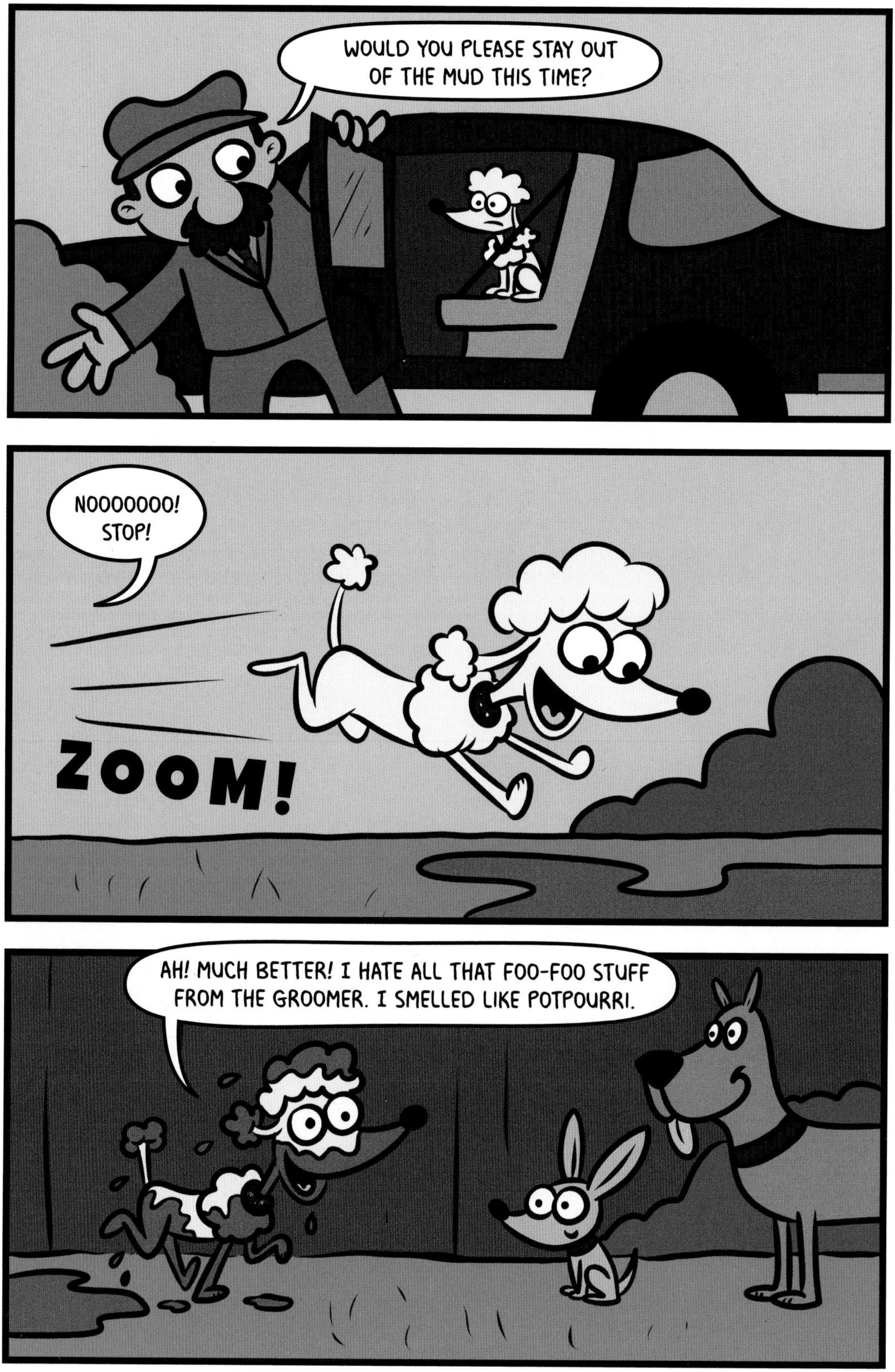
WOULD YOU PLEASE STAY OUT OF THE MUD THIS TIME?
NOOOOOOO! STOP!
ZOOM!
AH! MUCH BETTER! I HATE ALL THAT FOO-FOO STUFF FROM THE GROOMER. I SMELLED LIKE POTPOURRI.

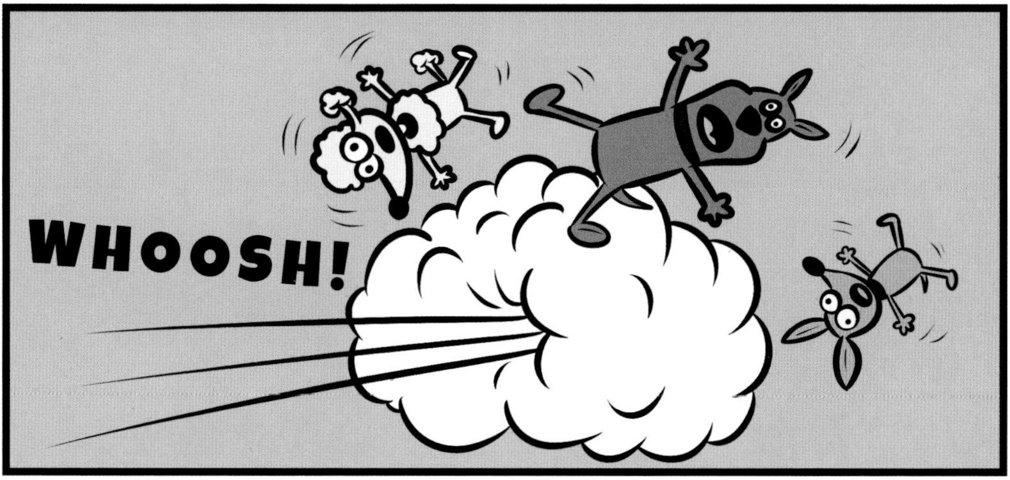
WHOOSH!

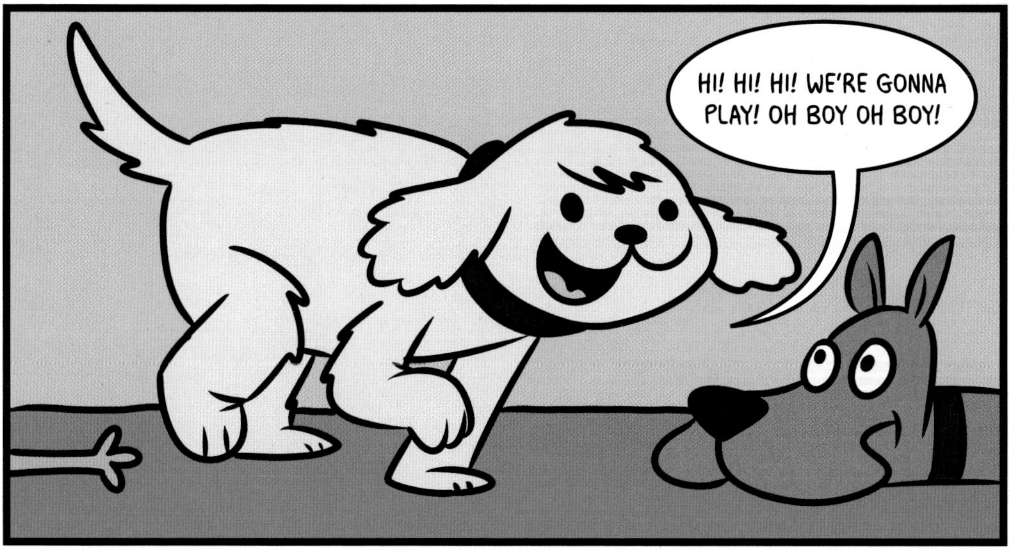
HI! HI! HI! WE'RE GONNA PLAY! OH BOY OH BOY!

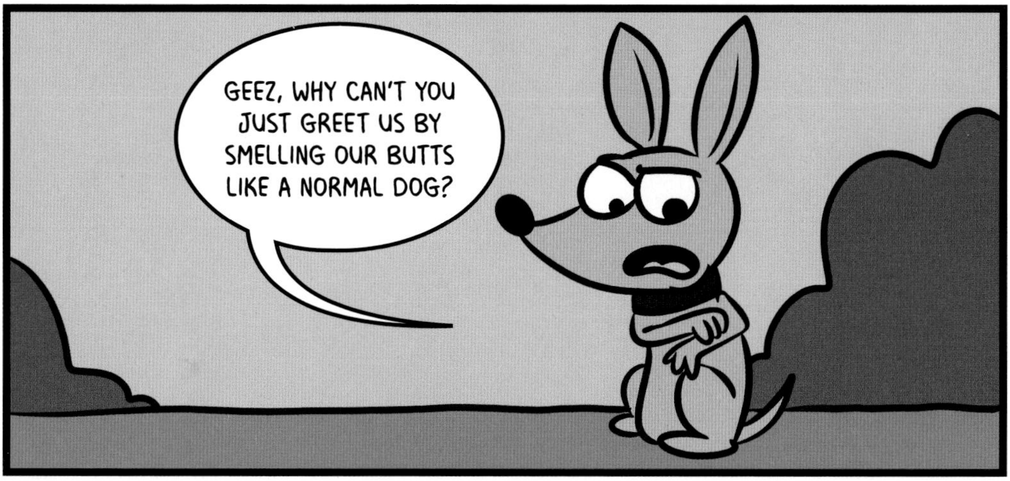
GEEZ, WHY CAN'T YOU JUST GREET US BY SMELLING OUR BUTTS LIKE A NORMAL DOG?

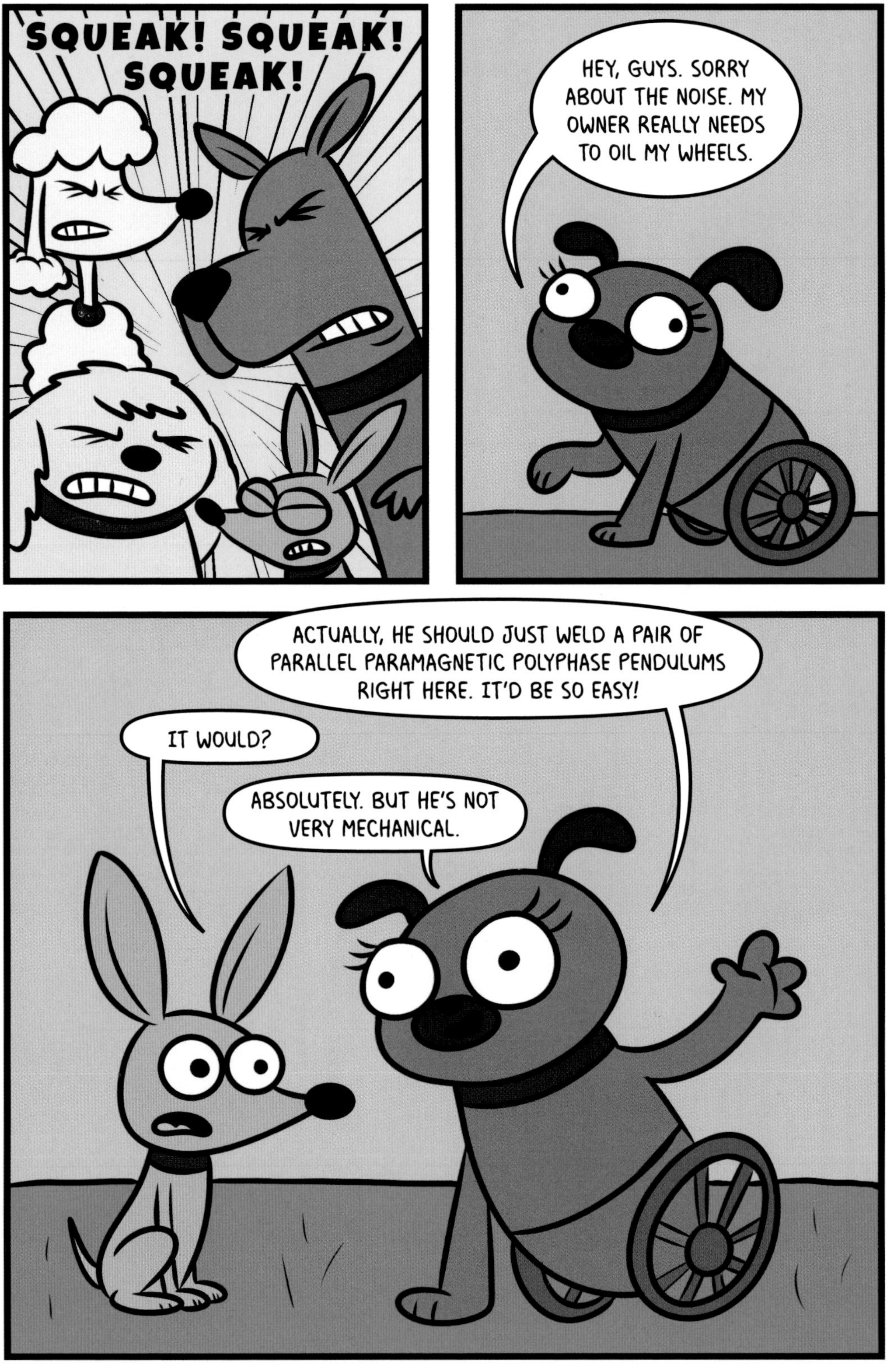
SQUEAK! SQUEAK! SQUEAK!
HEY, GUYS. SORRY ABOUT THE NOISE. MY OWNER REALLY NEEDS TO OIL MY WHEELS.
ACTUALLY, HE SHOULD JUST WELD A PAIR OF PARALLEL PARAMAGNETIC POLYPHASE PENDULUMS RIGHT HERE. IT'D BE SO EASY!
IT WOULD?
ABSOLUTELY. BUT HE'S NOT VERY MECHANICAL.

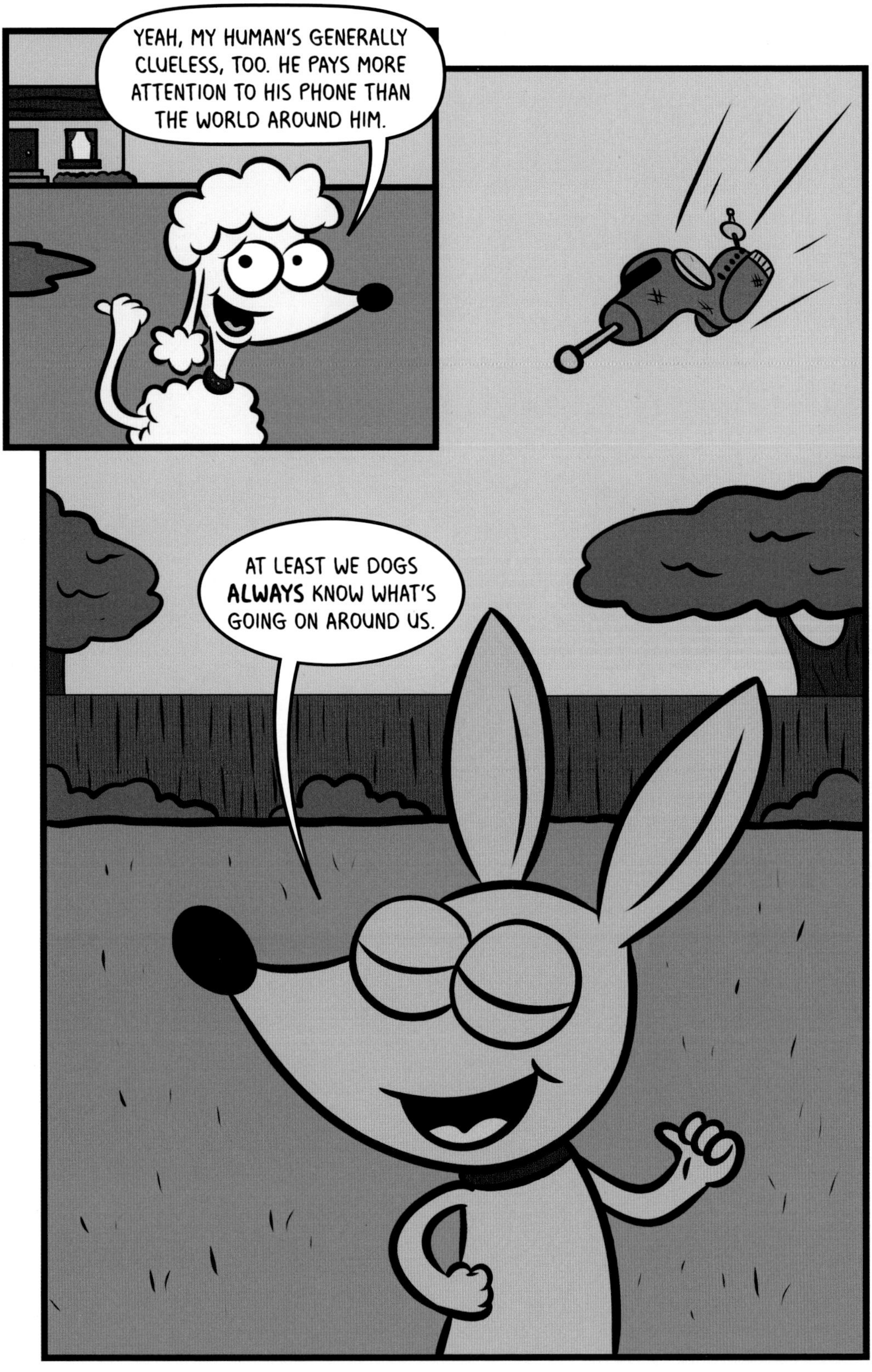
YEAH, MY HUMAN'S GENERALLY CLUELESS, TOO. HE PAYS MORE ATTENTION TO HIS PHONE THAN THE WORLD AROUND HIM.
AT LEAST WE DOGS **ALWAYS** KNOW WHAT'S GOING ON AROUND US.

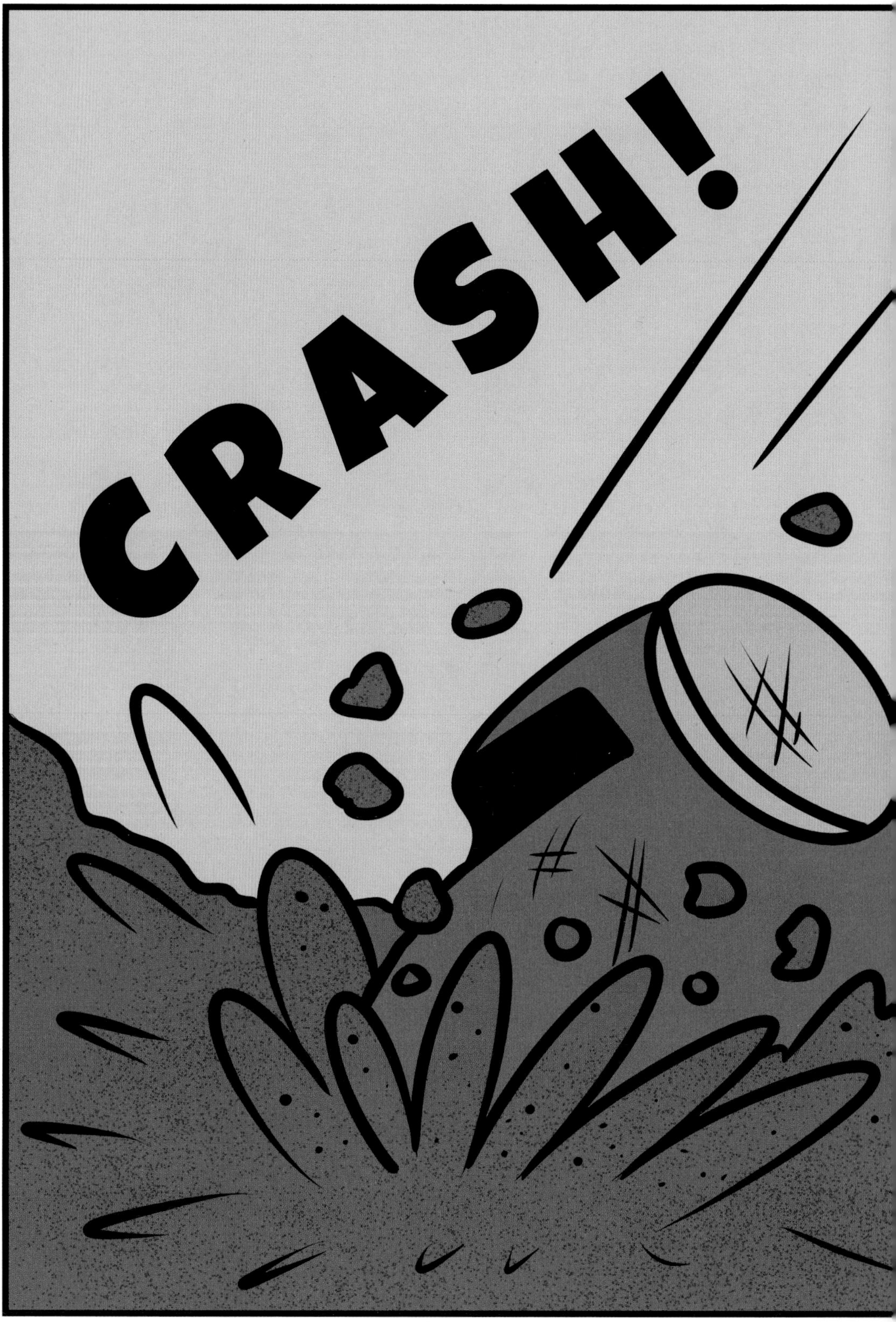
CRASH!

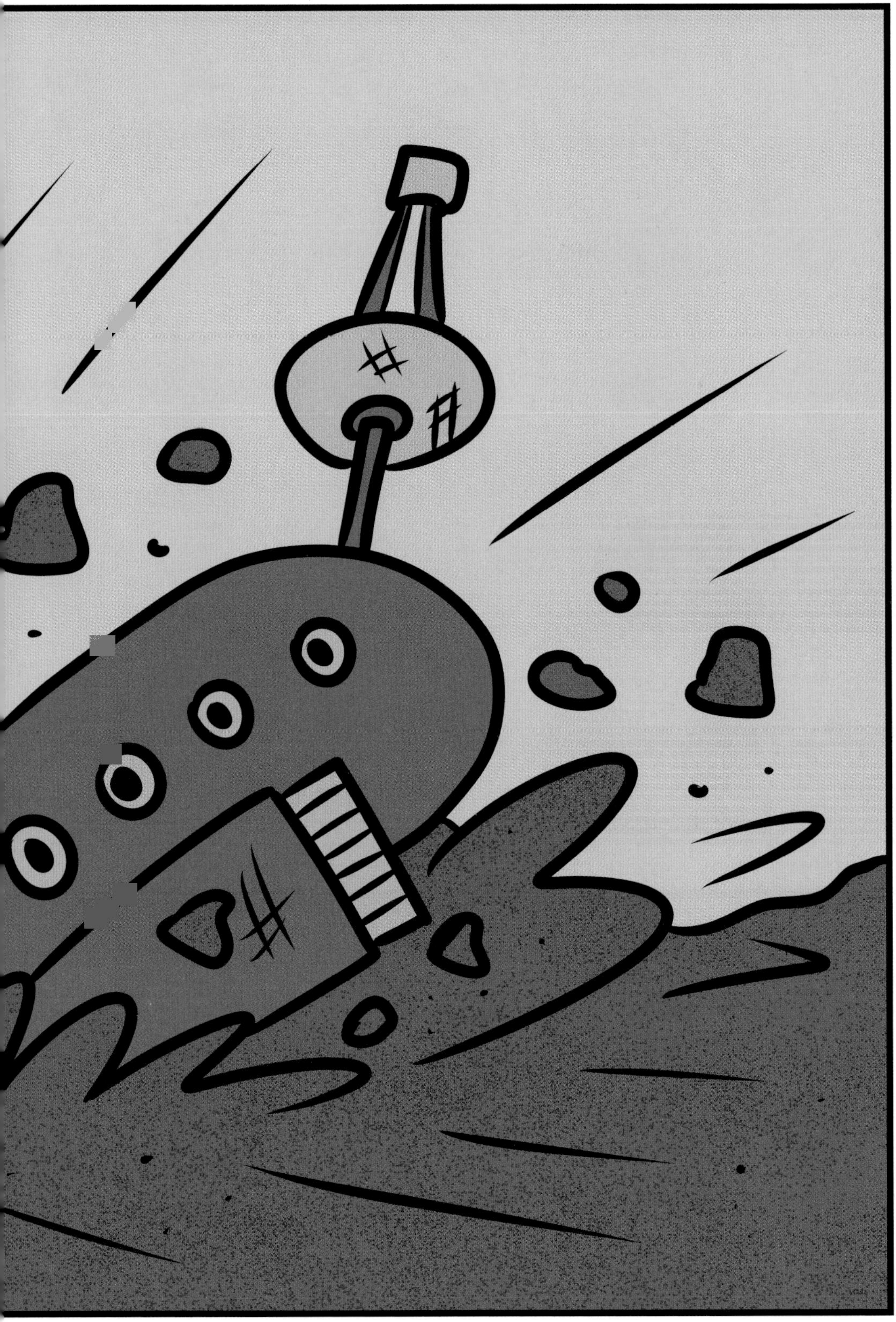

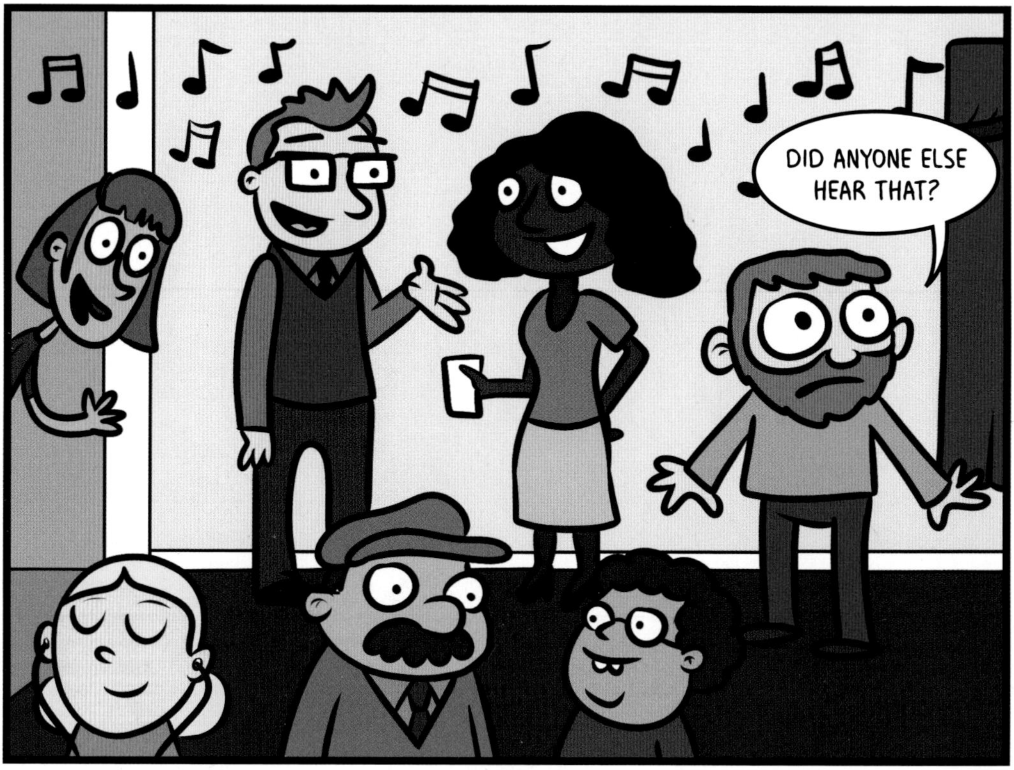
DID ANYONE ELSE HEAR THAT?

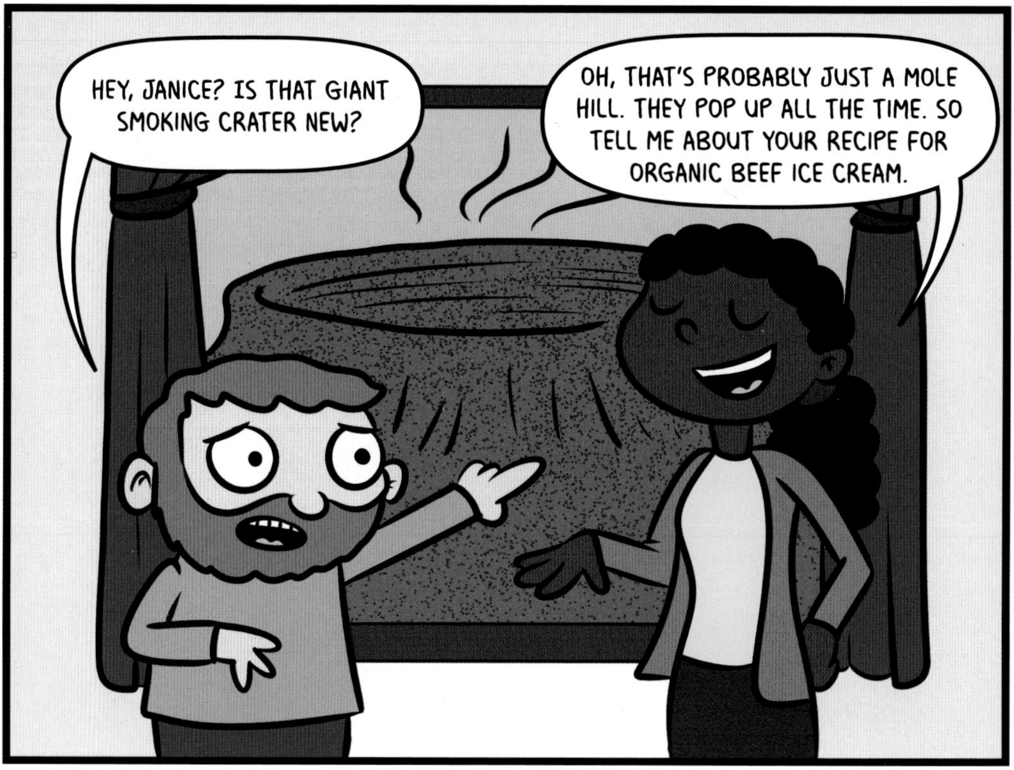
HEY, JANICE? IS THAT GIANT SMOKING CRATER NEW?
OH, THAT'S PROBABLY JUST A MOLE HILL. THEY POP UP ALL THE TIME. SO TELL ME ABOUT YOUR RECIPE FOR ORGANIC BEEF ICE CREAM.

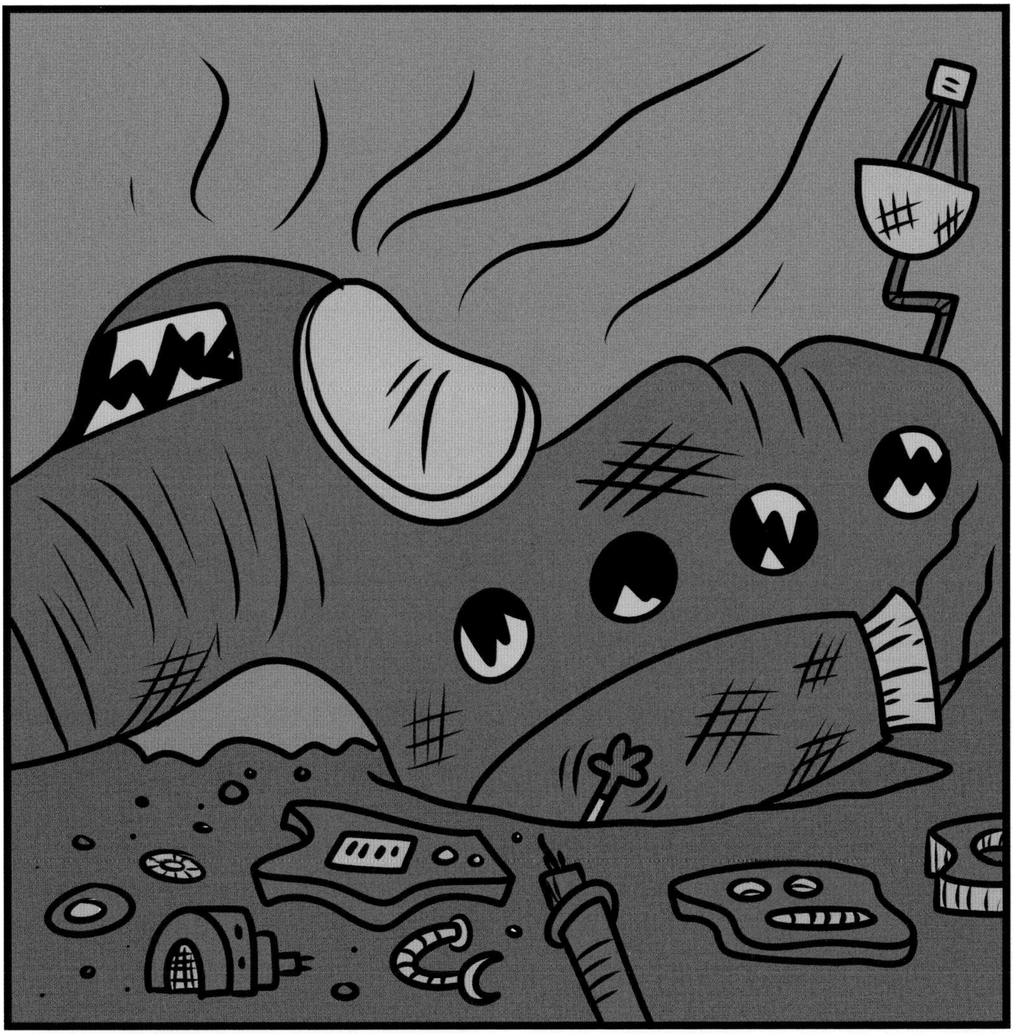

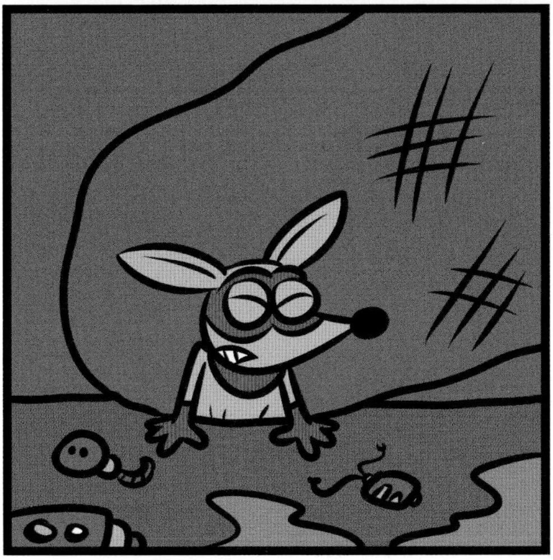

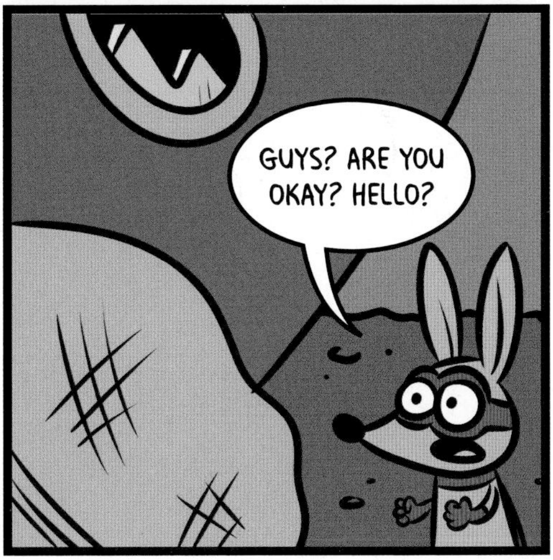
GUYS? ARE YOU OKAY? HELLO?

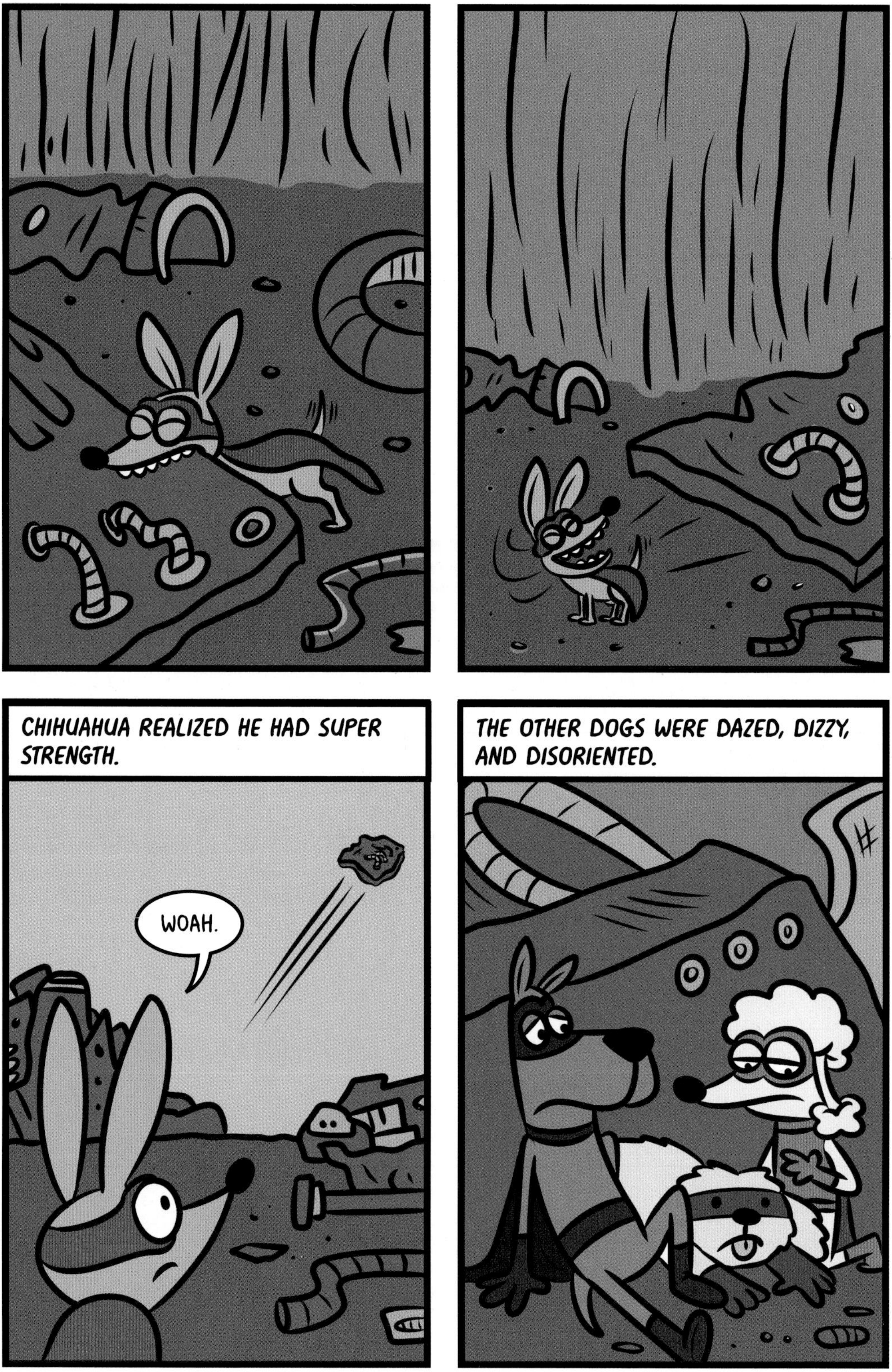
CHIHUAHUA REALIZED HE HAD SUPER STRENGTH.
WOAH.
THE OTHER DOGS WERE DAZED, DIZZY, AND DISORIENTED.

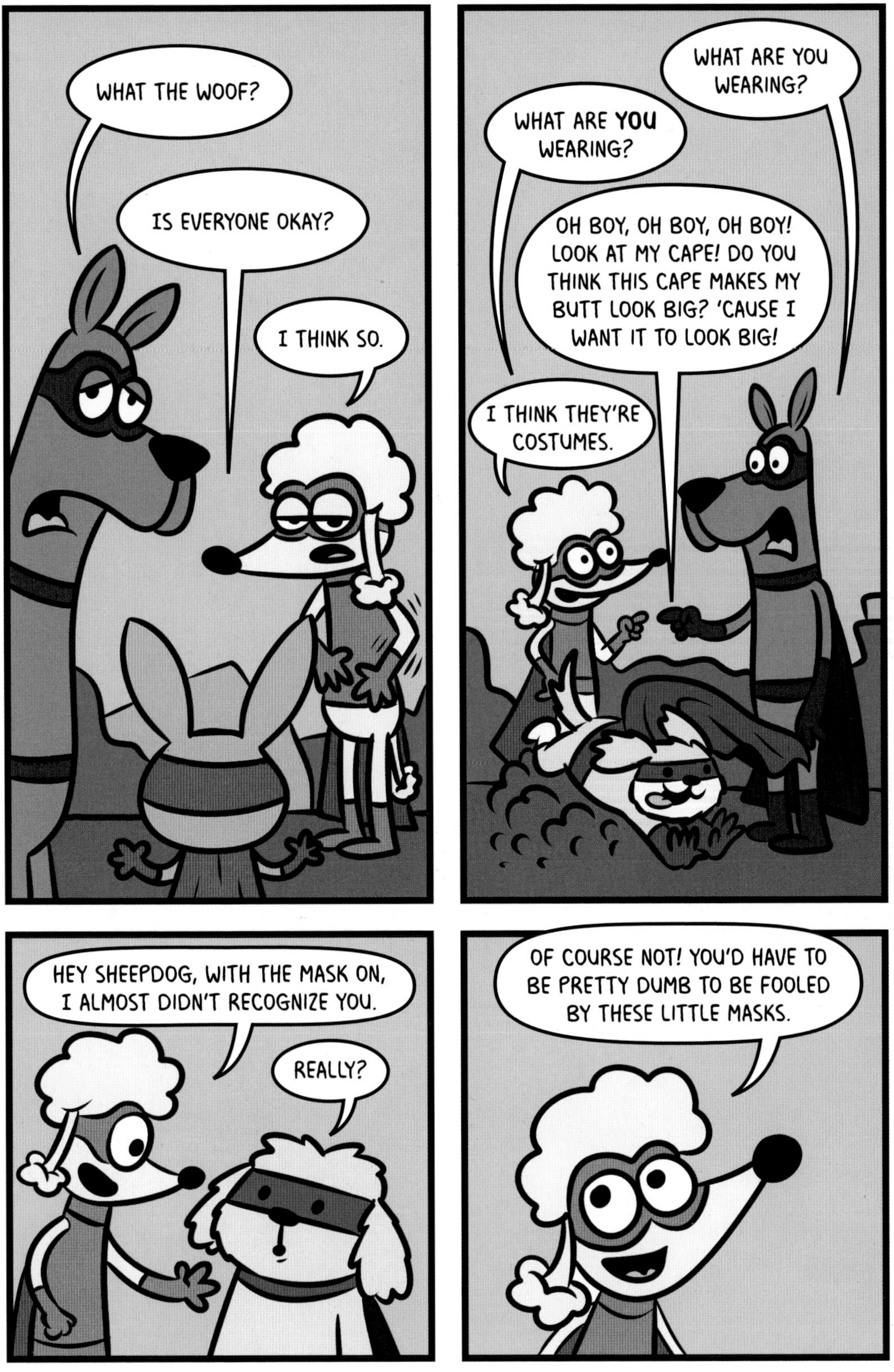
WHAT THE WOOF?
IS EVERYONE OKAY?
I THINK SO.
WHAT ARE YOU WEARING?
WHAT ARE YOU WEARING?
OH BOY, OH BOY, OH BOY! LOOK AT MY CAPE! DO YOU THINK THIS CAPE MAKES MY BUTT LOOK BIG? 'CAUSE I WANT IT TO LOOK BIG!
I THINK THEY'RE COSTUMES.
HEY SHEEPDOG, WITH THE MASK ON, I ALMOST DIDN'T RECOGNIZE YOU.
REALLY?
OF COURSE NOT! YOU'D HAVE TO BE PRETTY DUMB TO BE FOOLED BY THESE LITTLE MASKS.

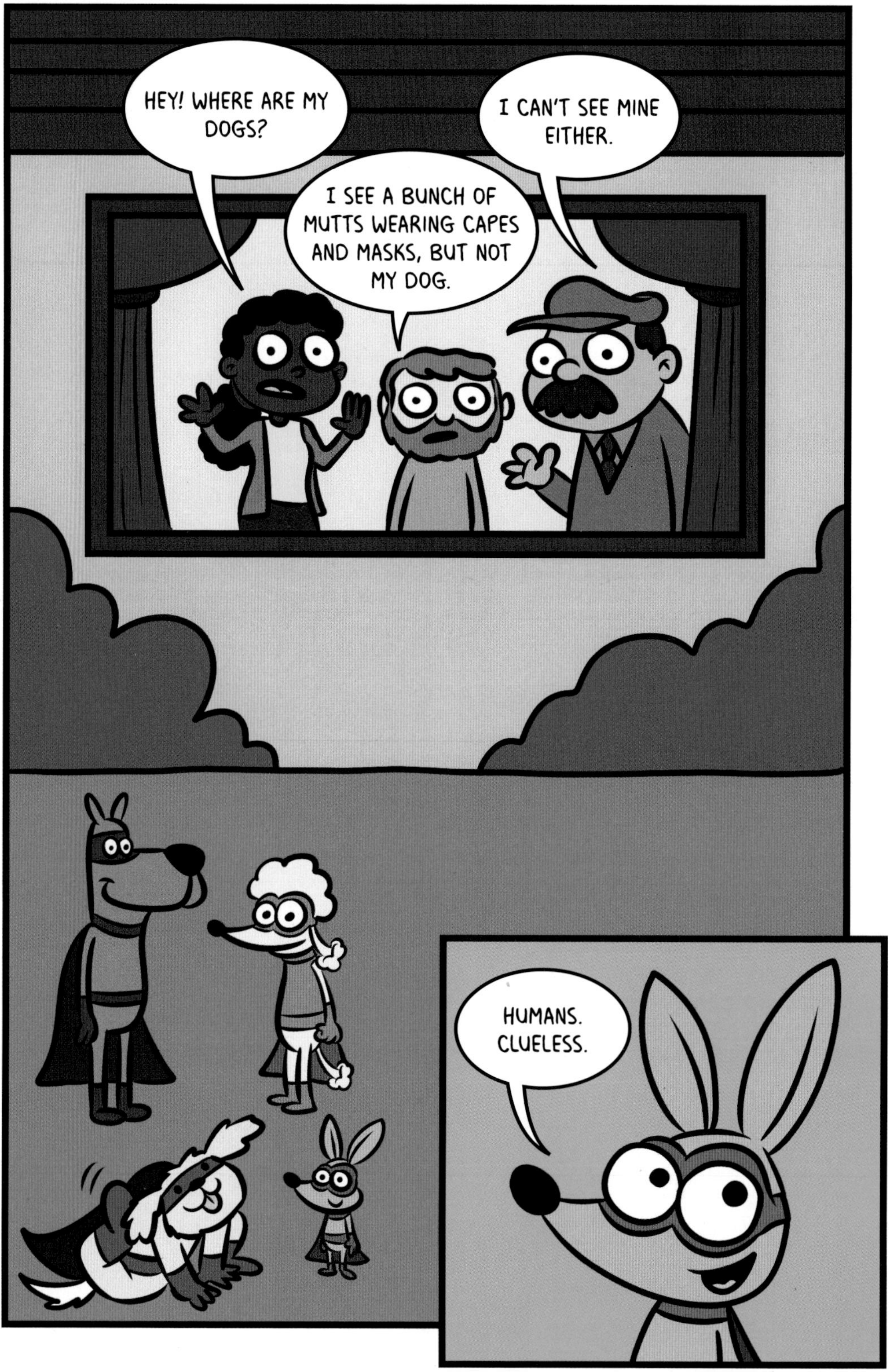
HEY! WHERE ARE MY DOGS?
I SEE A BUNCH OF MUTTS WEARING CAPES AND MASKS, BUT NOT MY DOG.
I CAN'T SEE MINE EITHER.
HUMANS. CLUELESS.

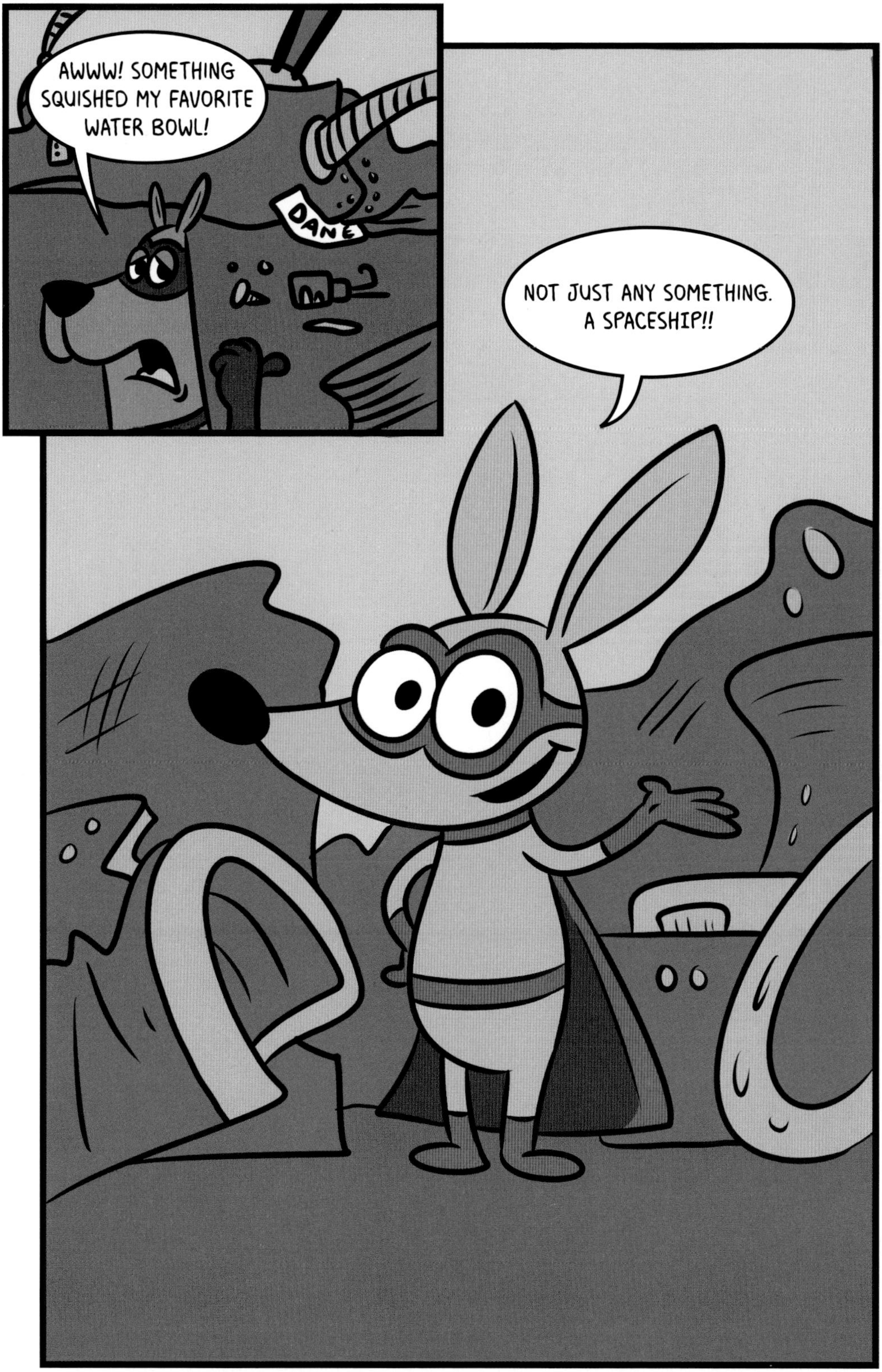
AWWW! SOMETHING SQUISHED MY FAVORITE WATER BOWL!
DANE
NOT JUST ANY SOMETHING. A SPACESHIP!!

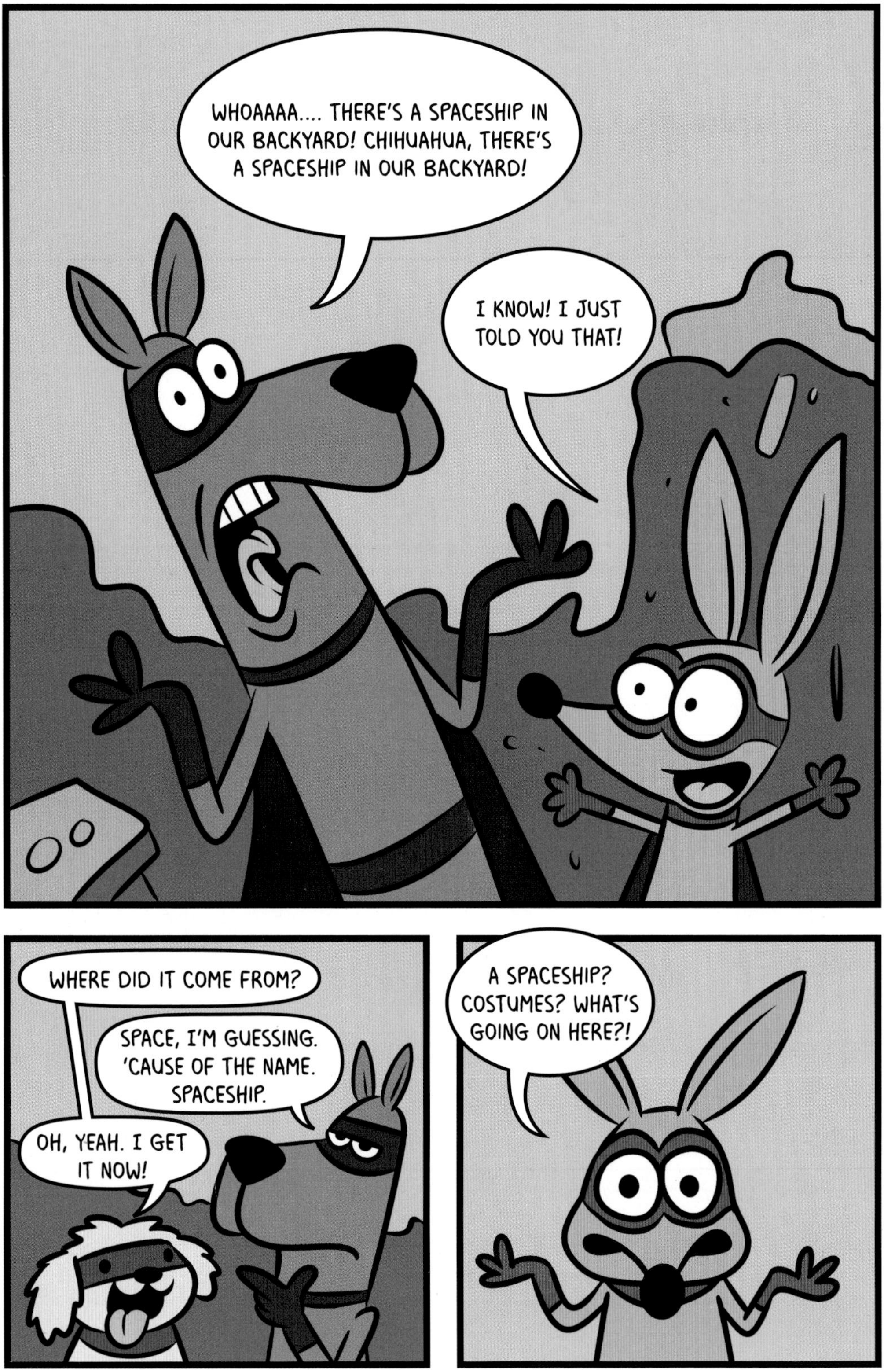
WHOAAAA.... THERE'S A SPACESHIP IN OUR BACKYARD! CHIHUAHUA, THERE'S A SPACESHIP IN OUR BACKYARD!
I KNOW! I JUST TOLD YOU THAT!
WHERE DID IT COME FROM?
SPACE, I'M GUESSING. 'CAUSE OF THE NAME. SPACESHIP.
OH, YEAH. I GET IT NOW!
A SPACESHIP? COSTUMES? WHAT'S GOING ON HERE?!

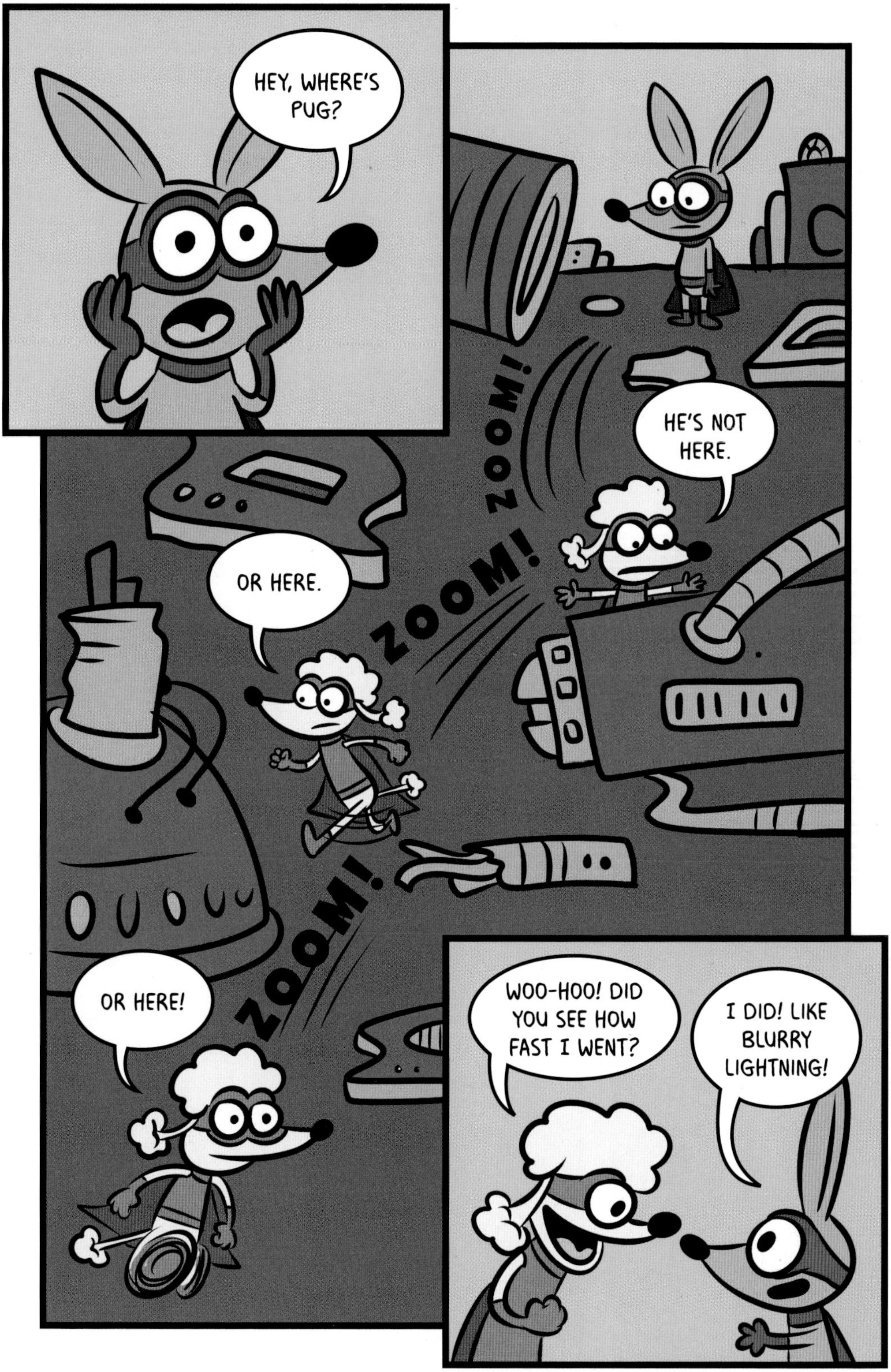
HEY, WHERE'S PUG?
HE'S NOT HERE.
ZOOM! ZOOM!
OR HERE.
ZOOM! ZOOM!
OR HERE!
WOO-HOO! DID YOU SEE HOW FAST I WENT?
I DID! LIKE BLURRY LIGHTNING!

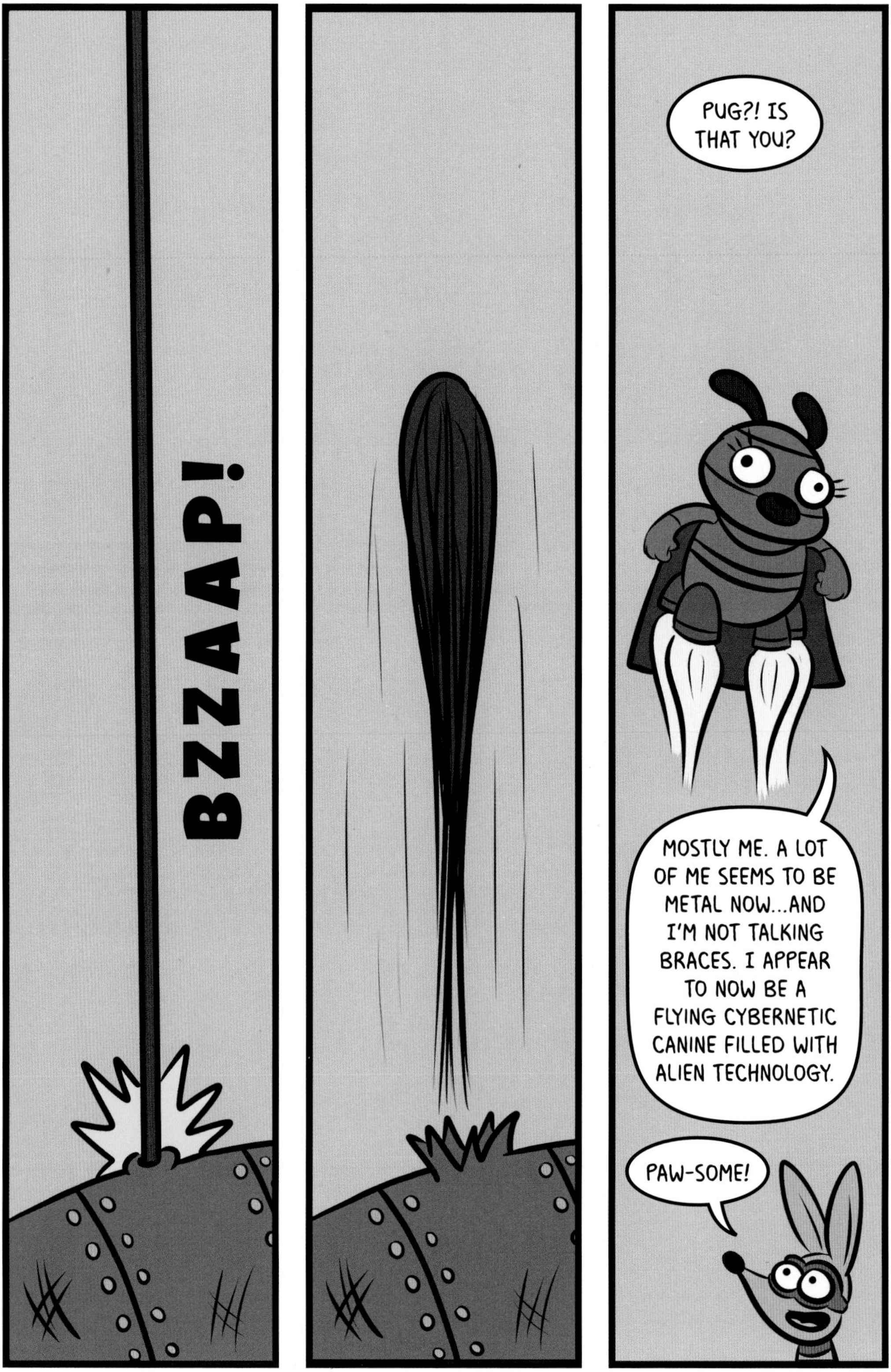
BZZAAP!
PUG?! IS THAT YOU?
MOSTLY ME. A LOT OF ME SEEMS TO BE METAL NOW...AND I'M NOT TALKING BRACES. I APPEAR TO NOW BE A FLYING CYBERNETIC CANINE FILLED WITH ALIEN TECHNOLOGY.
PAW-SOME!

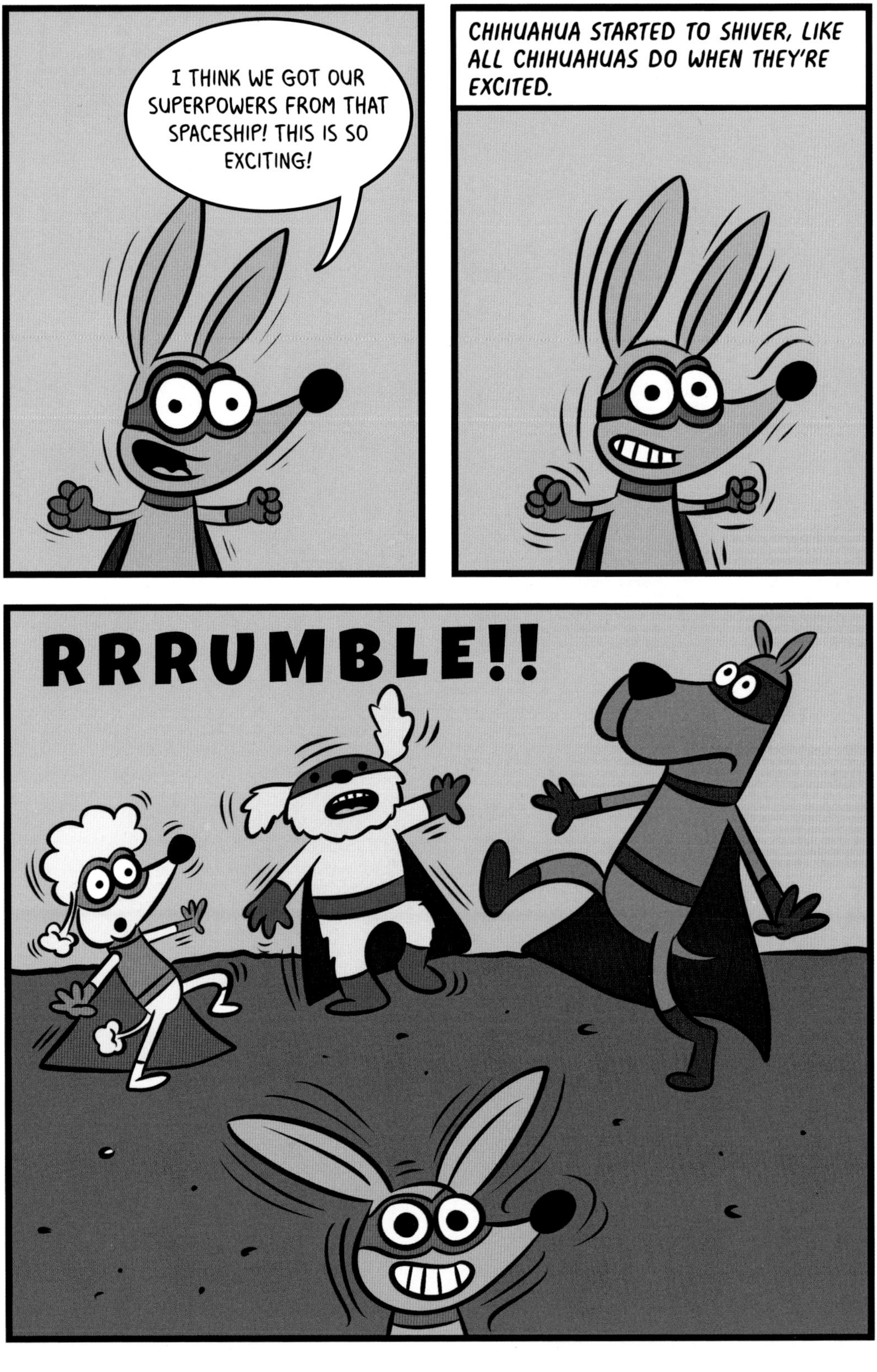
I THINK WE GOT OUR SUPERPOWERS FROM THAT SPACESHIP! THIS IS SO EXCITING!
CHIHUAHUA STARTED TO SHIVER, LIKE ALL CHIHUAHUAS DO WHEN THEY'RE EXCITED.
RRRUMBLE!!

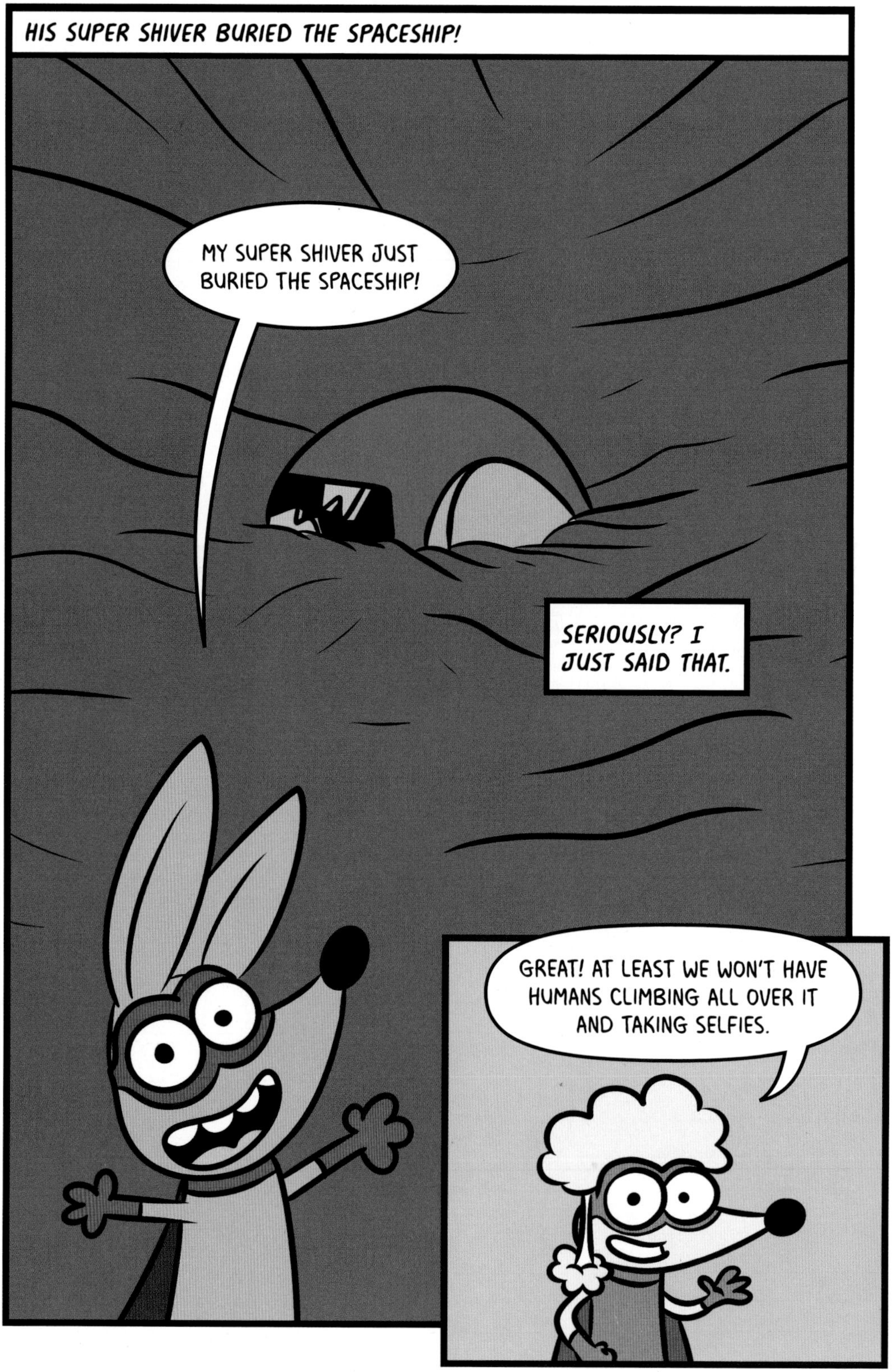
HIS SUPER SHIVER BURIED THE SPACESHIP!
MY SUPER SHIVER JUST BURIED THE SPACESHIP!
SERIOUSLY? I JUST SAID THAT.
GREAT! AT LEAST WE WON'T HAVE HUMANS CLIMBING ALL OVER IT AND TAKING SELFIES.

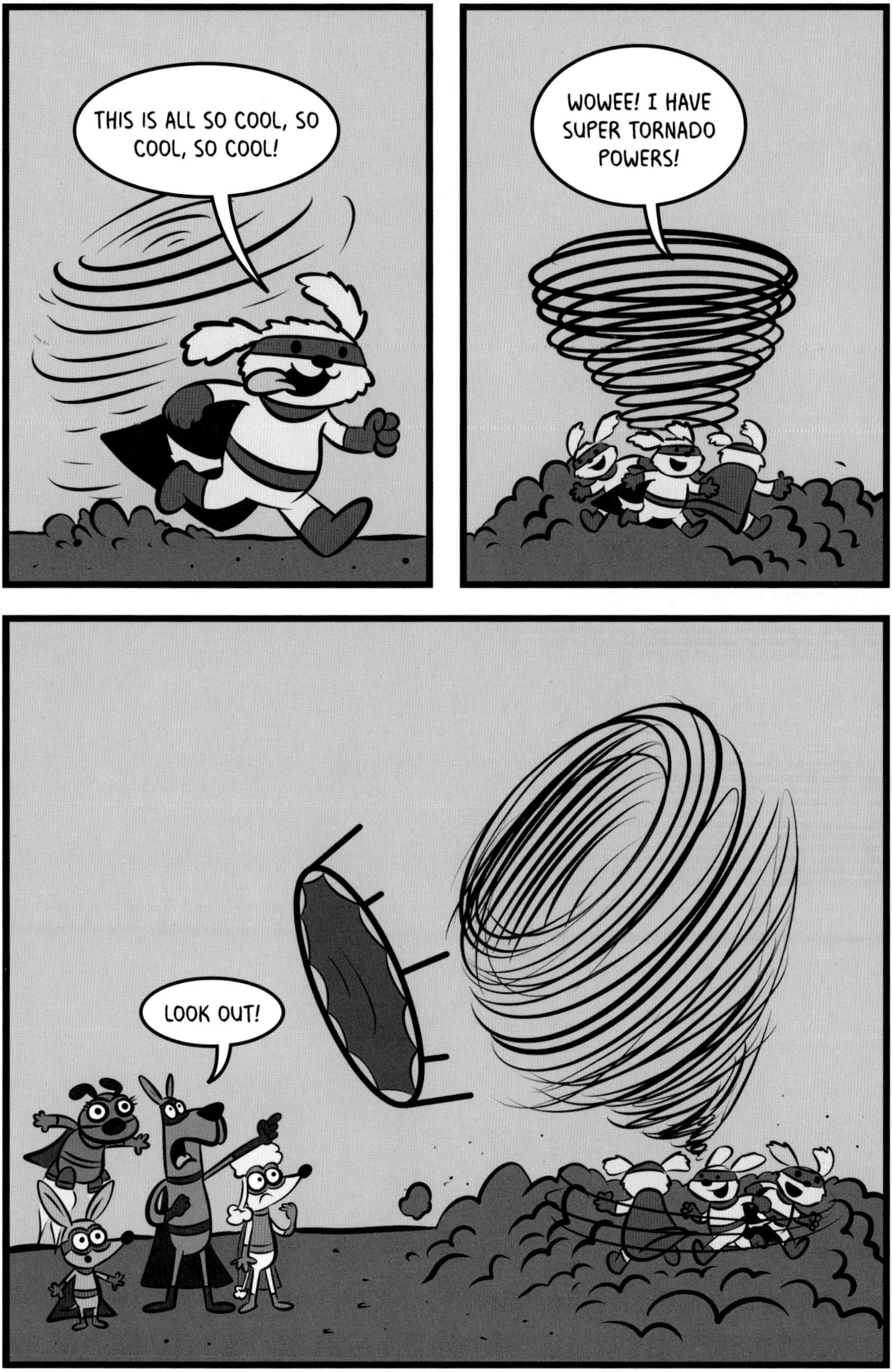
THIS IS ALL SO COOL, SO COOL, SO COOL!
WOWEE! I HAVE SUPER TORNADO POWERS!
LOOK OUT!

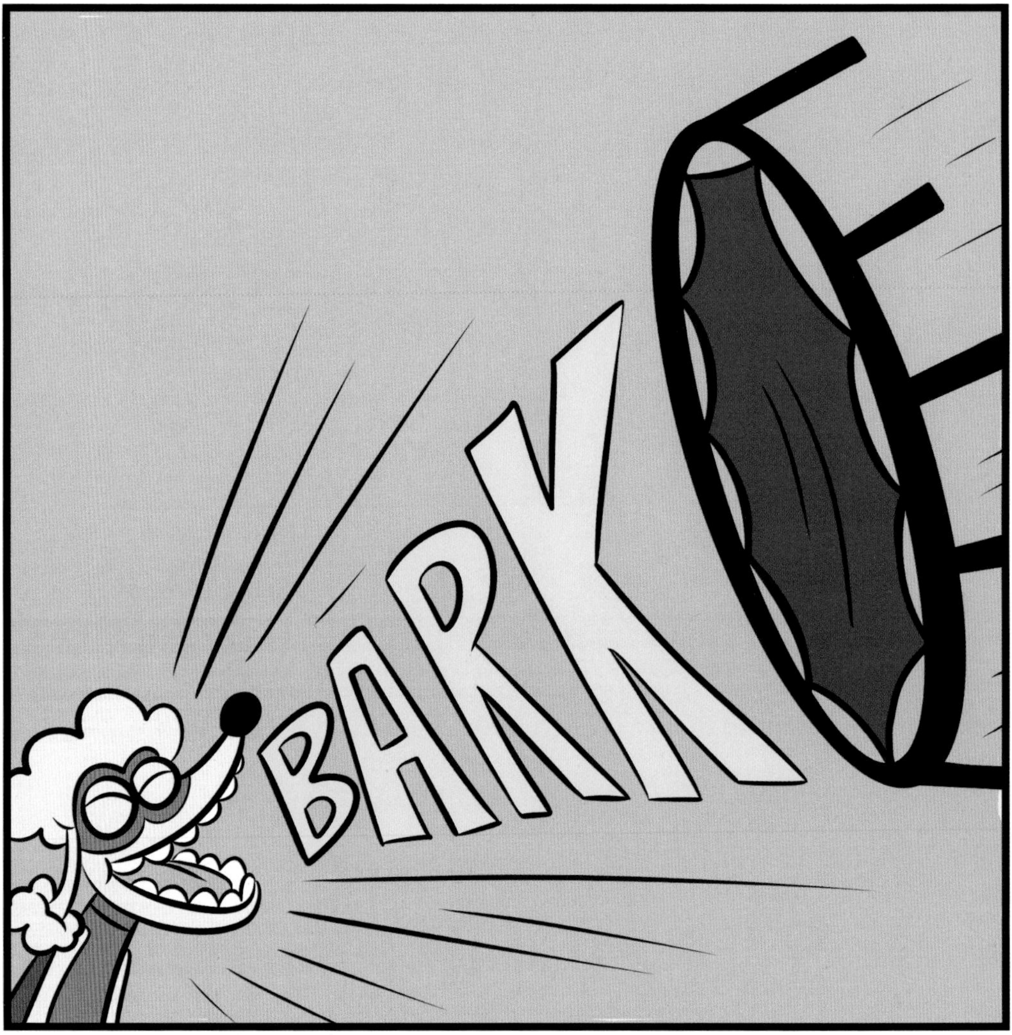
BARK

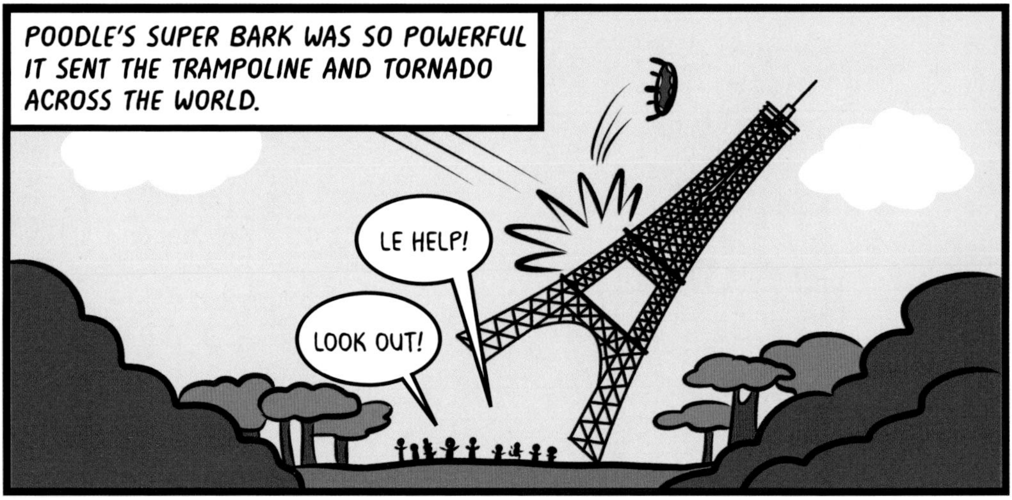
POODLE'S SUPER BARK WAS SO POWERFUL
IT SENT THE TRAMPOLINE AND TORNADO
ACROSS THE WORLD.
LE HELP!
LOOK OUT!

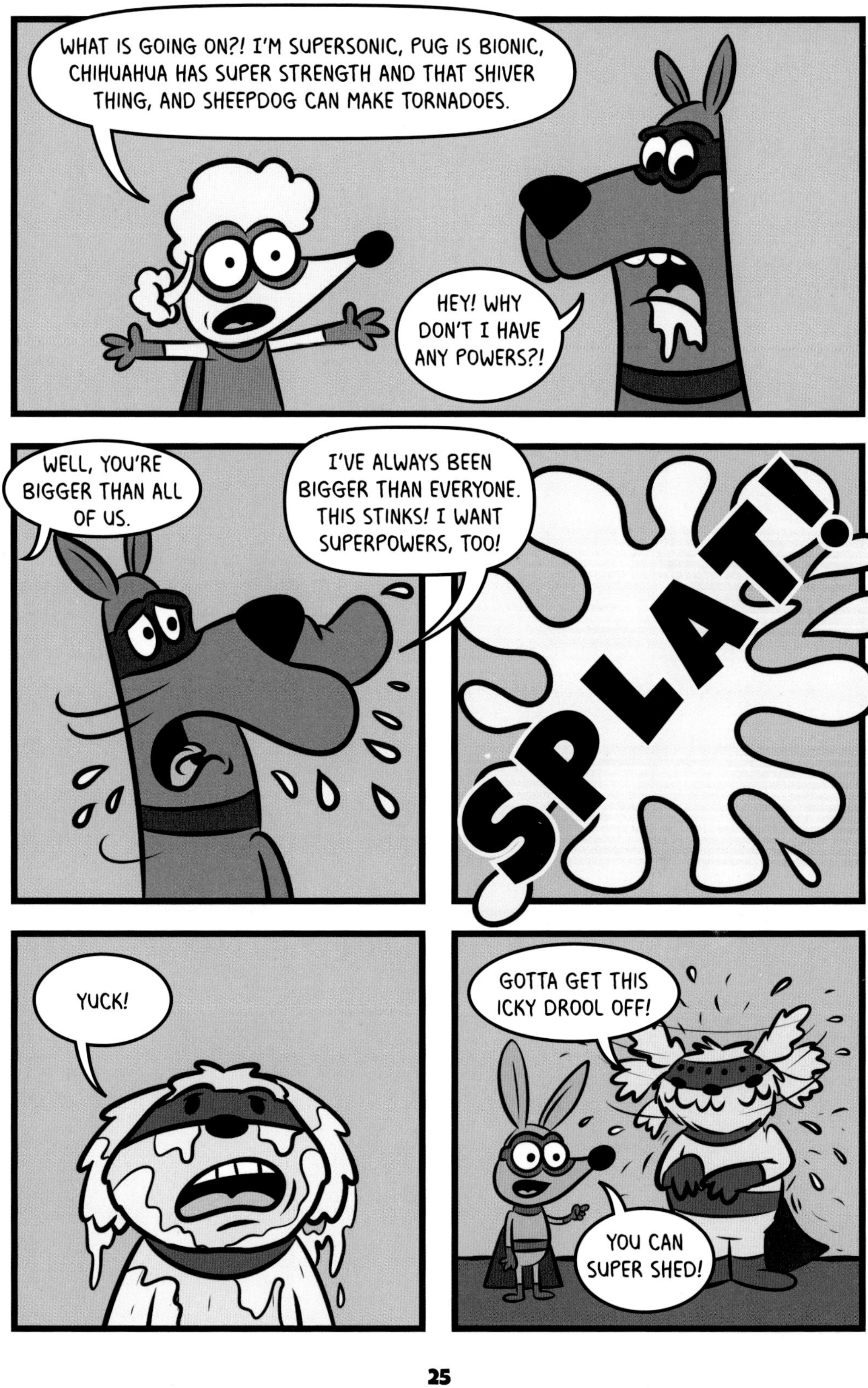
WHAT IS GOING ON?! I'M SUPERSONIC, PUG IS BIONIC, CHIHUAHUA HAS SUPER STRENGTH AND THAT SHIVER THING, AND SHEEPDOG CAN MAKE TORNADOES.
HEY! WHY DON'T I HAVE ANY POWERS?!
WELL, YOU'RE BIGGER THAN ALL OF US.
I'VE ALWAYS BEEN BIGGER THAN EVERYONE. THIS STINKS! I WANT SUPERPOWERS, TOO!
SPLAT!
YUCK!
GOTTA GET THIS ICKY DROOL OFF!
YOU CAN SUPER SHED!

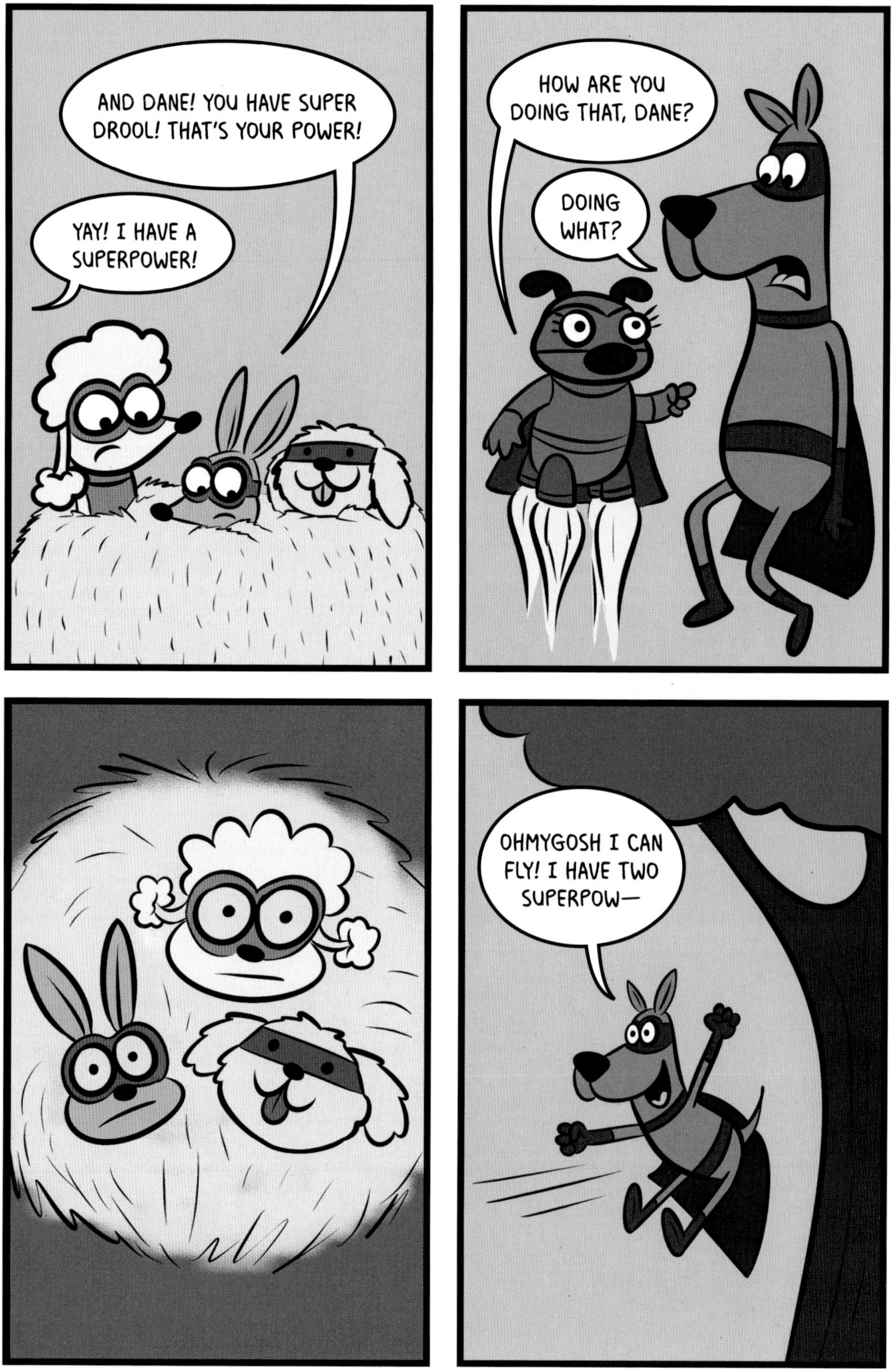
AND DANE! YOU HAVE SUPER DROOL! THAT'S YOUR POWER!
YAY! I HAVE A SUPERPOWER!
HOW ARE YOU DOING THAT, DANE?
DOING WHAT?
OHMYGOSH I CAN FLY! I HAVE TWO SUPERPOW—

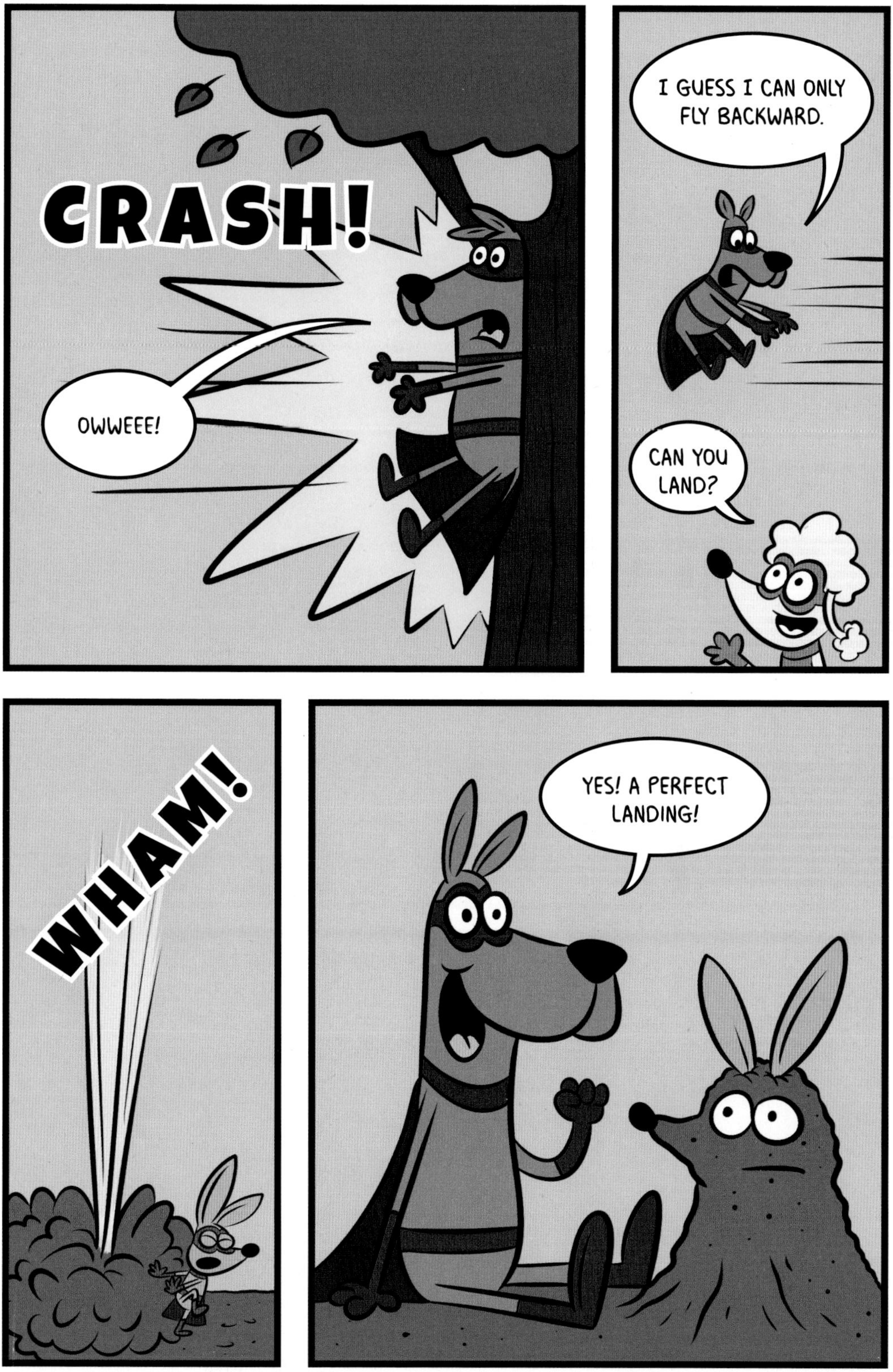
CRASH!
OWWEEE!
I GUESS I CAN ONLY FLY BACKWARD.
CAN YOU LAND?
WHAM!
YES! A PERFECT LANDING!

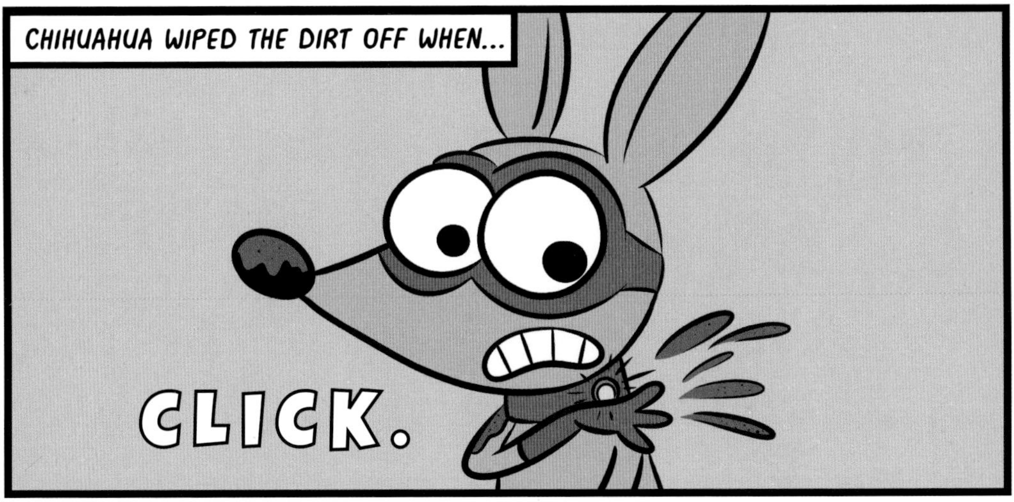
CHIHUAHUA WIPED THE DIRT OFF WHEN...
CLICK.

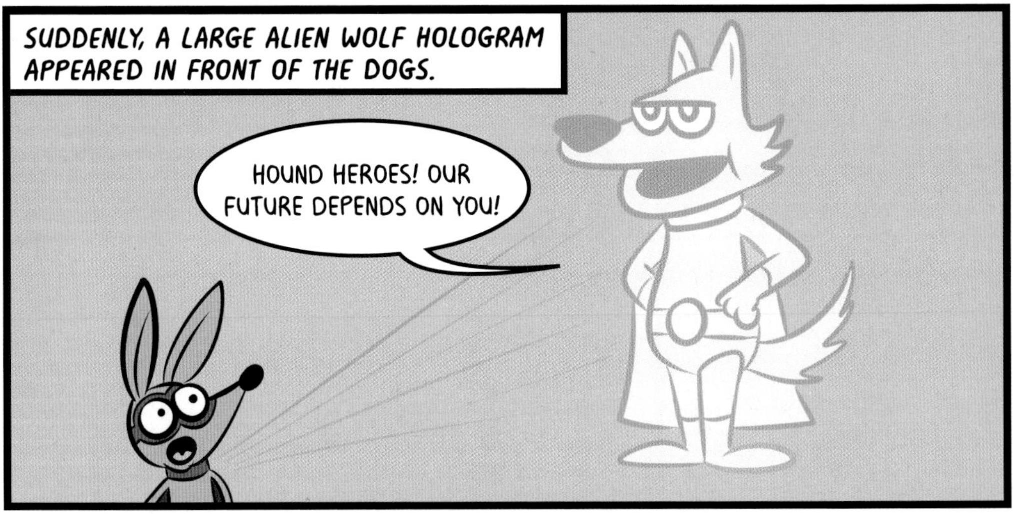
SUDDENLY, A LARGE ALIEN WOLF HOLOGRAM APPEARED IN FRONT OF THE DOGS.
HOUND HEROES! OUR FUTURE DEPENDS ON YOU!

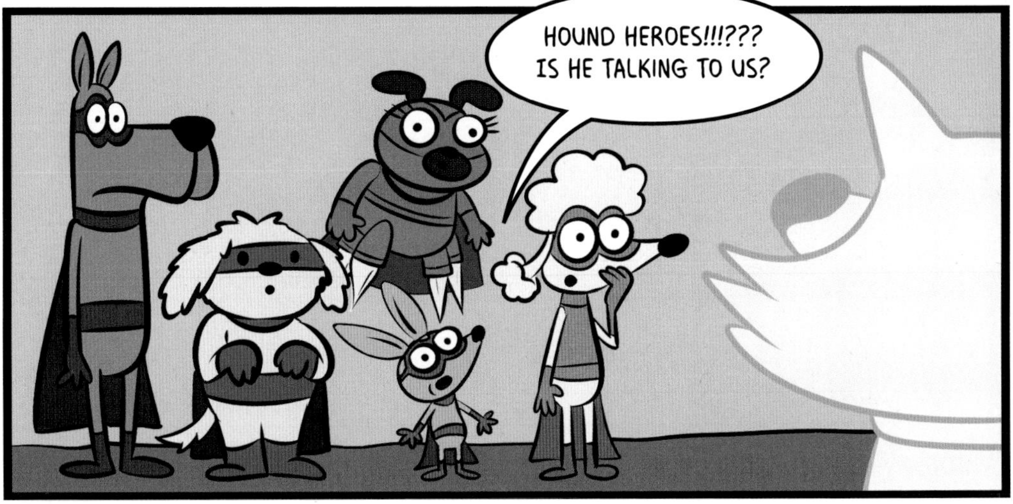
HOUND HEROES!!!??? IS HE TALKING TO US?

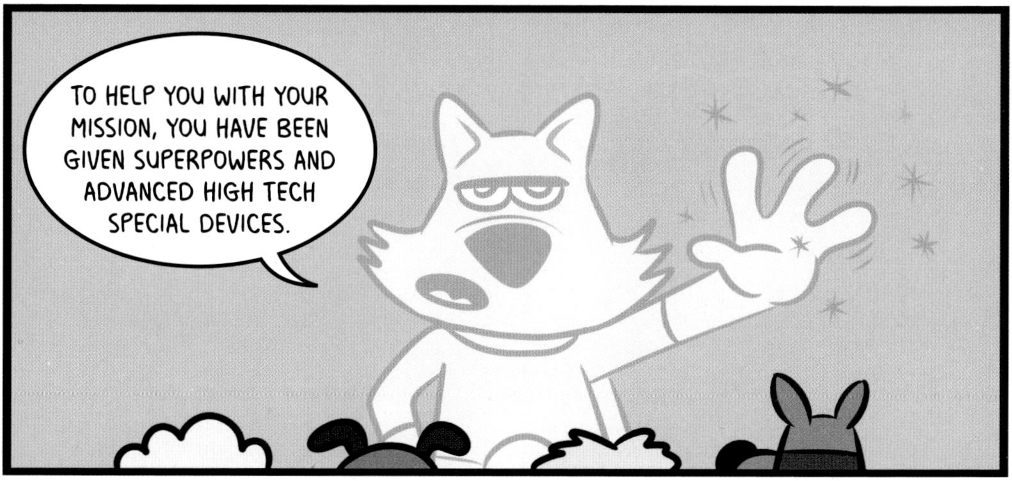
TO HELP YOU WITH YOUR MISSION, YOU HAVE BEEN GIVEN SUPERPOWERS AND ADVANCED HIGH TECH SPECIAL DEVICES.

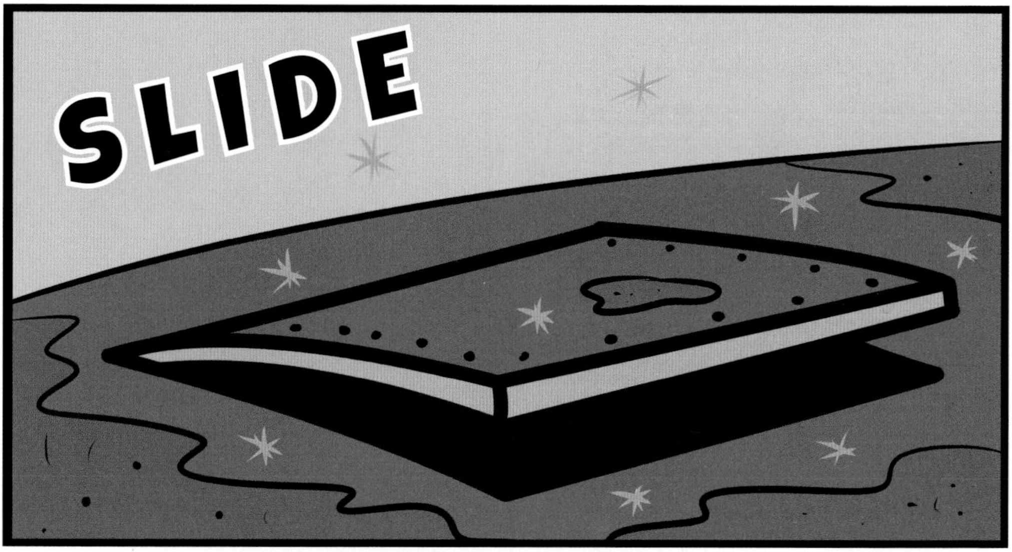
SLIDE

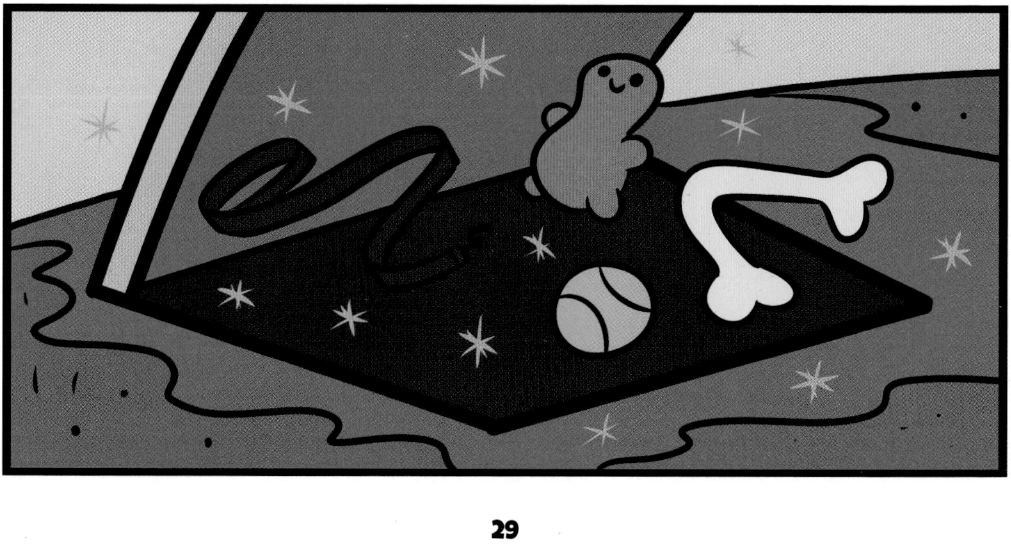

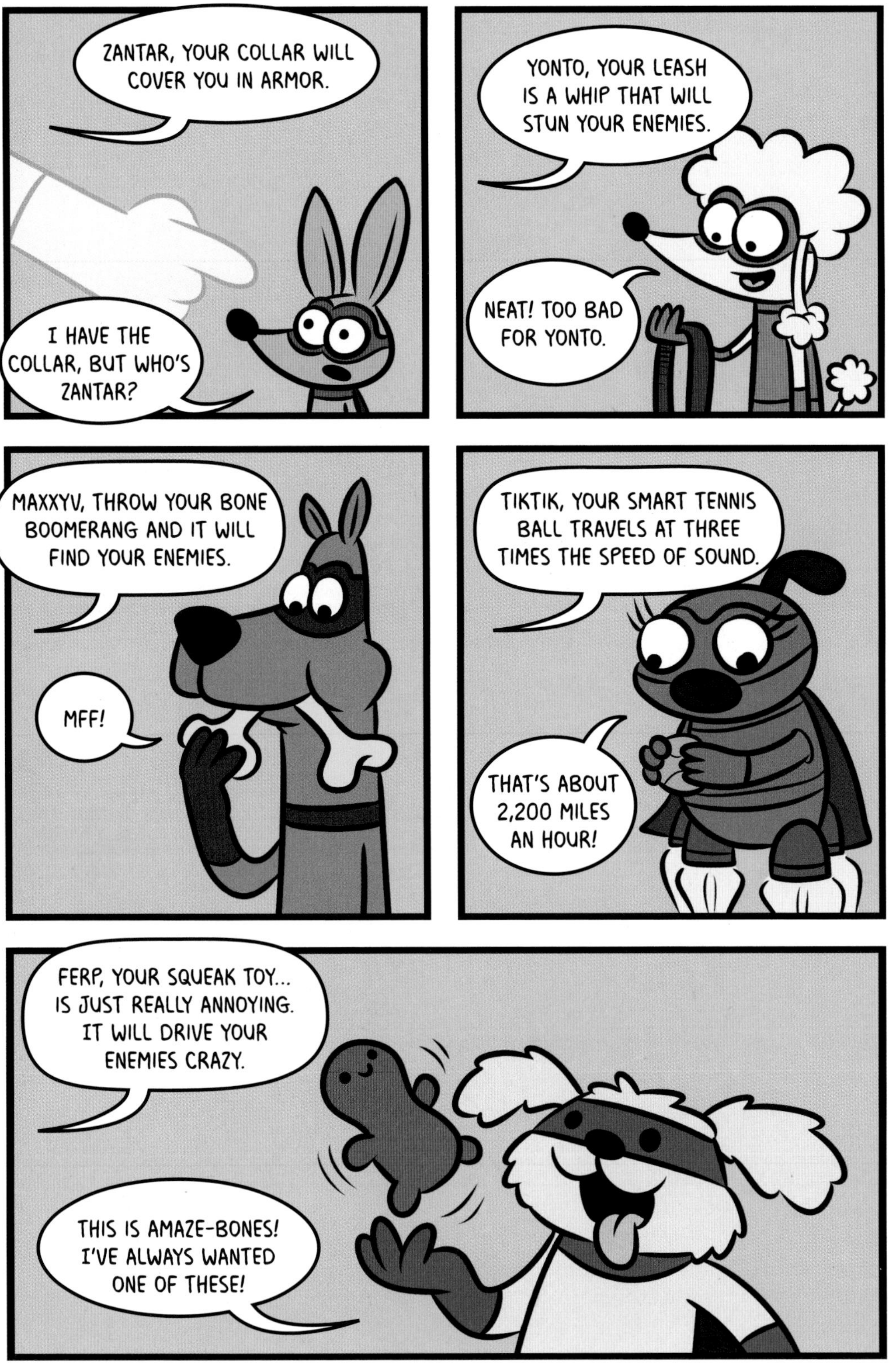
ZANTAR, YOUR COLLAR WILL COVER YOU IN ARMOR.
I HAVE THE COLLAR, BUT WHO'S ZANTAR?
YONTO, YOUR LEASH IS A WHIP THAT WILL STUN YOUR ENEMIES.
NEAT! TOO BAD FOR YONTO.
MAXXYV, THROW YOUR BONE BOOMERANG AND IT WILL FIND YOUR ENEMIES.
MFF!
TIKTIK, YOUR SMART TENNIS BALL TRAVELS AT THREE TIMES THE SPEED OF SOUND.
THAT'S ABOUT 2,200 MILES AN HOUR!
FERP, YOUR SQUEAK TOY... IS JUST REALLY ANNOYING. IT WILL DRIVE YOUR ENEMIES CRAZY.
THIS IS AMAZE-BONES! I'VE ALWAYS WANTED ONE OF THESE!

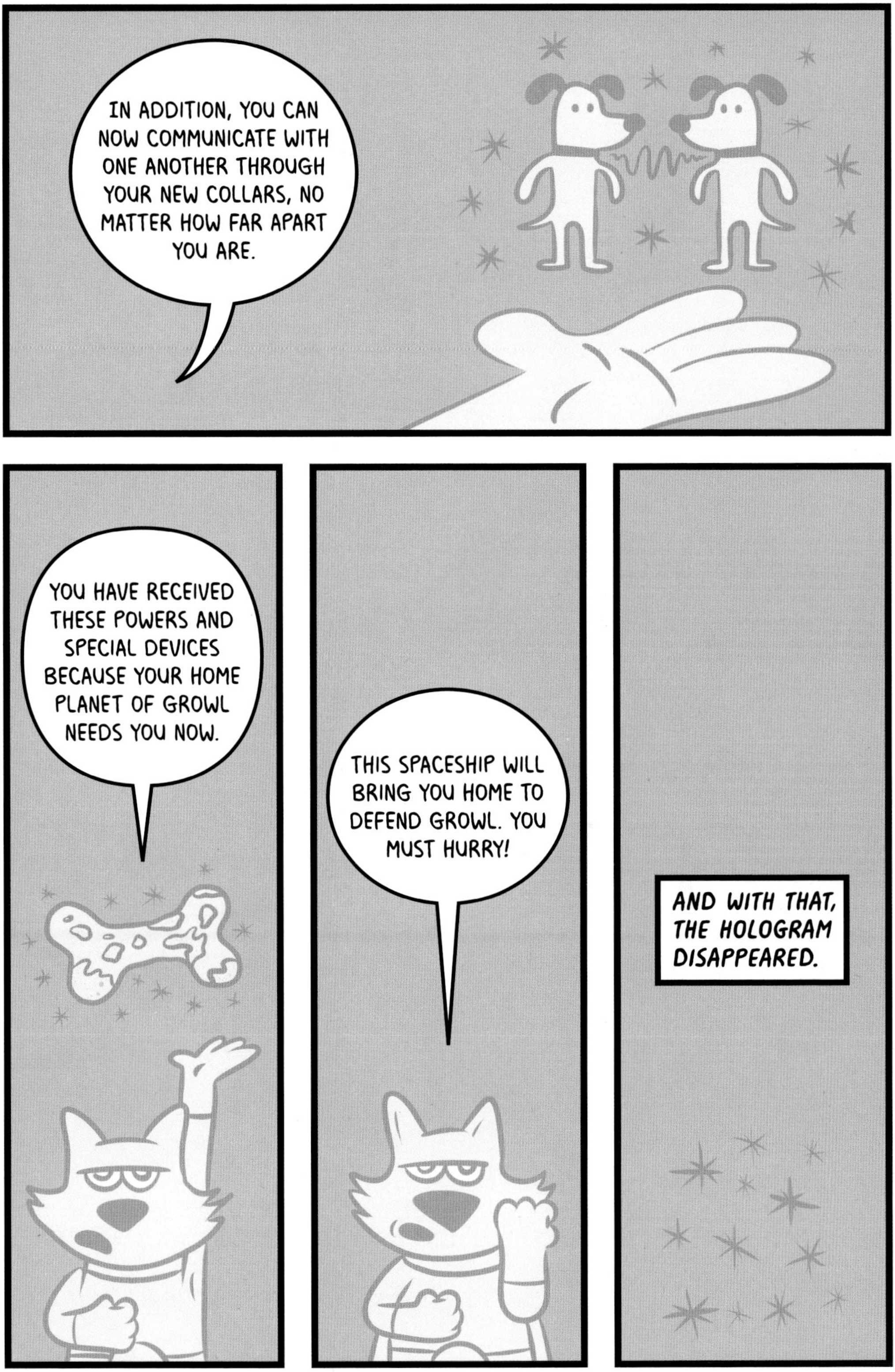
IN ADDITION, YOU CAN NOW COMMUNICATE WITH ONE ANOTHER THROUGH YOUR NEW COLLARS, NO MATTER HOW FAR APART YOU ARE.
YOU HAVE RECEIVED THESE POWERS AND SPECIAL DEVICES BECAUSE YOUR HOME PLANET OF GROWL NEEDS YOU NOW.
THIS SPACESHIP WILL BRING YOU HOME TO DEFEND GROWL. YOU MUST HURRY!
AND WITH THAT, THE HOLOGRAM DISAPPEARED.

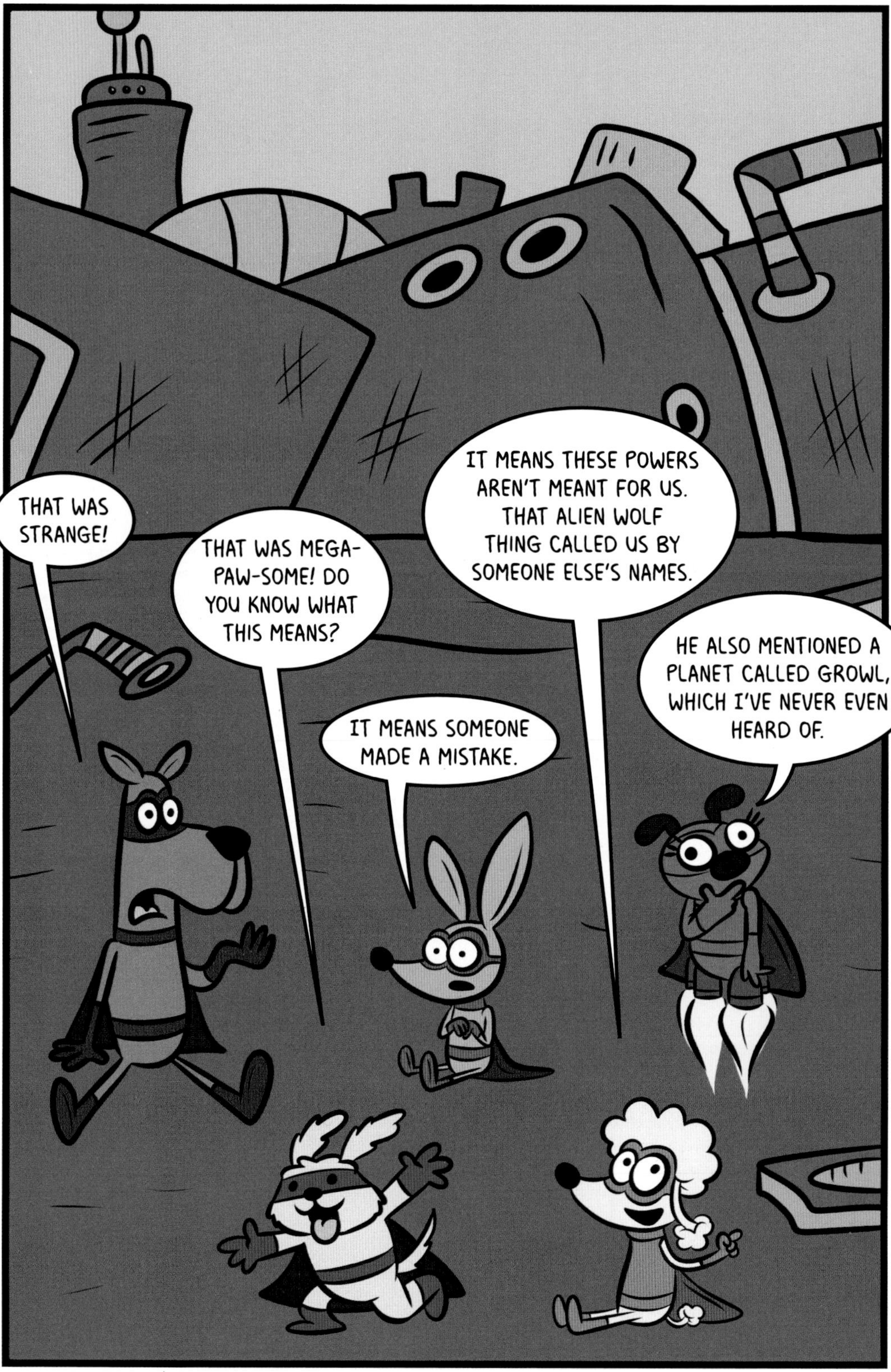
THAT WAS STRANGE!
THAT WAS MEGA-PAW-SOME! DO YOU KNOW WHAT THIS MEANS?
IT MEANS SOMEONE MADE A MISTAKE.
IT MEANS THESE POWERS AREN'T MEANT FOR US. THAT ALIEN WOLF THING CALLED US BY SOMEONE ELSE'S NAMES.
HE ALSO MENTIONED A PLANET CALLED GROWL, WHICH I'VE NEVER EVEN HEARD OF.

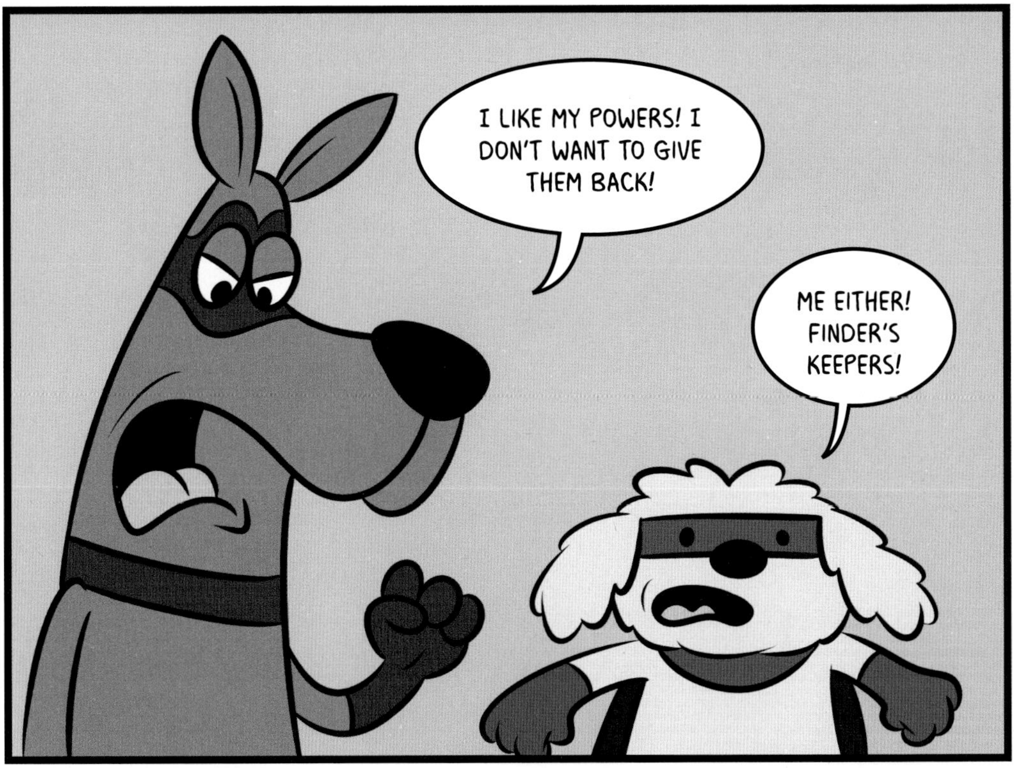
I LIKE MY POWERS! I DON'T WANT TO GIVE THEM BACK!
ME EITHER! FINDER'S KEEPERS!

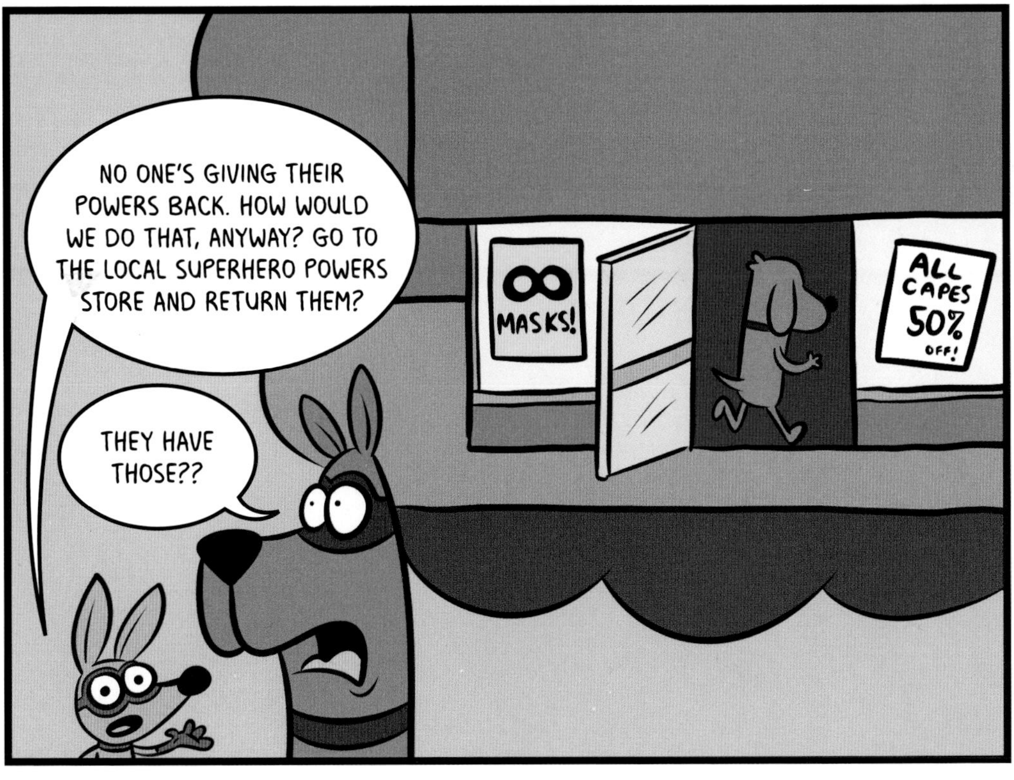
NO ONE'S GIVING THEIR POWERS BACK. HOW WOULD WE DO THAT, ANYWAY? GO TO THE LOCAL SUPERHERO POWERS STORE AND RETURN THEM?
MASKS!
ALL CAPES 50% OFF!
THEY HAVE THOSE??

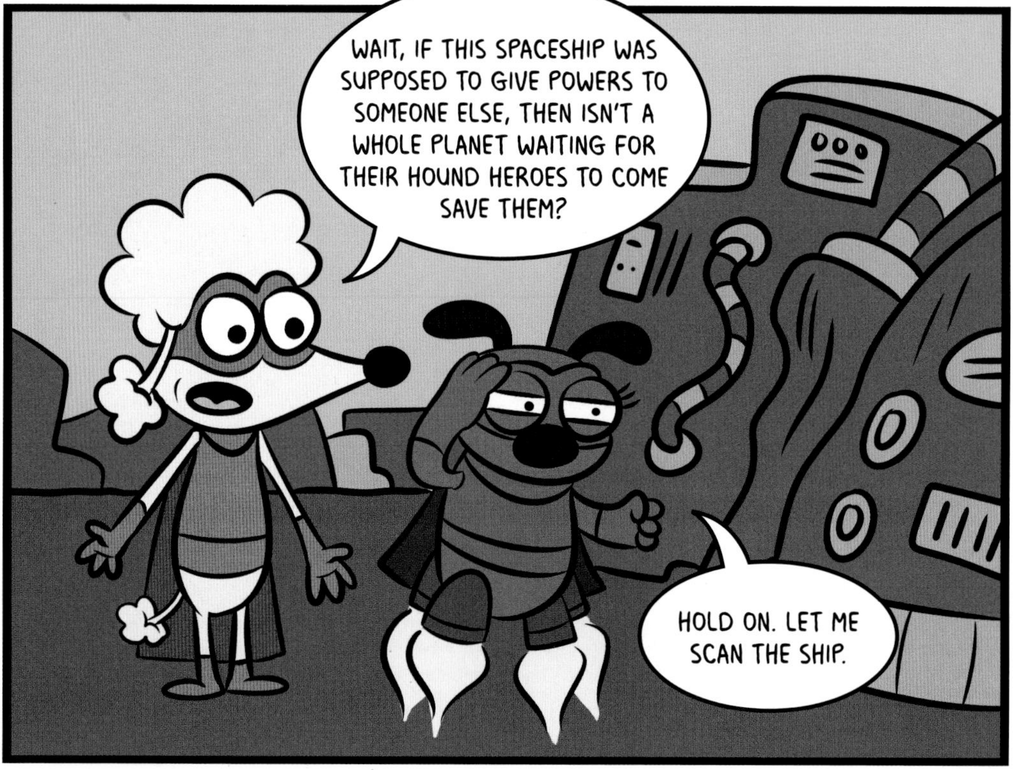
WAIT, IF THIS SPACESHIP WAS SUPPOSED TO GIVE POWERS TO SOMEONE ELSE, THEN ISN'T A WHOLE PLANET WAITING FOR THEIR HOUND HEROES TO COME SAVE THEM?
HOLD ON. LET ME SCAN THE SHIP.

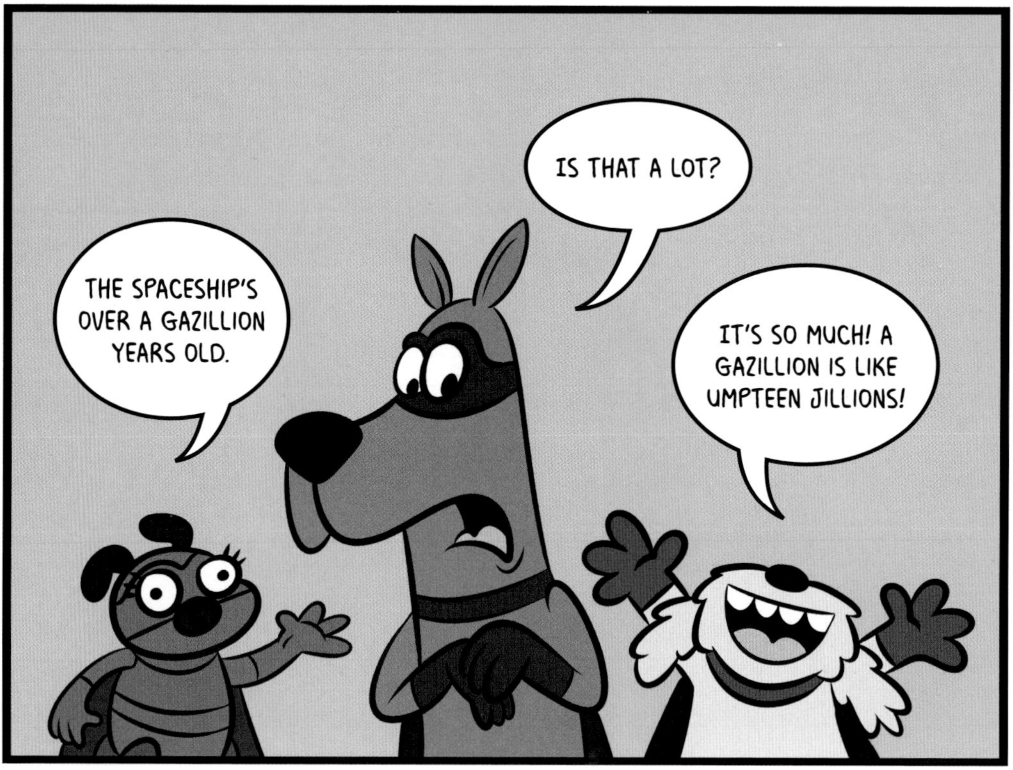
THE SPACESHIP'S OVER A GAZILLION YEARS OLD.
IS THAT A LOT?
IT'S SO MUCH! A GAZILLION IS LIKE UMPTEEN JILLIONS!

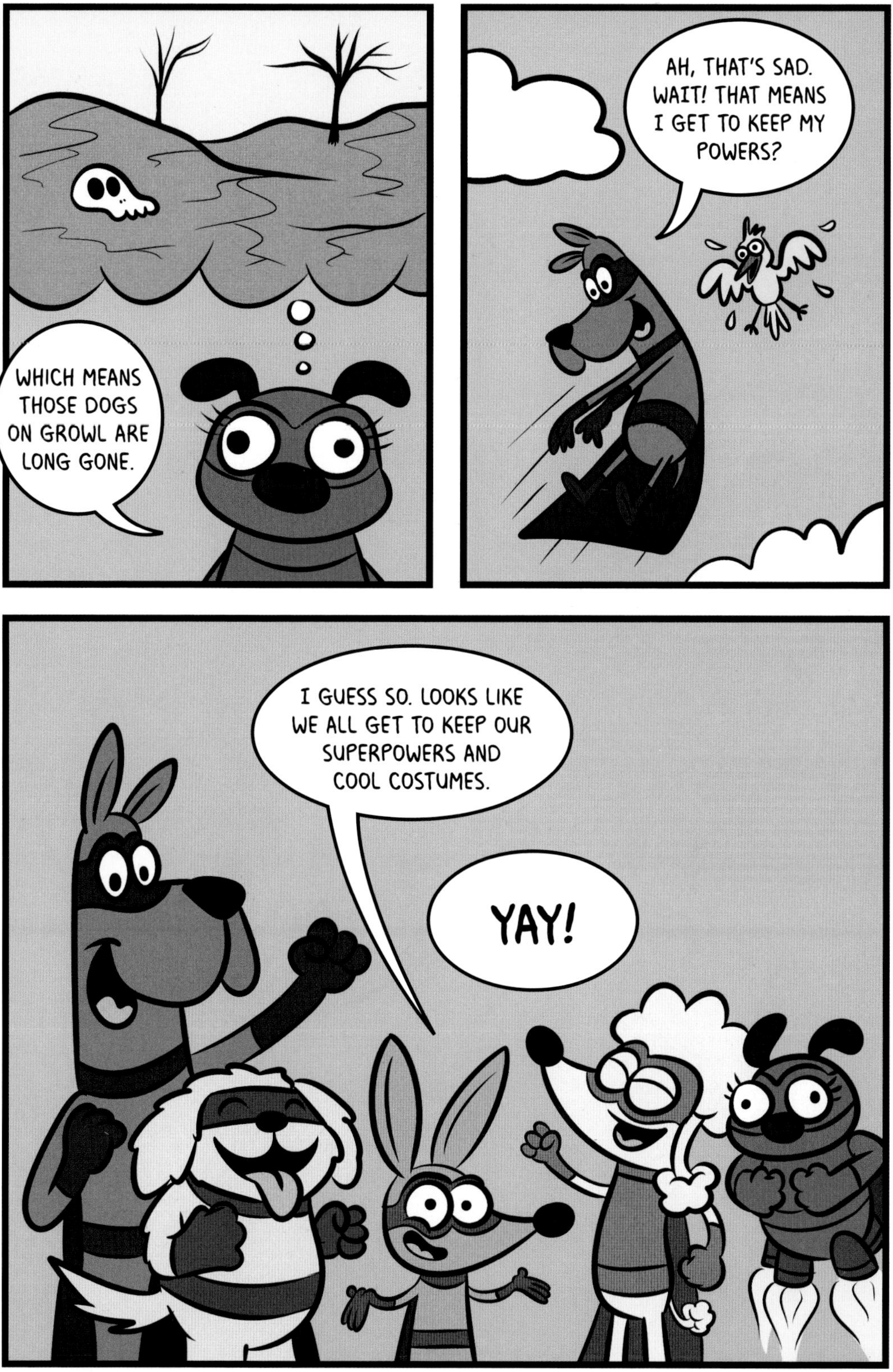
WHICH MEANS THOSE DOGS ON GROWL ARE LONG GONE.
AH, THAT'S SAD. WAIT! THAT MEANS I GET TO KEEP MY POWERS?
I GUESS SO. LOOKS LIKE WE ALL GET TO KEEP OUR SUPERPOWERS AND COOL COSTUMES.
YAY!

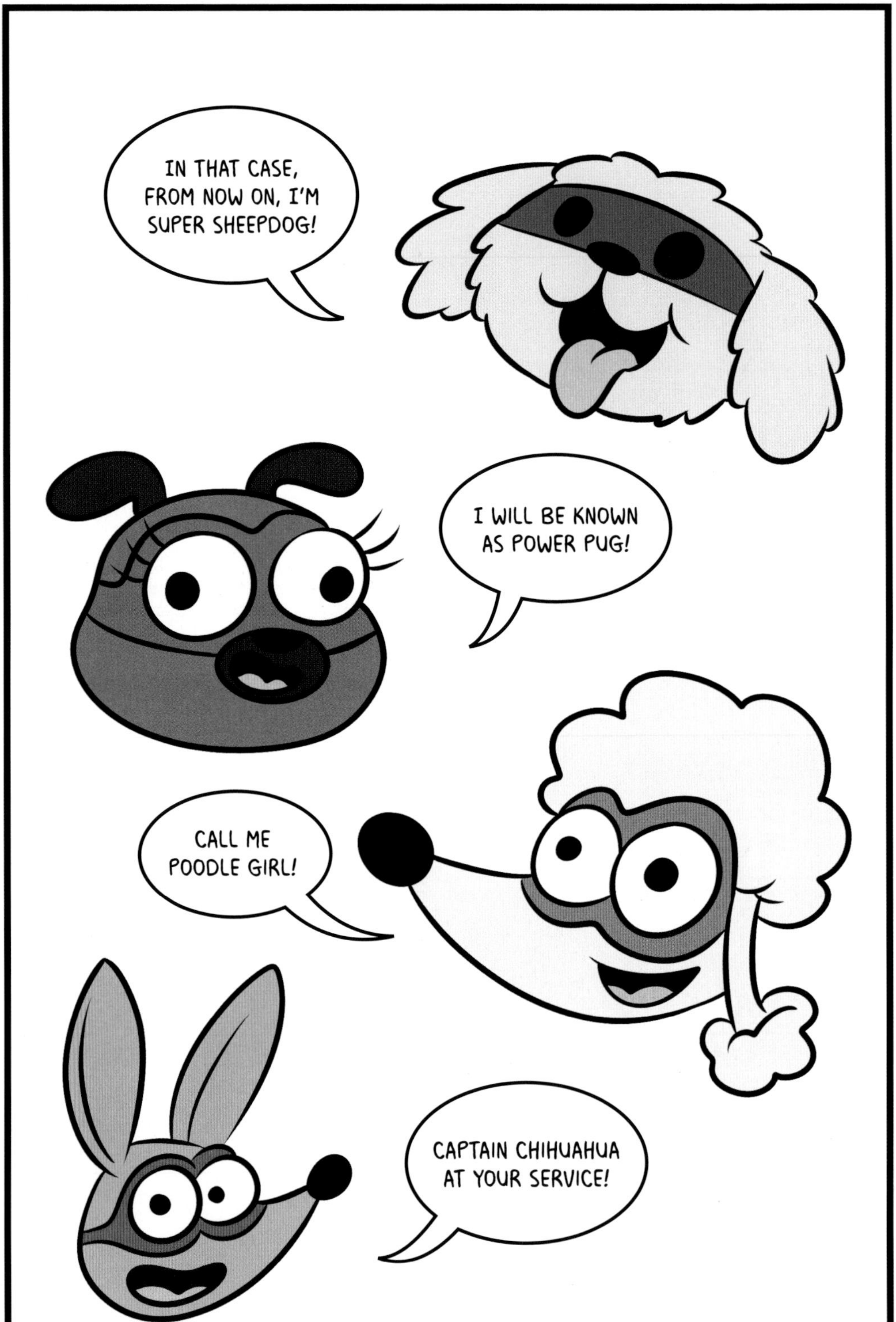
IN THAT CASE, FROM NOW ON, I'M SUPER SHEEPDOG!
I WILL BE KNOWN AS POWER PUG!
CALL ME POODLE GIRL!
CAPTAIN CHIHUAHUA AT YOUR SERVICE!

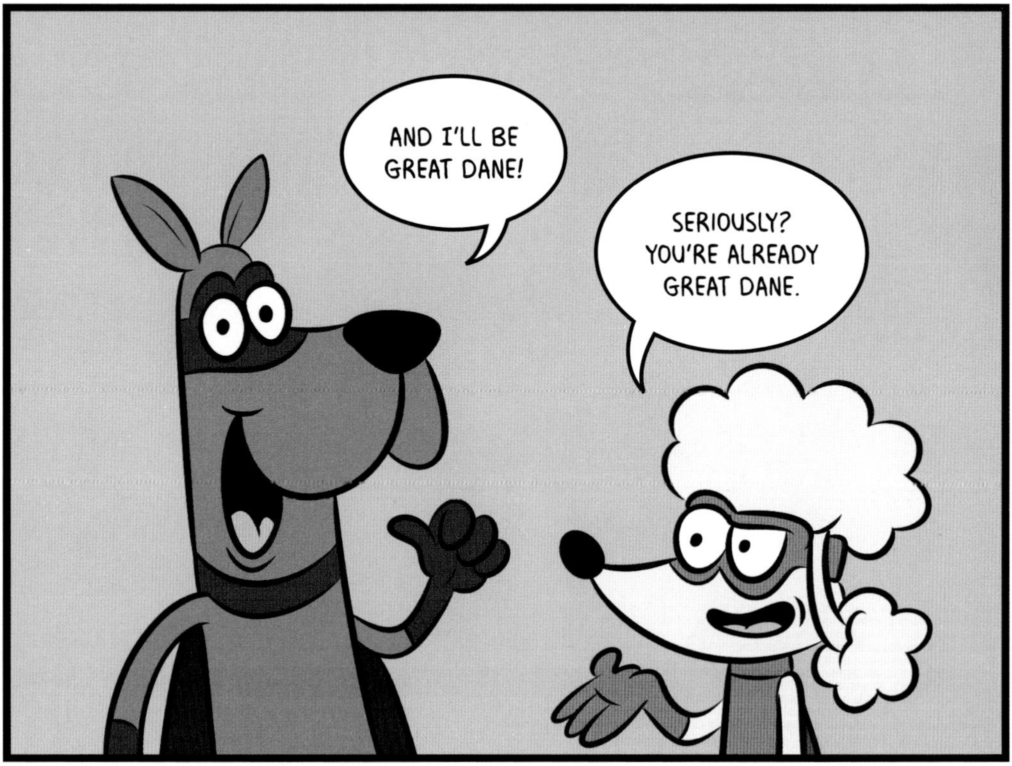
AND I'LL BE GREAT DANE!
SERIOUSLY? YOU'RE ALREADY GREAT DANE.

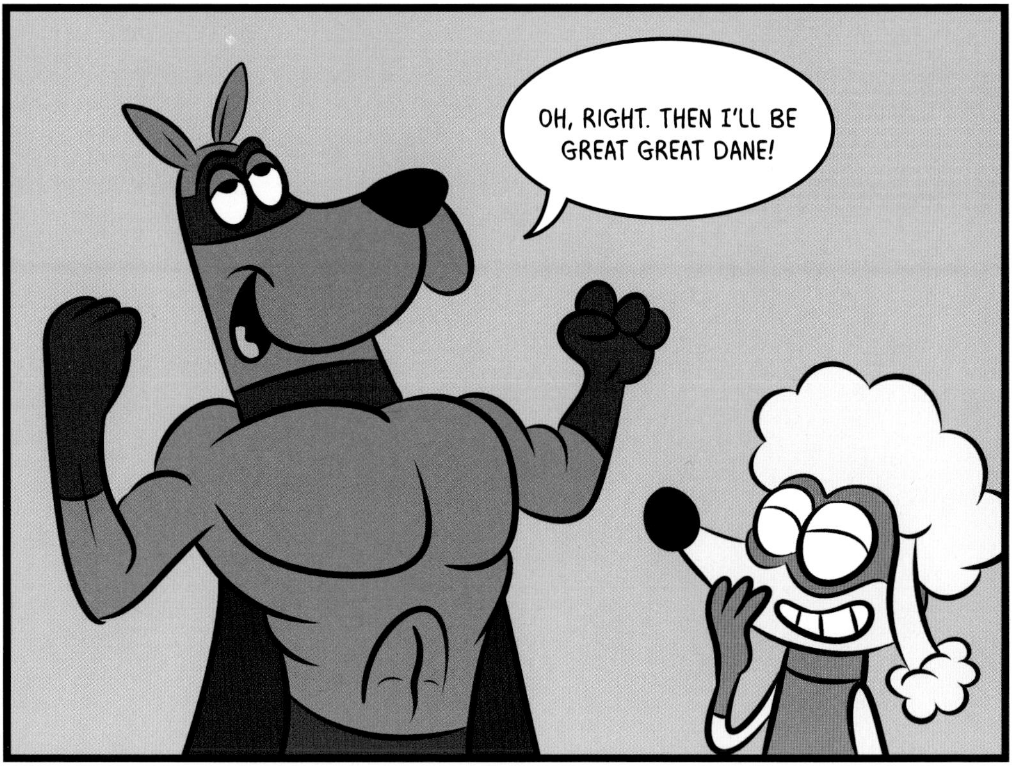
OH, RIGHT. THEN I'LL BE GREAT GREAT DANE!

MEET THE HOUND HEROES!

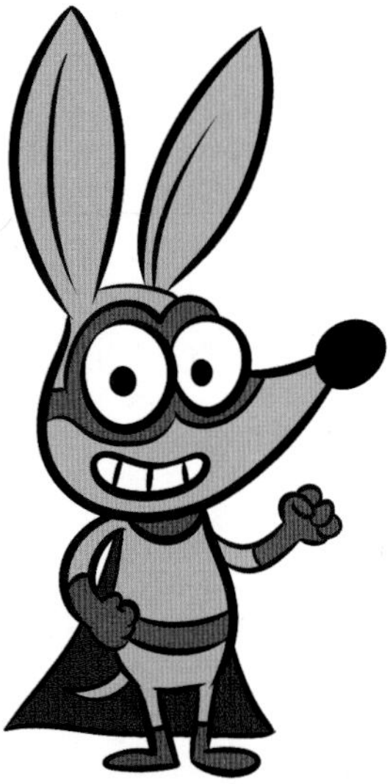

CAPTAIN CHIHUAHUA

- SUPER STRENGTH
- SUPER SHIVER
- COLLAR THAT TURNS ON FULL-BODY ARMOR

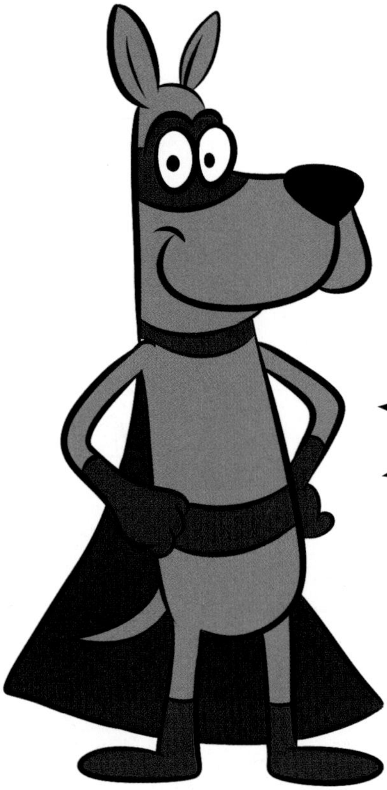

GREAT GREAT DANE

- HE CAN FLY (BACKWARD)
- SUPER DROOL
- BONE BOOMERANG TO TAKE OUT BAD GUYS

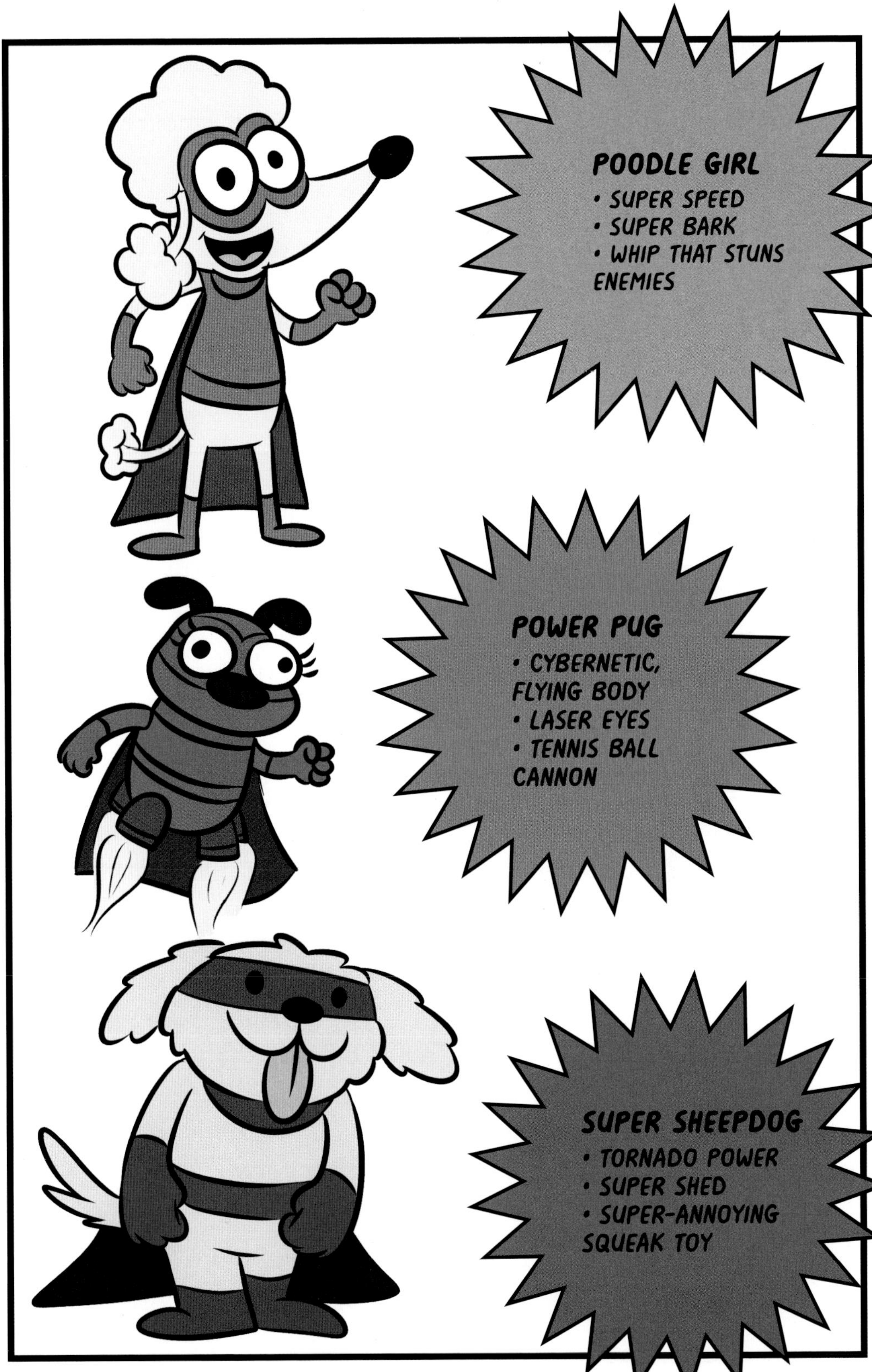
POODLE GIRL
• SUPER SPEED
• SUPER BARK
• WHIP THAT STUNS ENEMIES
POWER PUG
• CYBERNETIC, FLYING BODY
• LASER EYES
• TENNIS BALL CANNON
SUPER SHEEPDOG
• TORNADO POWER
• SUPER SHED
• SUPER-ANNOYING SQUEAK TOY

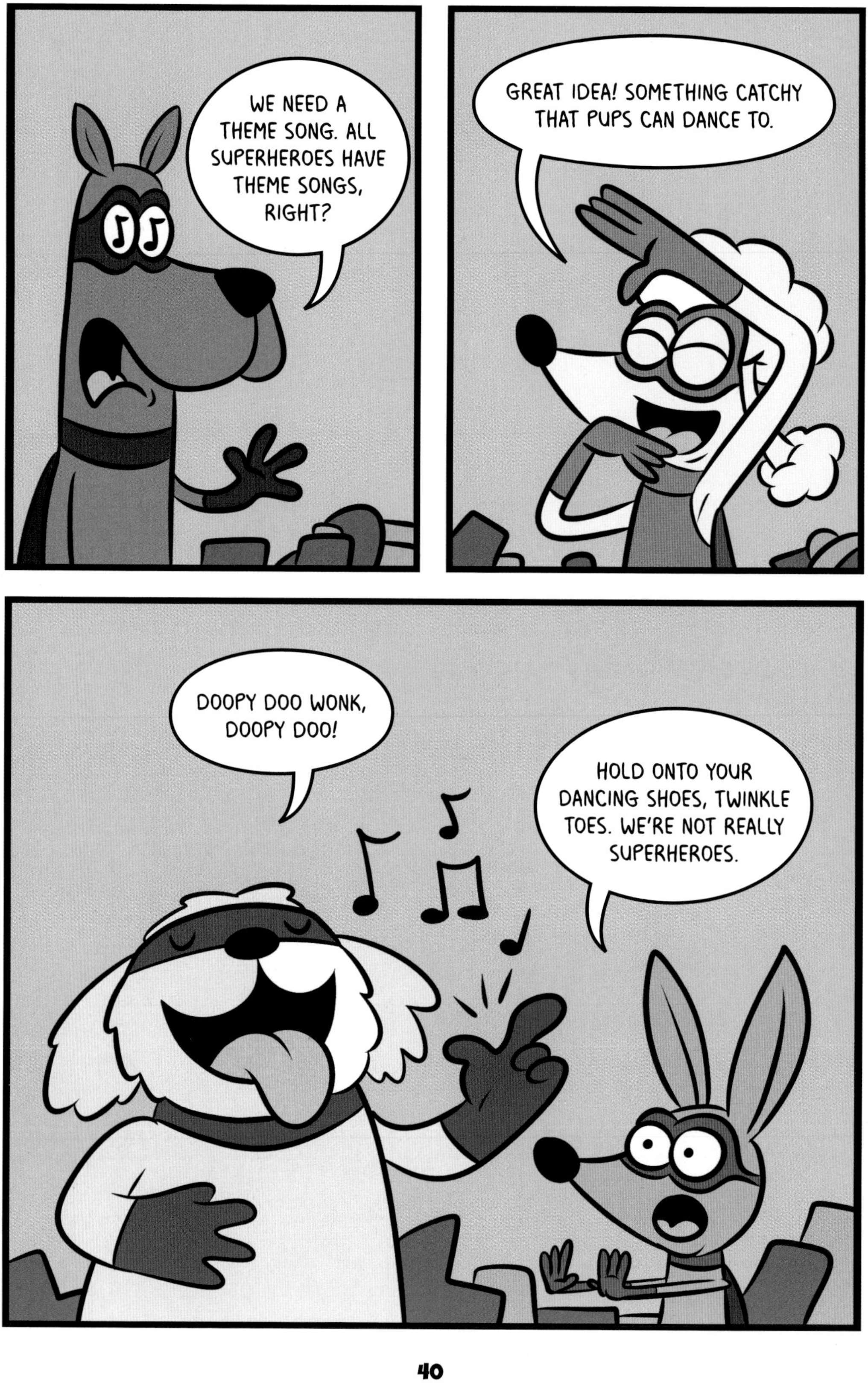
WE NEED A THEME SONG. ALL SUPERHEROES HAVE THEME SONGS, RIGHT?
GREAT IDEA! SOMETHING CATCHY THAT PUPS CAN DANCE TO.
DOOPY DOO WONK, DOOPY DOO!
HOLD ONTO YOUR DANCING SHOES, TWINKLE TOES. WE'RE NOT REALLY SUPERHEROES.

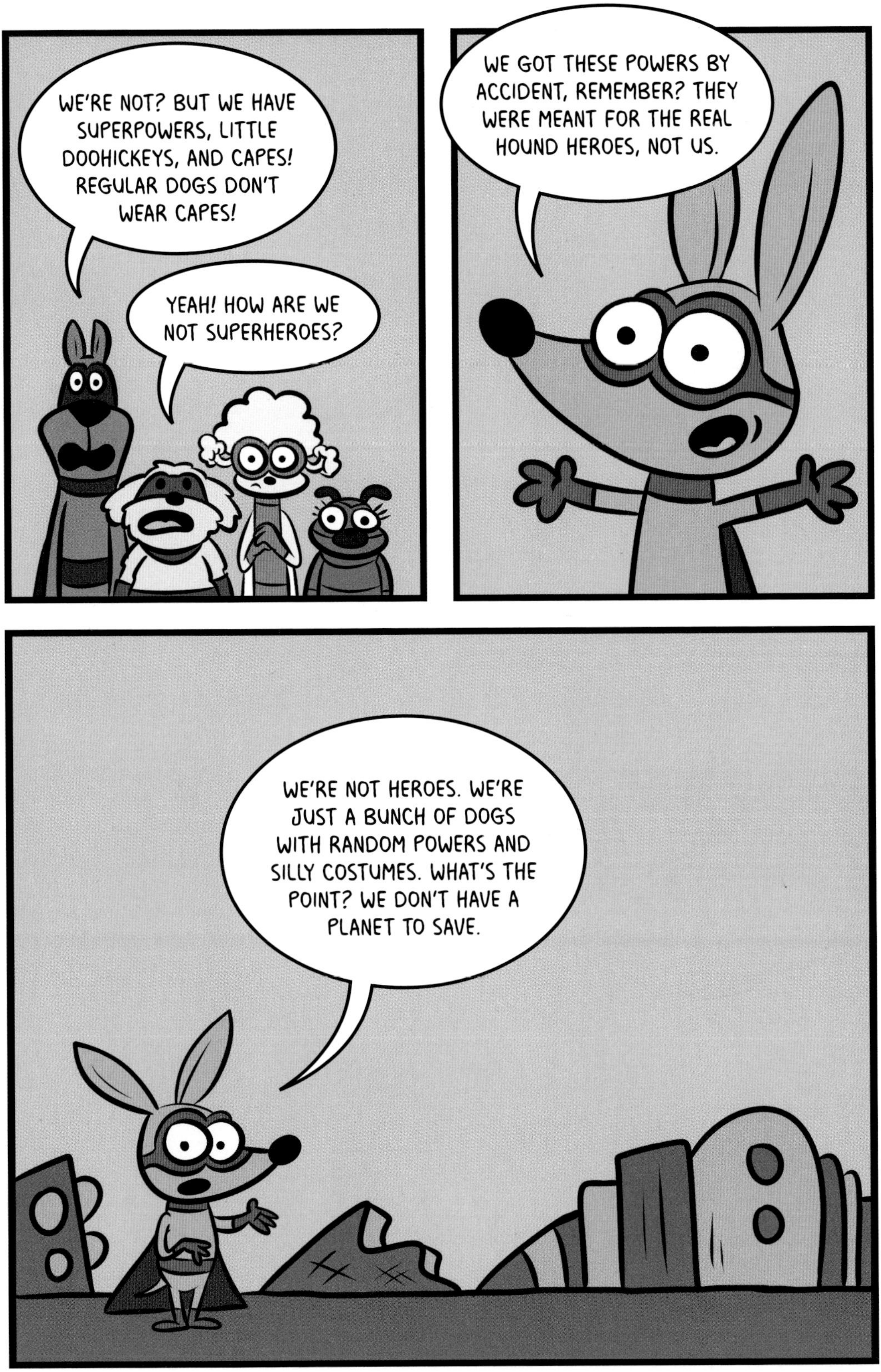
WE'RE NOT? BUT WE HAVE SUPERPOWERS, LITTLE DOOHICKEYS, AND CAPES! REGULAR DOGS DON'T WEAR CAPES!
YEAH! HOW ARE WE NOT SUPERHEROES?
WE GOT THESE POWERS BY ACCIDENT, REMEMBER? THEY WERE MEANT FOR THE REAL HOUND HEROES, NOT US.
WE'RE NOT HEROES. WE'RE JUST A BUNCH OF DOGS WITH RANDOM POWERS AND SILLY COSTUMES. WHAT'S THE POINT? WE DON'T HAVE A PLANET TO SAVE.

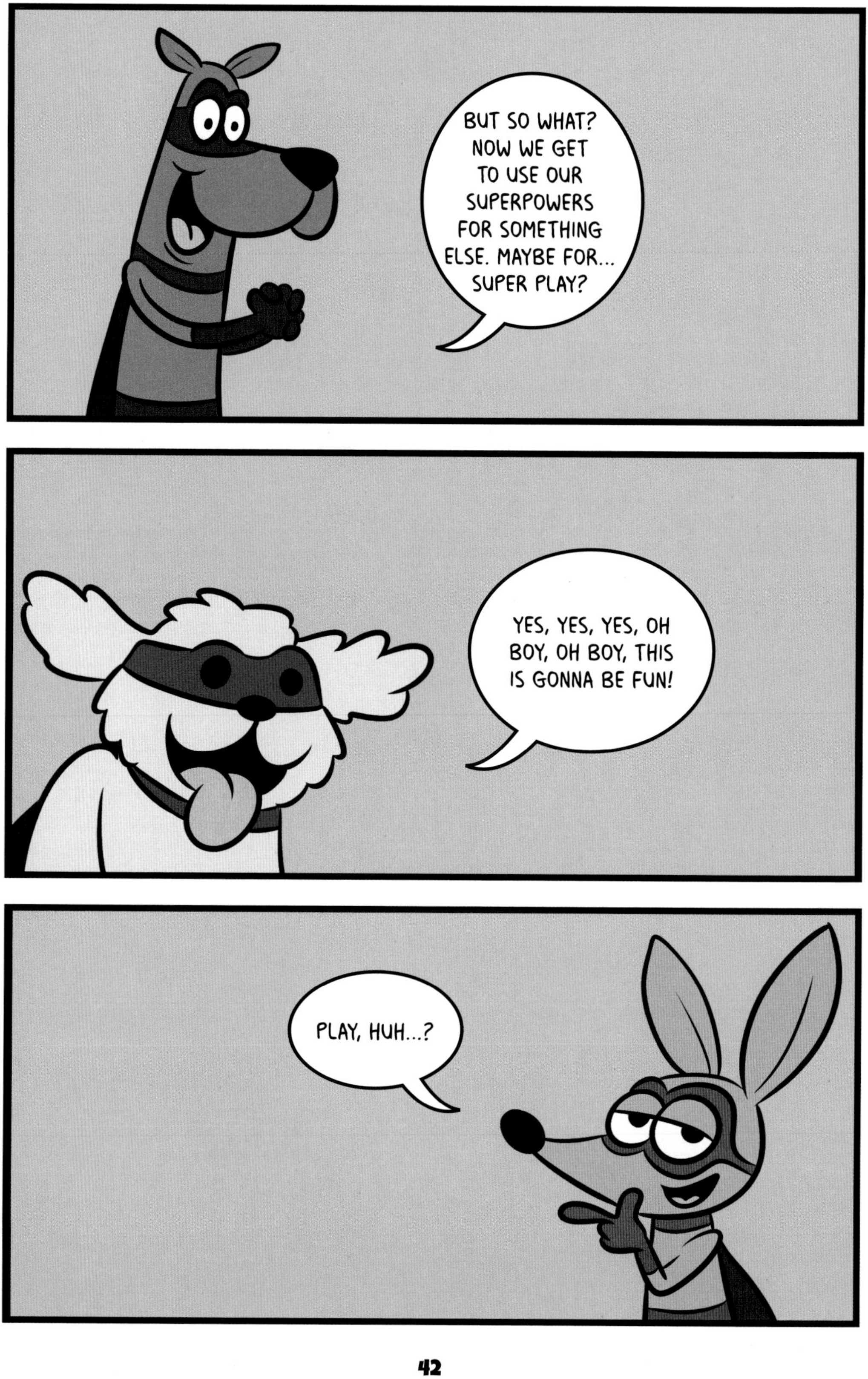
BUT SO WHAT? NOW WE GET TO USE OUR SUPERPOWERS FOR SOMETHING ELSE. MAYBE FOR... SUPER PLAY?
YES, YES, YES, OH BOY, OH BOY, THIS IS GONNA BE FUN!
PLAY, HUH...?

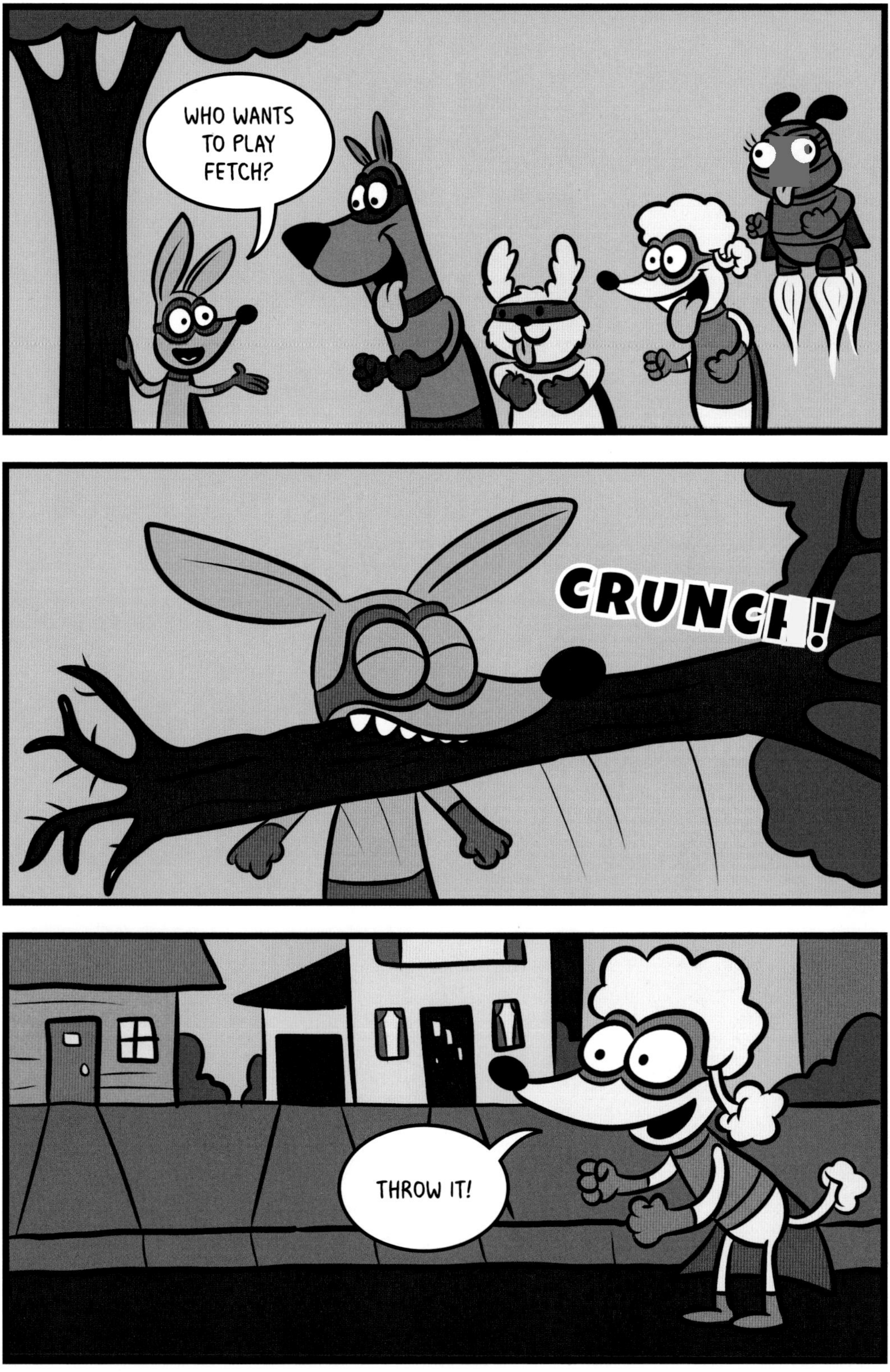
WHO WANTS TO PLAY FETCH?
CRUNCH!
THROW IT!

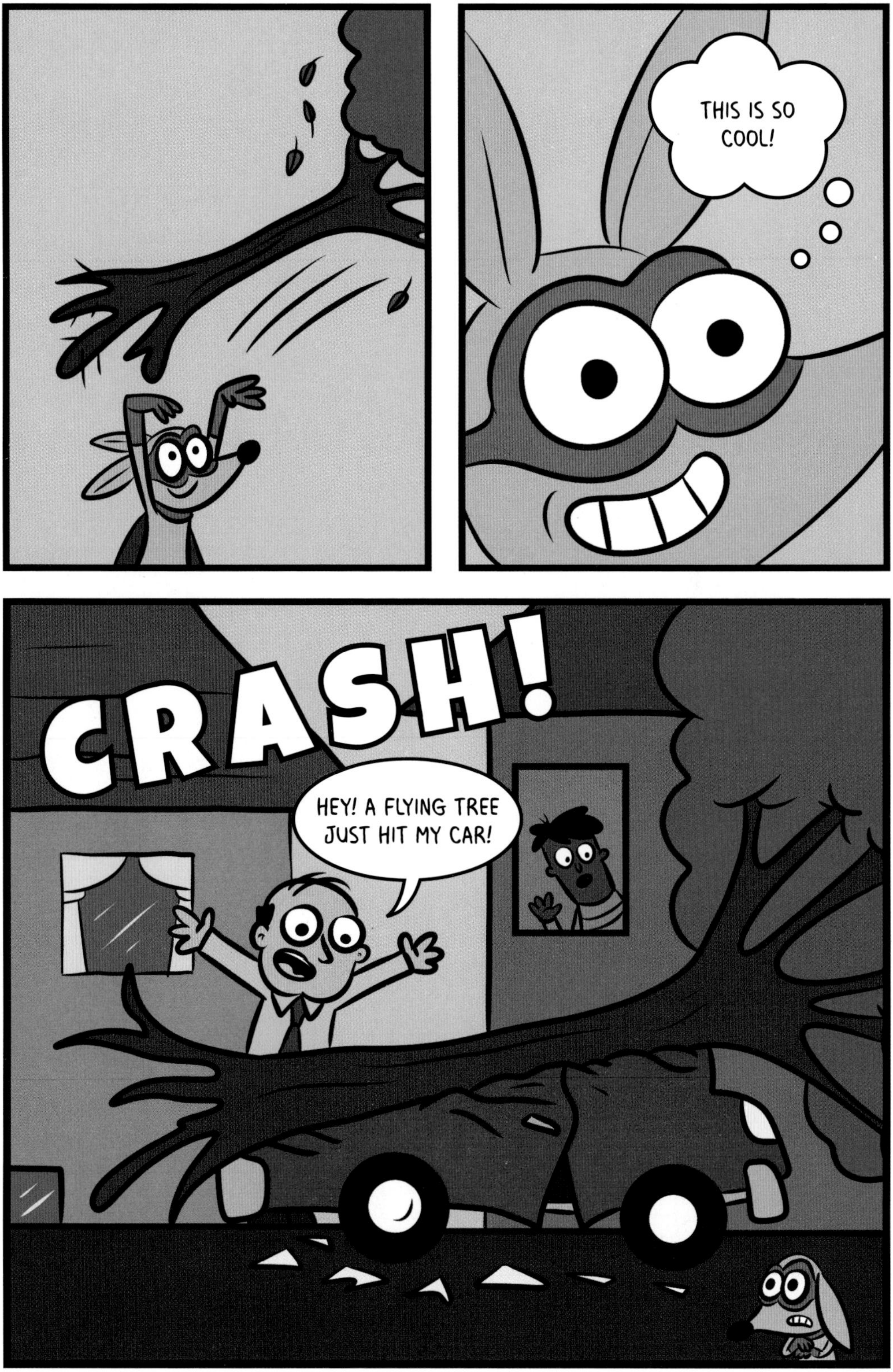
THIS IS SO COOL!
CRASH!
HEY! A FLYING TREE JUST HIT MY CAR!

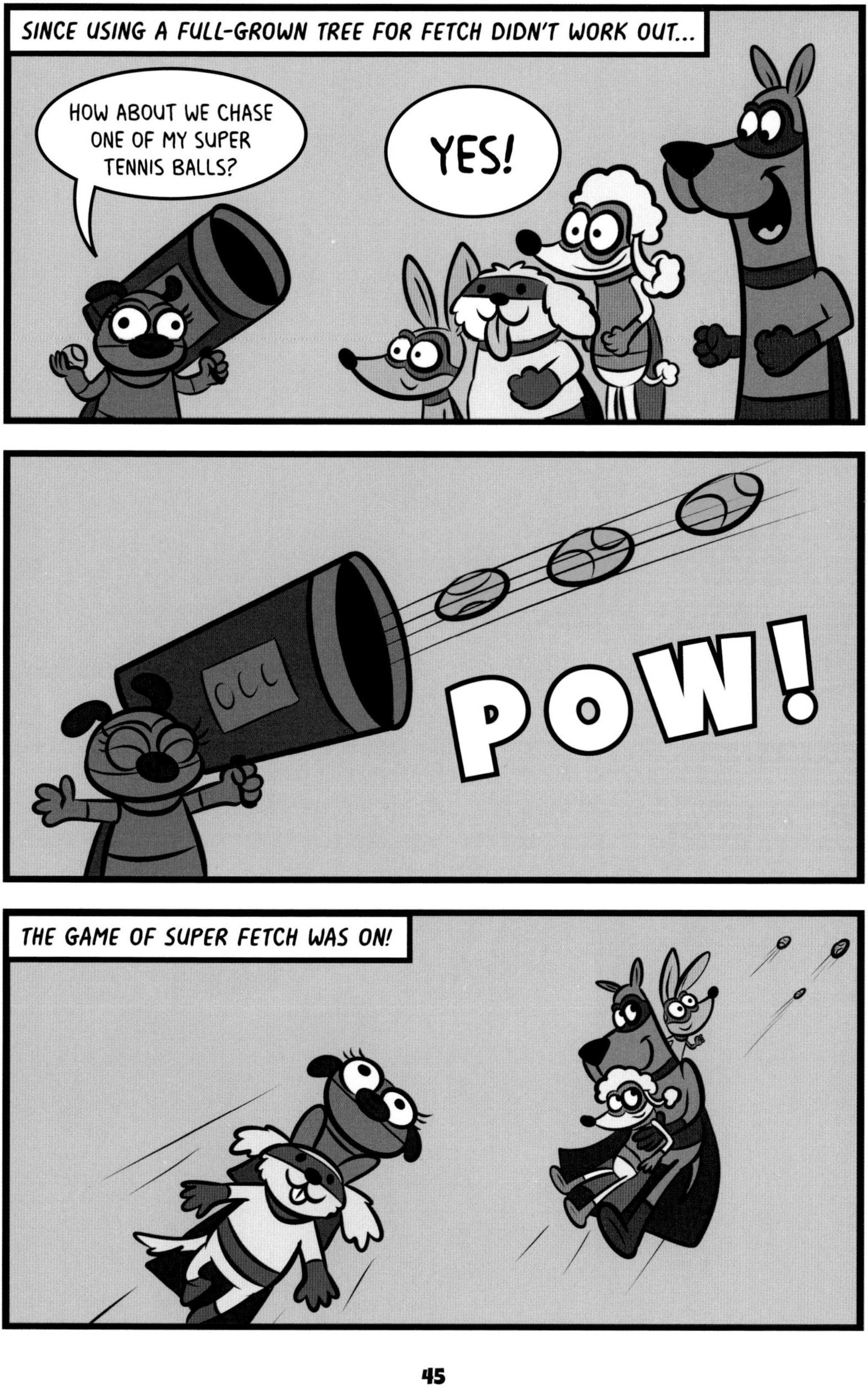
SINCE USING A FULL-GROWN TREE FOR FETCH DIDN'T WORK OUT...
HOW ABOUT WE CHASE ONE OF MY SUPER TENNIS BALLS?
YES!
POW!
THE GAME OF SUPER FETCH WAS ON!

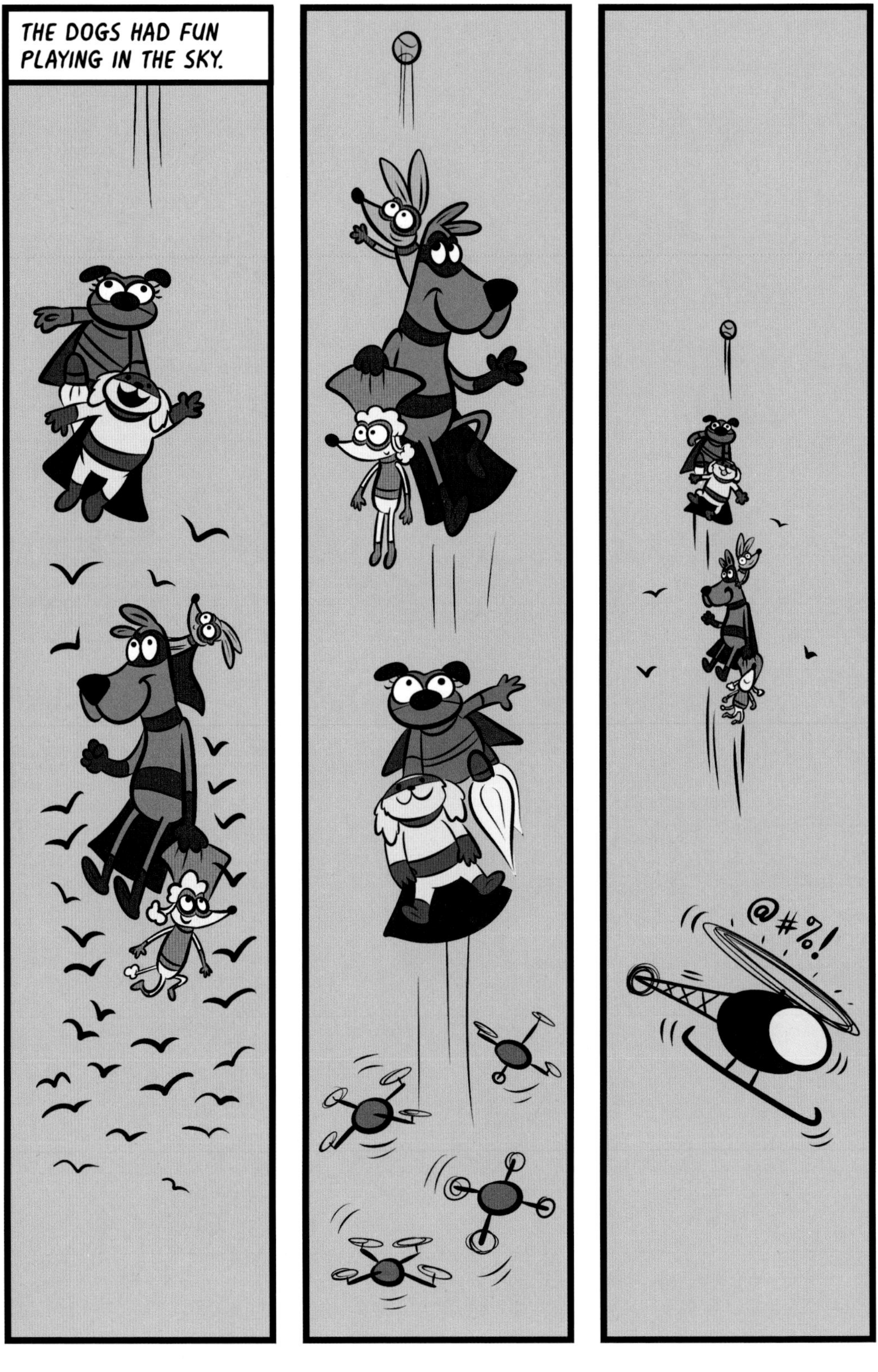
THE DOGS HAD FUN PLAYING IN THE SKY.
@#%!

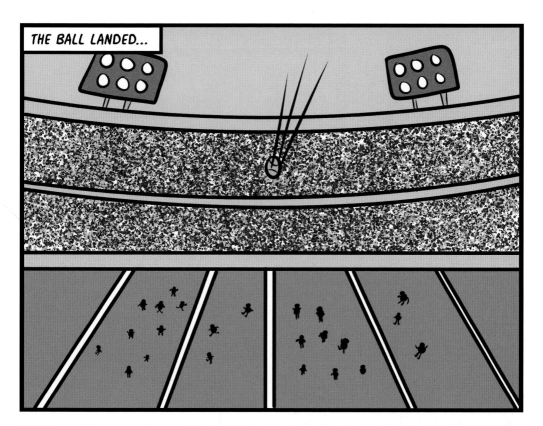

THE BALL LANDED...

AND SO DID THE DOGS.

I GOT THE BALL! I GOT IT I GOT IT I GOT IT!

SHEEPDOG'S SPINNING SENT THE PLAYERS SOARING!

WHOA! SOMEONE MUST HAVE HIT ME REALLY HARD!

HELP!

I SHOULD HAVE GONE INTO BASEBALL.

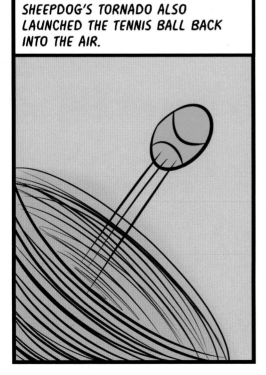

SHEEPDOG'S TORNADO ALSO LAUNCHED THE TENNIS BALL BACK INTO THE AIR.

WHERE'S THE BALL?

OVER THERE!

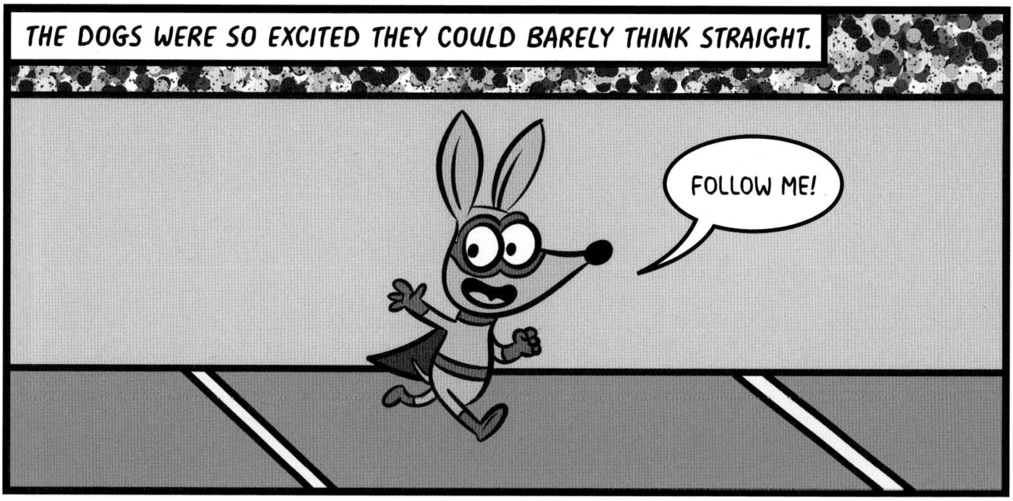
THE DOGS WERE SO EXCITED THEY COULD BARELY THINK STRAIGHT.
FOLLOW ME!

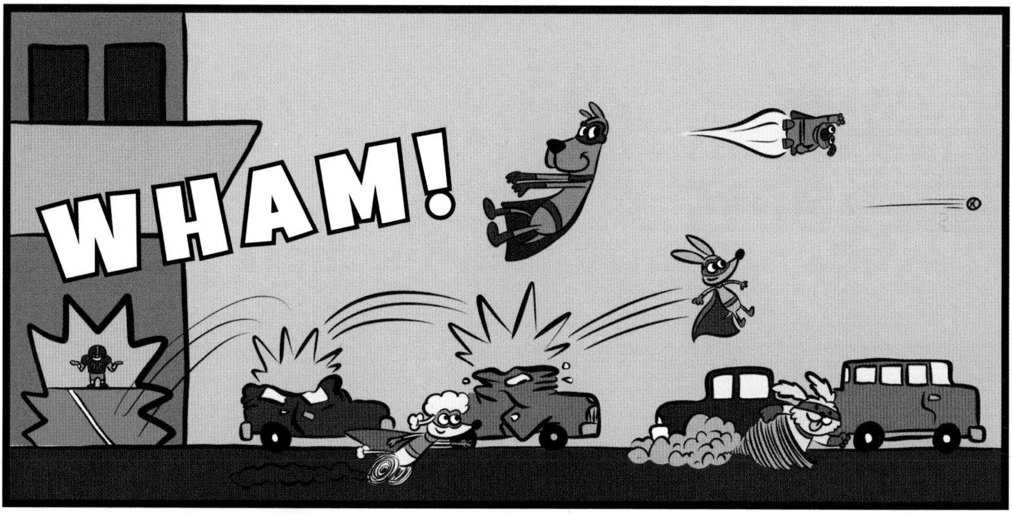
WHAM!

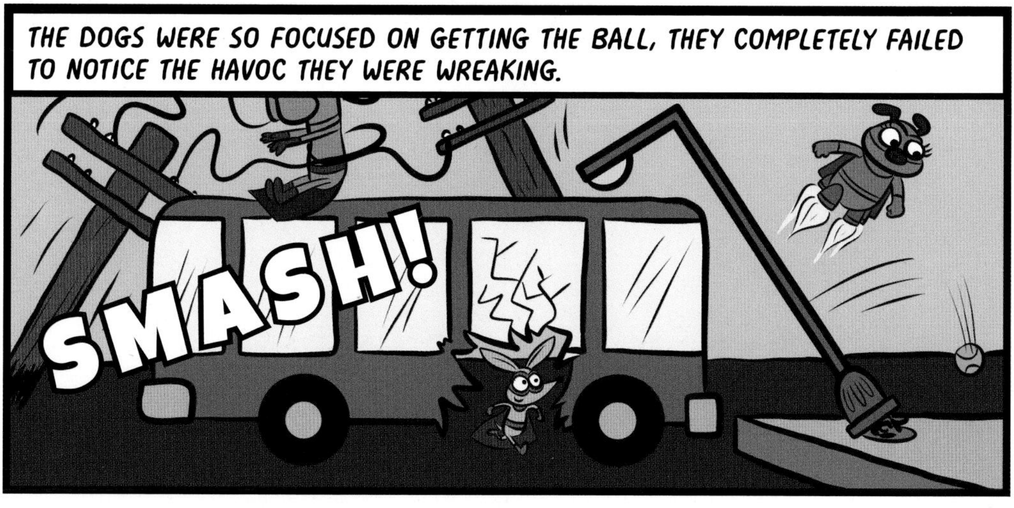
THE DOGS WERE SO FOCUSED ON GETTING THE BALL, THEY COMPLETELY FAILED TO NOTICE THE HAVOC THEY WERE WREAKING.
SMASH!

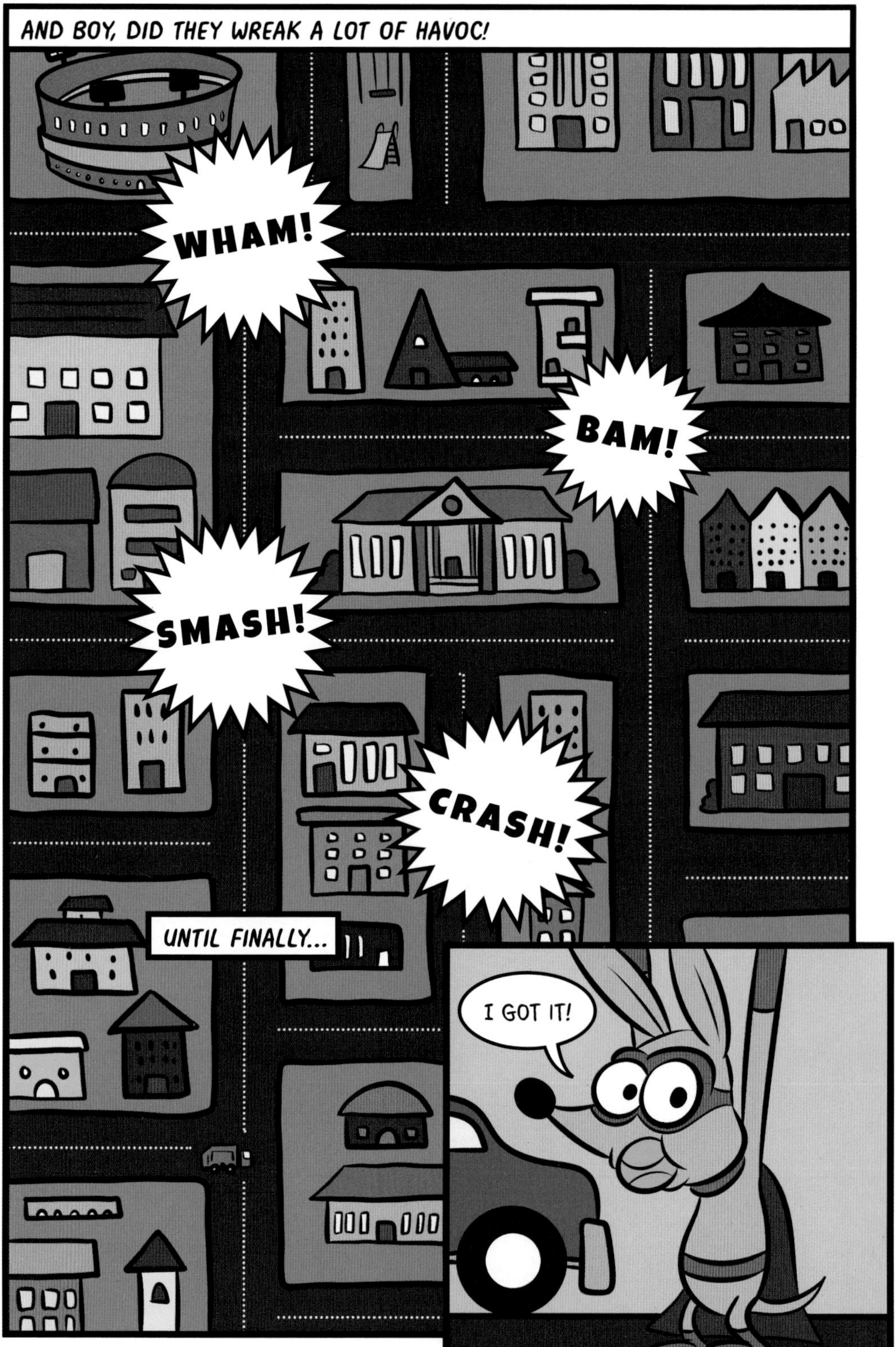
AND BOY, DID THEY WREAK A LOT OF HAVOC!
WHAM!
BAM!
SMASH!
CRASH!
UNTIL FINALLY...
I GOT IT!

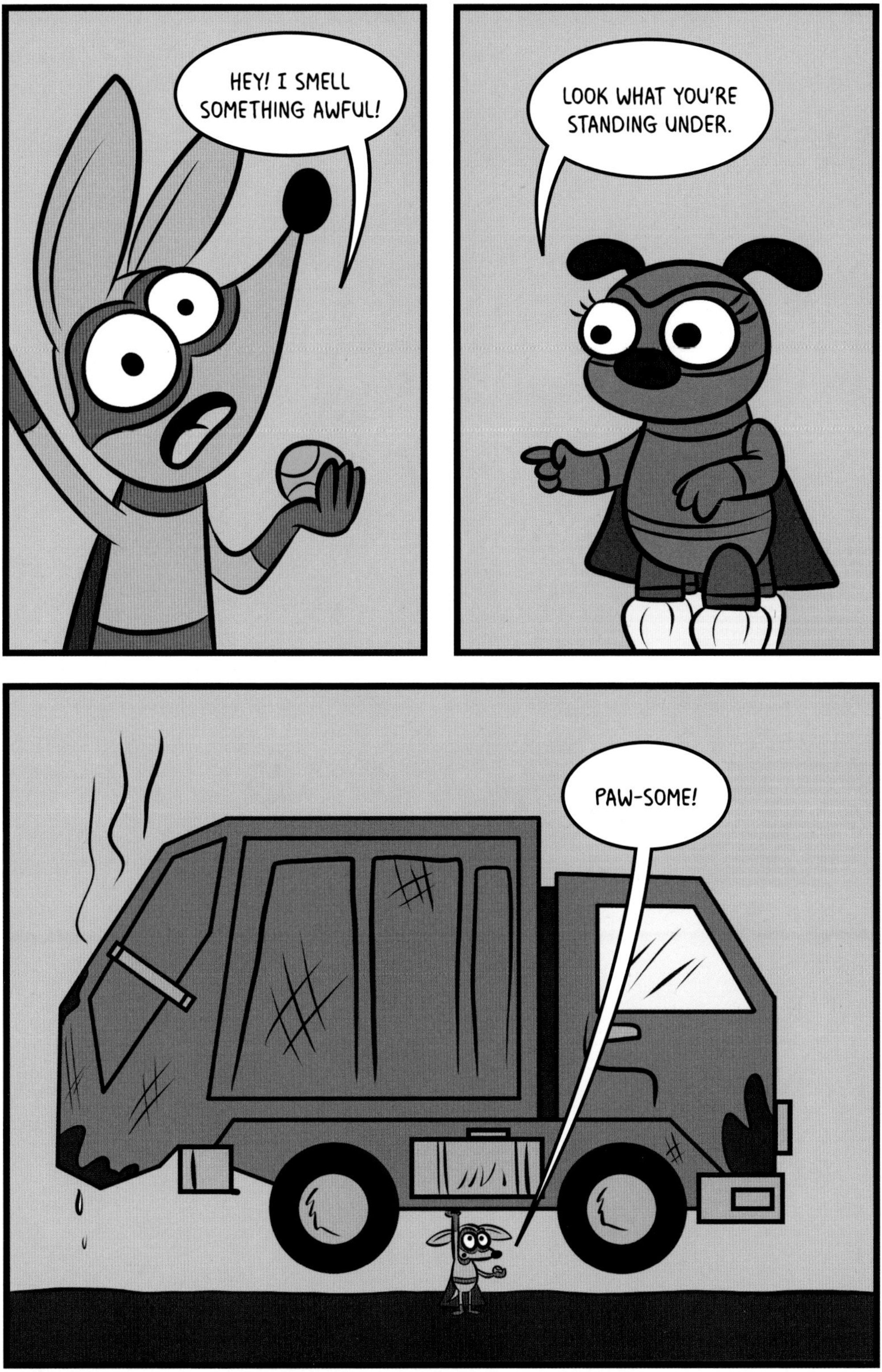
HEY! I SMELL SOMETHING AWFUL!
LOOK WHAT YOU'RE STANDING UNDER.
PAW-SOME!

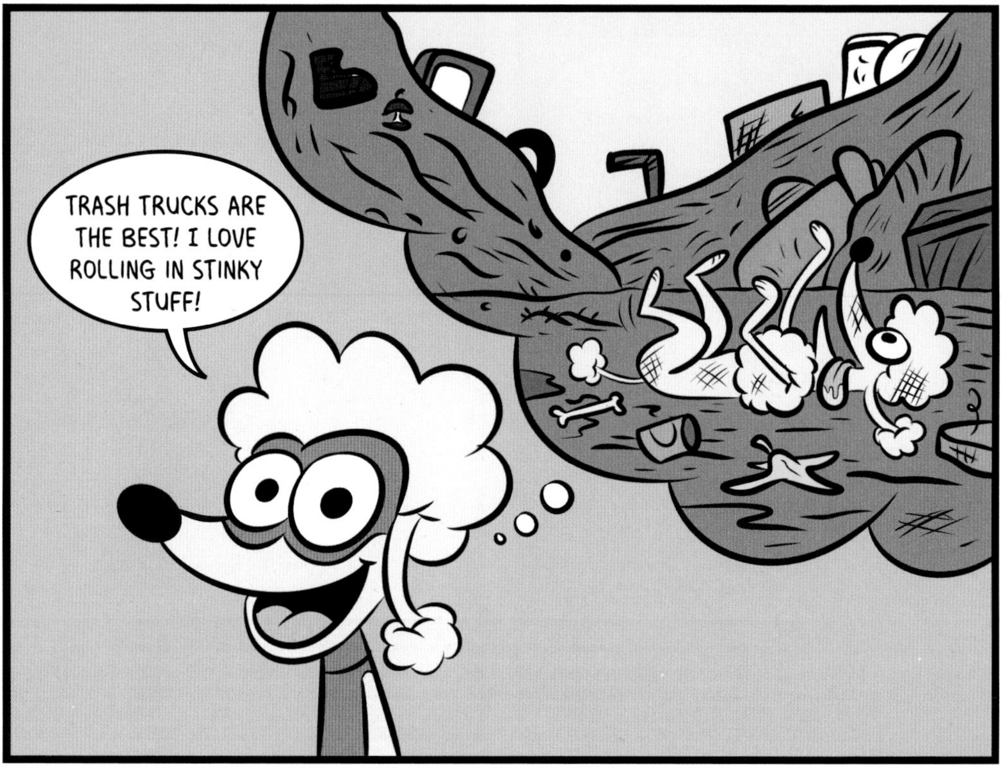
TRASH TRUCKS ARE THE BEST! I LOVE ROLLING IN STINKY STUFF!

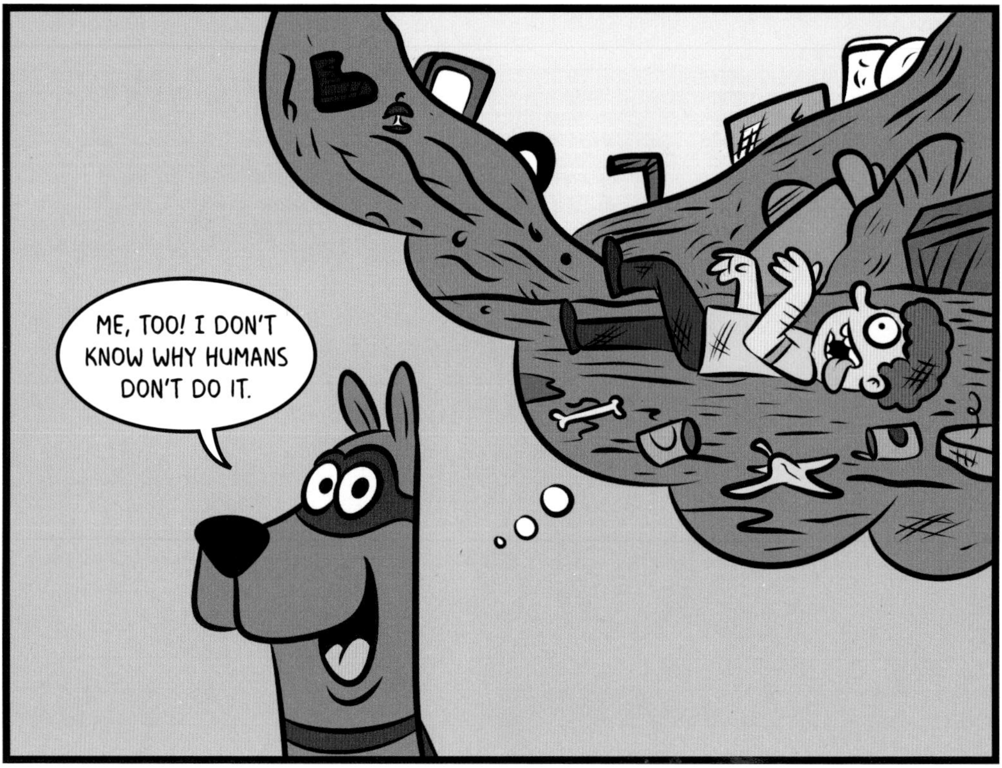
ME, TOO! I DON'T KNOW WHY HUMANS DON'T DO IT.

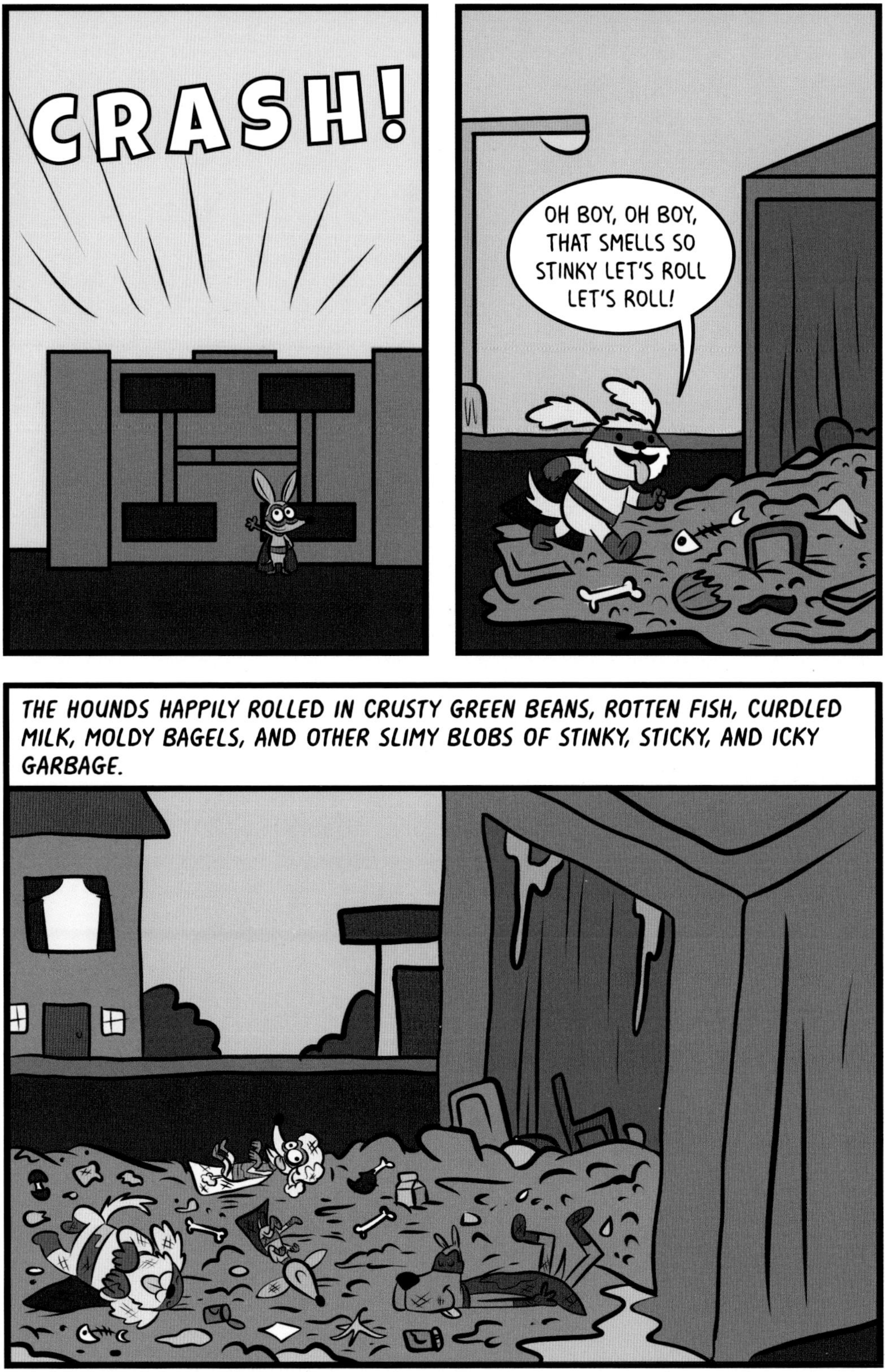
CRASH!
OH BOY, OH BOY, THAT SMELLS SO STINKY LET'S ROLL LET'S ROLL!
THE HOUNDS HAPPILY ROLLED IN CRUSTY GREEN BEANS, ROTTEN FISH, CURDLED MILK, MOLDY BAGELS, AND OTHER SLIMY BLOBS OF STINKY, STICKY, AND ICKY GARBAGE.

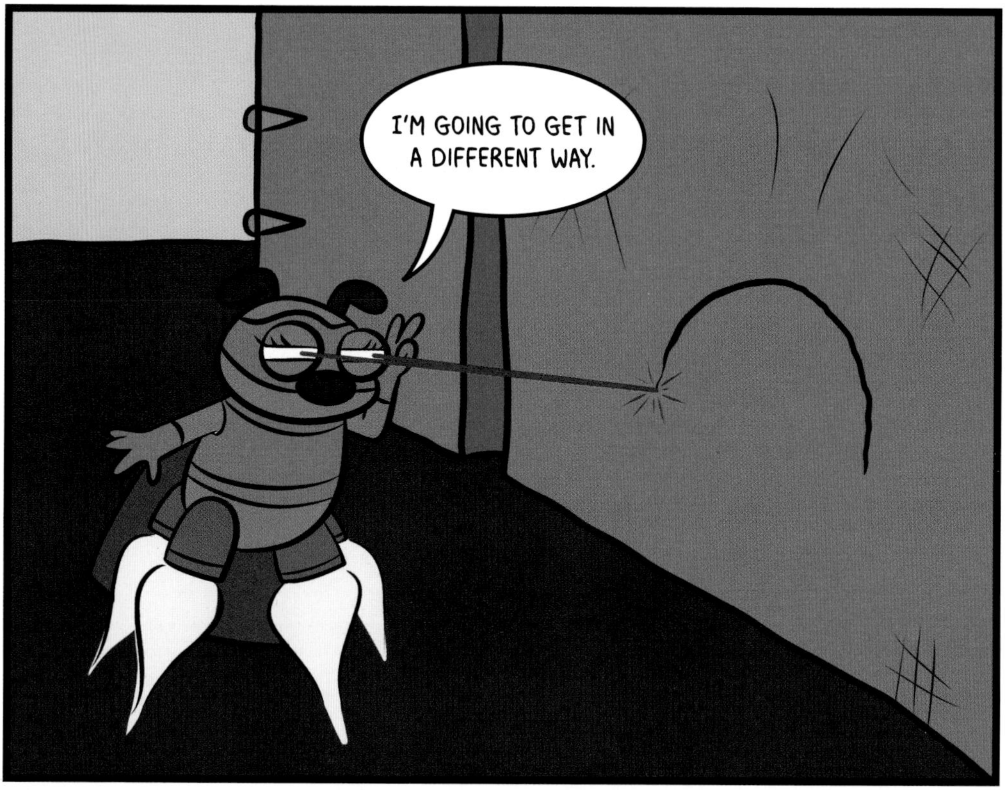
I'M GOING TO GET IN A DIFFERENT WAY.

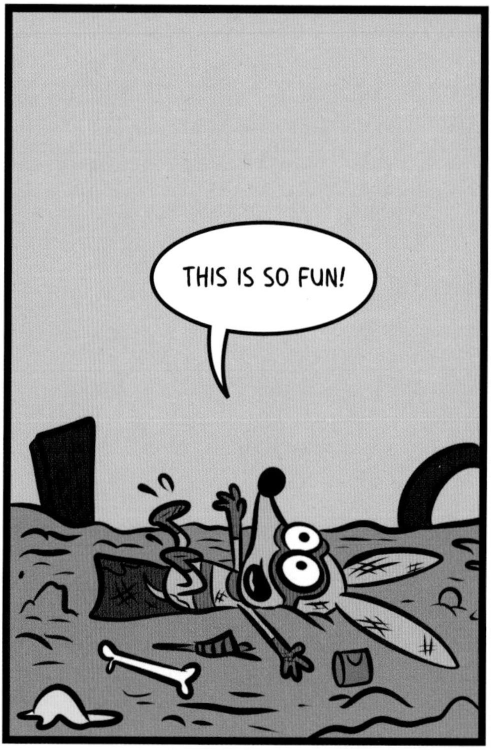
THIS IS SO FUN!

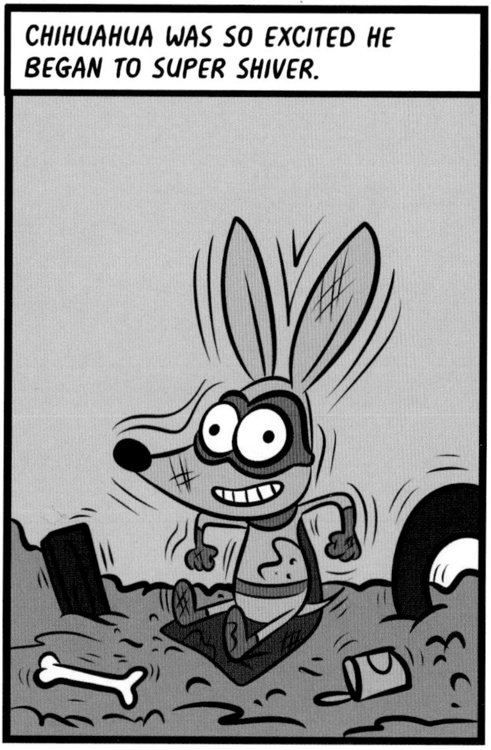
CHIHUAHUA WAS SO EXCITED HE BEGAN TO SUPER SHIVER.

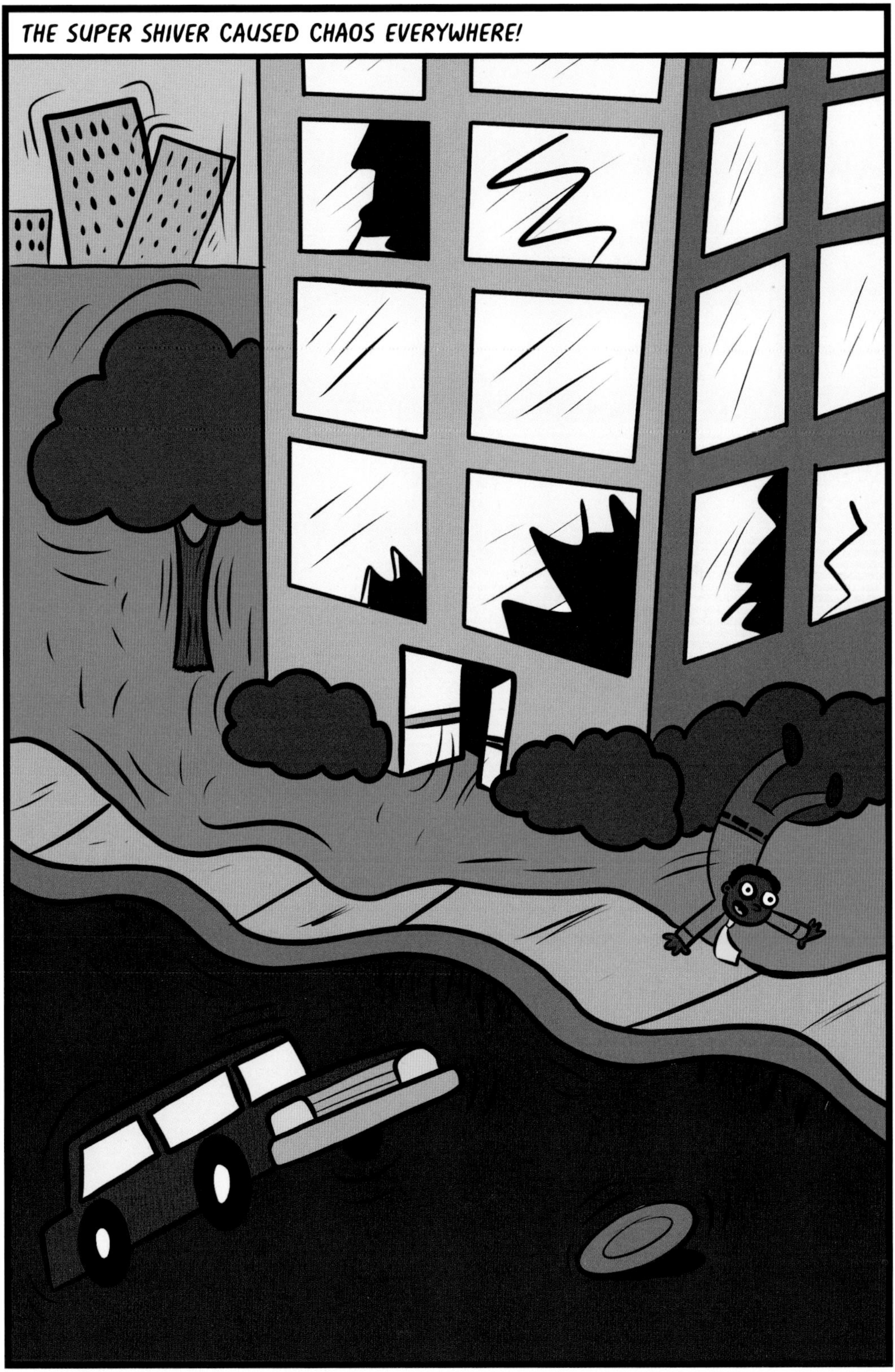
THE SUPER SHIVER CAUSED CHAOS EVERYWHERE!

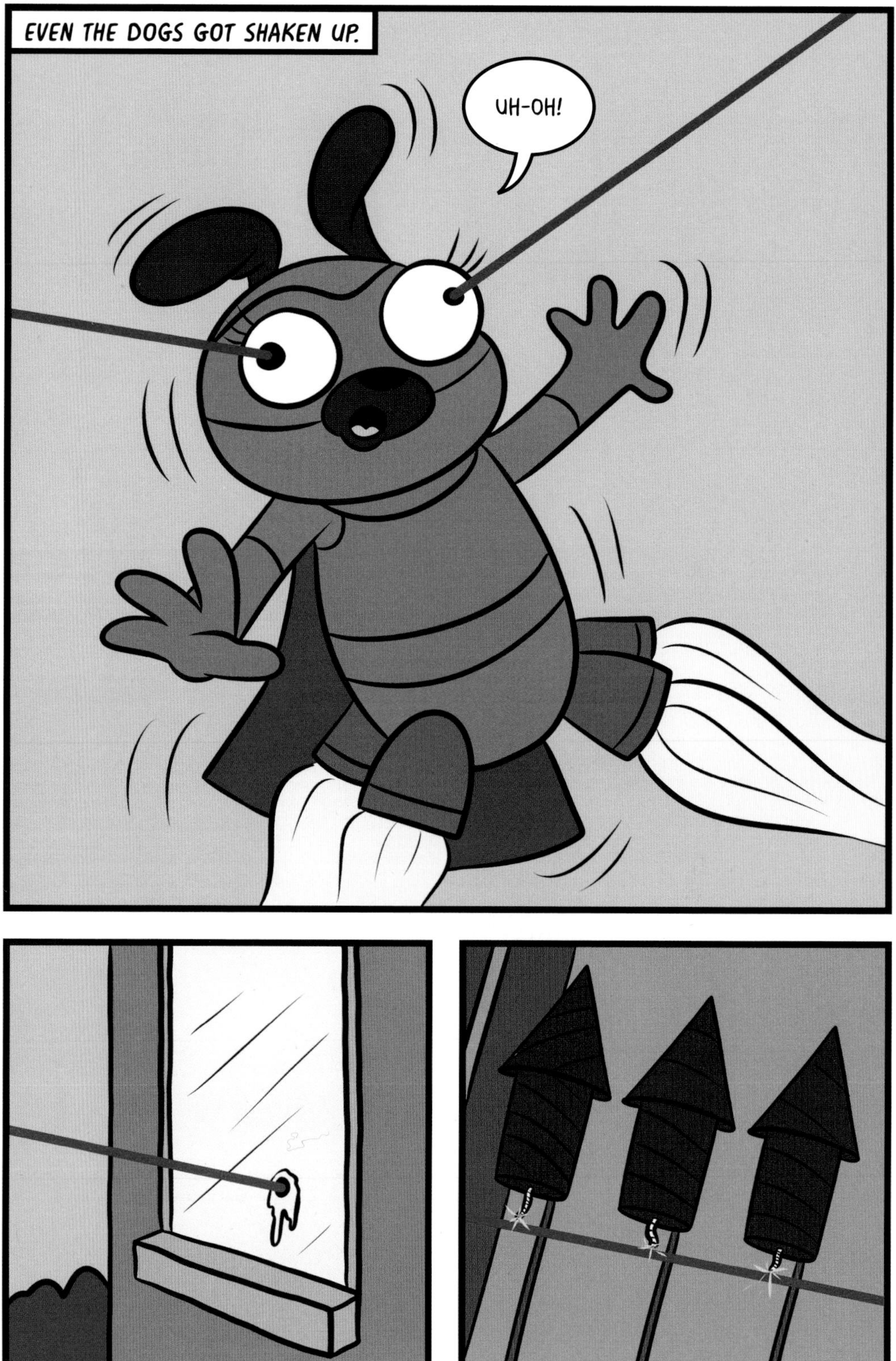
EVEN THE DOGS GOT SHAKEN UP.
UH-OH!

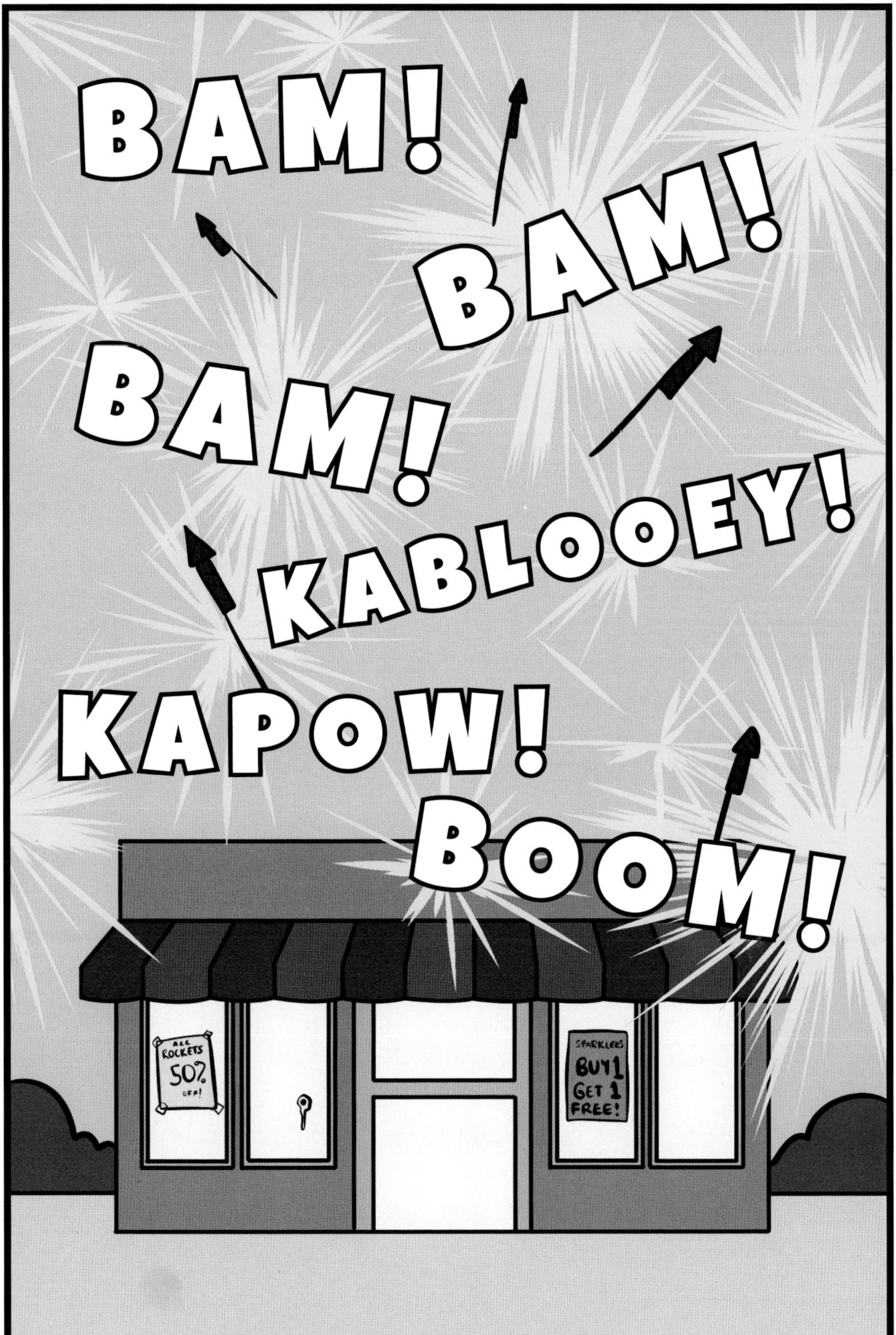
BAM!
BAM!
BAM!
KABLOOEY!
KAPOW!
BOOM!
ALL ROCKETS 50% OFF!
SPARKLERS BUY 1 GET 1 FREE!

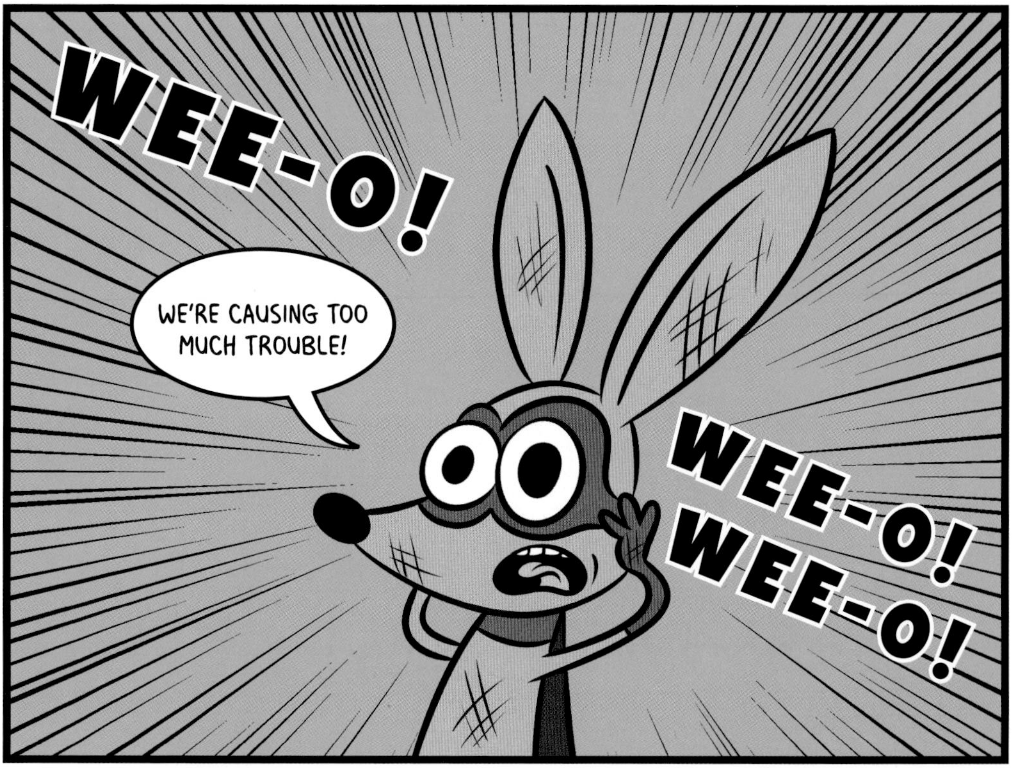
WEE-O!
WE'RE CAUSING TOO MUCH TROUBLE!
WEE-O! WEE-O!

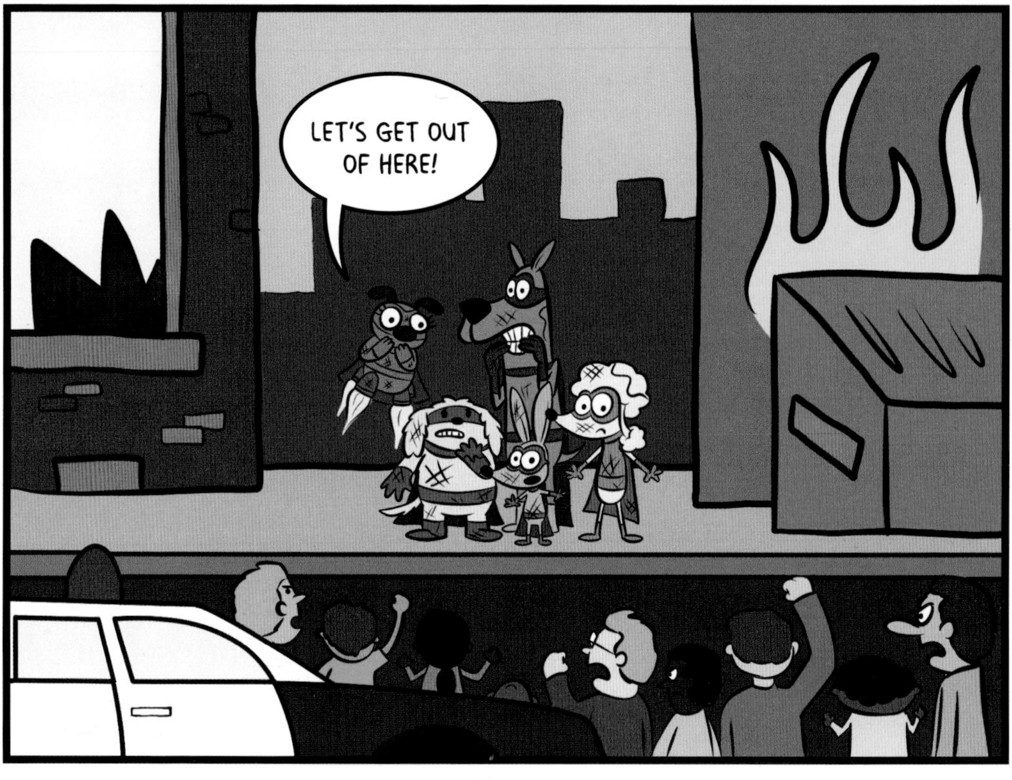
LET'S GET OUT OF HERE!

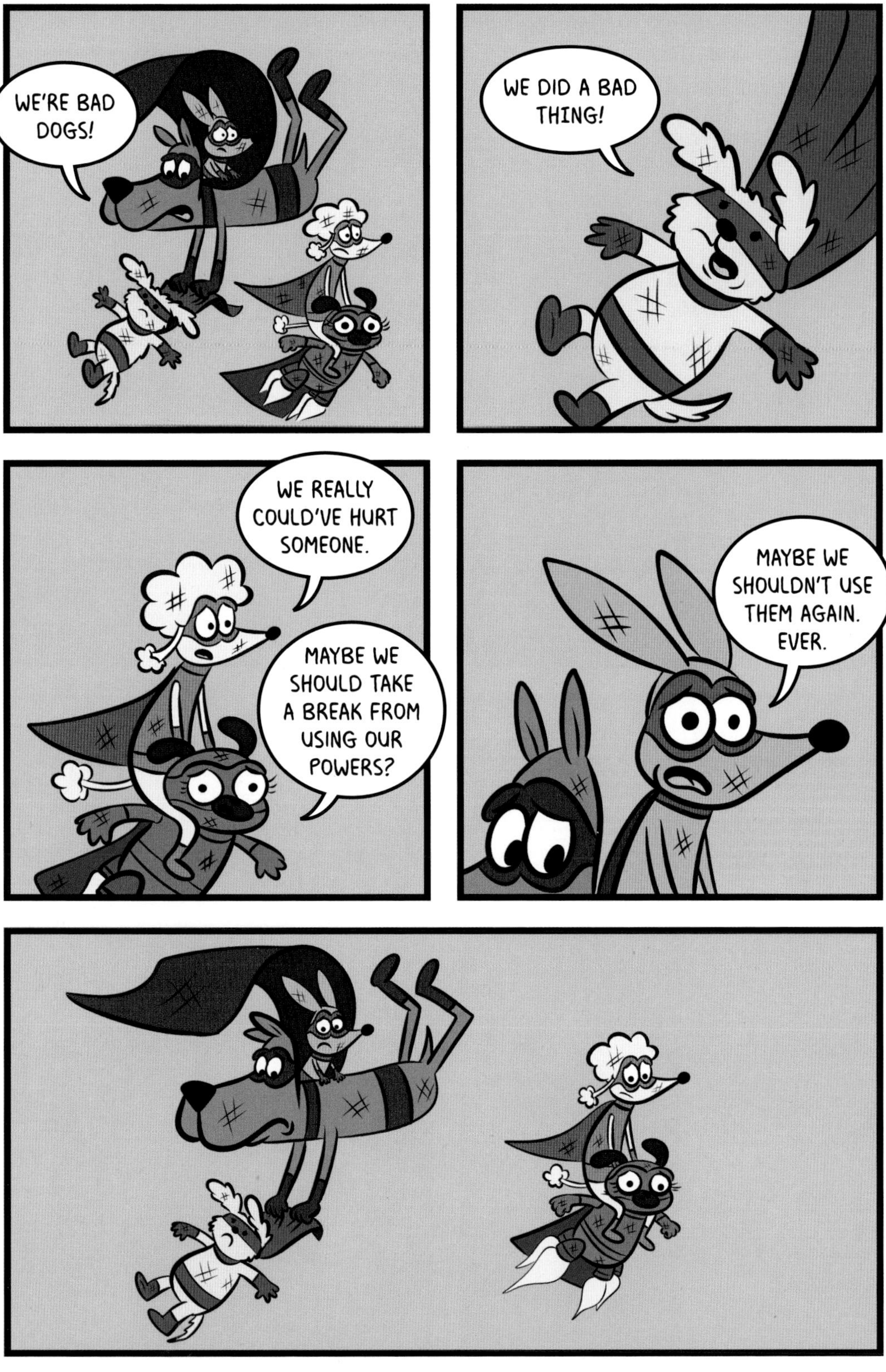
WE'RE BAD DOGS!
WE DID A BAD THING!
WE REALLY COULD'VE HURT SOMEONE.
MAYBE WE SHOULD TAKE A BREAK FROM USING OUR POWERS?
MAYBE WE SHOULDN'T USE THEM AGAIN. EVER.

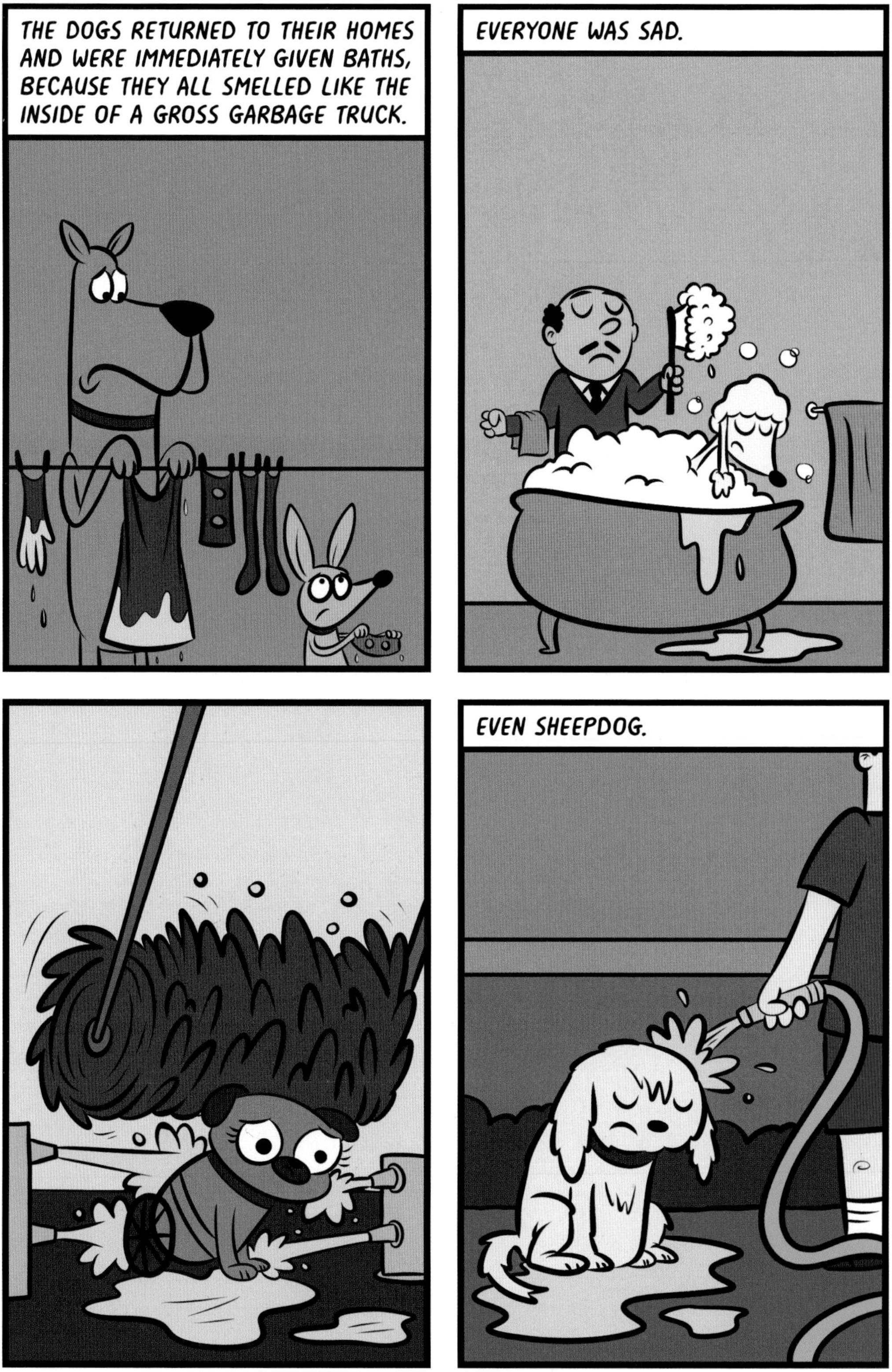
THE DOGS RETURNED TO THEIR HOMES AND WERE IMMEDIATELY GIVEN BATHS, BECAUSE THEY ALL SMELLED LIKE THE INSIDE OF A GROSS GARBAGE TRUCK.
EVERYONE WAS SAD.
EVEN SHEEPDOG.

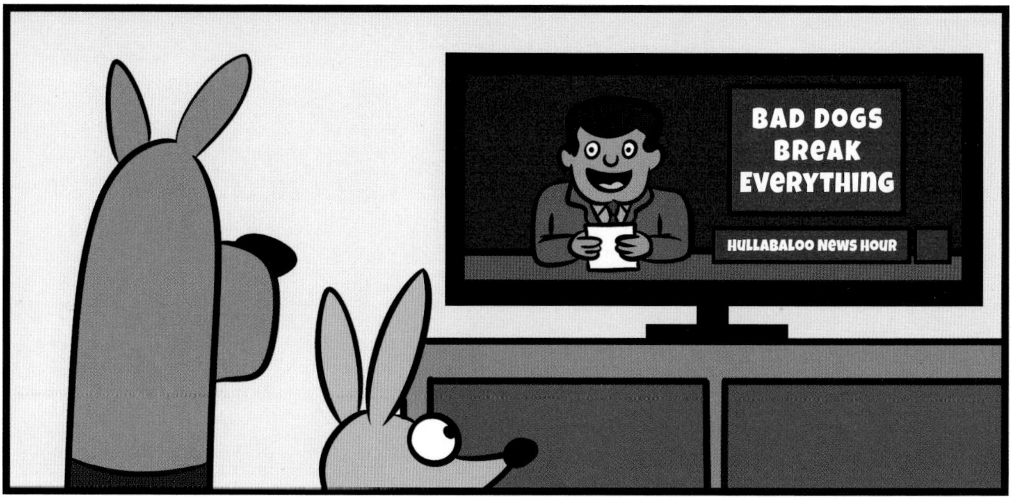
BAD DOGS BREAK EVERYTHING
HULLABALOO NEWS HOUR

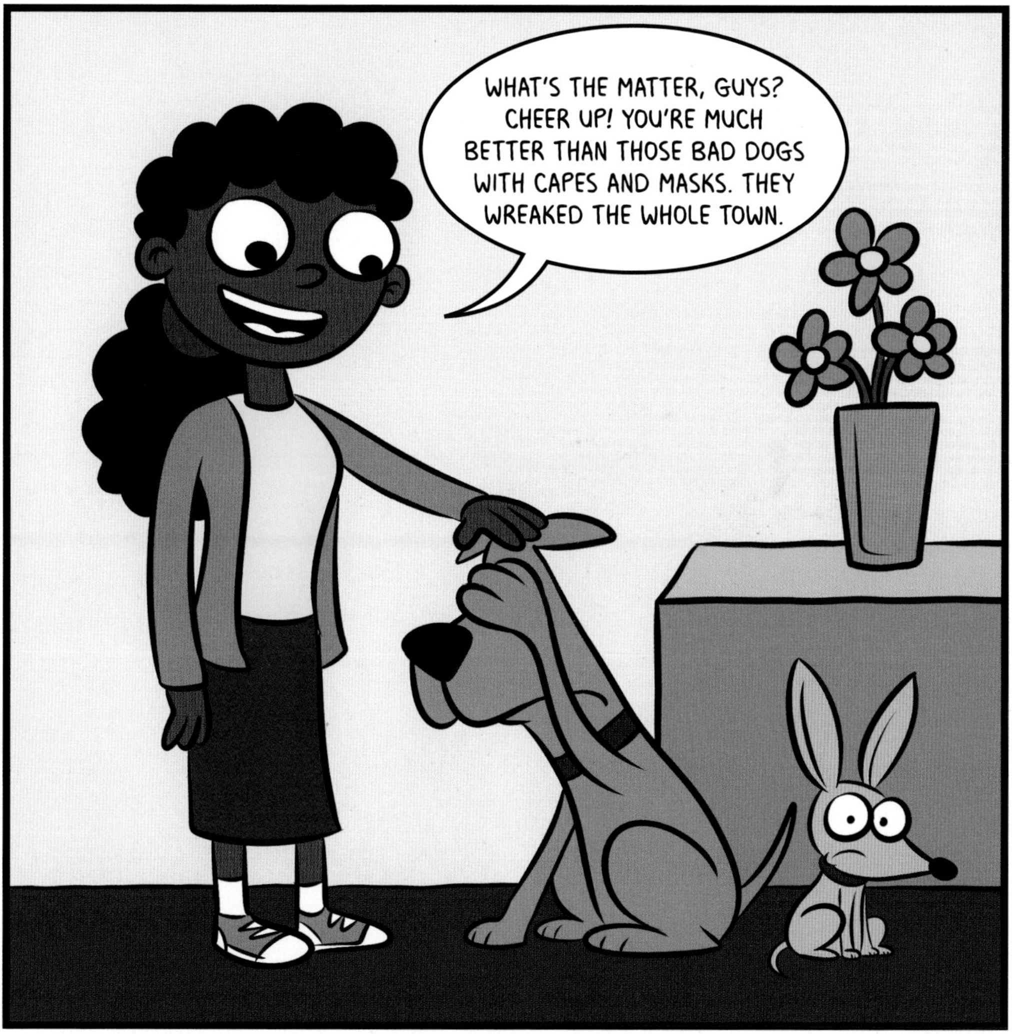
WHAT'S THE MATTER, GUYS? CHEER UP! YOU'RE MUCH BETTER THAN THOSE BAD DOGS WITH CAPES AND MASKS. THEY WREAKED THE WHOLE TOWN.

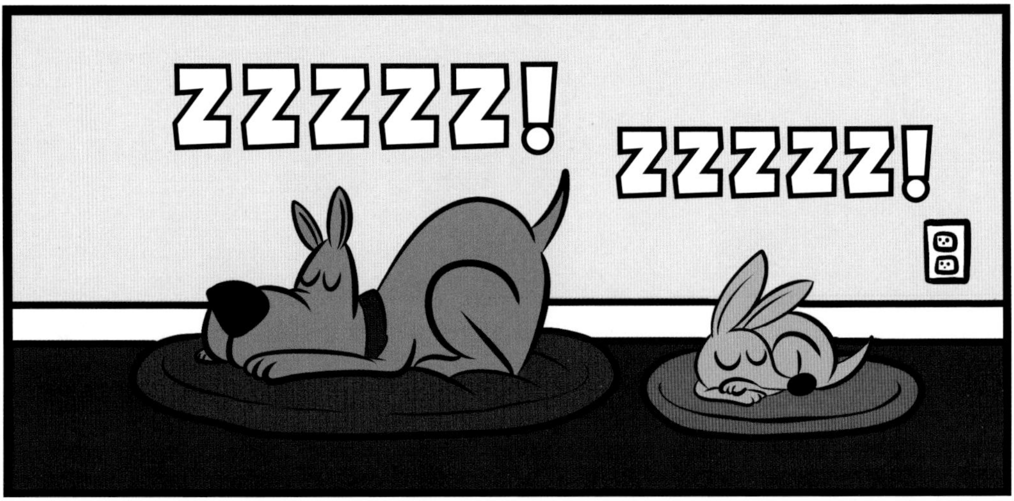
ZZZZZ!
ZZZZZ!

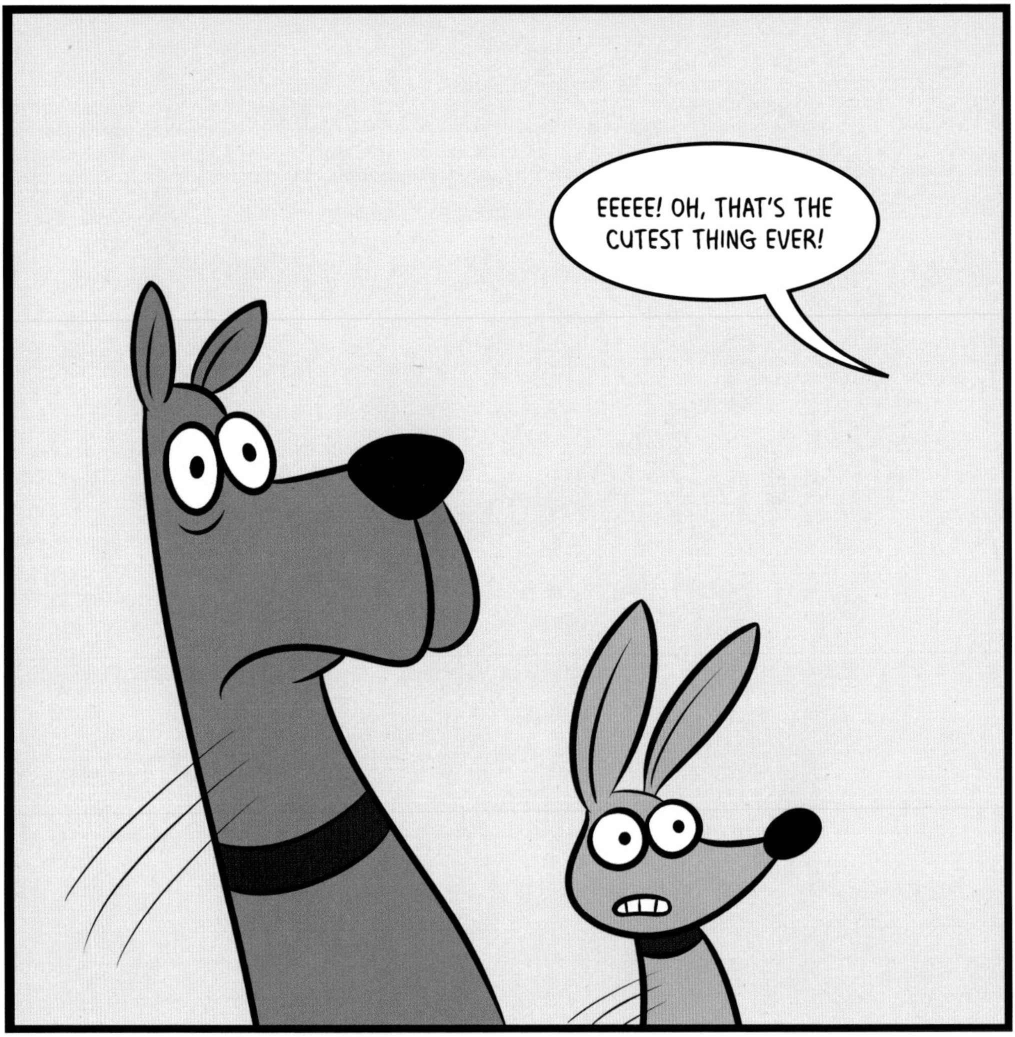
EEEEE! OH, THAT'S THE CUTEST THING EVER!

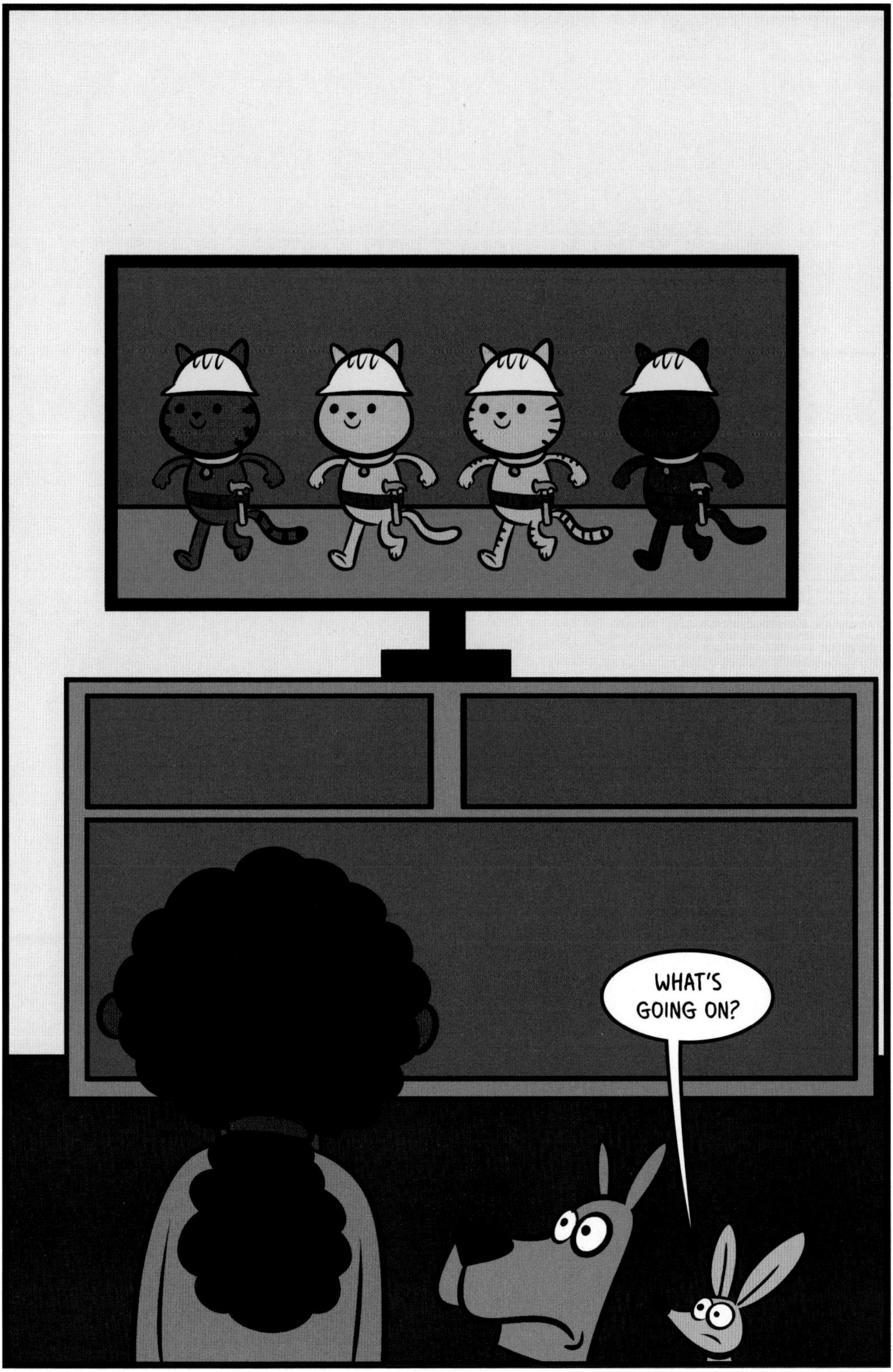
WHAT'S GOING ON?

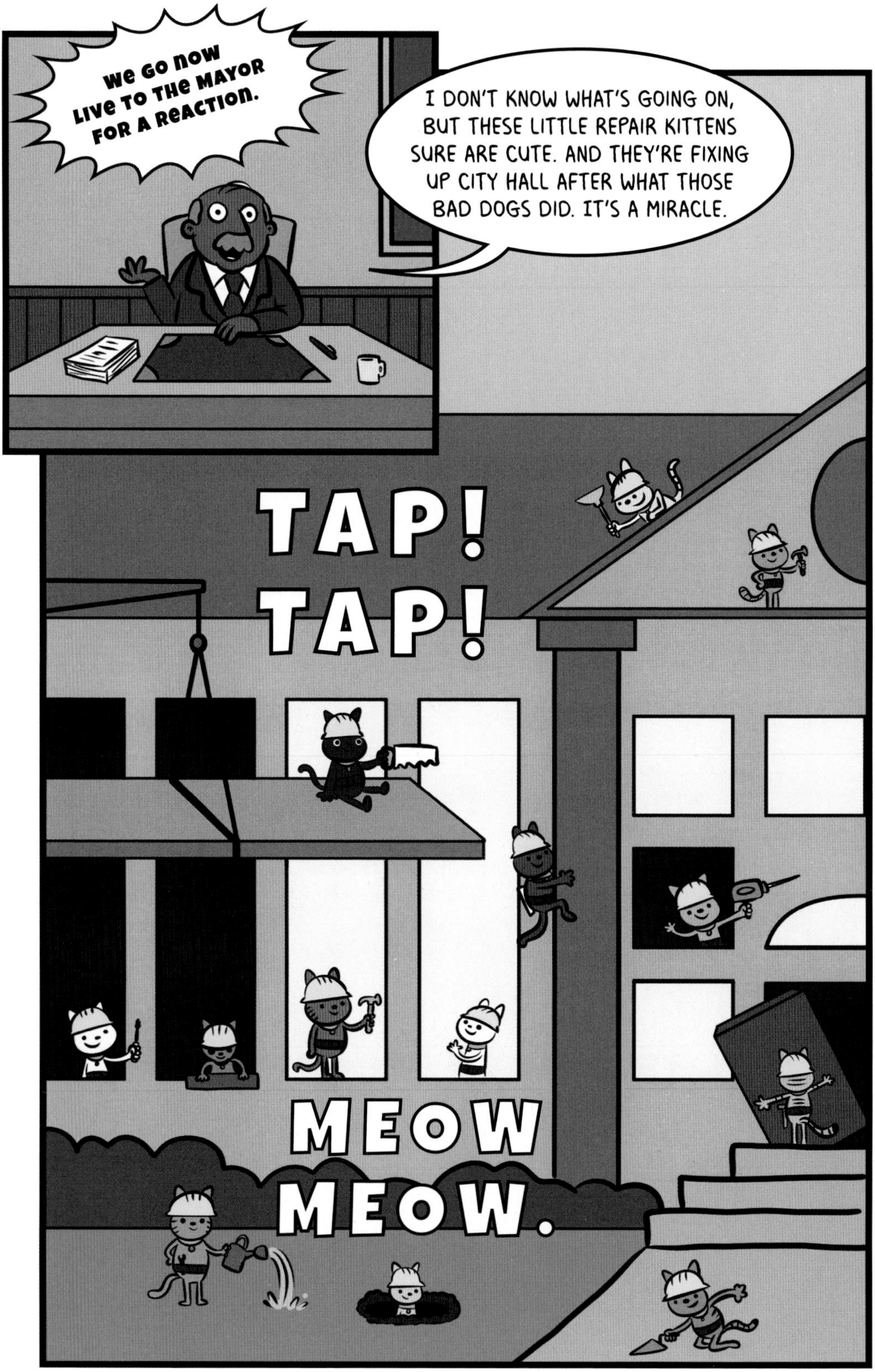
WE GO NOW LIVE TO THE MAYOR FOR A REACTION.
I DON'T KNOW WHAT'S GOING ON, BUT THESE LITTLE REPAIR KITTENS SURE ARE CUTE. AND THEY'RE FIXING UP CITY HALL AFTER WHAT THOSE BAD DOGS DID. IT'S A MIRACLE.
TAP! TAP!
MEOW MEOW.

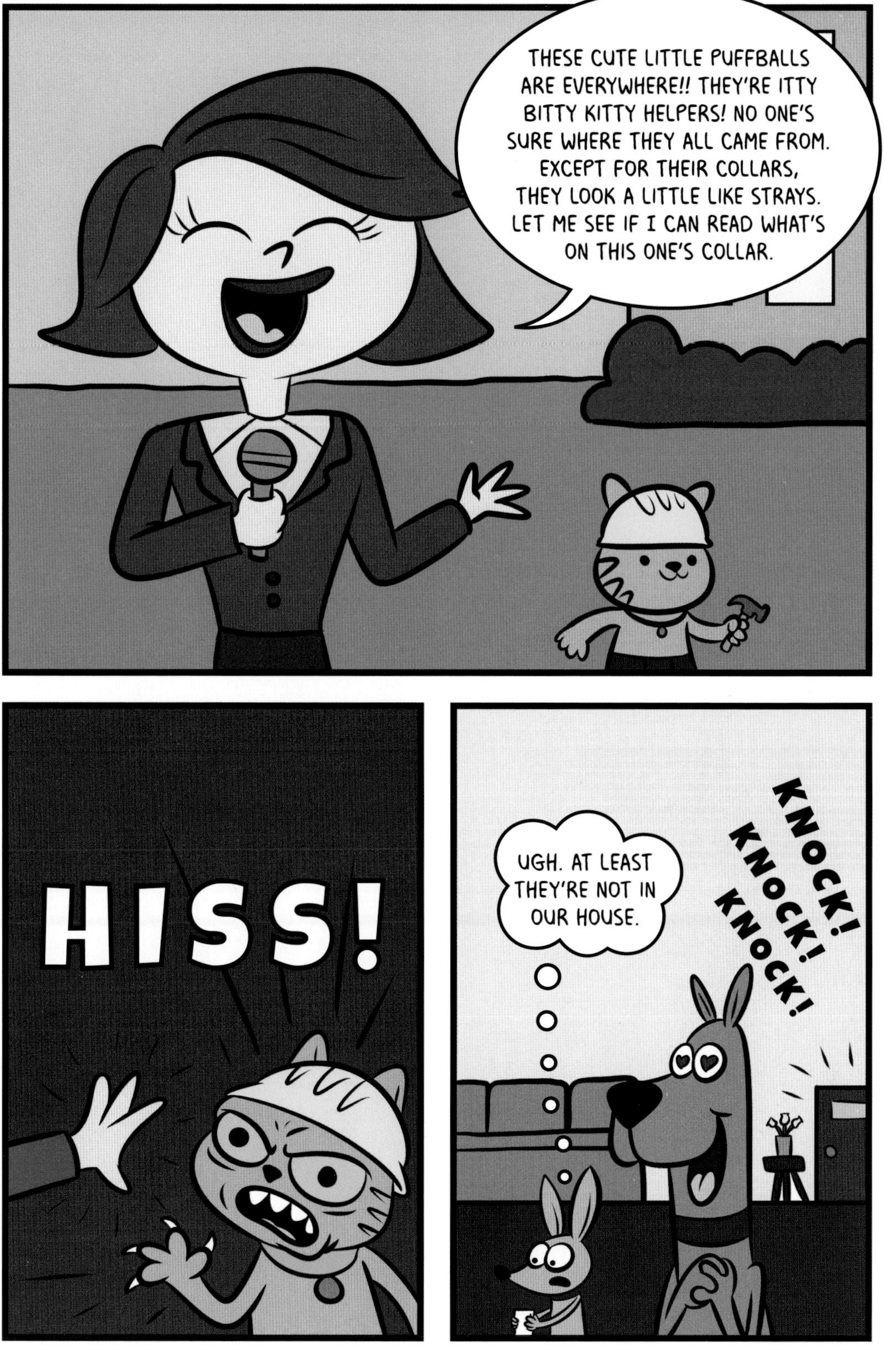
THESE CUTE LITTLE PUFFBALLS ARE EVERYWHERE!! THEY'RE ITTY BITTY KITTY HELPERS! NO ONE'S SURE WHERE THEY ALL CAME FROM. EXCEPT FOR THEIR COLLARS, THEY LOOK A LITTLE LIKE STRAYS. LET ME SEE IF I CAN READ WHAT'S ON THIS ONE'S COLLAR.
HISS!
UGH. AT LEAST THEY'RE NOT IN OUR HOUSE.
KNOCK! KNOCK! KNOCK!

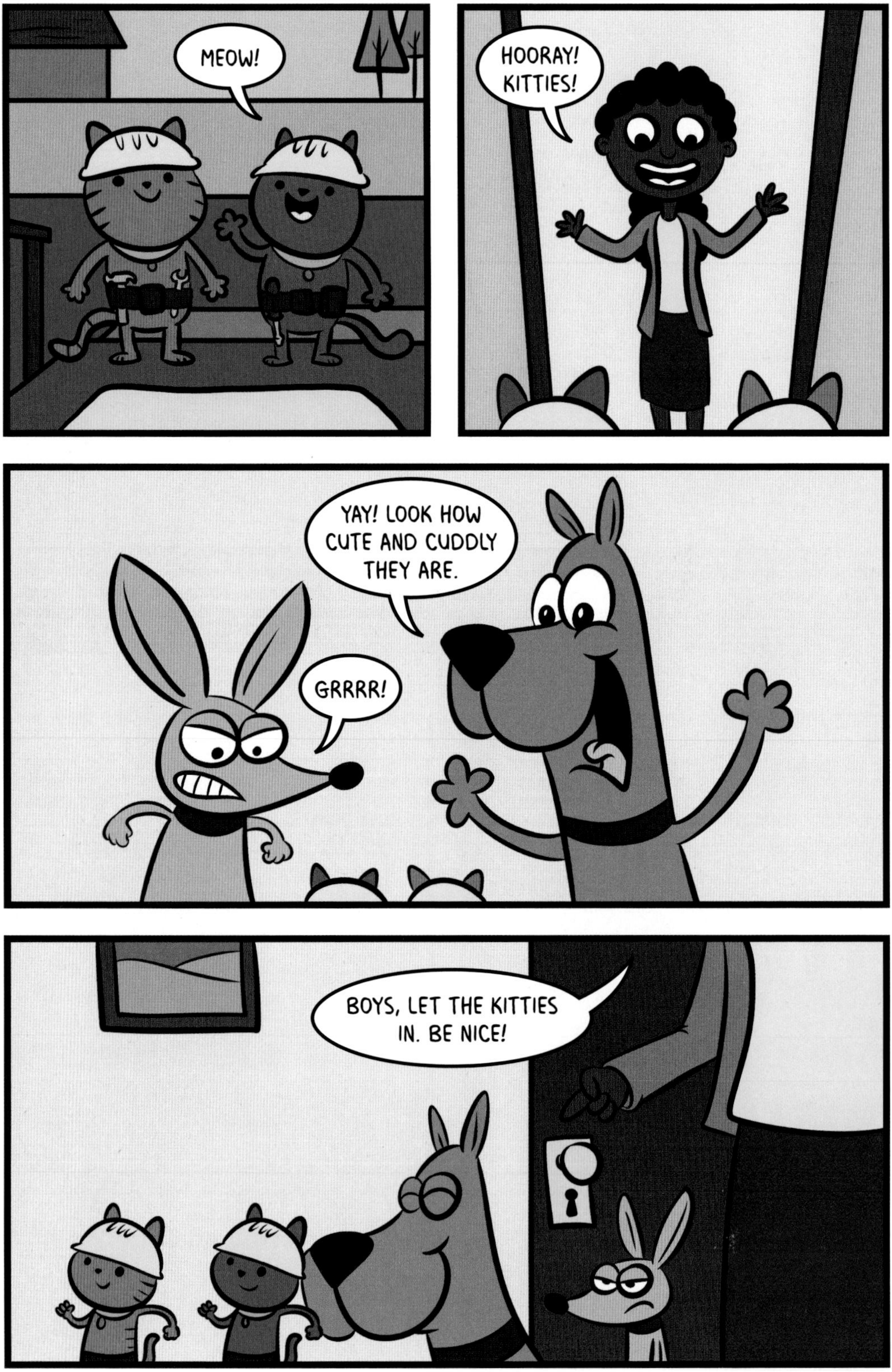
MEOW!
HOORAY! KITTIES!
YAY! LOOK HOW CUTE AND CUDDLY THEY ARE.
GRRRR!
BOYS, LET THE KITTIES IN. BE NICE!

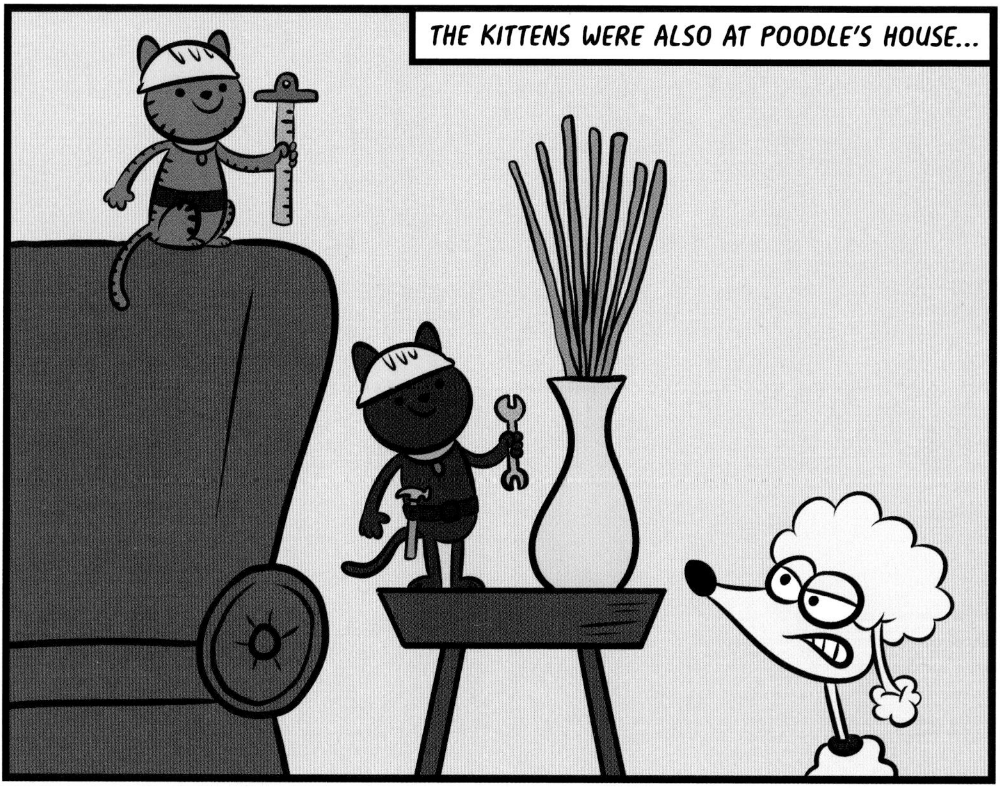
THE KITTENS WERE ALSO AT POODLE'S HOUSE...

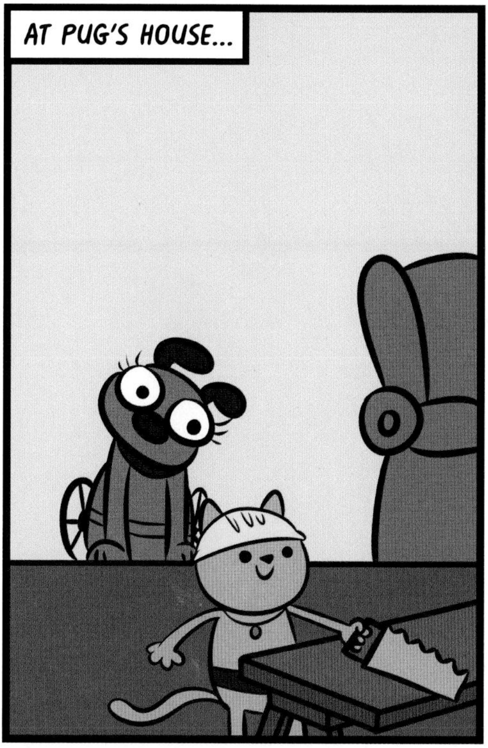
AT PUG'S HOUSE...

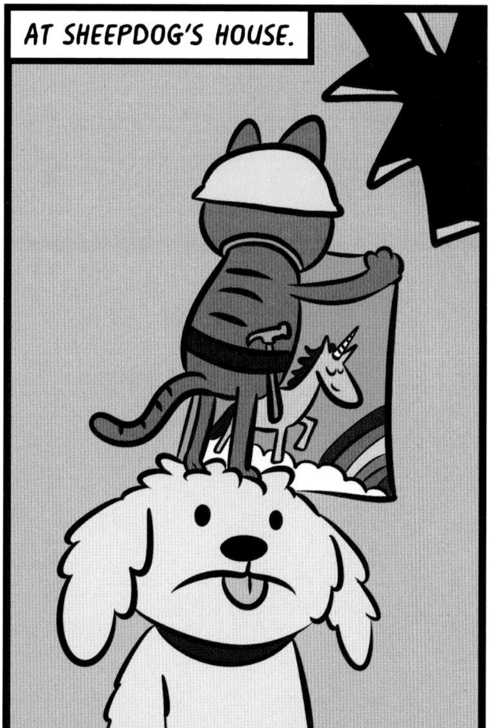
AT SHEEPDOG'S HOUSE.

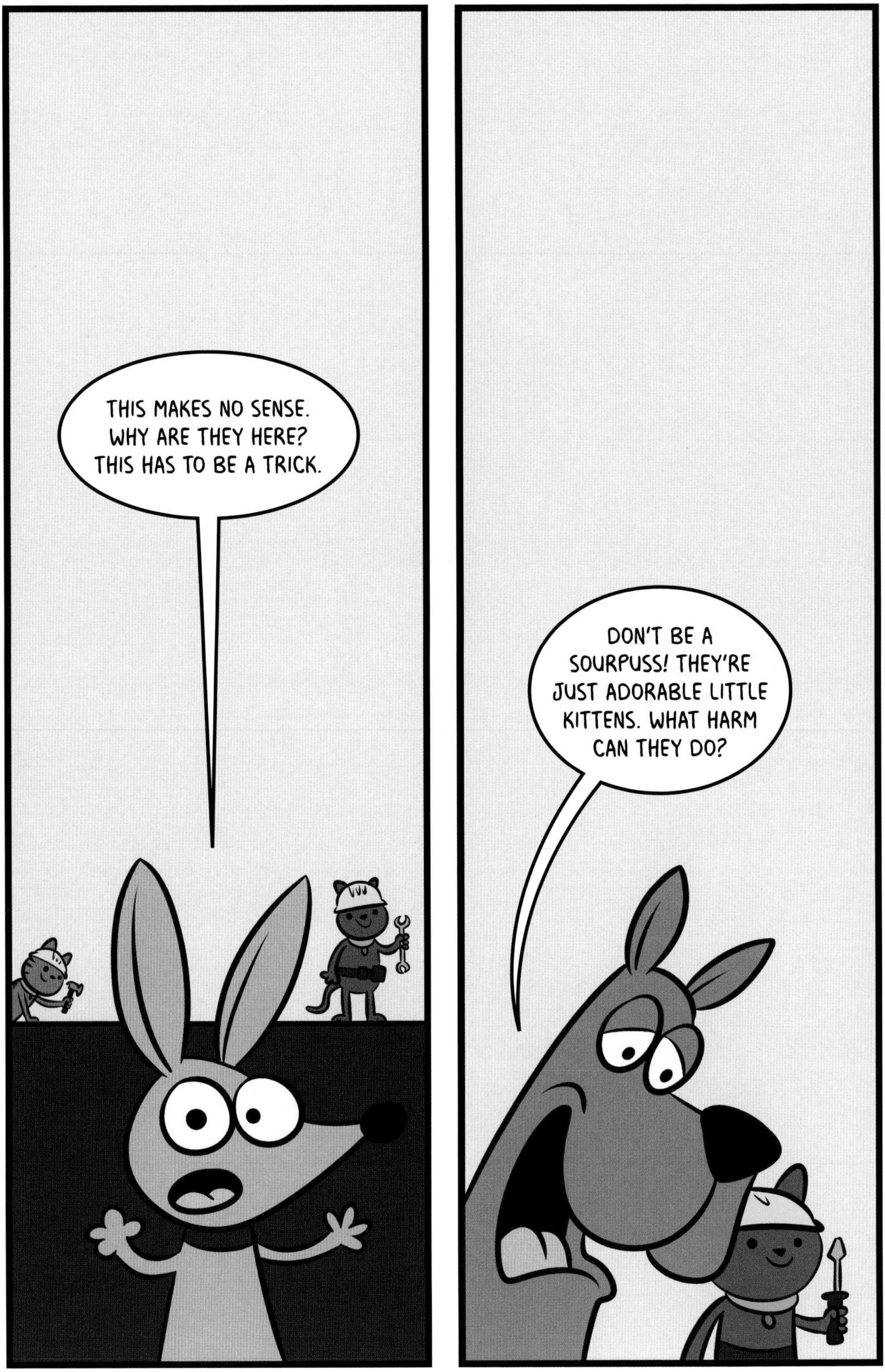
THIS MAKES NO SENSE. WHY ARE THEY HERE? THIS HAS TO BE A TRICK.
DON'T BE A SOURPUSS! THEY'RE JUST ADORABLE LITTLE KITTENS. WHAT HARM CAN THEY DO?

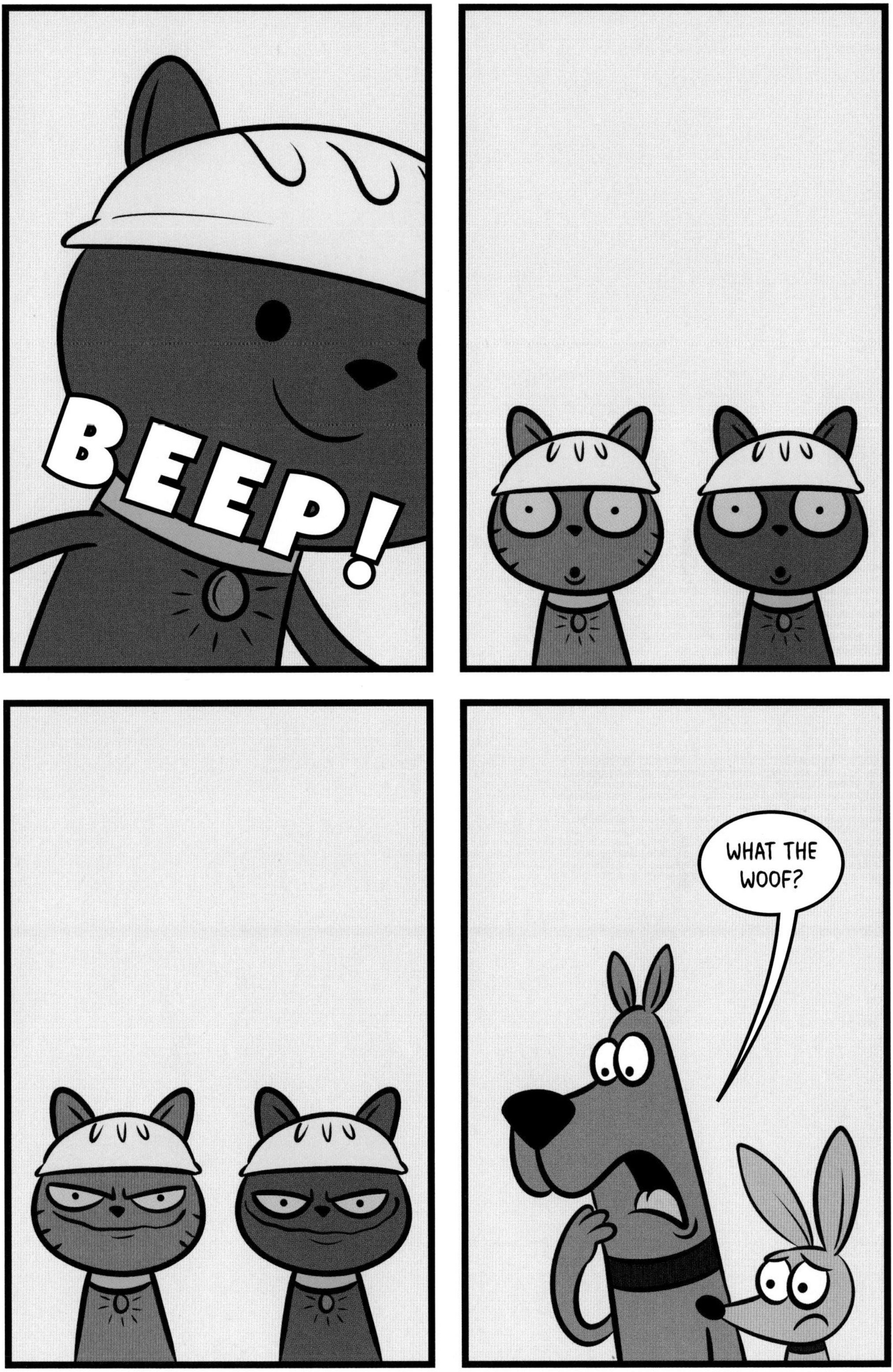
BEEP!
WHAT THE WOOF?

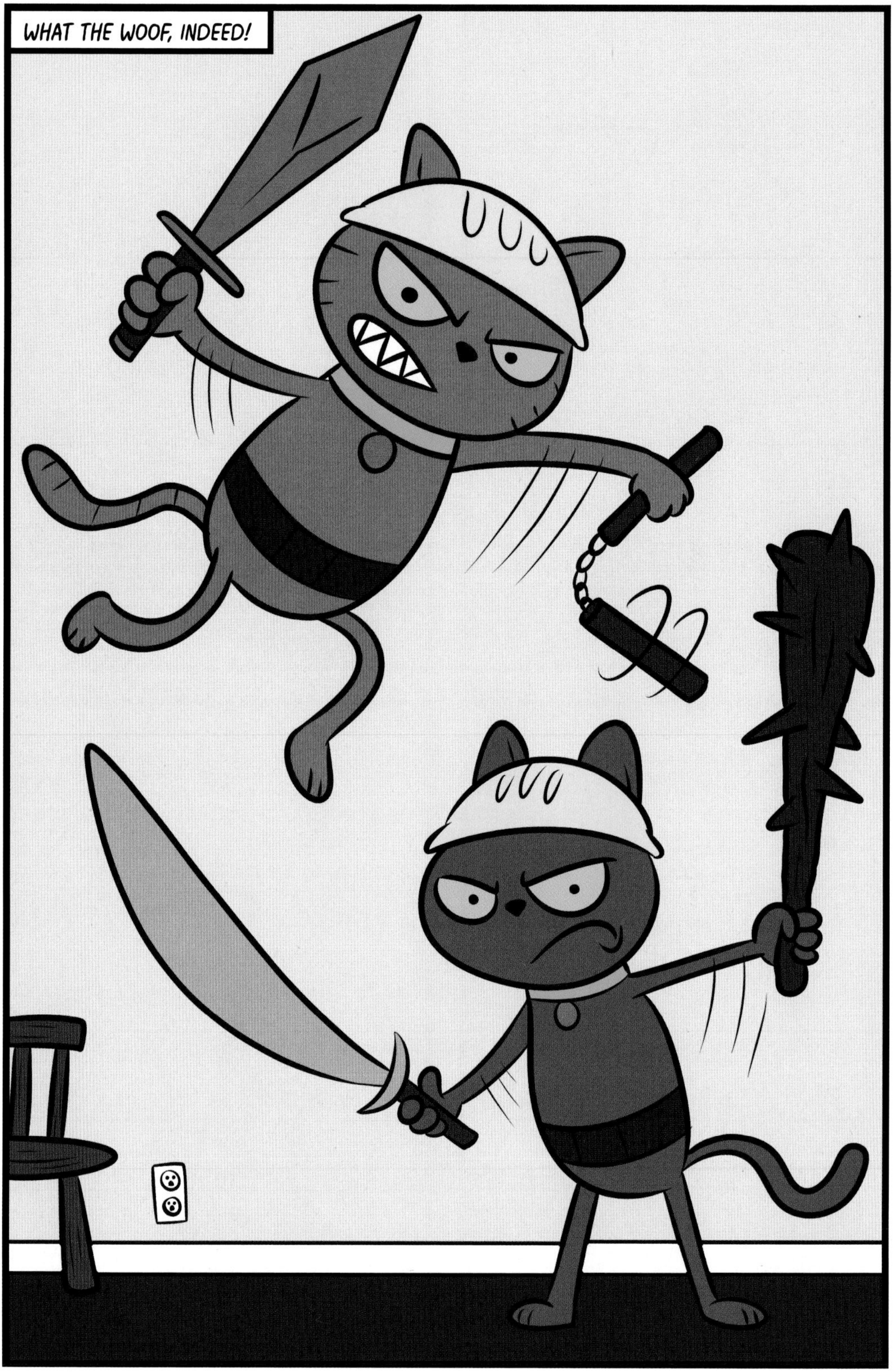
WHAT THE WOOF, INDEED!

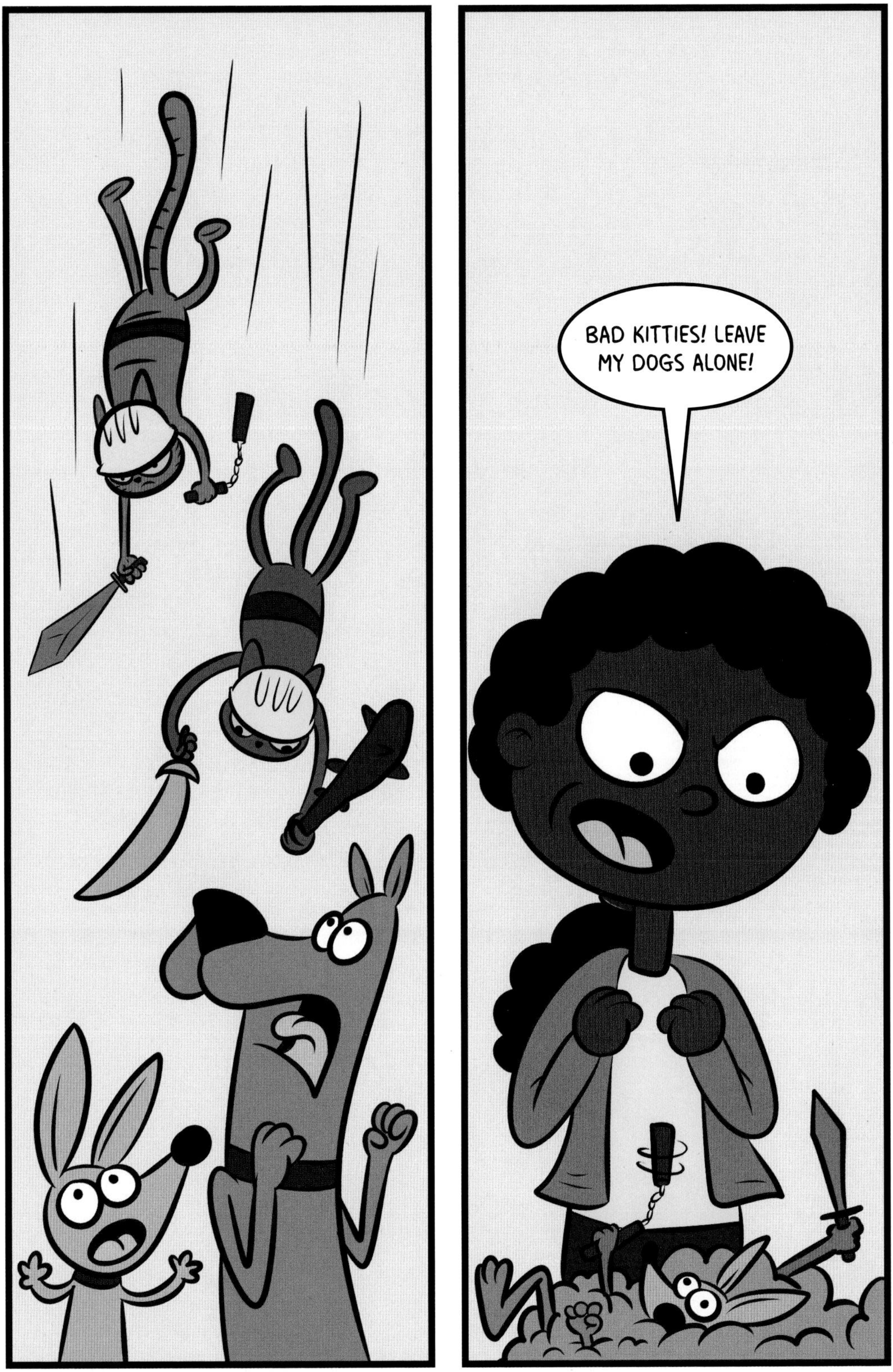
BAD KITTIES! LEAVE MY DOGS ALONE!

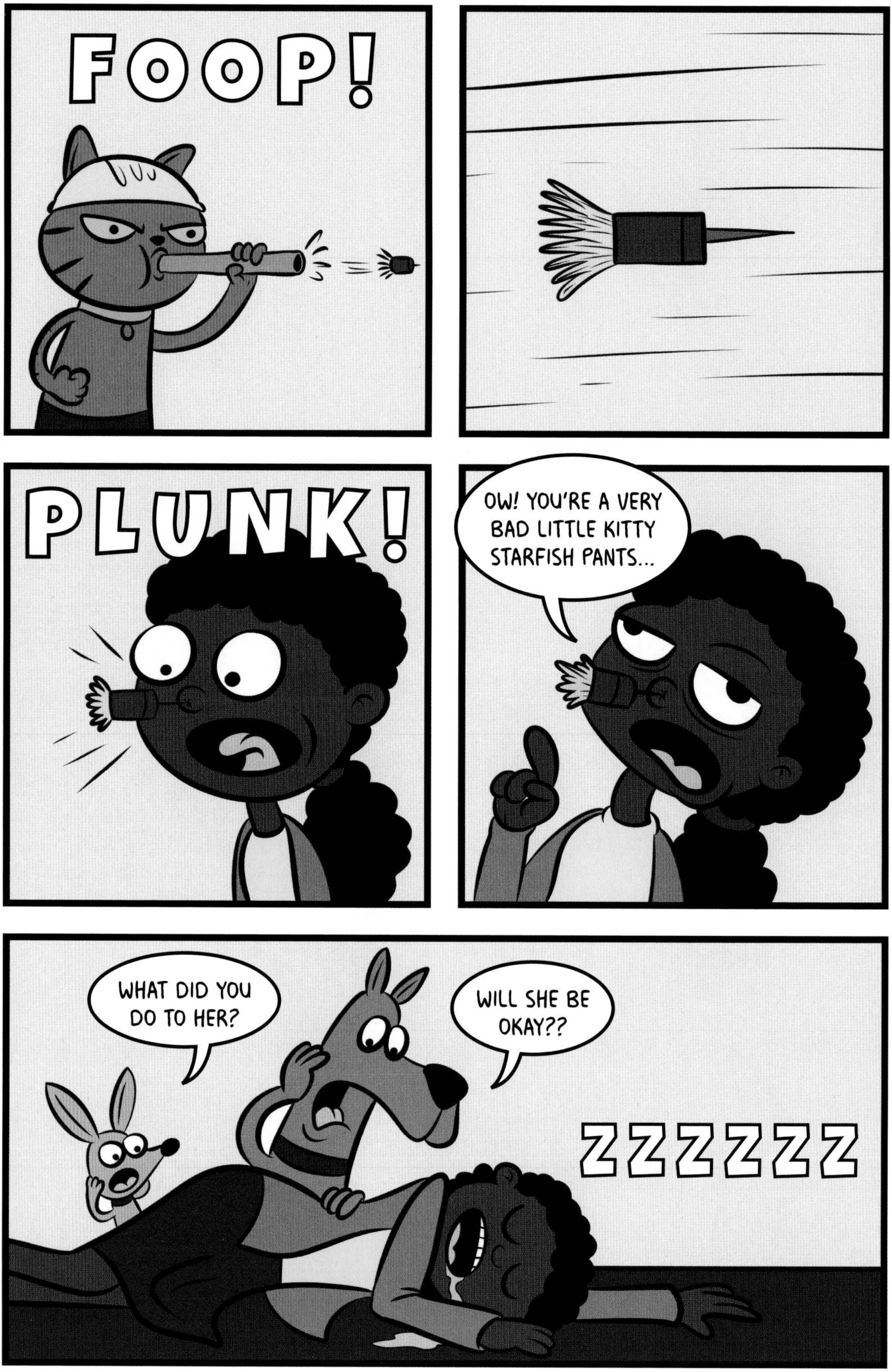
FOOP!
PLUNK!
OW! YOU'RE A VERY BAD LITTLE KITTY STARFISH PANTS...
WHAT DID YOU DO TO HER?
WILL SHE BE OKAY??
ZZZZZZ

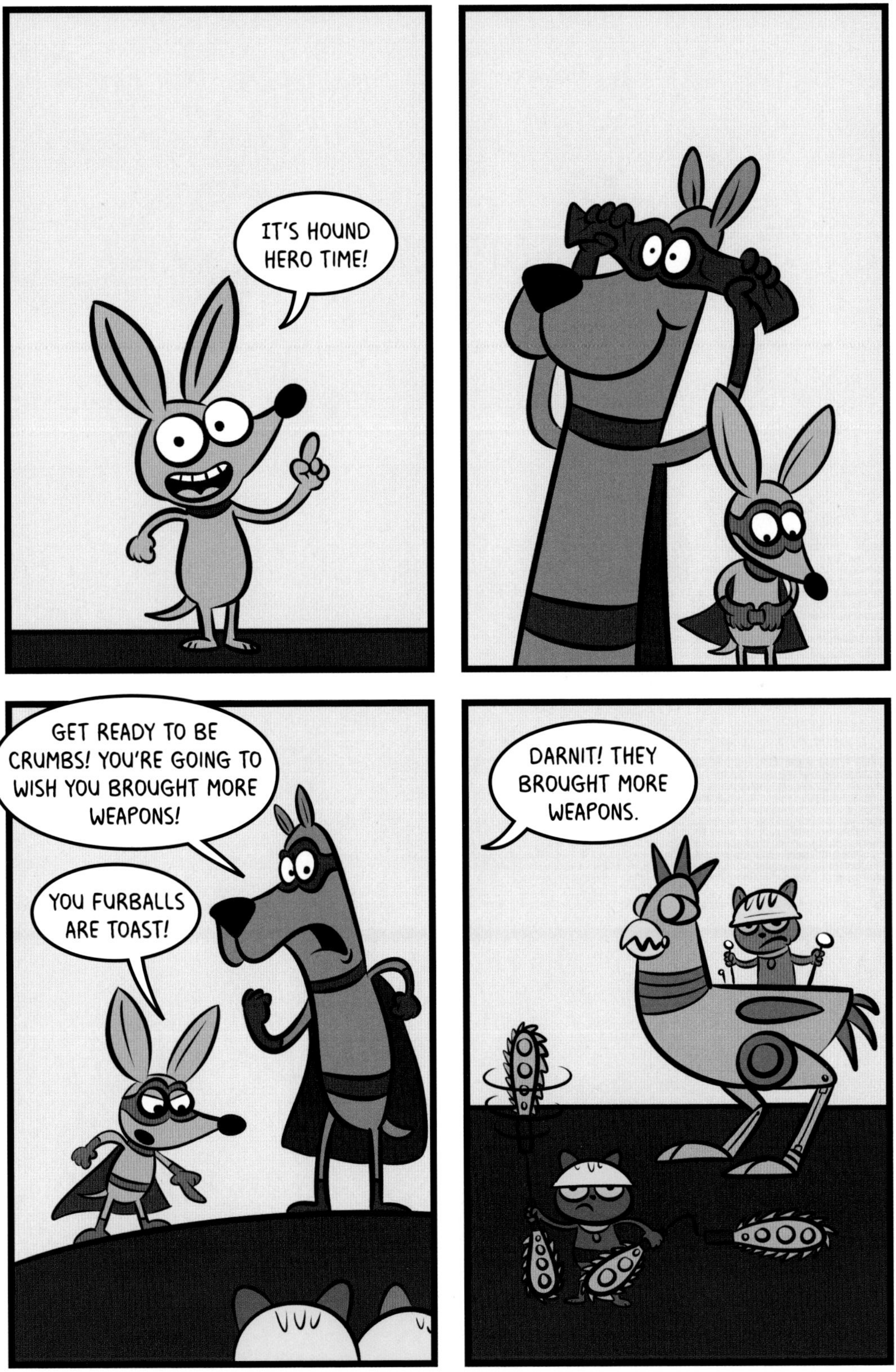
IT'S HOUND HERO TIME!
GET READY TO BE CRUMBS! YOU'RE GOING TO WISH YOU BROUGHT MORE WEAPONS!
YOU FURBALLS ARE TOAST!
DARNIT! THEY BROUGHT MORE WEAPONS.

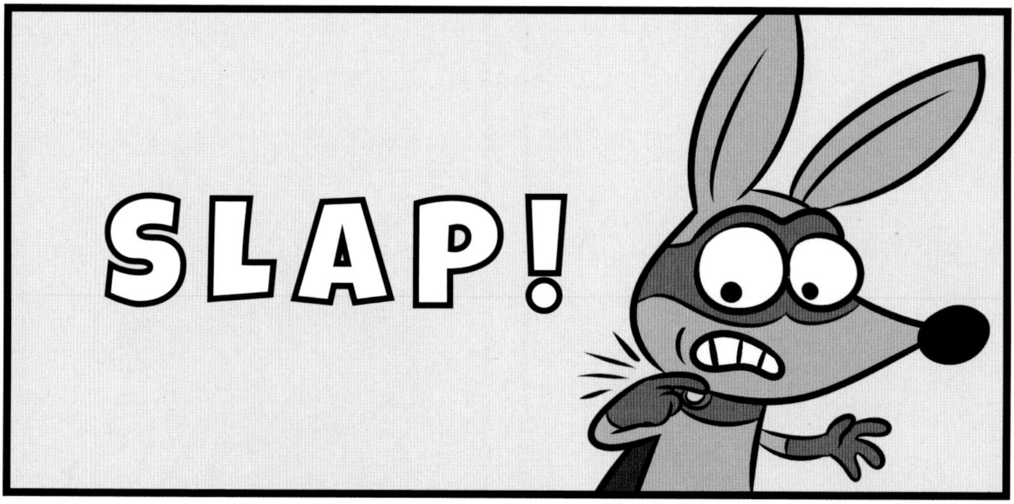
SLAP!

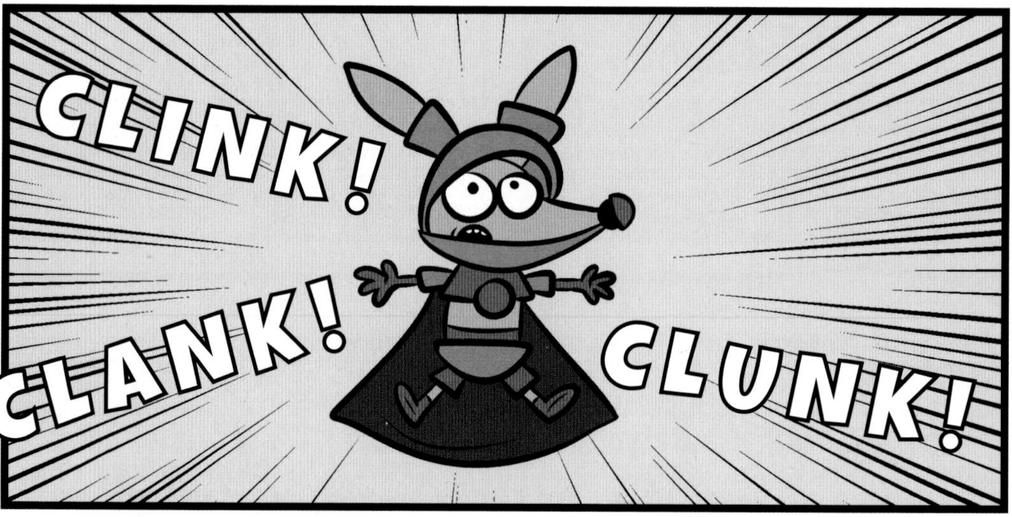
CLINK!
CLANK!
CLUNK!

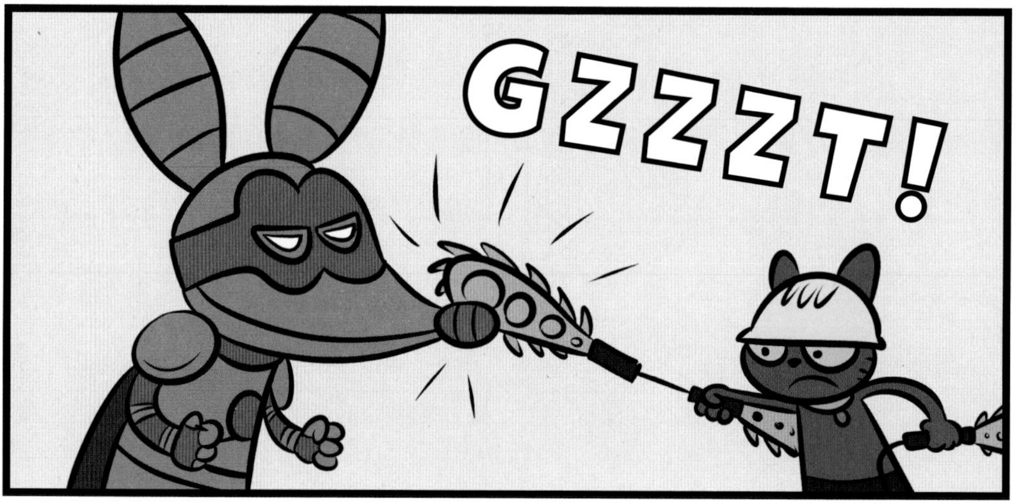
GZZZT!

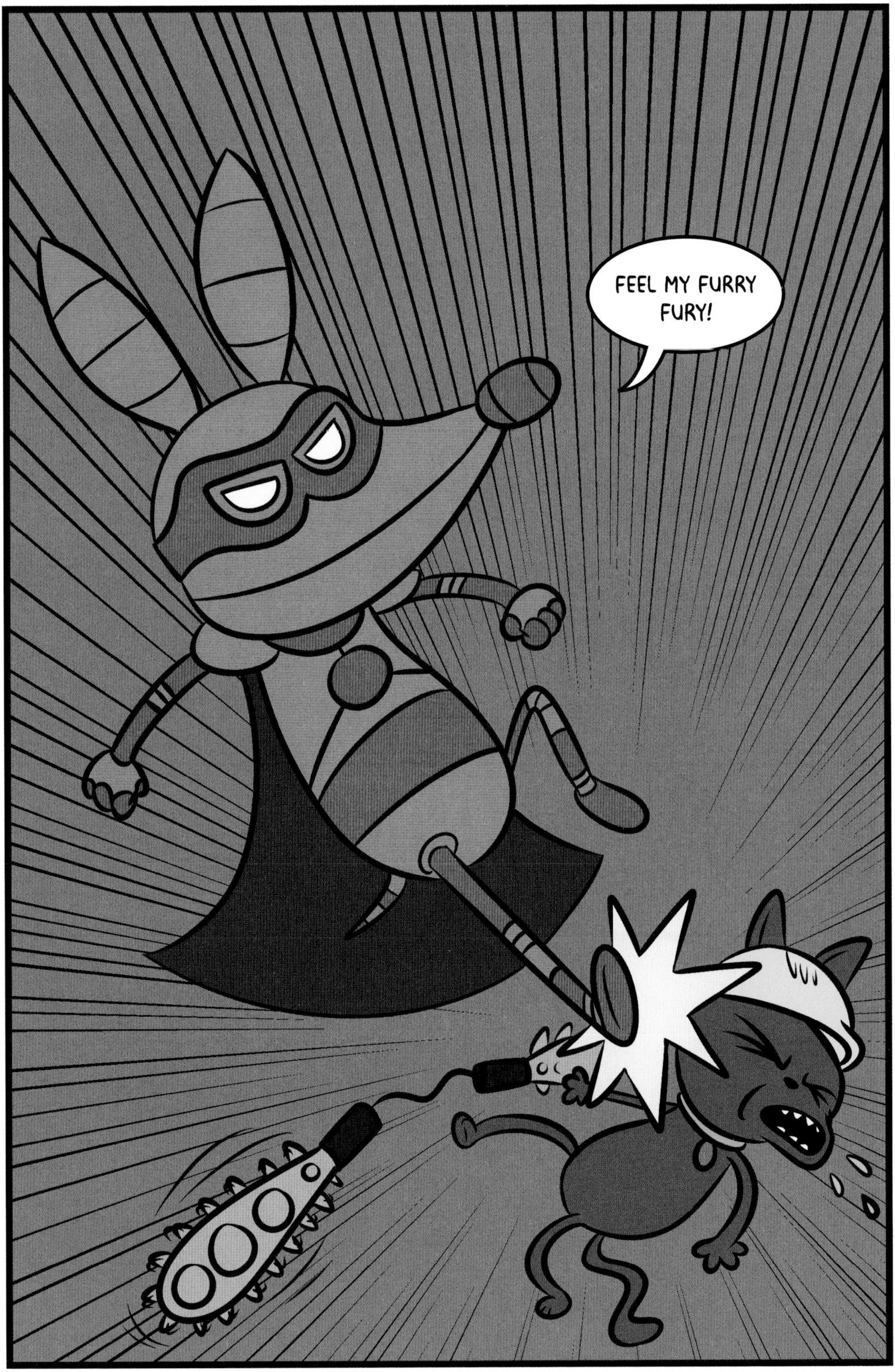
FEEL MY FURRY FURY!

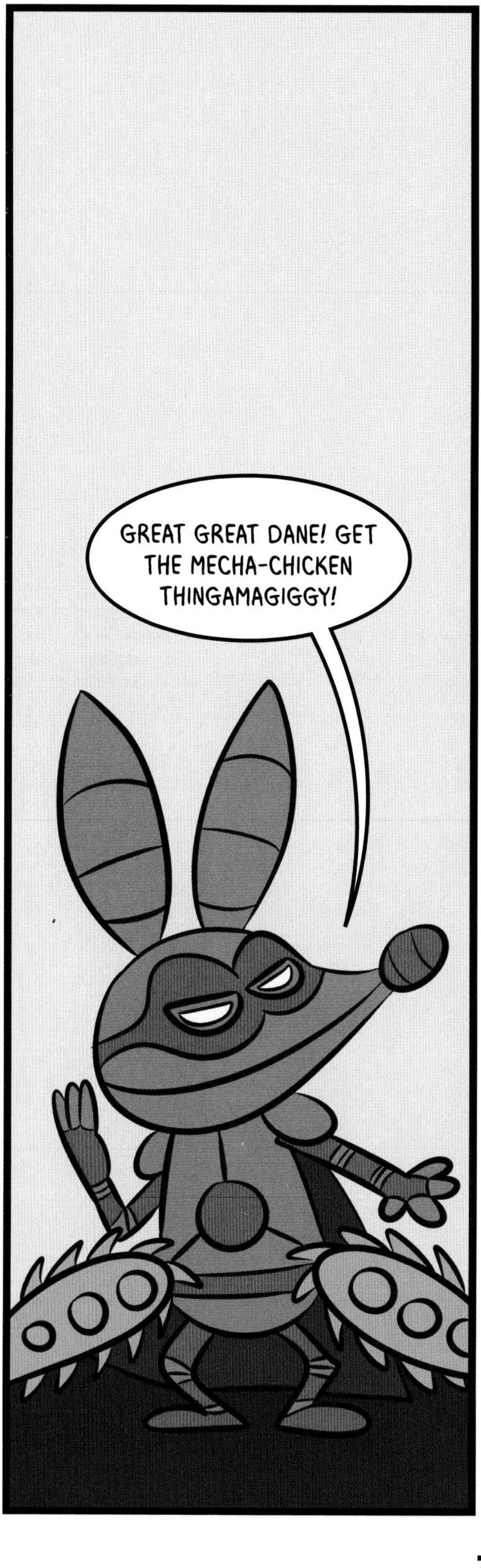
GREAT GREAT DANE! GET THE MECHA-CHICKEN THINGAMAGIGGY!

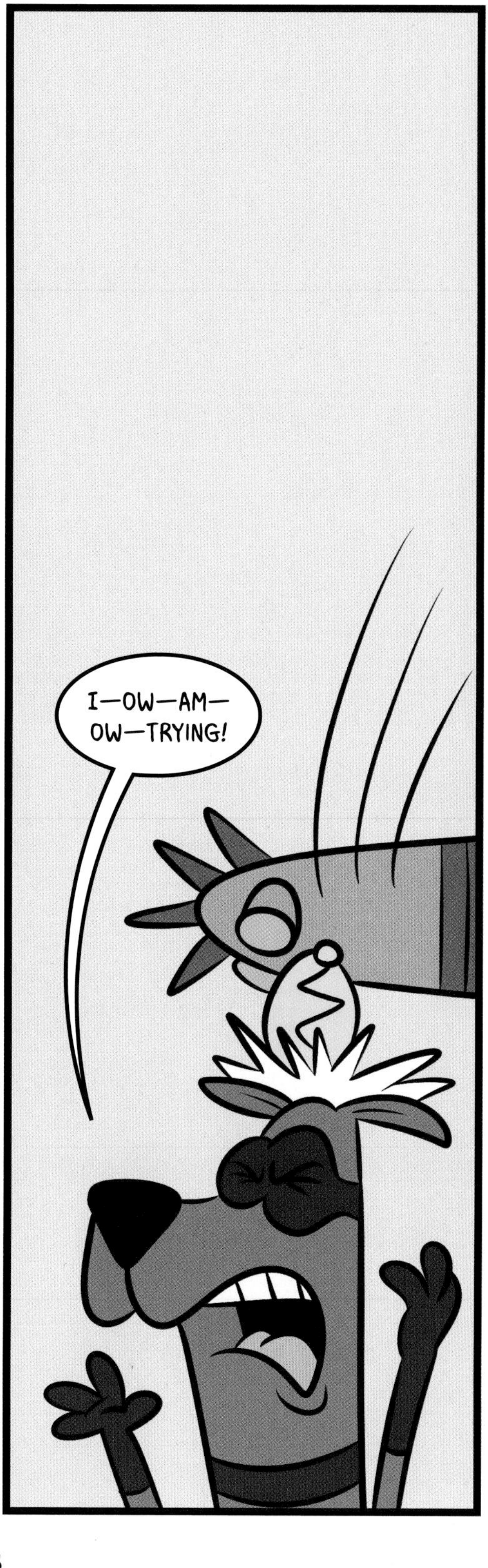
I—OW—AM—OW—TRYING!

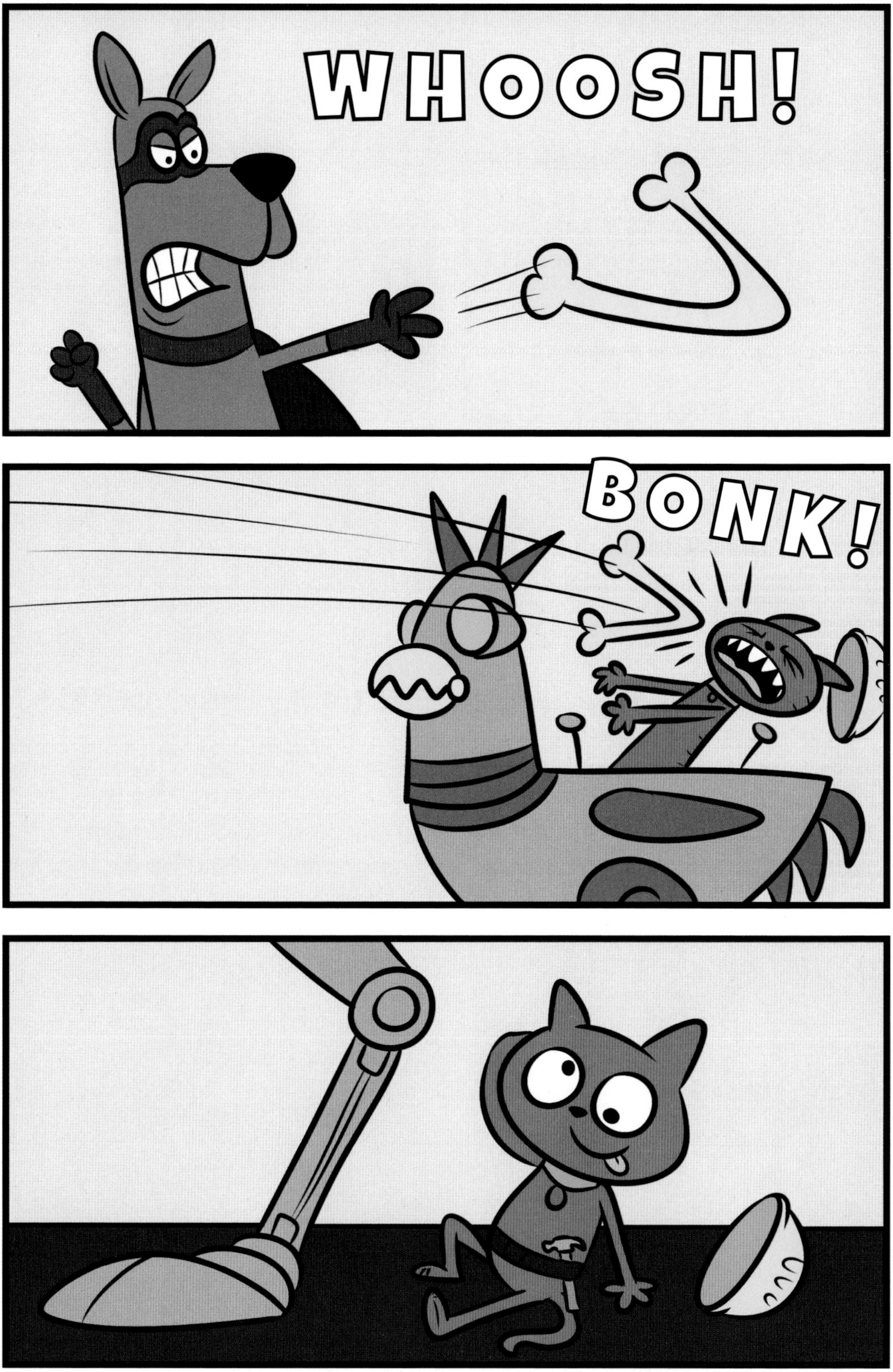
WHOOSH!
BONK!

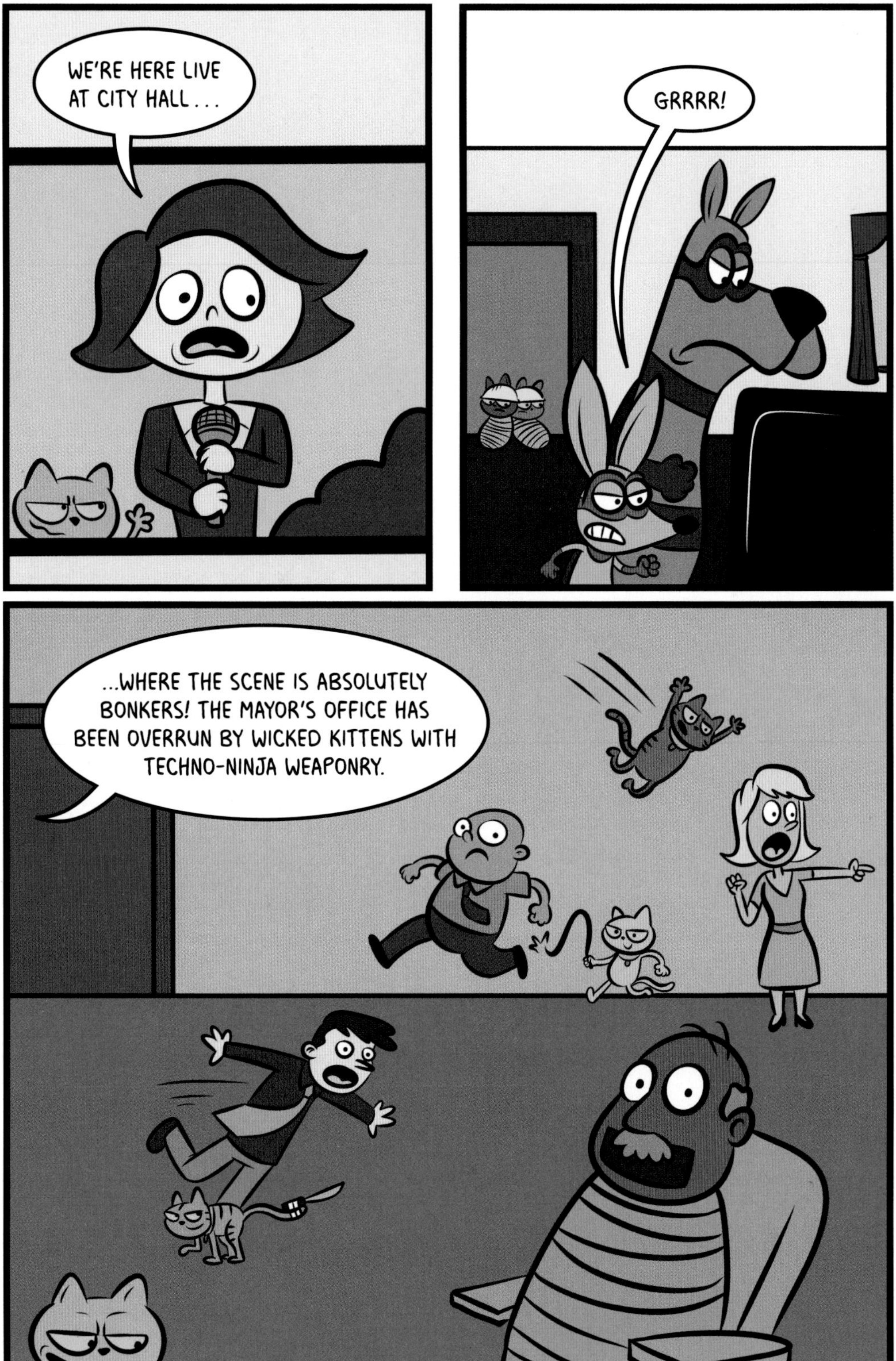
WE'RE HERE LIVE AT CITY HALL . . .
GRRRR!
...WHERE THE SCENE IS ABSOLUTELY BONKERS! THE MAYOR'S OFFICE HAS BEEN OVERRUN BY WICKED KITTENS WITH TECHNO-NINJA WEAPONRY.

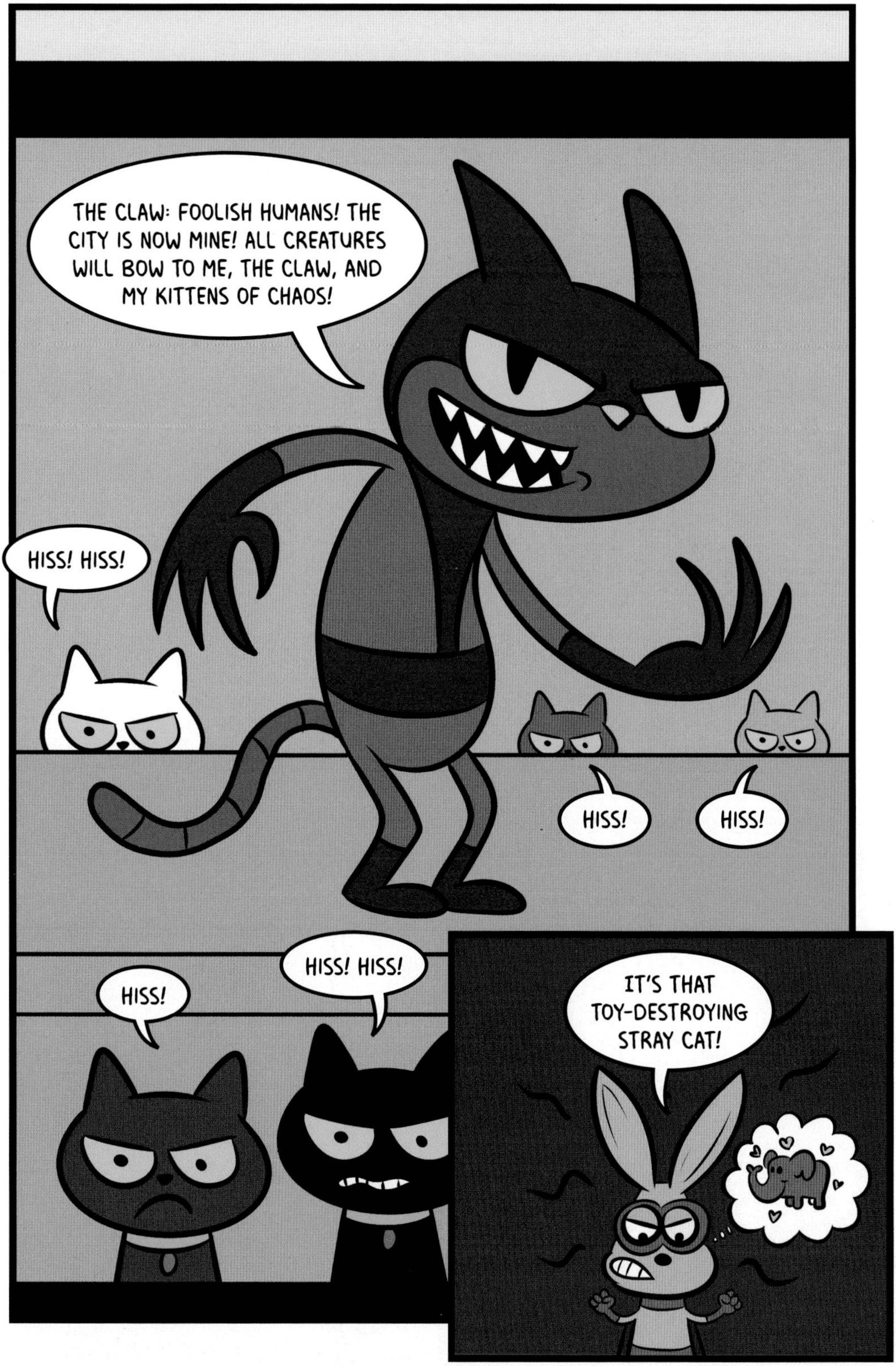

THE CLAW: FOOLISH HUMANS! THE CITY IS NOW MINE! ALL CREATURES WILL BOW TO ME, THE CLAW, AND MY KITTENS OF CHAOS!
HISS! HISS!
HISS!
HISS!
HISS!
HISS! HISS!
IT'S THAT TOY-DESTROYING STRAY CAT!

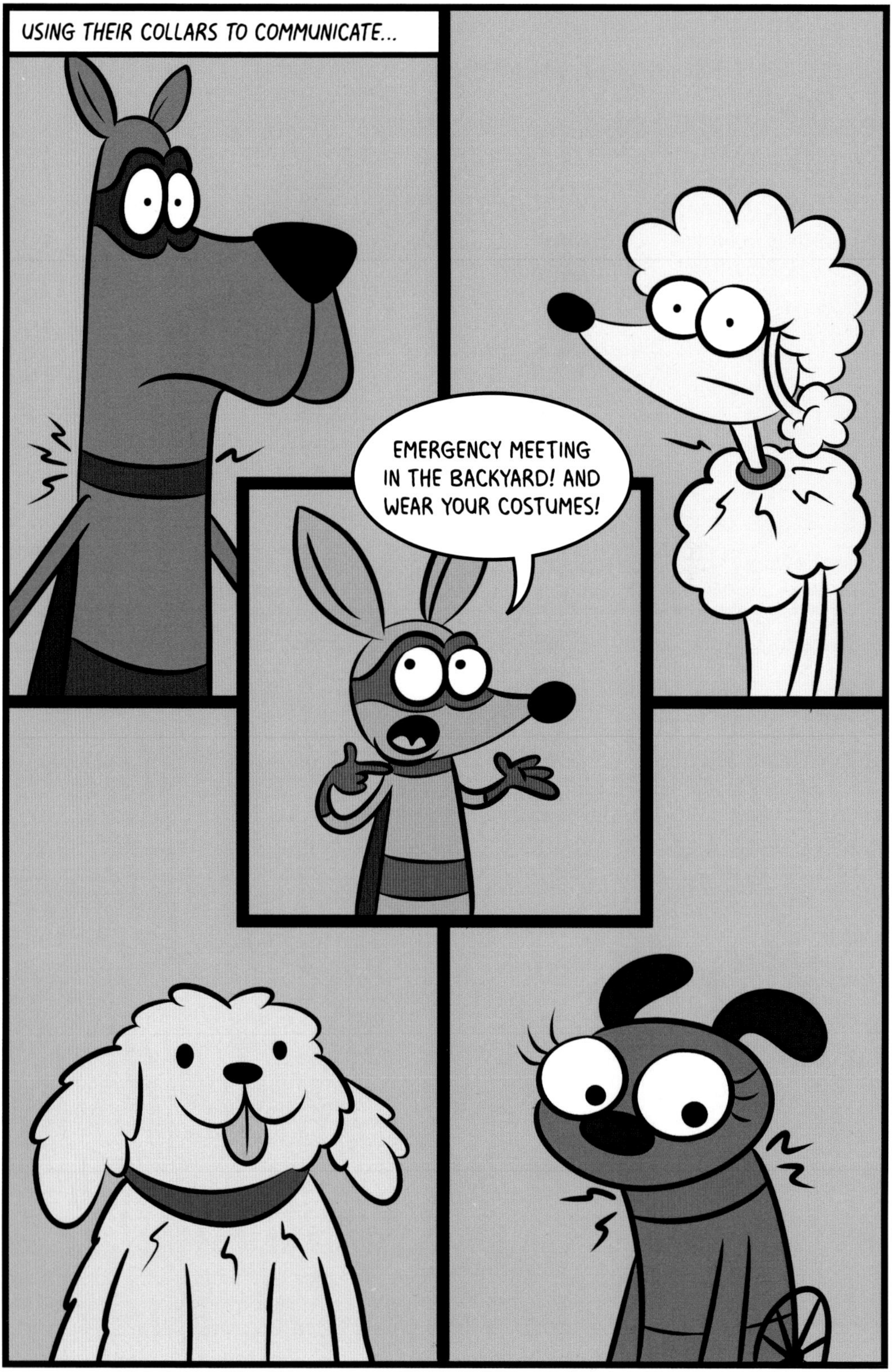
USING THEIR COLLARS TO COMMUNICATE...
EMERGENCY MEETING IN THE BACKYARD! AND WEAR YOUR COSTUMES!

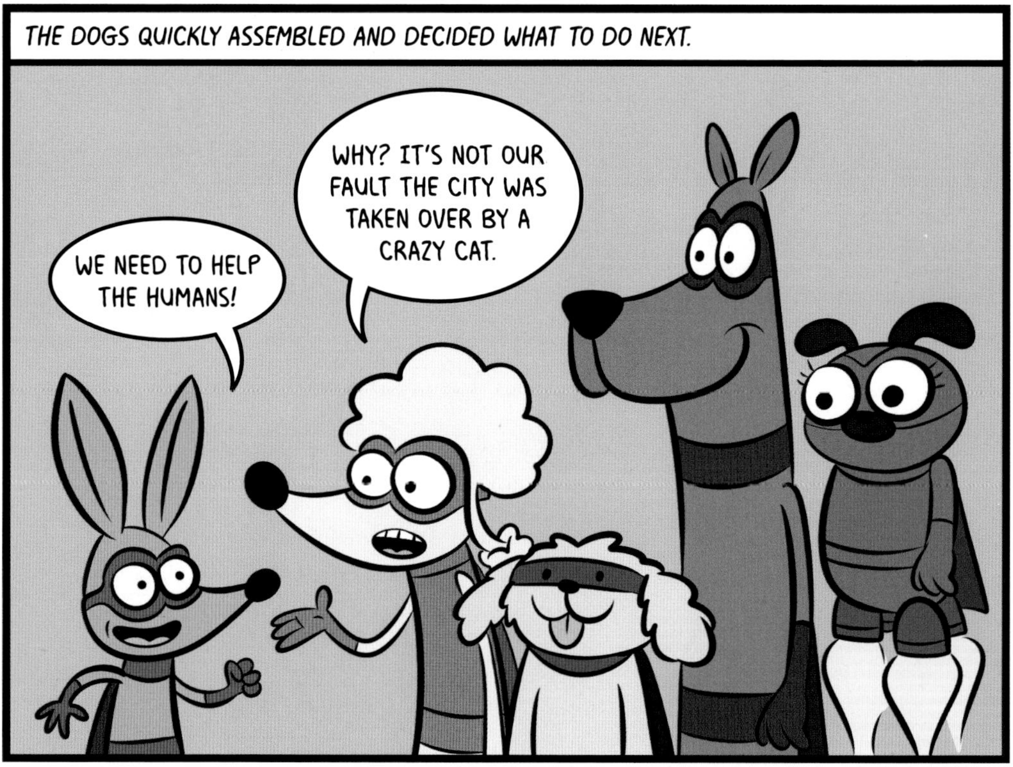
THE DOGS QUICKLY ASSEMBLED AND DECIDED WHAT TO DO NEXT.
WE NEED TO HELP THE HUMANS!
WHY? IT'S NOT OUR FAULT THE CITY WAS TAKEN OVER BY A CRAZY CAT.

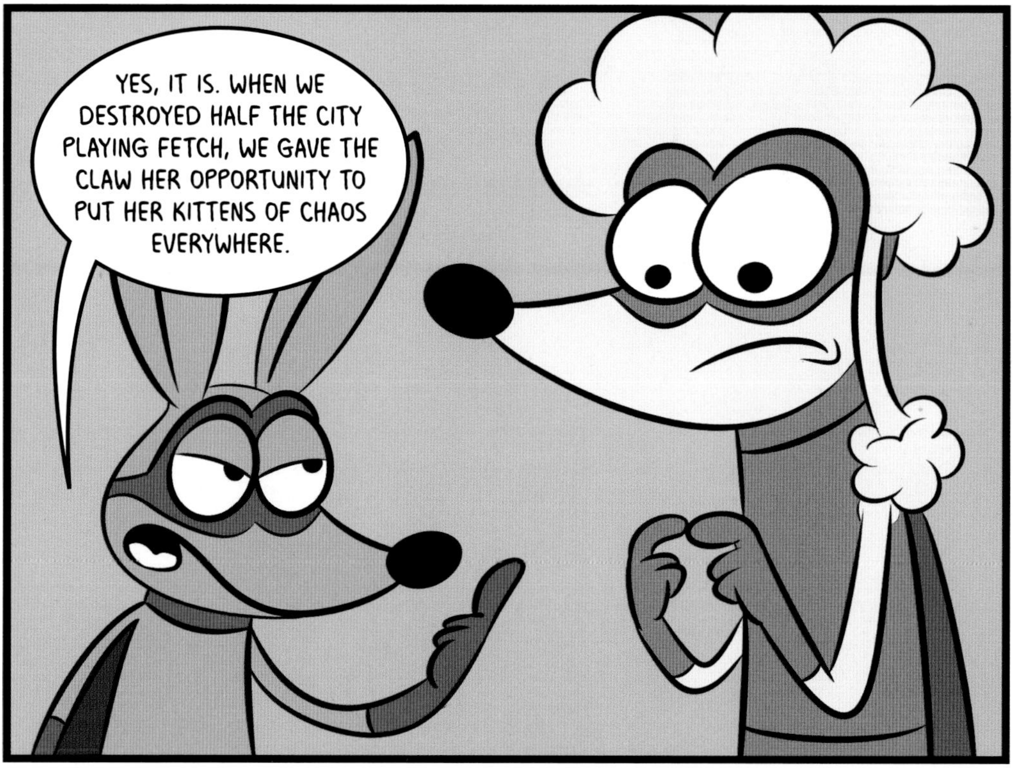
YES, IT IS. WHEN WE DESTROYED HALF THE CITY PLAYING FETCH, WE GAVE THE CLAW HER OPPORTUNITY TO PUT HER KITTENS OF CHAOS EVERYWHERE.

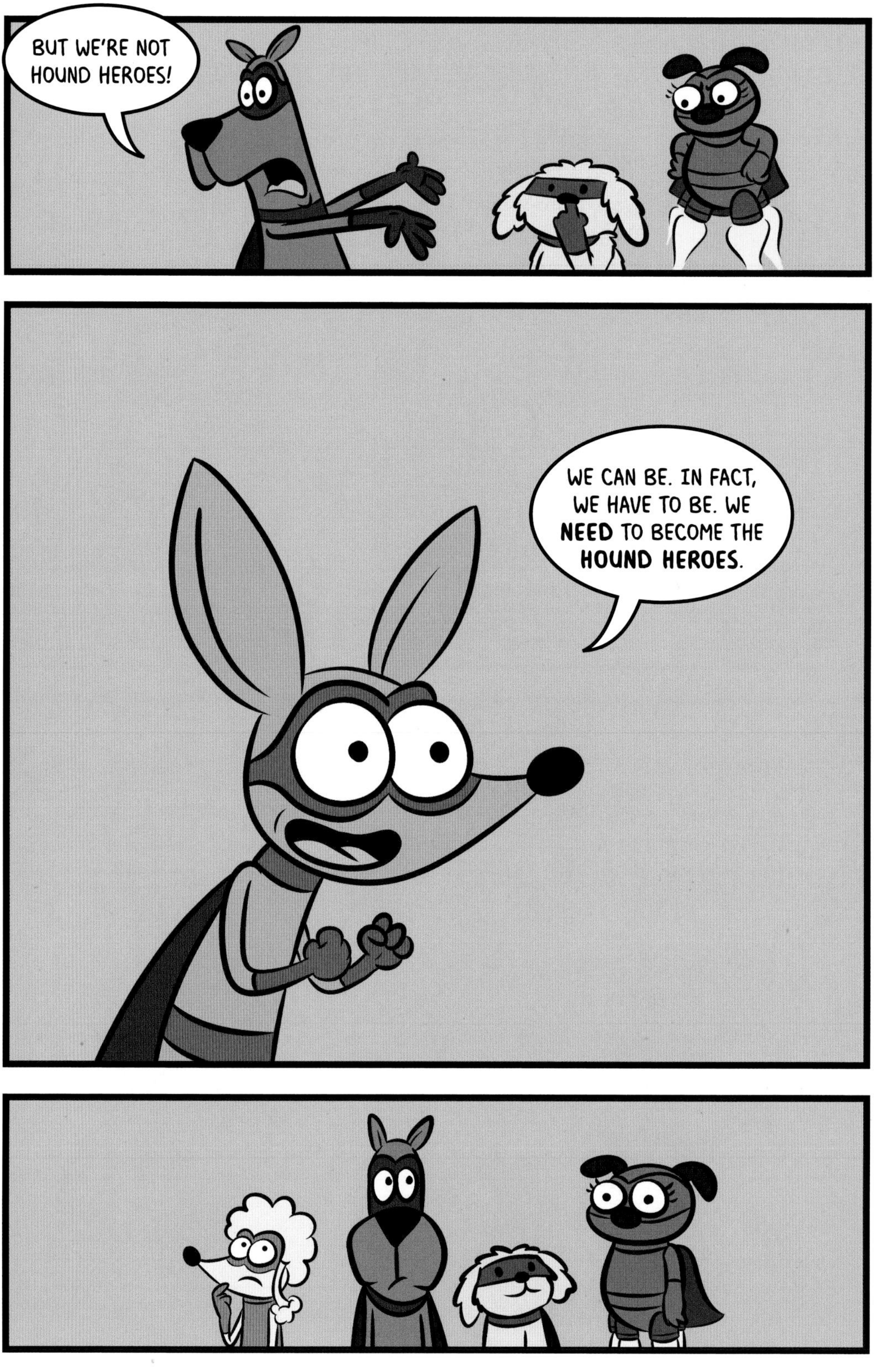
BUT WE'RE NOT HOUND HEROES!
WE CAN BE. IN FACT, WE HAVE TO BE. WE **NEED** TO BECOME THE **HOUND HEROES**.

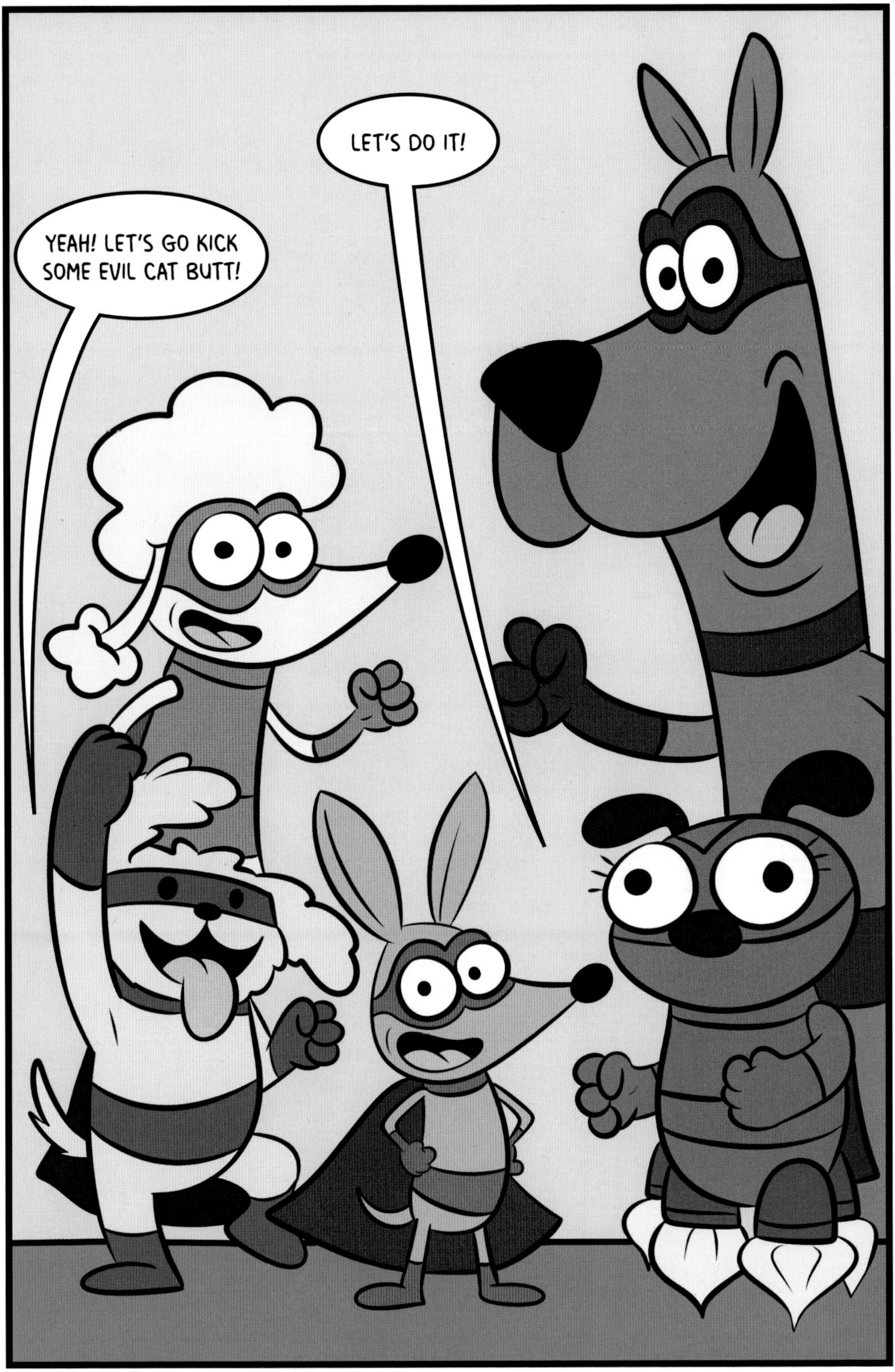
YEAH! LET'S GO KICK SOME EVIL CAT BUTT!
LET'S DO IT!

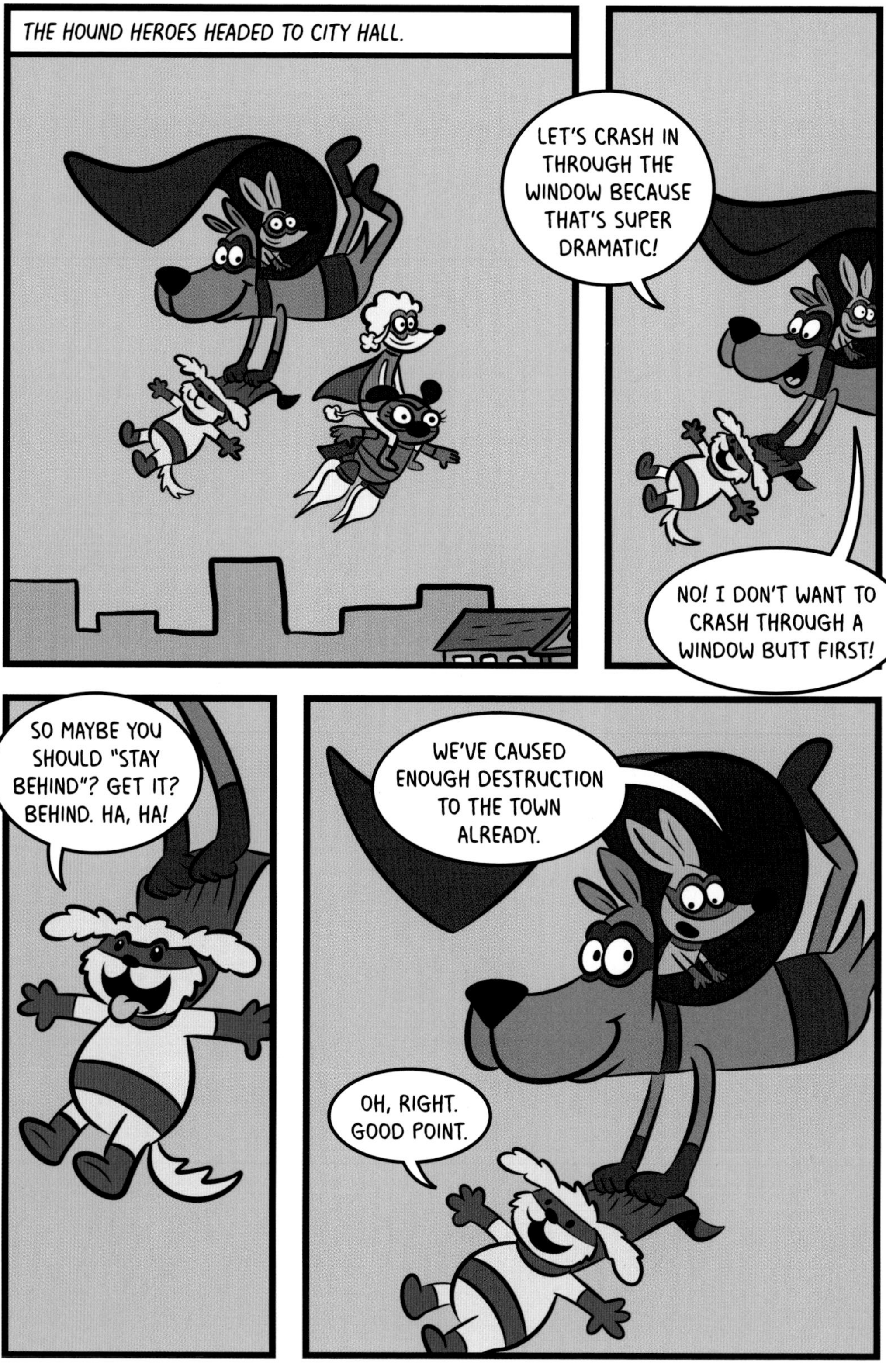
THE HOUND HEROES HEADED TO CITY HALL.
LET'S CRASH IN THROUGH THE WINDOW BECAUSE THAT'S SUPER DRAMATIC!
NO! I DON'T WANT TO CRASH THROUGH A WINDOW BUTT FIRST!
SO MAYBE YOU SHOULD "STAY BEHIND"? GET IT? BEHIND. HA, HA!
WE'VE CAUSED ENOUGH DESTRUCTION TO THE TOWN ALREADY.
OH, RIGHT. GOOD POINT.

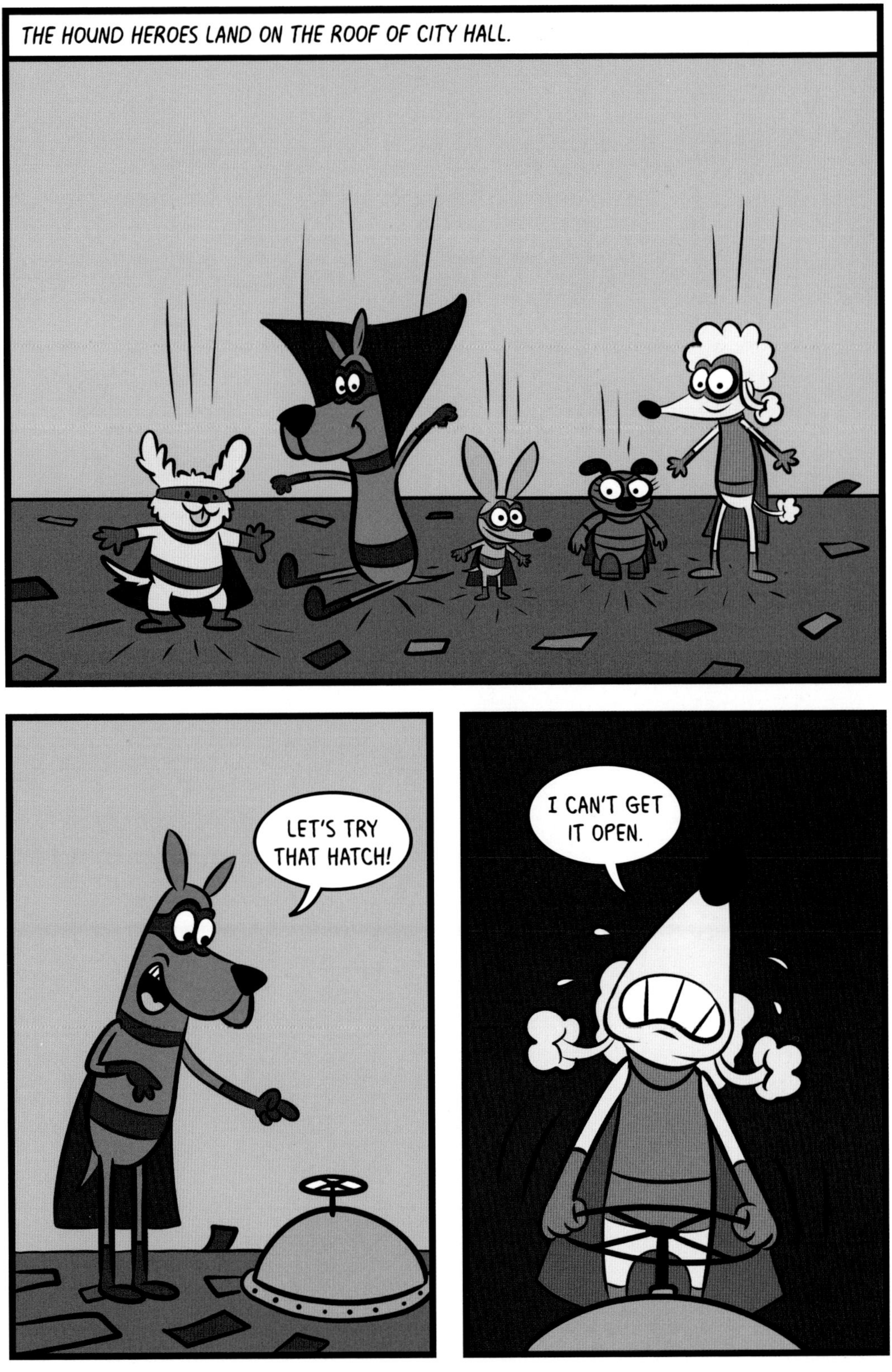
THE HOUND HEROES LAND ON THE ROOF OF CITY HALL.
LET'S TRY THAT HATCH!
I CAN'T GET IT OPEN.

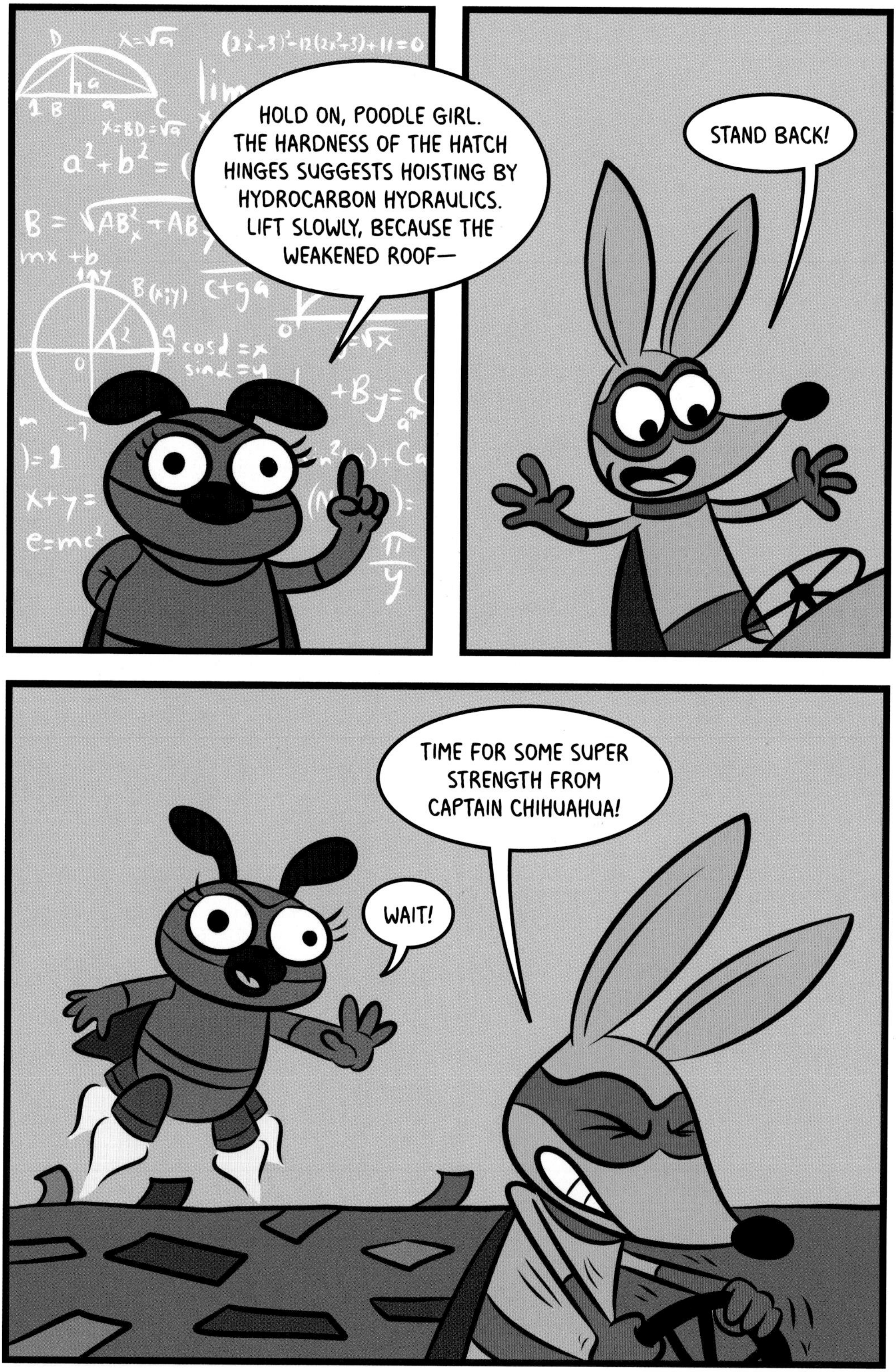
HOLD ON, POODLE GIRL. THE HARDNESS OF THE HATCH HINGES SUGGESTS HOISTING BY HYDROCARBON HYDRAULICS. LIFT SLOWLY, BECAUSE THE WEAKENED ROOF—
STAND BACK!
TIME FOR SOME SUPER STRENGTH FROM CAPTAIN CHIHUAHUA!
WAIT!

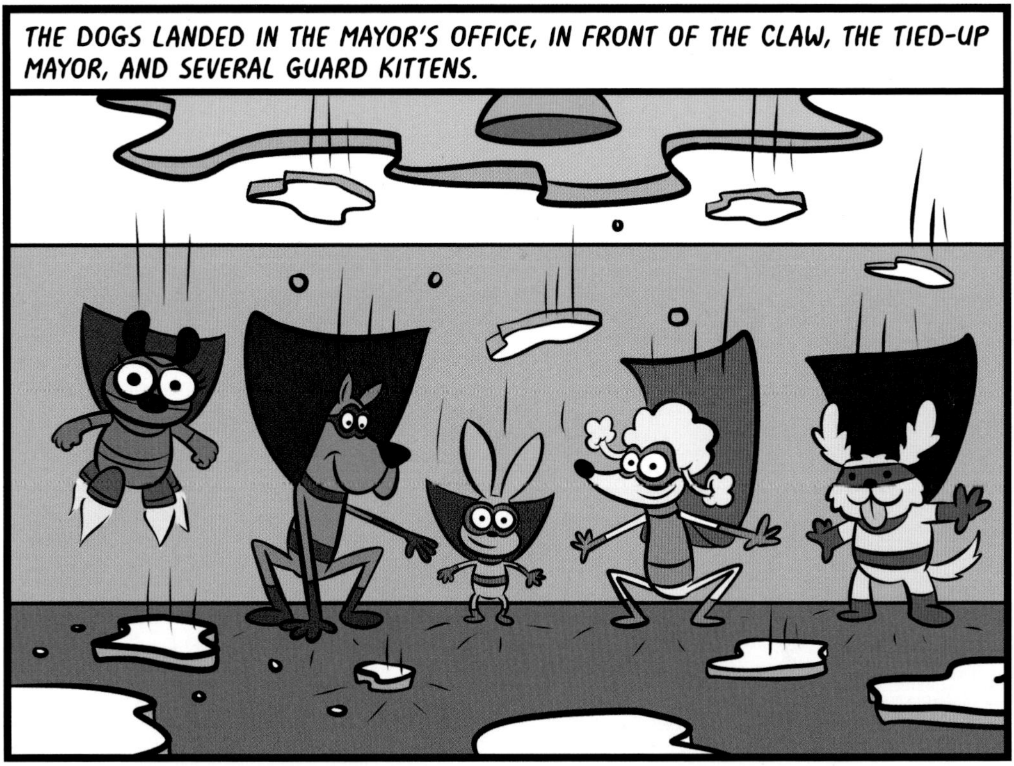
THE DOGS LANDED IN THE MAYOR'S OFFICE, IN FRONT OF THE CLAW, THE TIED-UP MAYOR, AND SEVERAL GUARD KITTENS.

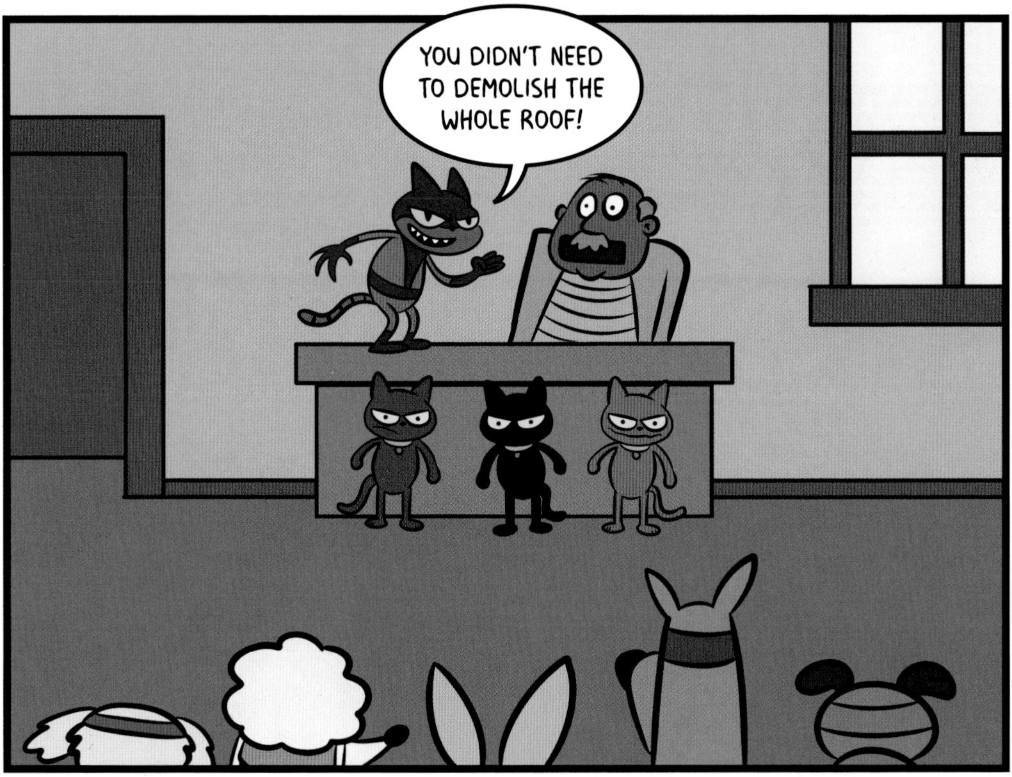
YOU DIDN'T NEED TO DEMOLISH THE WHOLE ROOF!

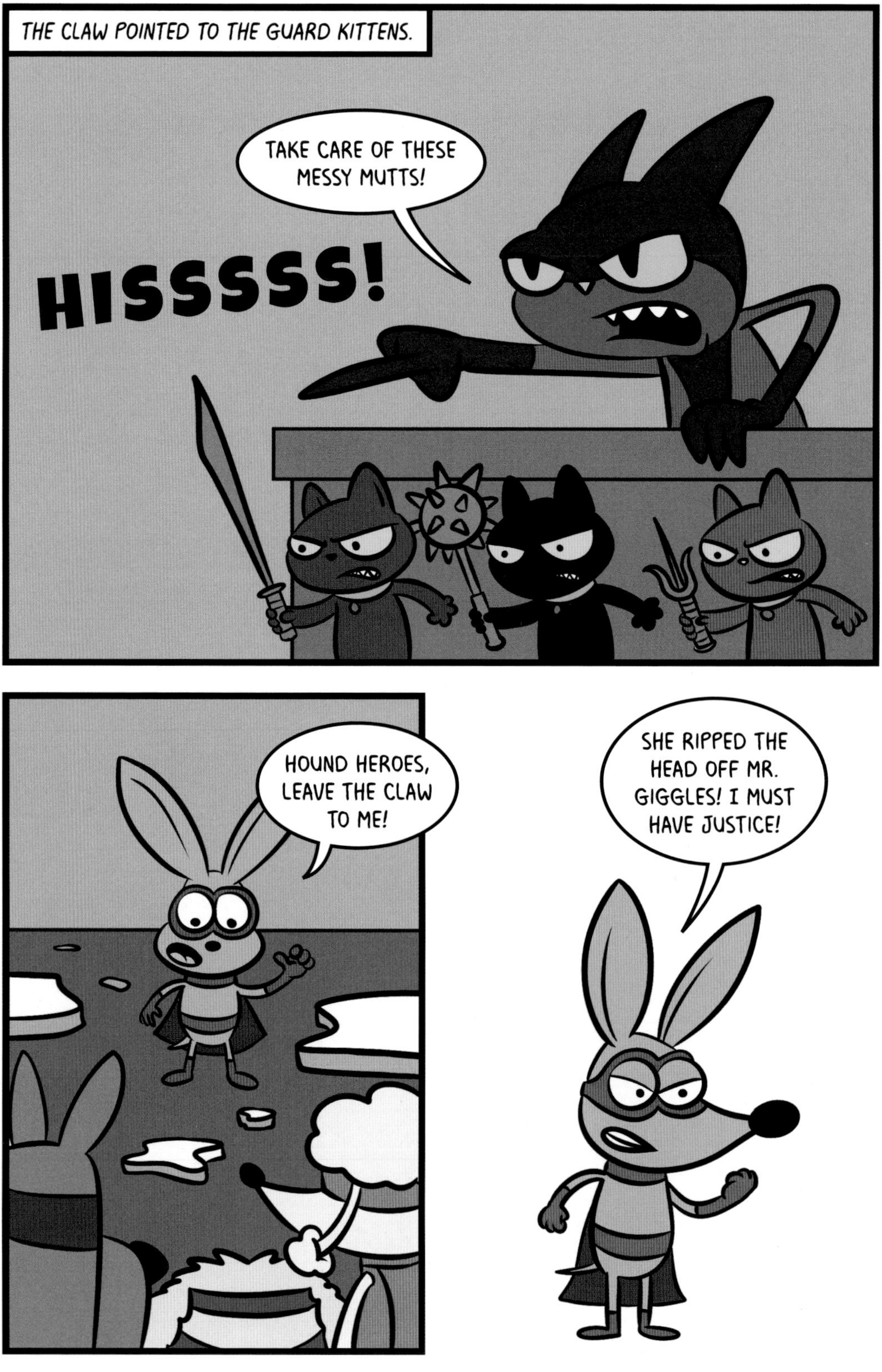
THE CLAW POINTED TO THE GUARD KITTENS.
TAKE CARE OF THESE MESSY MUTTS!
HISSSSS!
HOUND HEROES, LEAVE THE CLAW TO ME!
SHE RIPPED THE HEAD OFF MR. GIGGLES! I MUST HAVE JUSTICE!

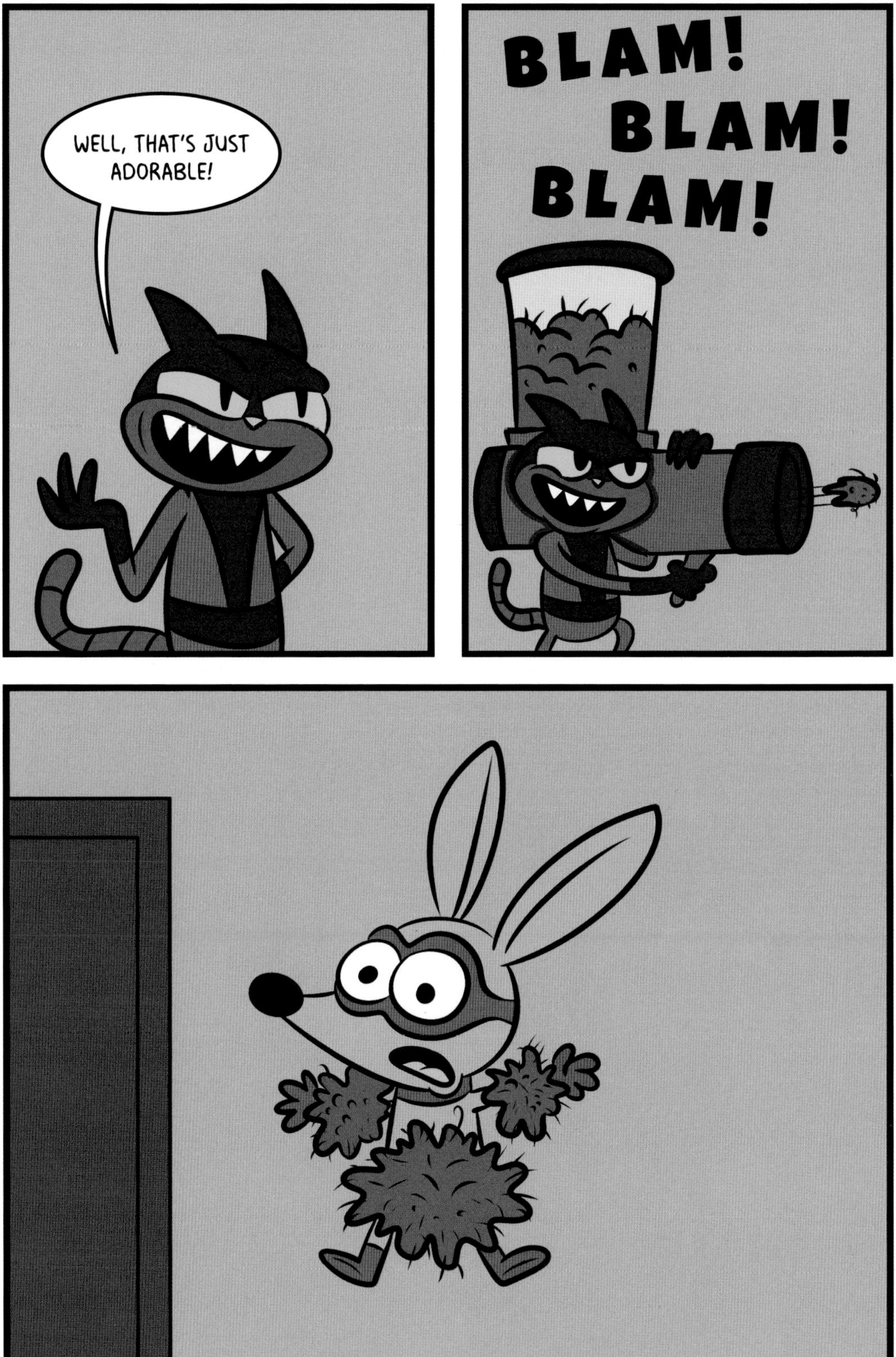
WELL, THAT'S JUST ADORABLE!
BLAM!
BLAM!
BLAM!

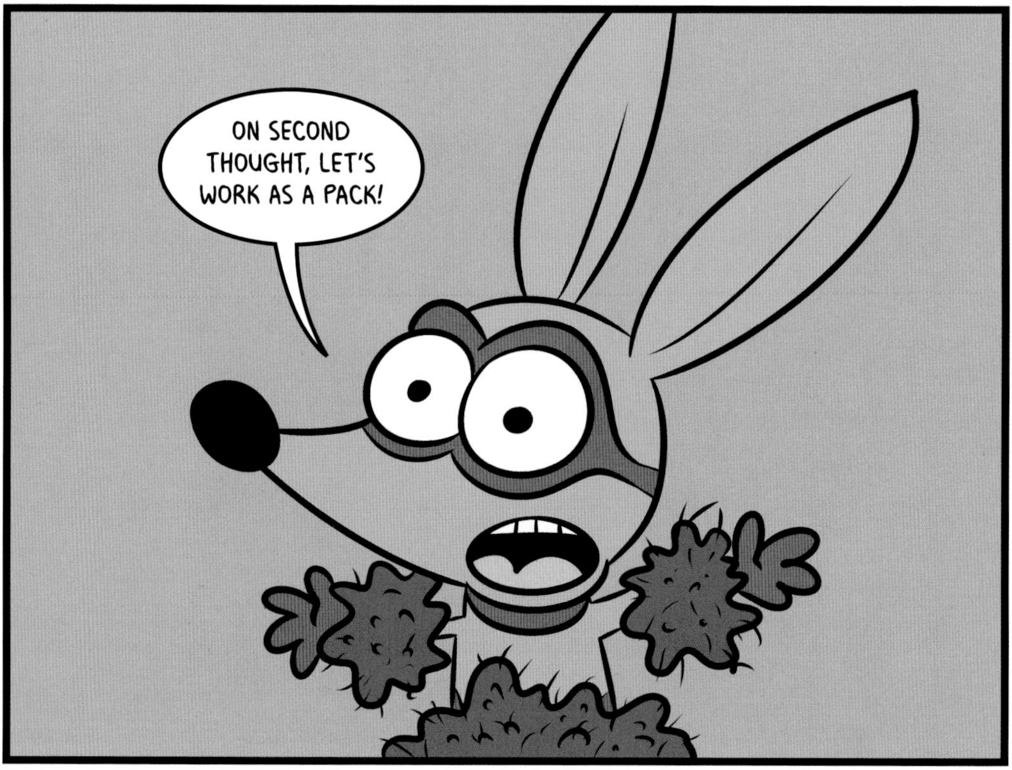
ON SECOND THOUGHT, LET'S WORK AS A PACK!

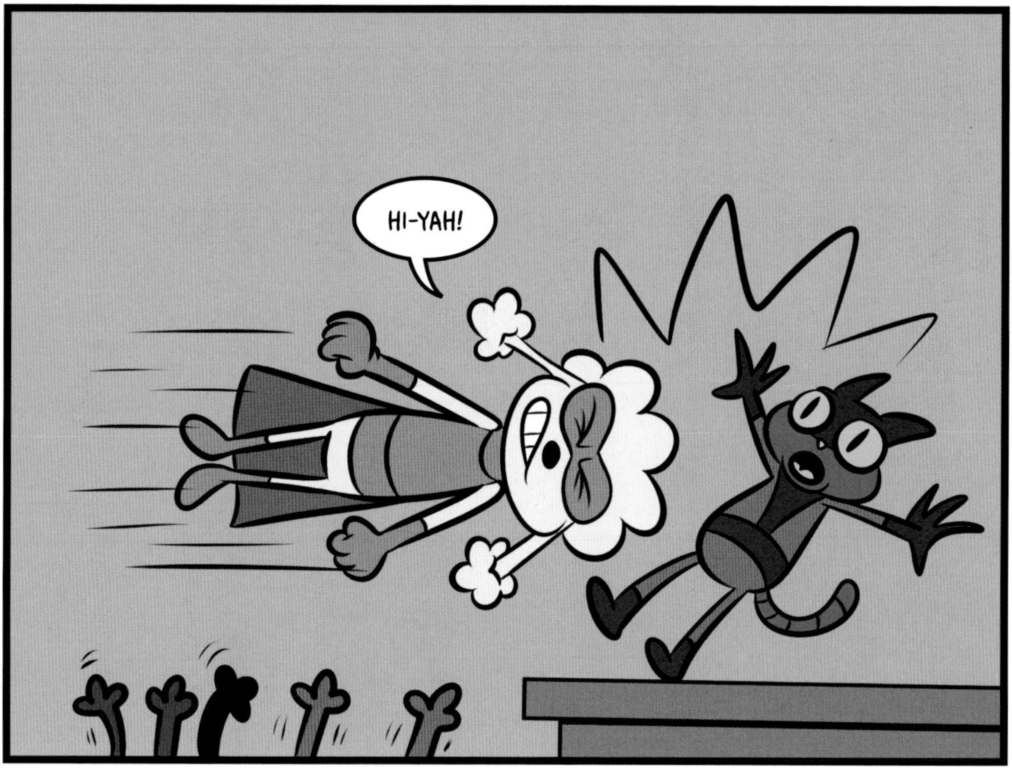
HI-YAH!

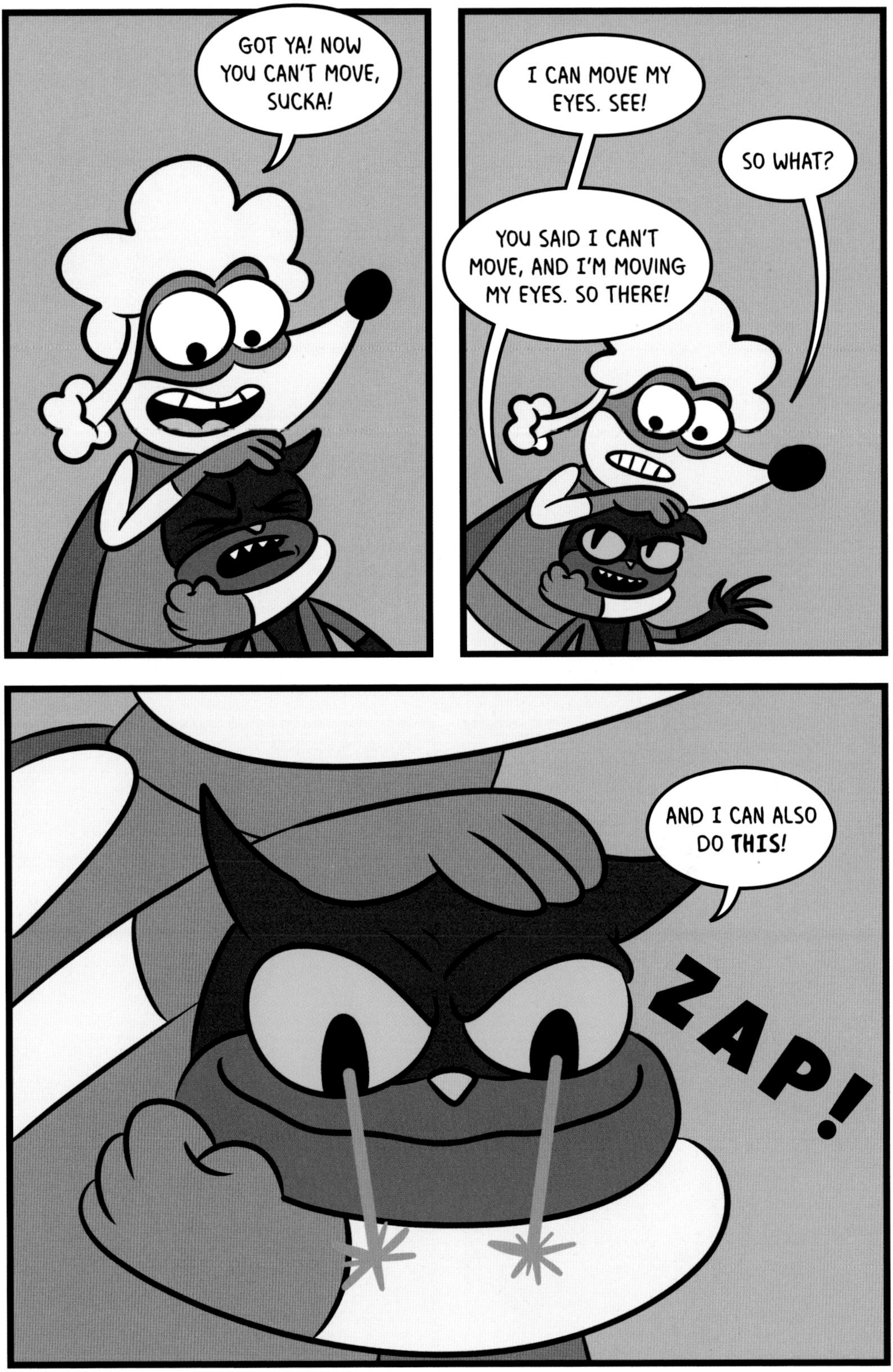
GOT YA! NOW YOU CAN'T MOVE, SUCKA!
I CAN MOVE MY EYES. SEE!
SO WHAT?
YOU SAID I CAN'T MOVE, AND I'M MOVING MY EYES. SO THERE!
AND I CAN ALSO DO **THIS!**
ZAP!

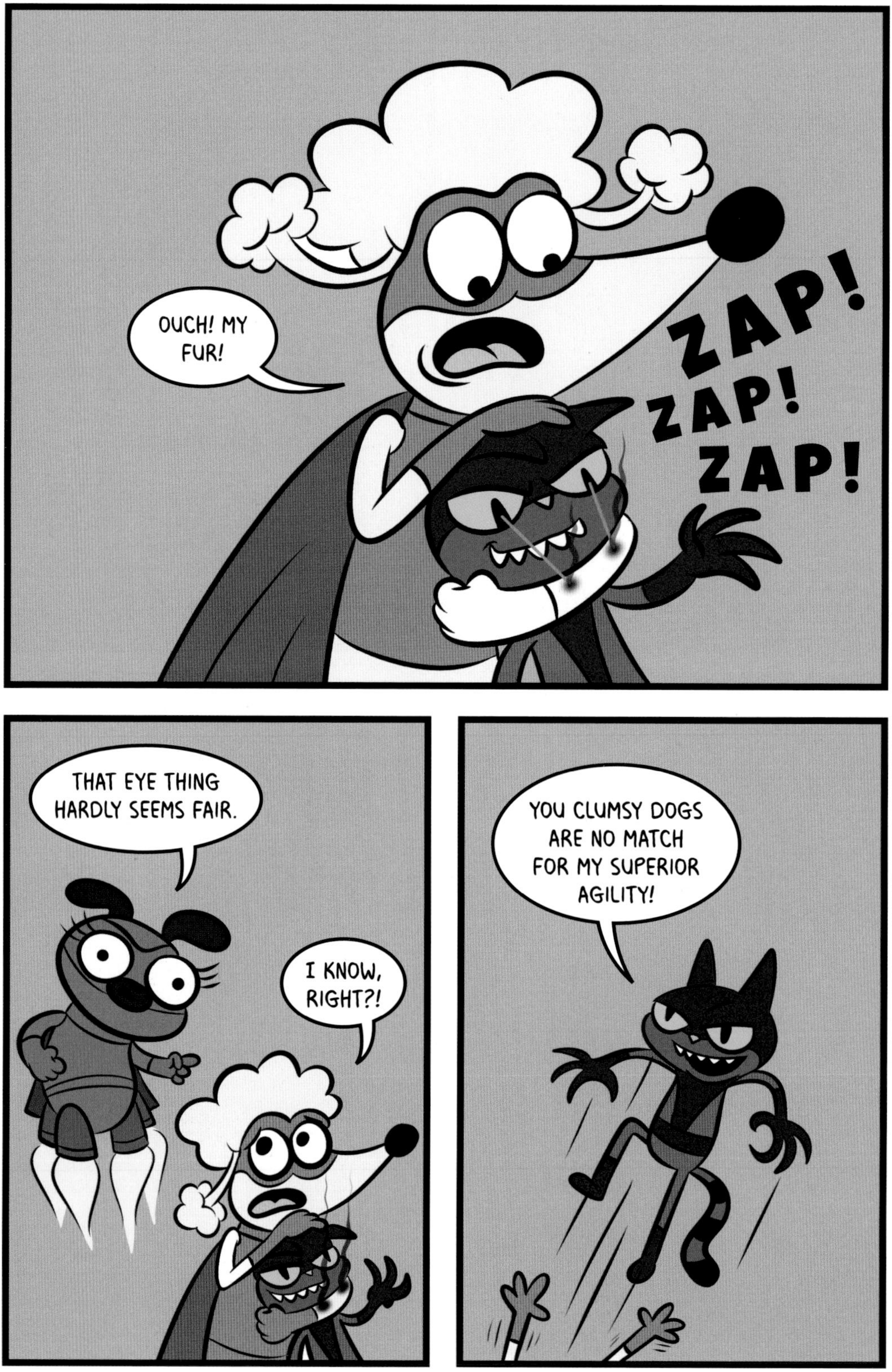
OUCH! MY FUR!
ZAP!
ZAP!
ZAP!
THAT EYE THING HARDLY SEEMS FAIR.
I KNOW, RIGHT?!
YOU CLUMSY DOGS ARE NO MATCH FOR MY SUPERIOR AGILITY!

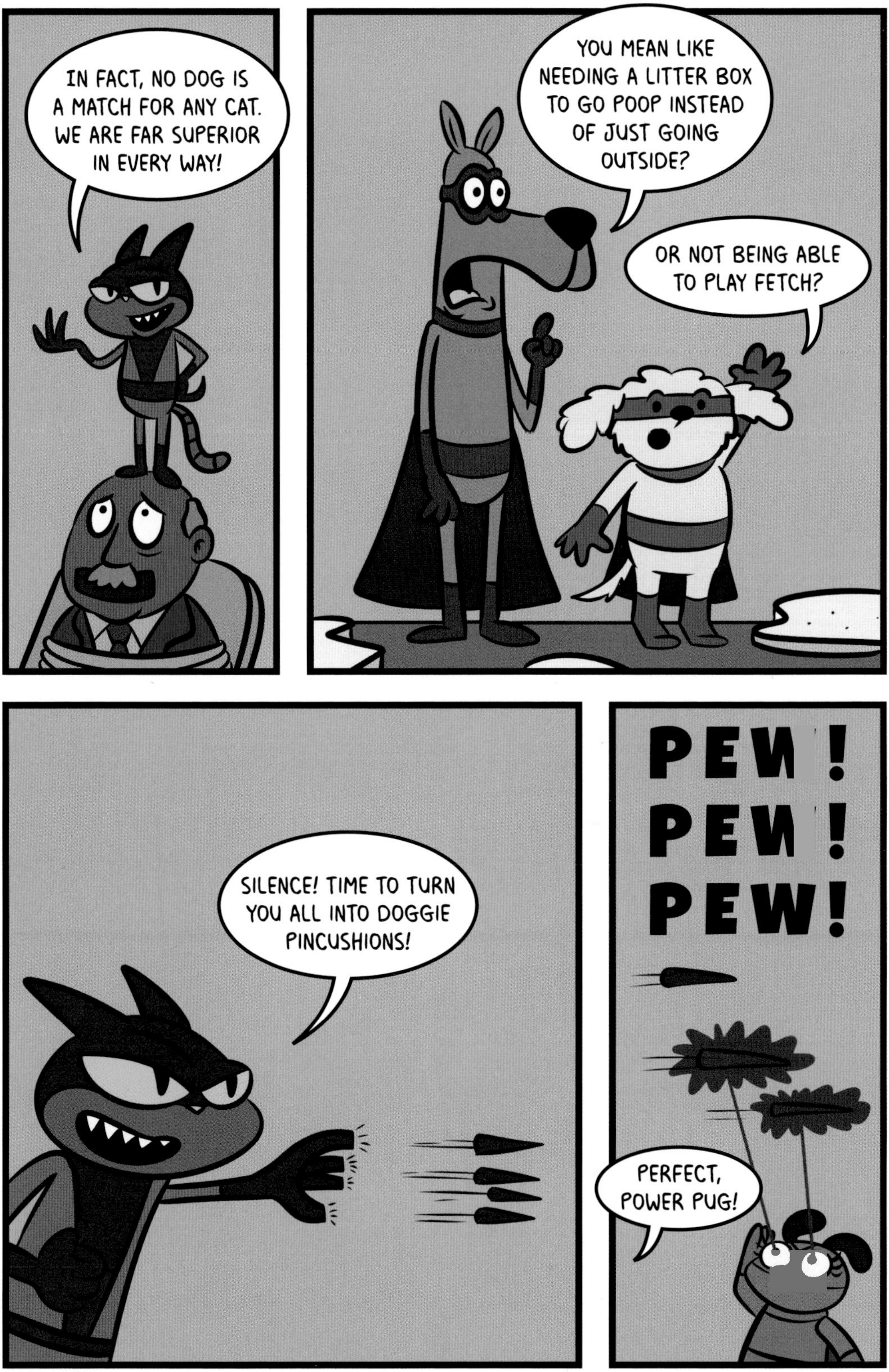
IN FACT, NO DOG IS A MATCH FOR ANY CAT. WE ARE FAR SUPERIOR IN EVERY WAY!
YOU MEAN LIKE NEEDING A LITTER BOX TO GO POOP INSTEAD OF JUST GOING OUTSIDE?
OR NOT BEING ABLE TO PLAY FETCH?
SILENCE! TIME TO TURN YOU ALL INTO DOGGIE PINCUSHIONS!
PEW! PEW! PEW!
PERFECT, POWER PUG!

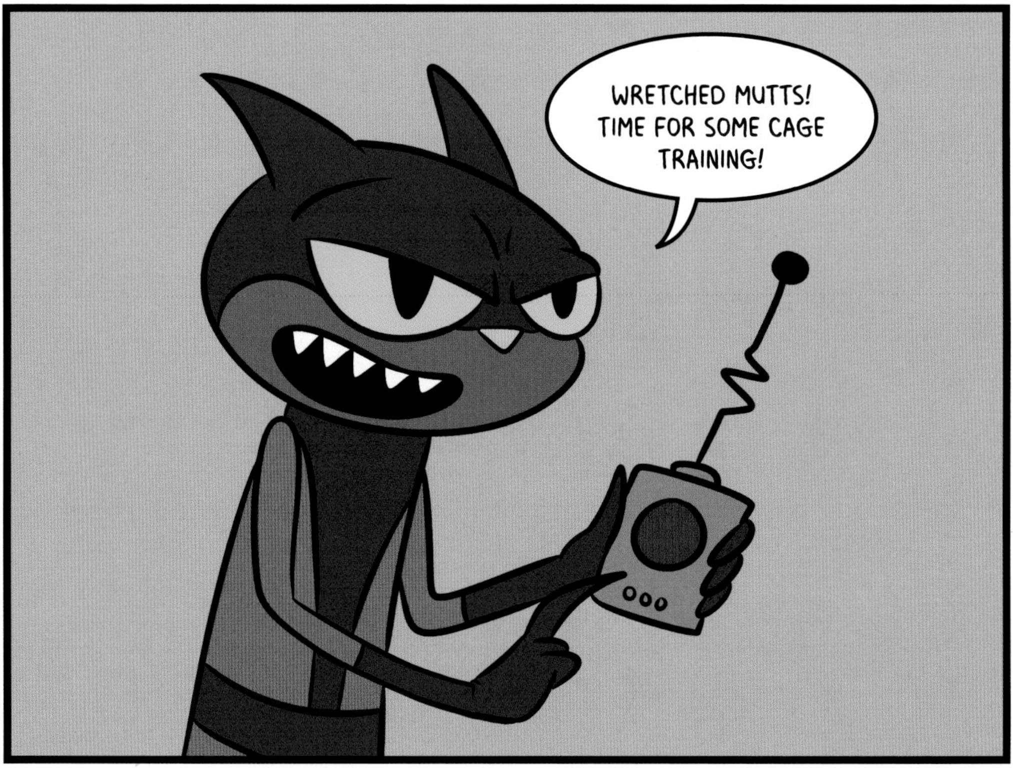
WRETCHED MUTTS! TIME FOR SOME CAGE TRAINING!

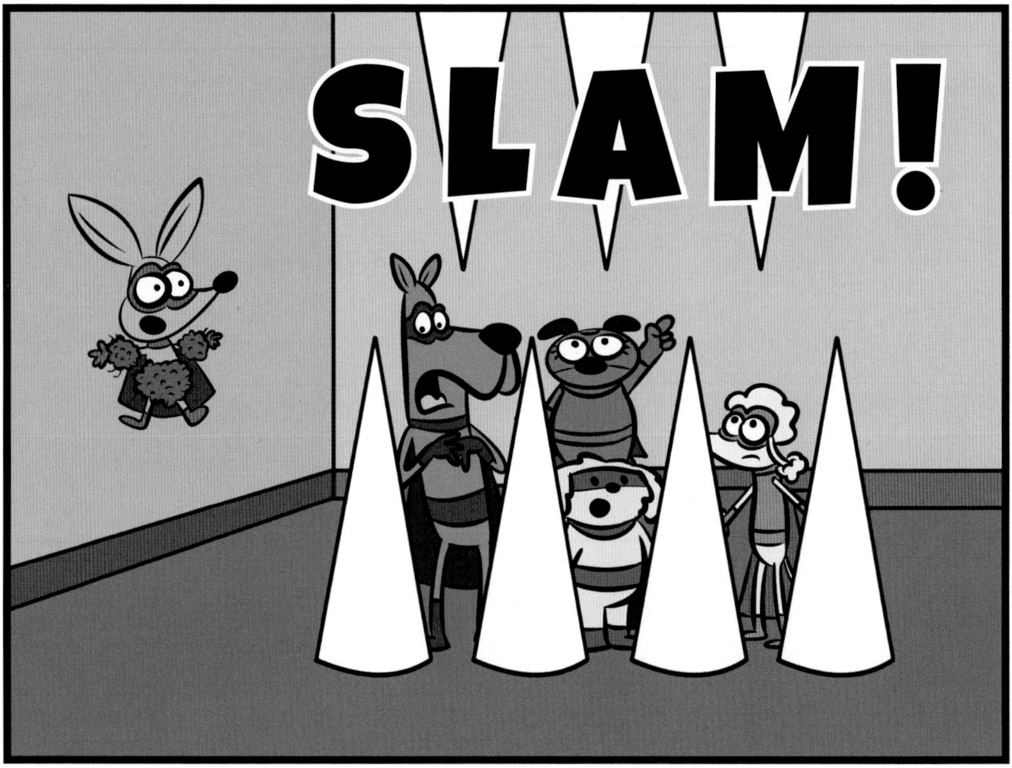
SLAM!

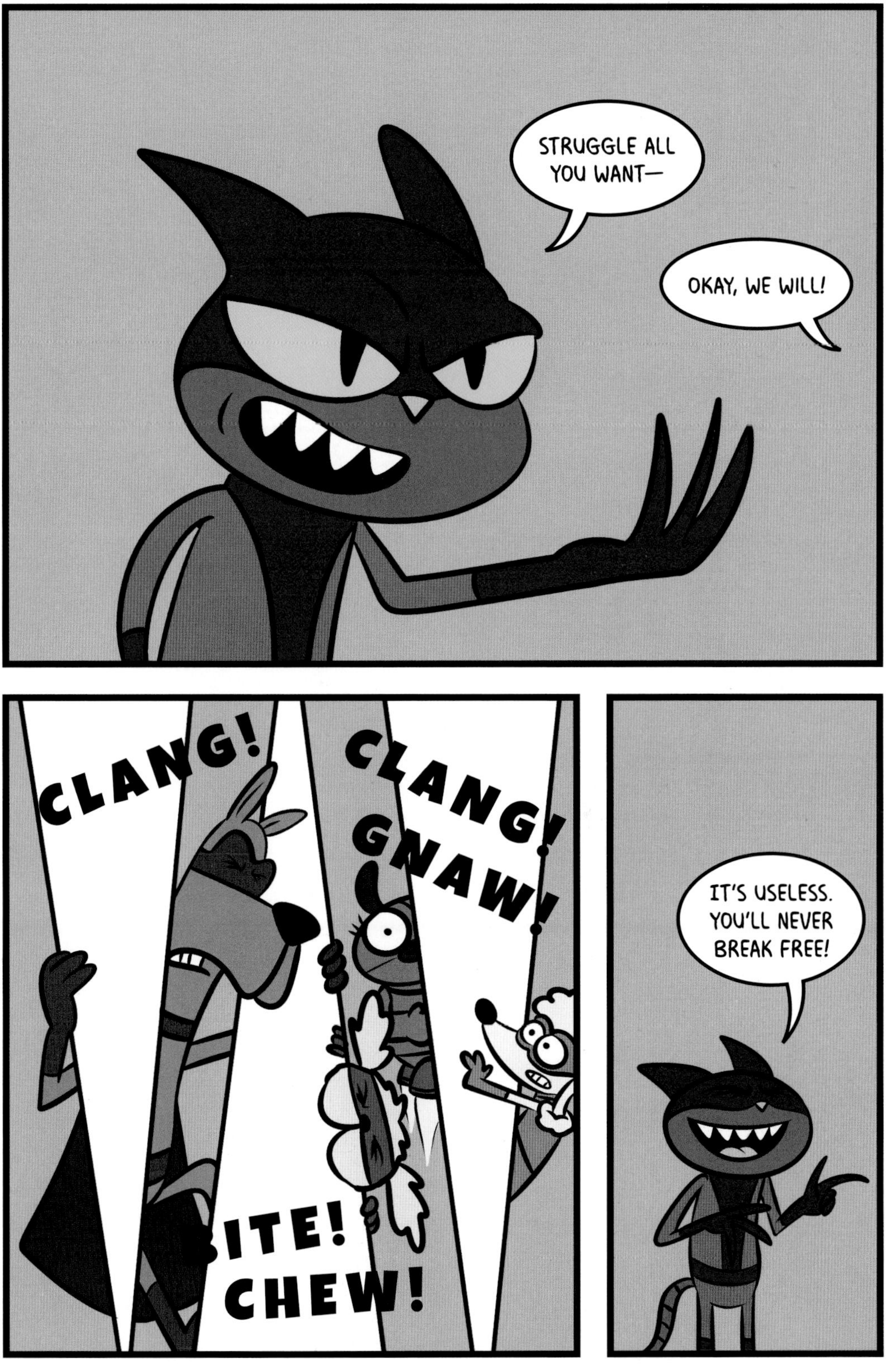
STRUGGLE ALL YOU WANT—
OKAY, WE WILL!
CLANG!
CLANG!
GNAW!
BITE!
CHEW!
IT'S USELESS. YOU'LL NEVER BREAK FREE!

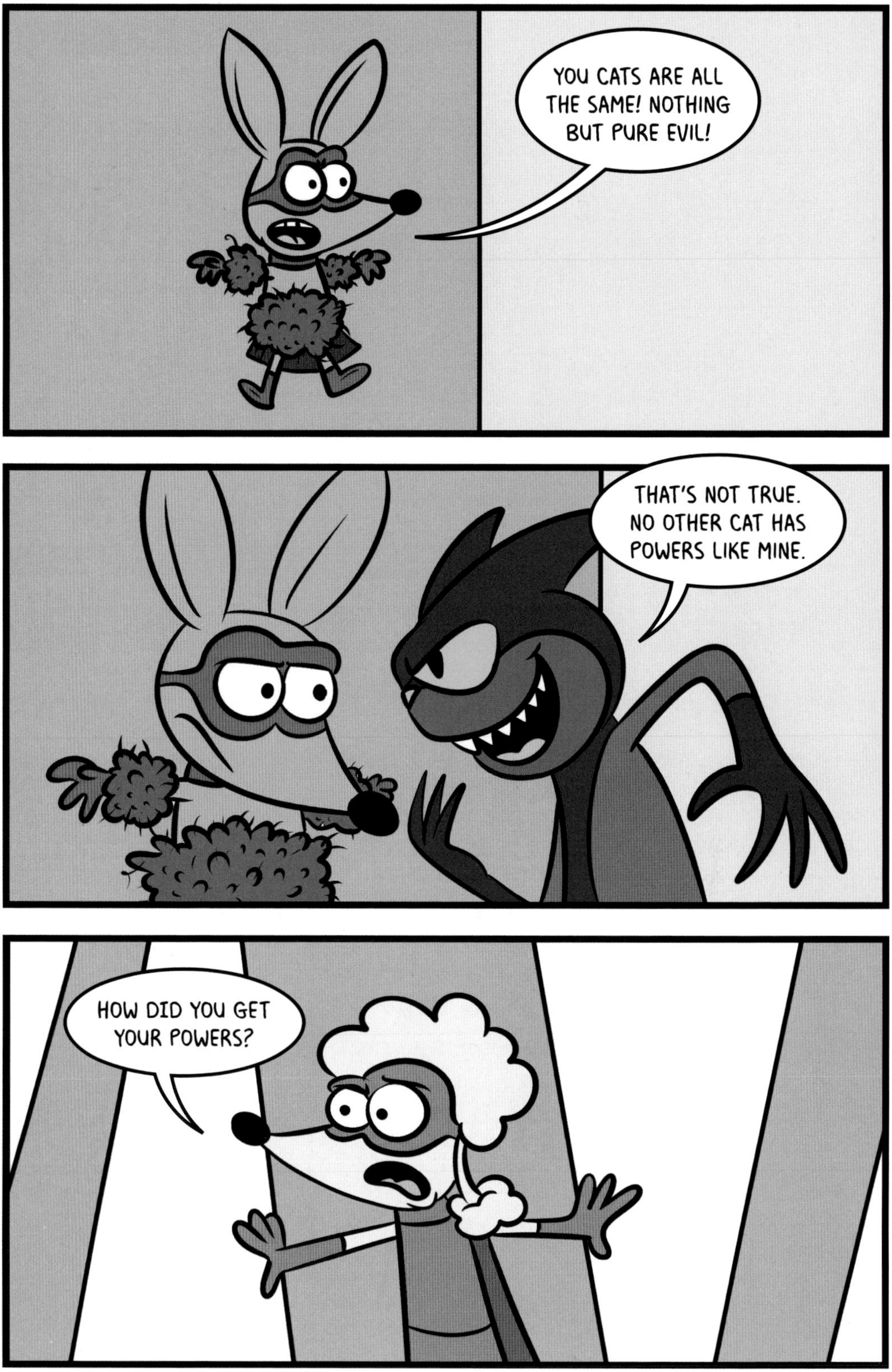
YOU CATS ARE ALL THE SAME! NOTHING BUT PURE EVIL!
THAT'S NOT TRUE. NO OTHER CAT HAS POWERS LIKE MINE.
HOW DID YOU GET YOUR POWERS?

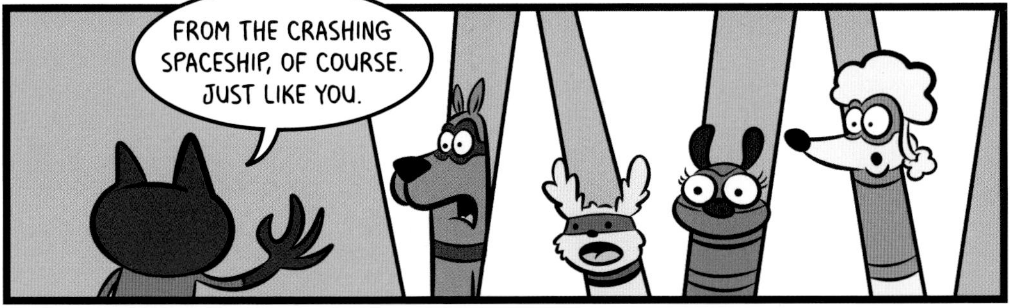
FROM THE CRASHING SPACESHIP, OF COURSE. JUST LIKE YOU.

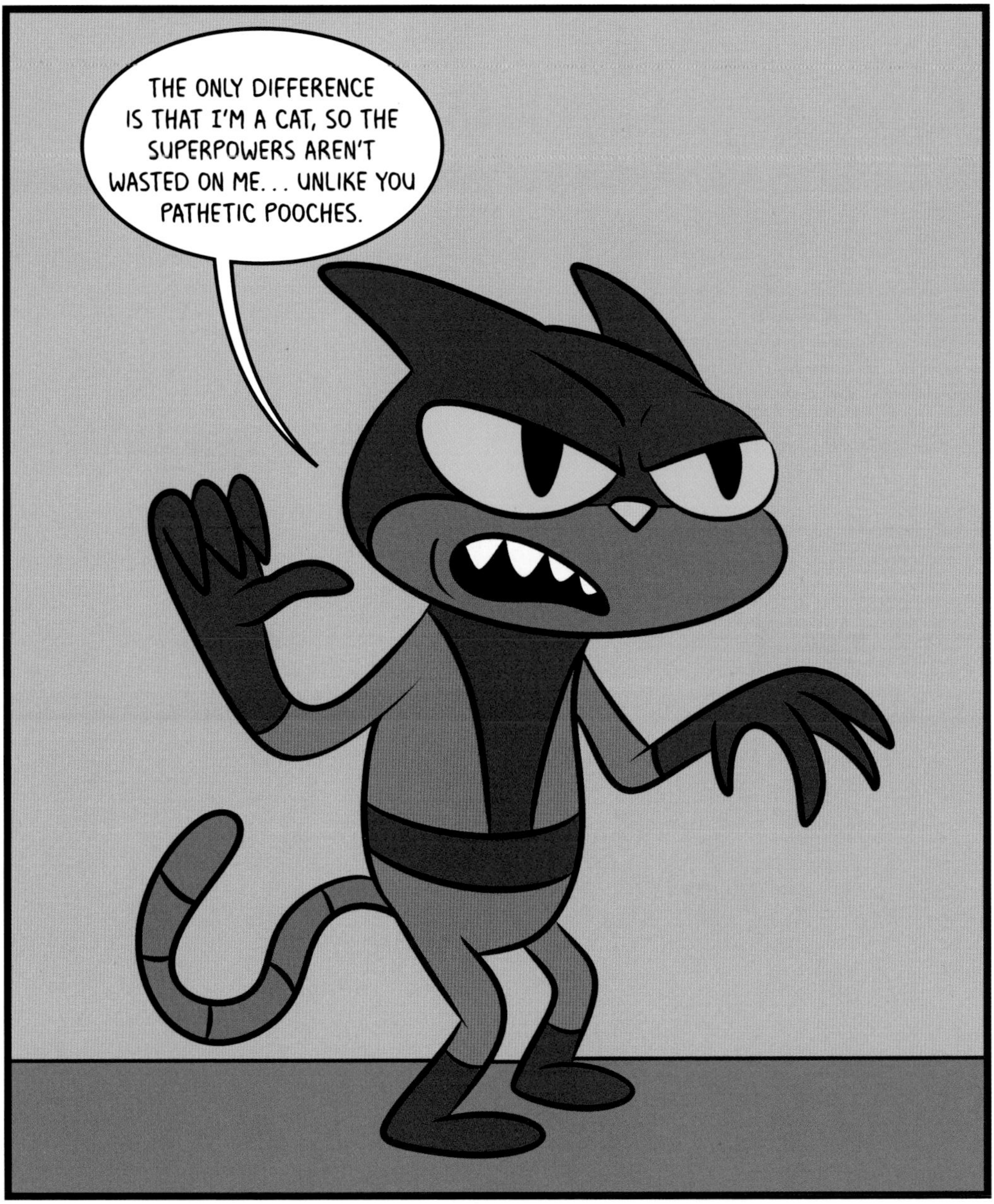
THE ONLY DIFFERENCE IS THAT I'M A CAT, SO THE SUPERPOWERS AREN'T WASTED ON ME... UNLIKE YOU PATHETIC POOCHES.

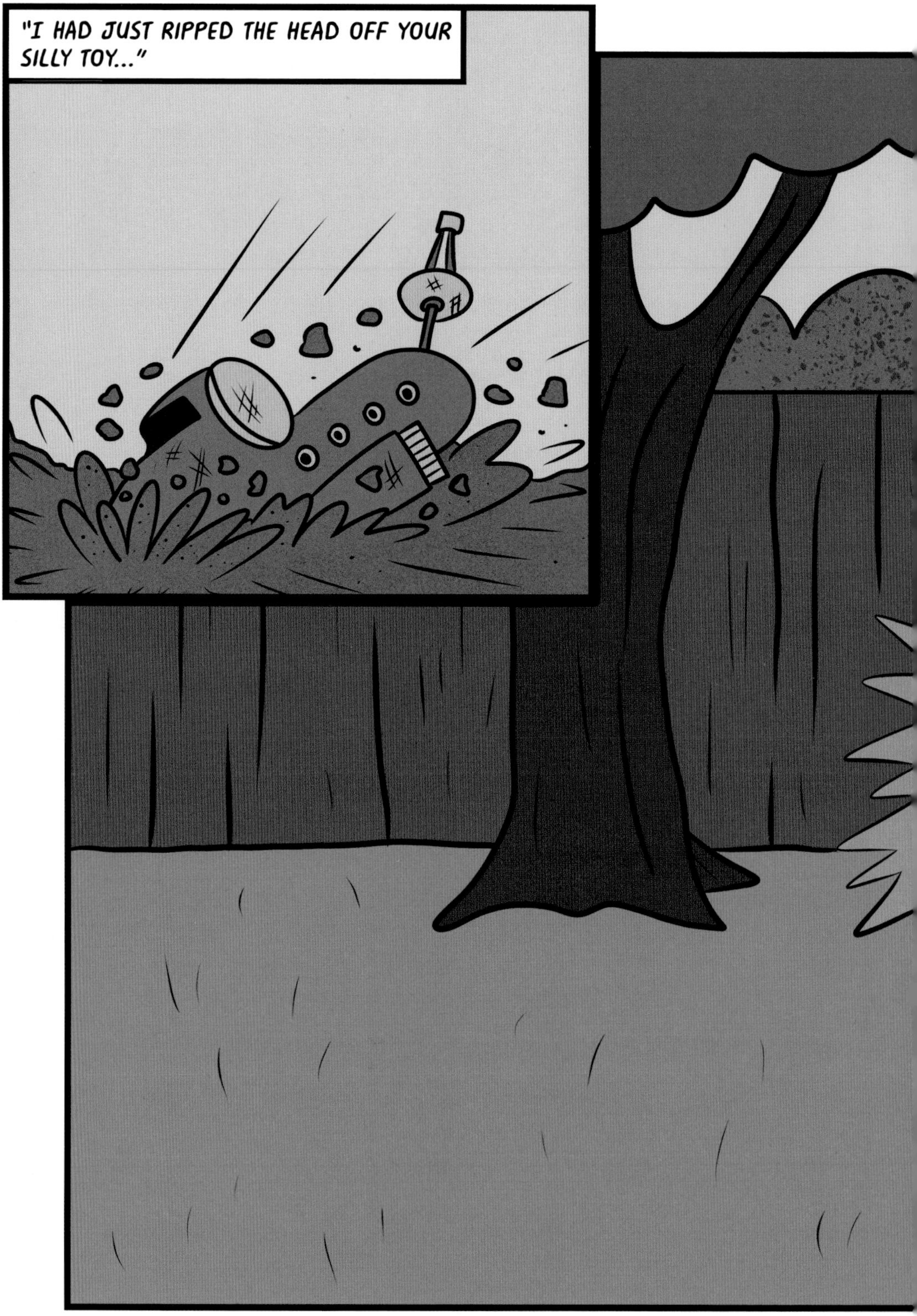
"I HAD JUST RIPPED THE HEAD OFF YOUR SILLY TOY..."

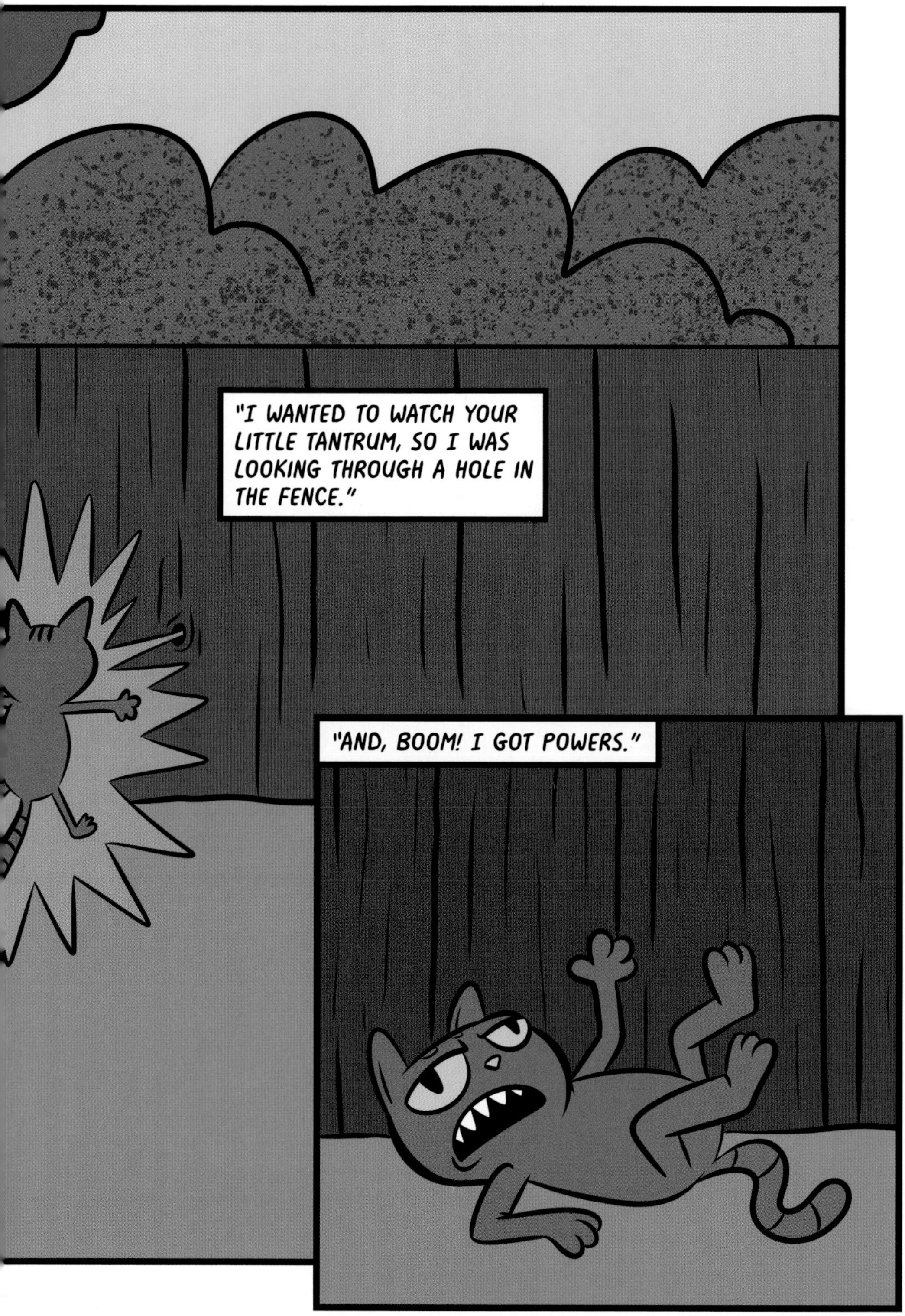
"I WANTED TO WATCH YOUR LITTLE TANTRUM, SO I WAS LOOKING THROUGH A HOLE IN THE FENCE."
"AND, BOOM! I GOT POWERS."

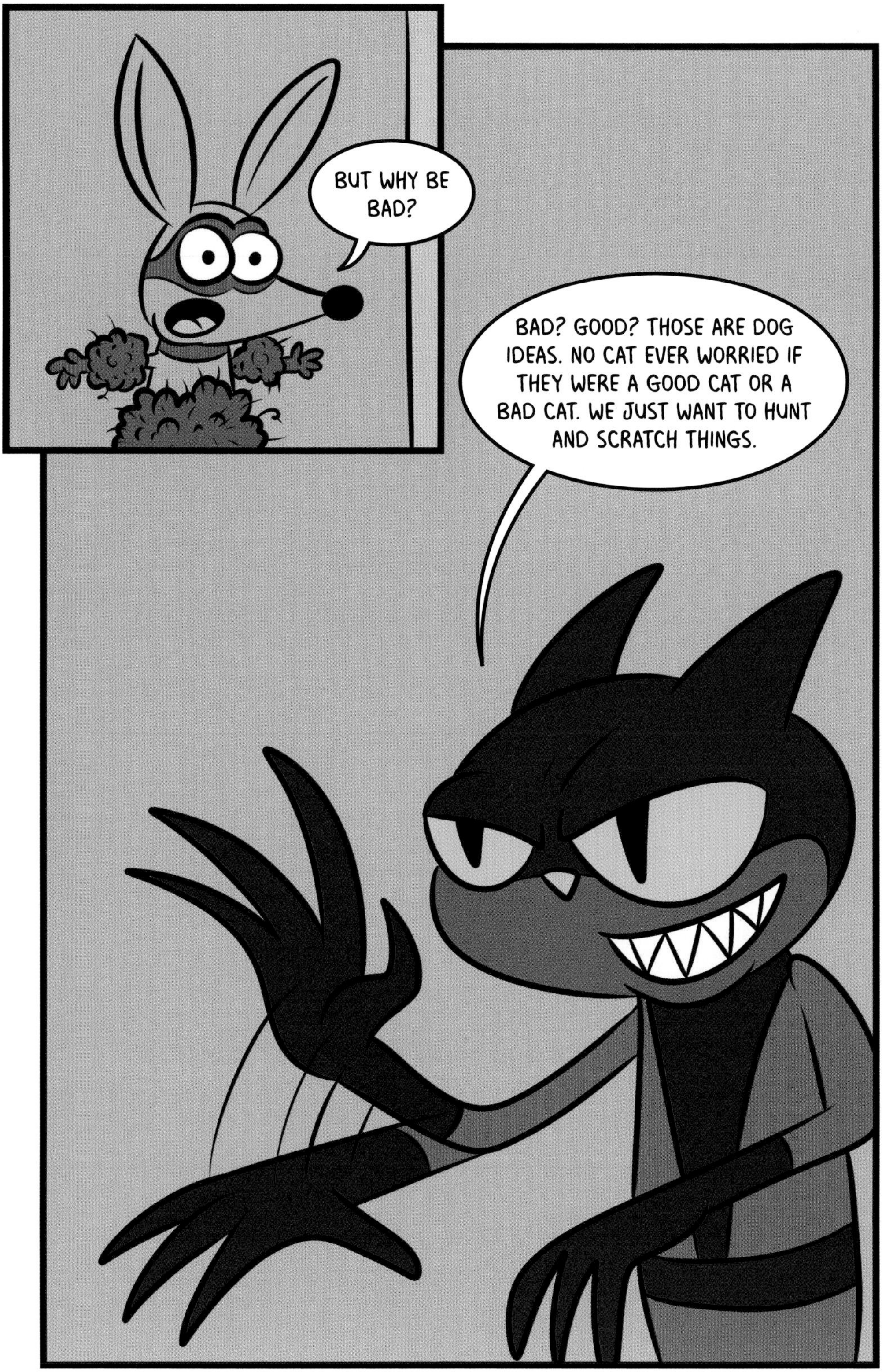
BUT WHY BE BAD?
BAD? GOOD? THOSE ARE DOG IDEAS. NO CAT EVER WORRIED IF THEY WERE A GOOD CAT OR A BAD CAT. WE JUST WANT TO HUNT AND SCRATCH THINGS.

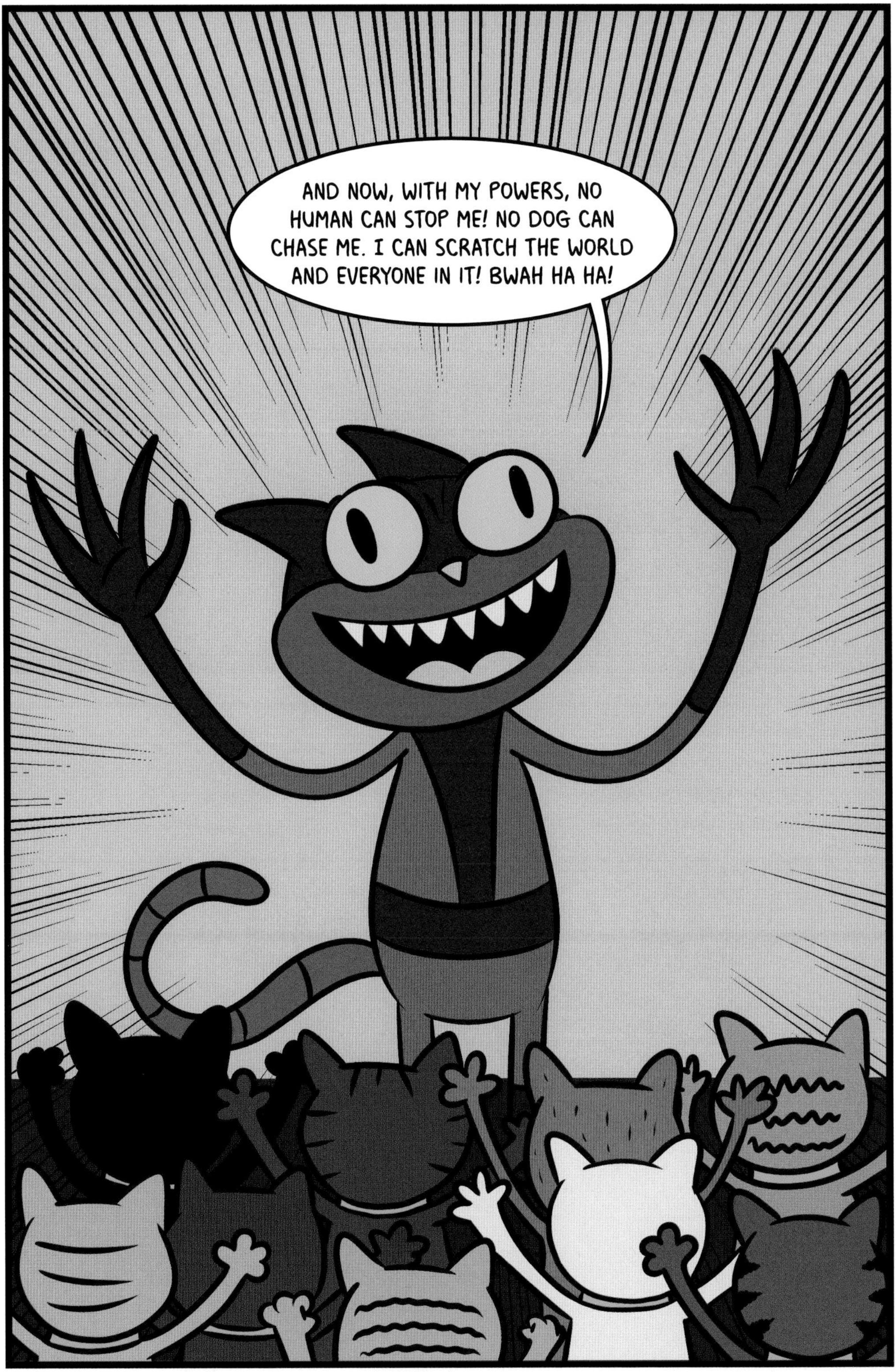
AND NOW, WITH MY POWERS, NO HUMAN CAN STOP ME! NO DOG CAN CHASE ME. I CAN SCRATCH THE WORLD AND EVERYONE IN IT! BWAH HA HA!

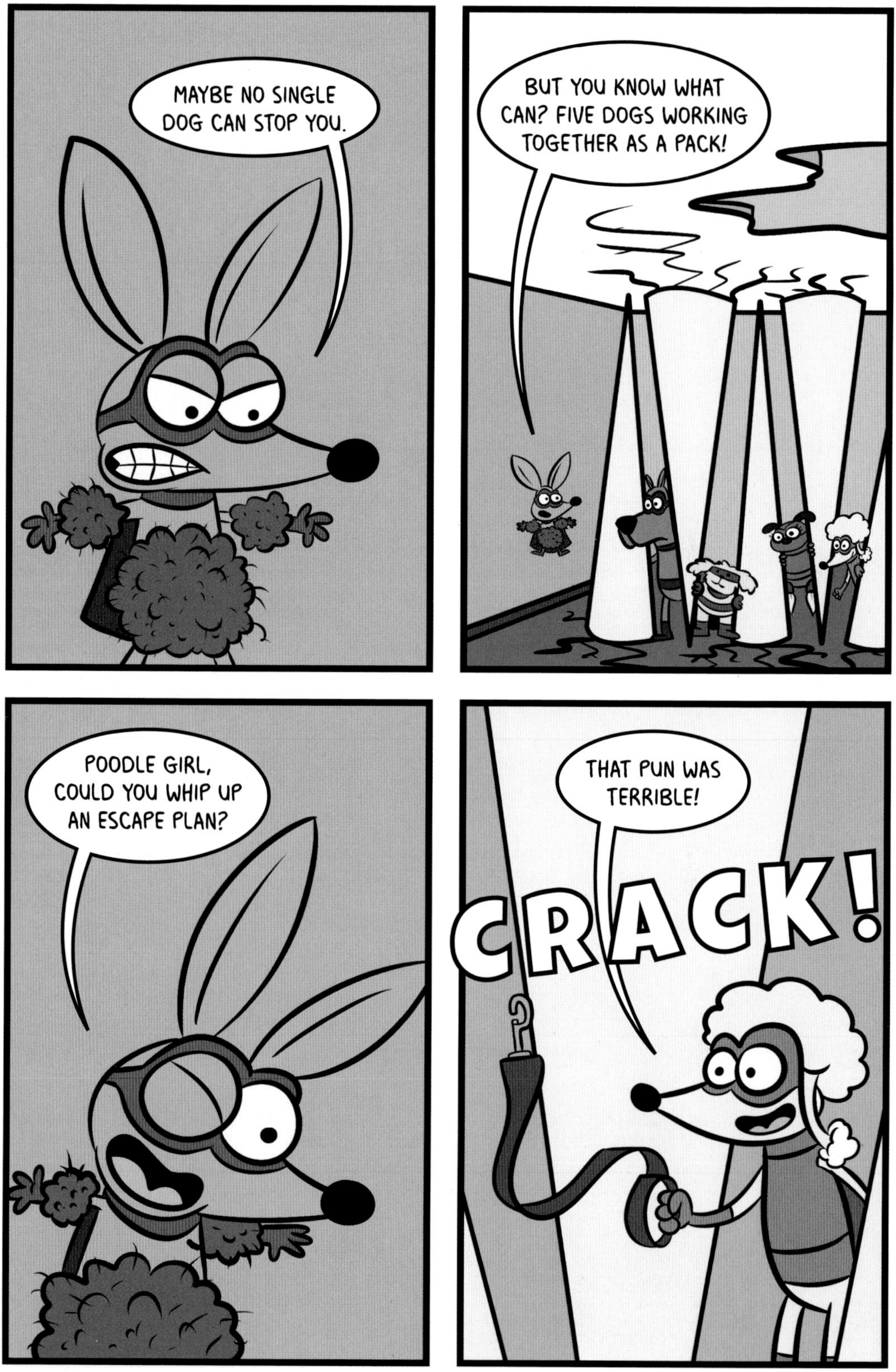
MAYBE NO SINGLE DOG CAN STOP YOU.
BUT YOU KNOW WHAT CAN? FIVE DOGS WORKING TOGETHER AS A PACK!
POODLE GIRL, COULD YOU WHIP UP AN ESCAPE PLAN?
THAT PUN WAS TERRIBLE!
CRACK!

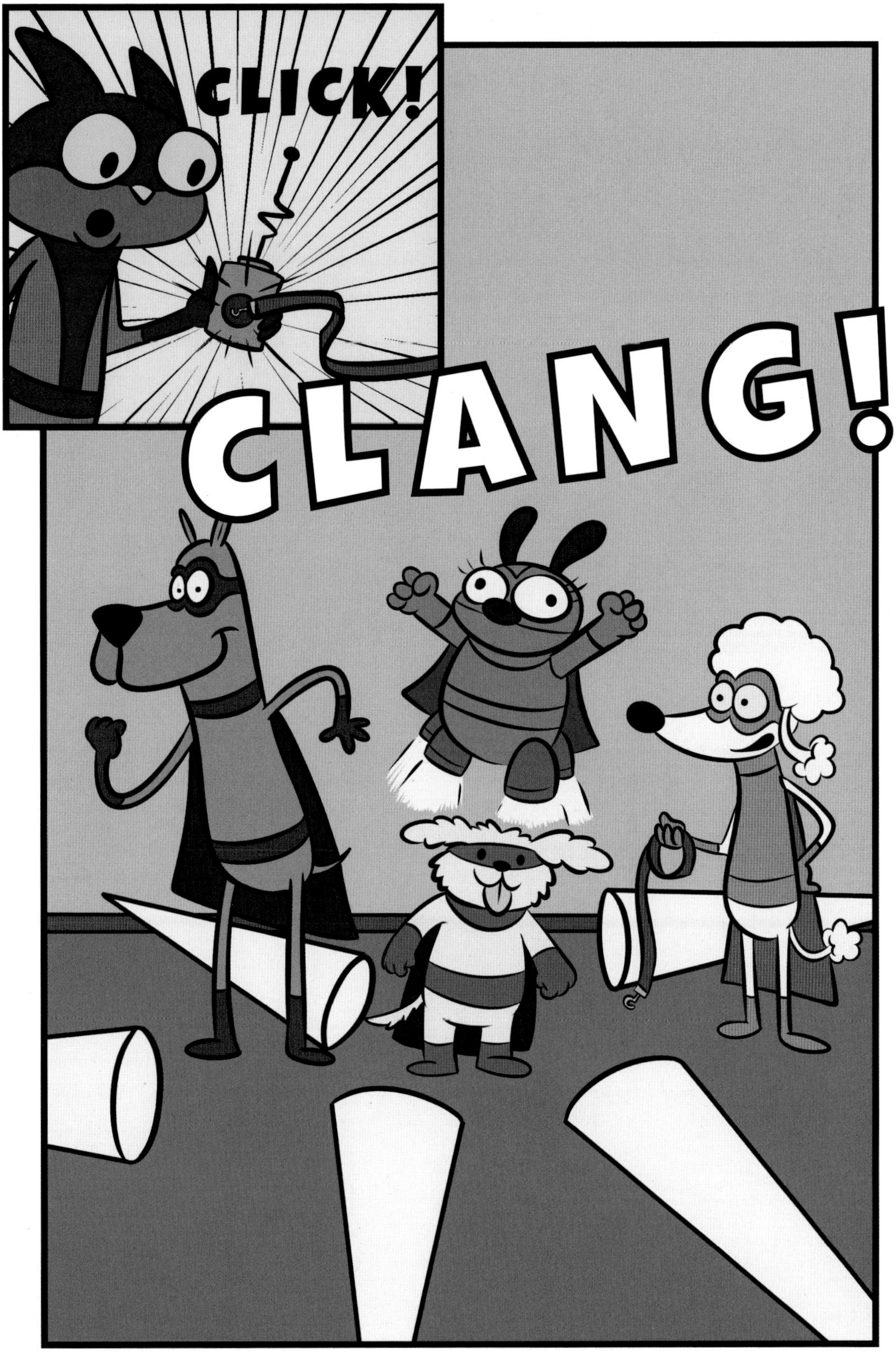
CLICK!
CLANG!

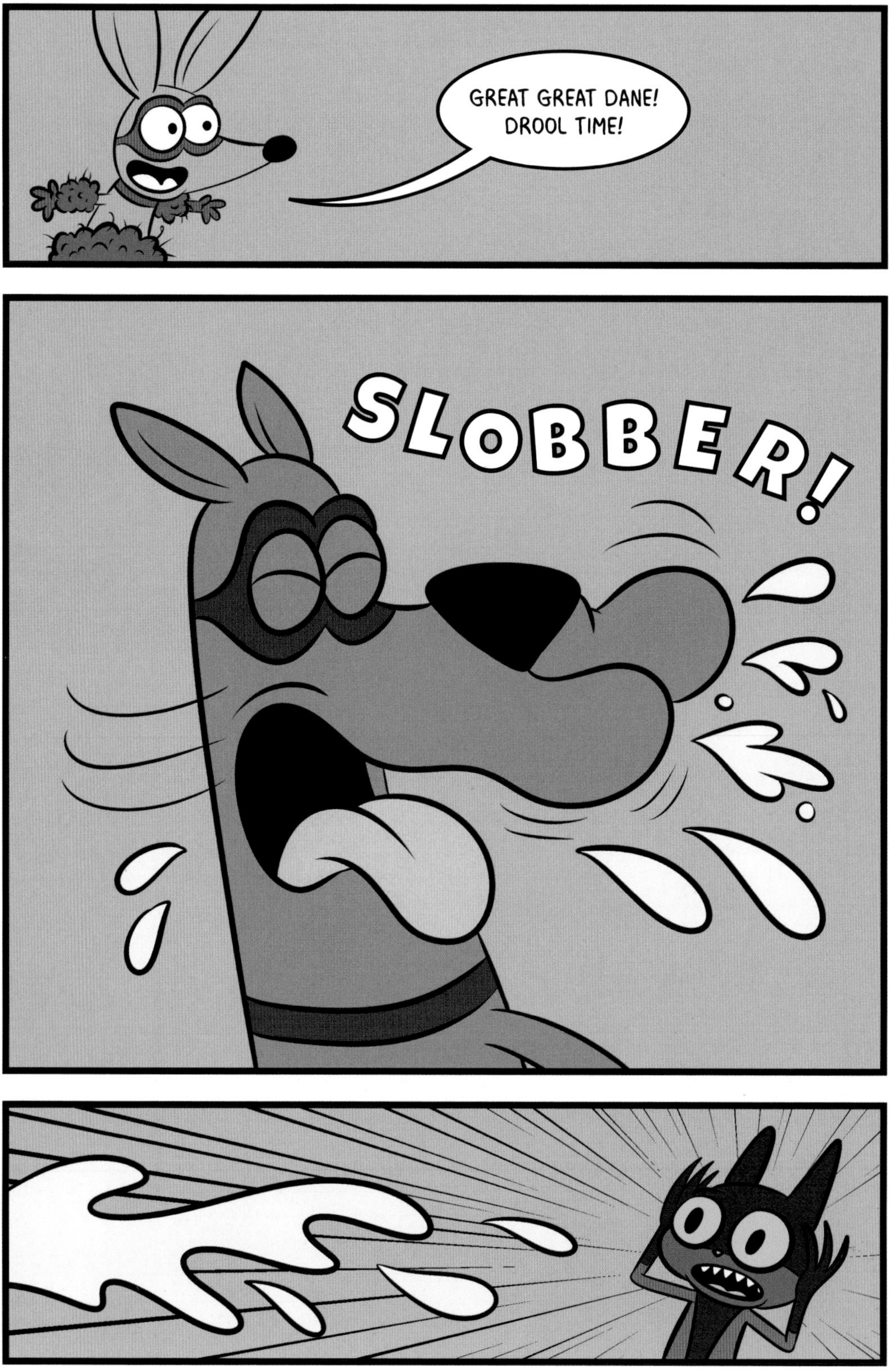
GREAT GREAT DANE!
DROOL TIME!
SLOBBER!

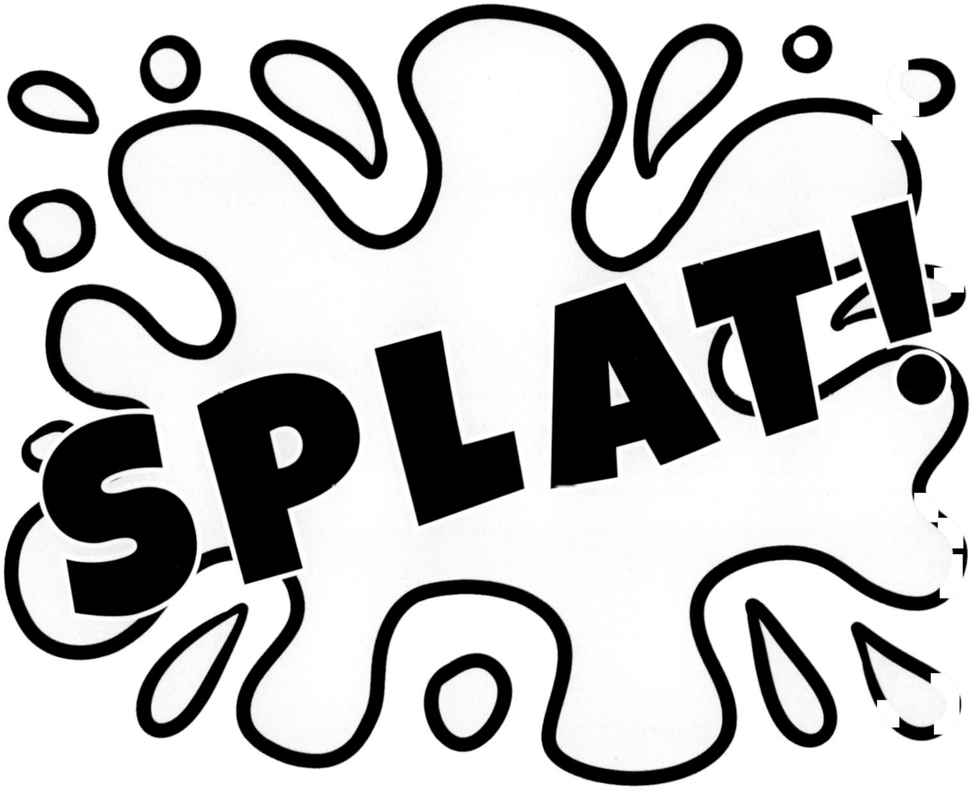
SPLAT!

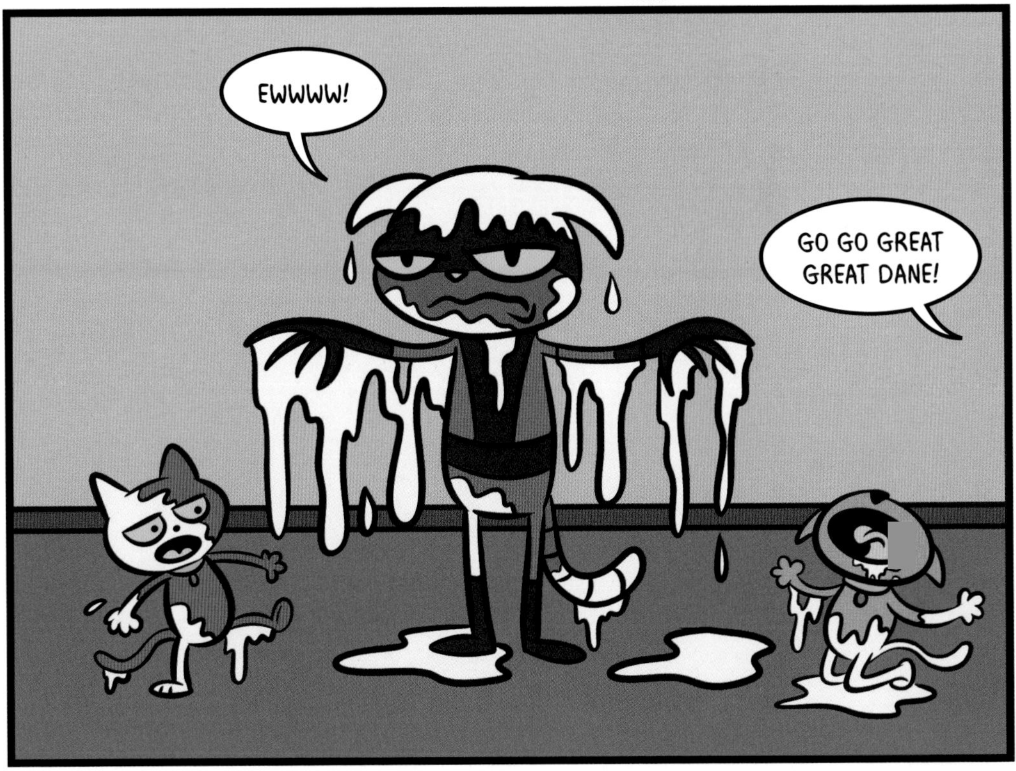
EWWWW!
GO GO GREAT GREAT DANE!

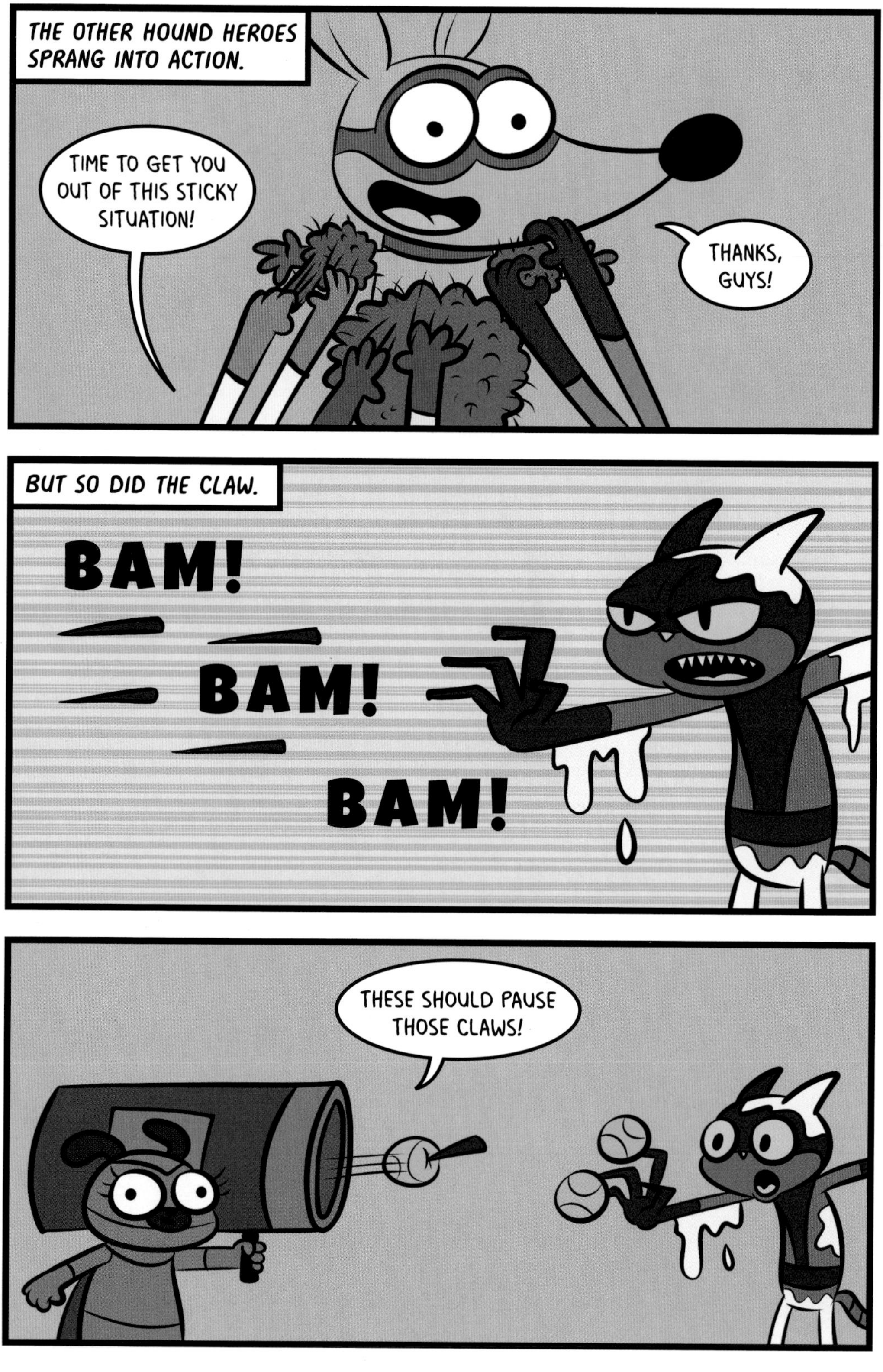
THE OTHER HOUND HEROES SPRANG INTO ACTION.
TIME TO GET YOU OUT OF THIS STICKY SITUATION!
THANKS, GUYS!
BUT SO DID THE CLAW.
BAM!
BAM!
BAM!
THESE SHOULD PAUSE THOSE CLAWS!

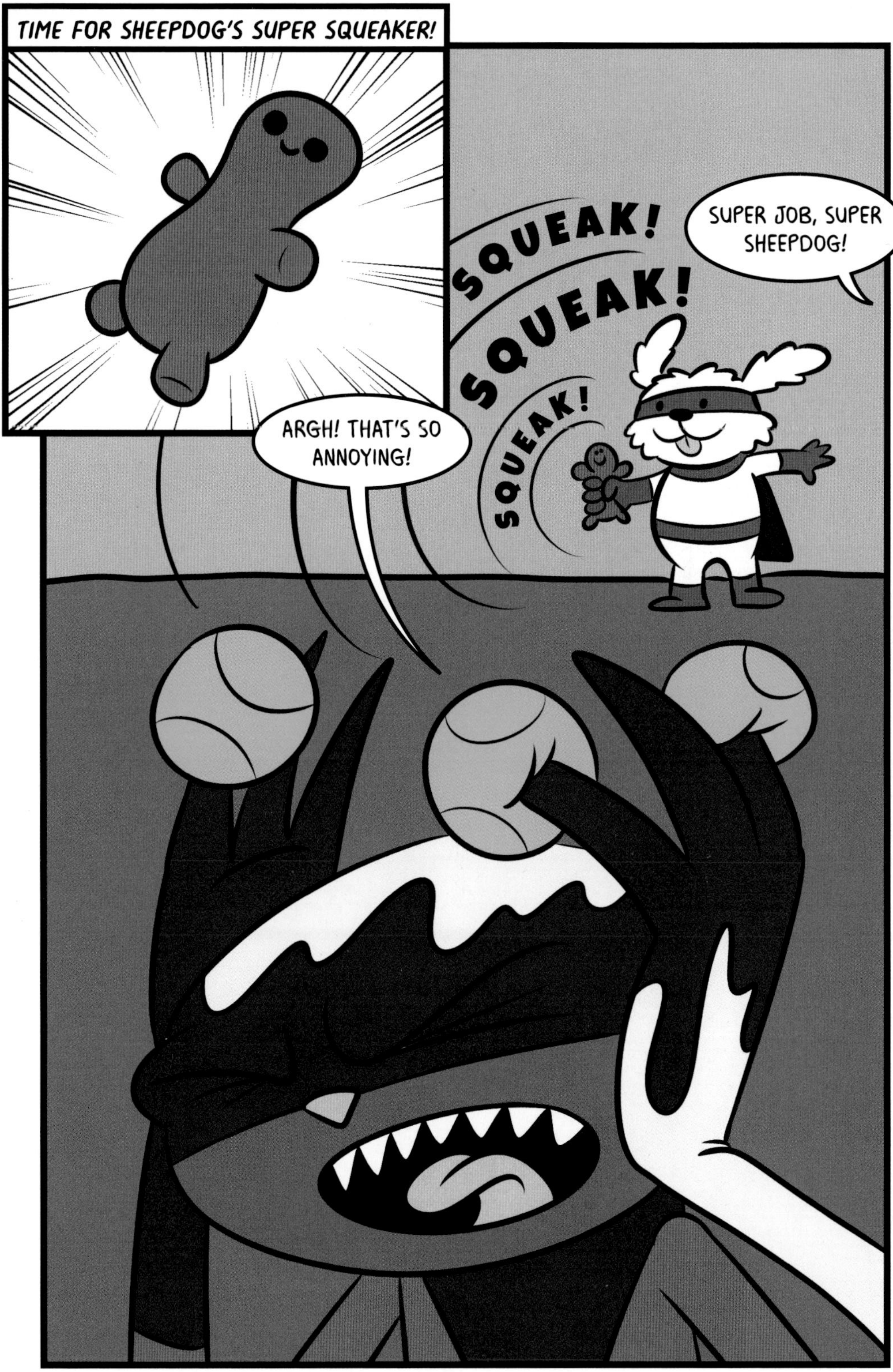
TIME FOR SHEEPDOG'S SUPER SQUEAKER!
SQUEAK!
SQUEAK!
SQUEAK!
SUPER JOB, SUPER SHEEPDOG!
ARGH! THAT'S SO ANNOYING!

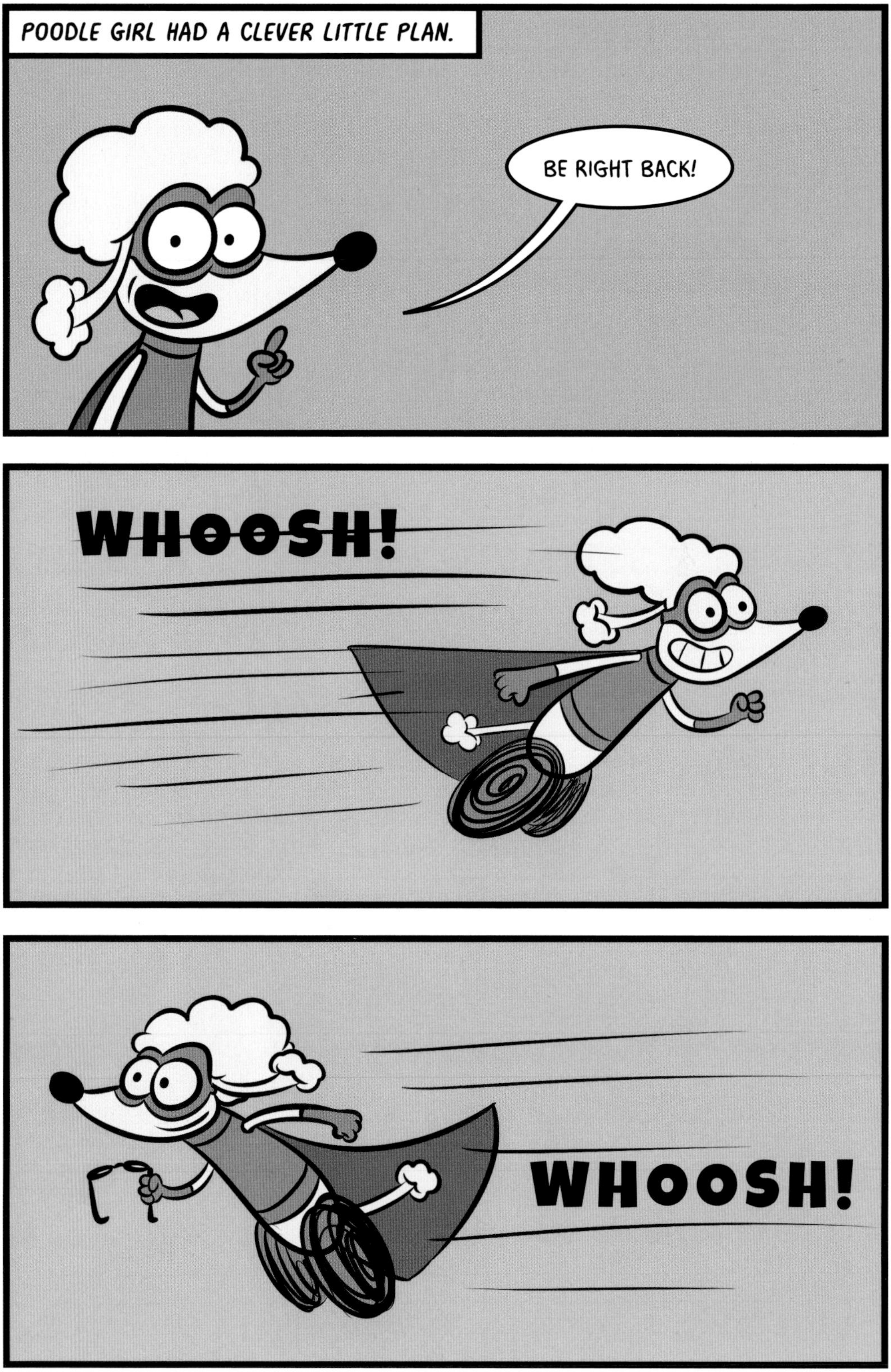
POODLE GIRL HAD A CLEVER LITTLE PLAN.
BE RIGHT BACK!
WHOOSH!
WHOOSH!

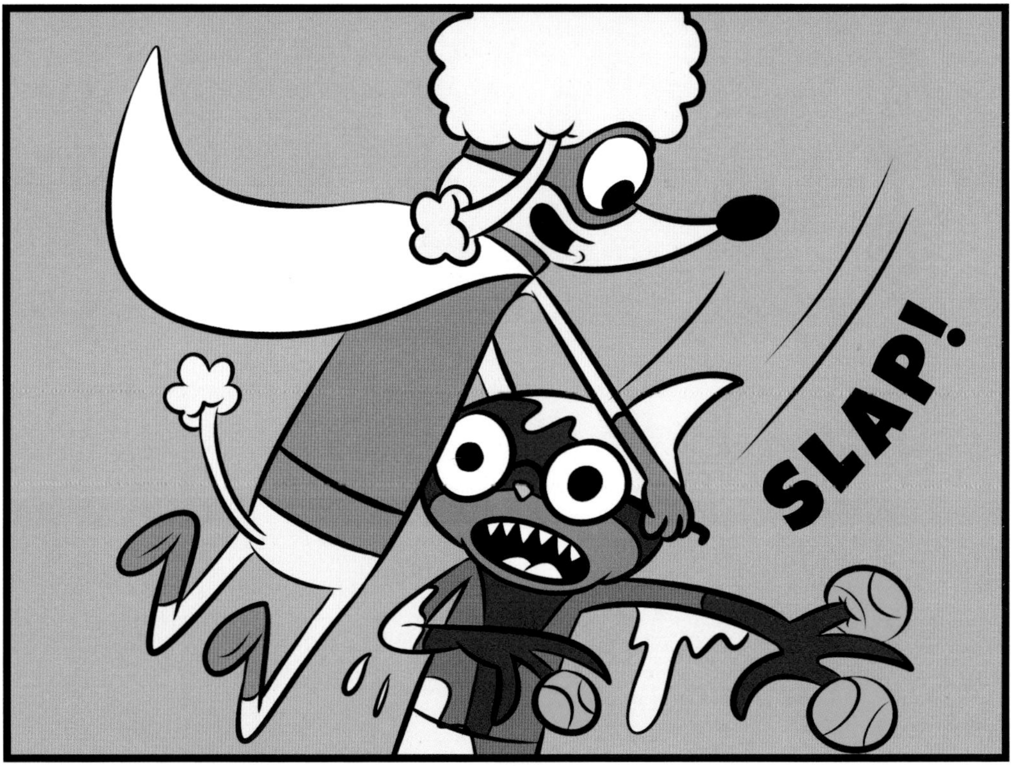
SLAP!

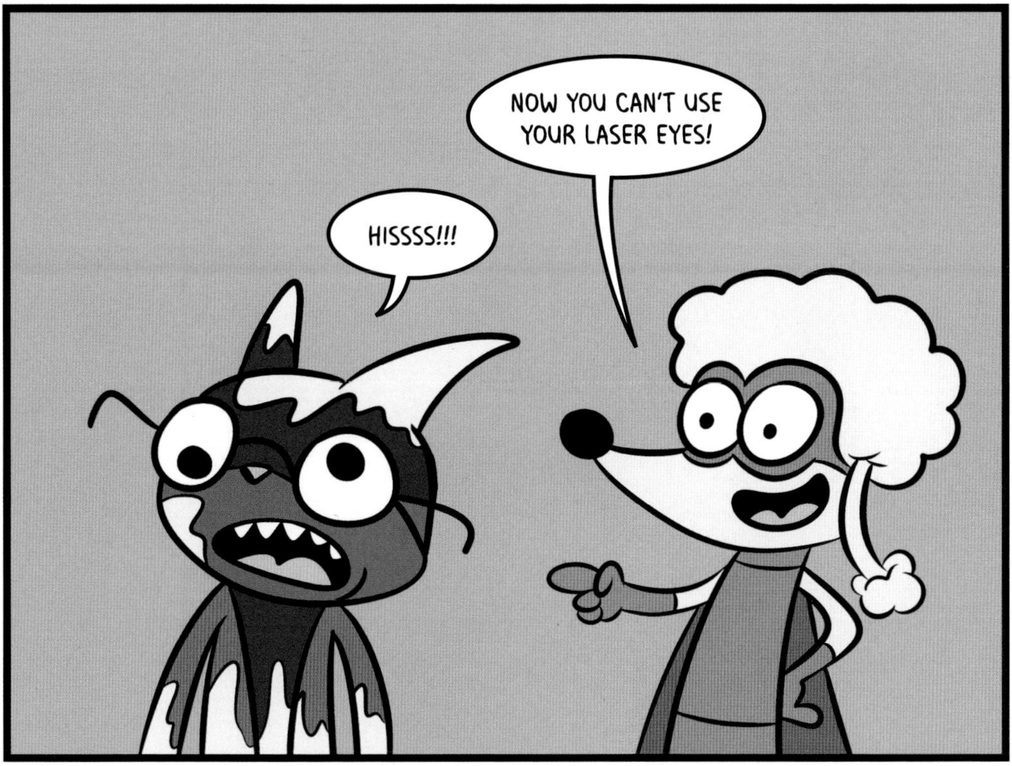
NOW YOU CAN'T USE YOUR LASER EYES!
HISSSS!!!

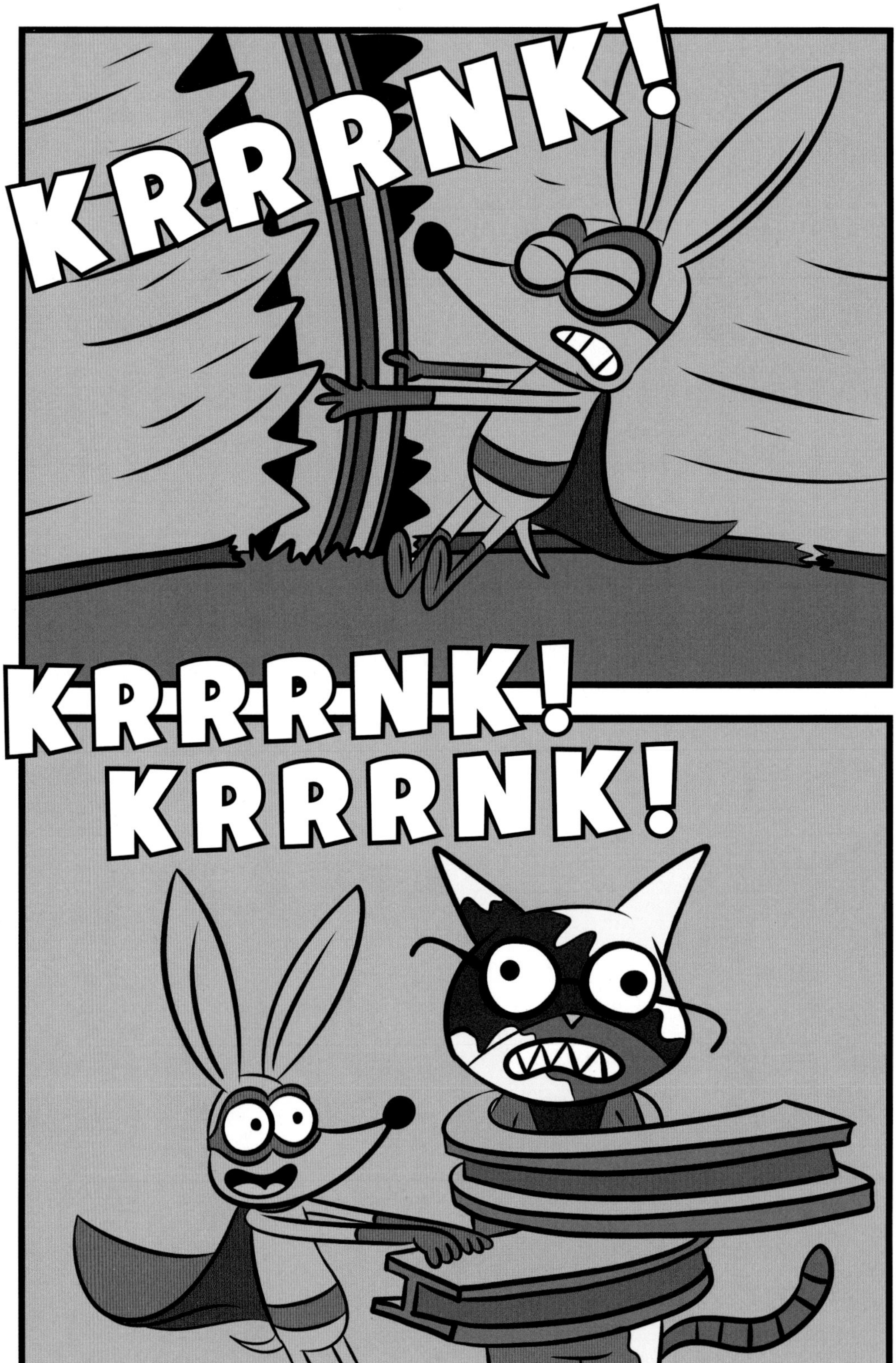
KRRRNK!
KRRRNK!
KRRRNK!

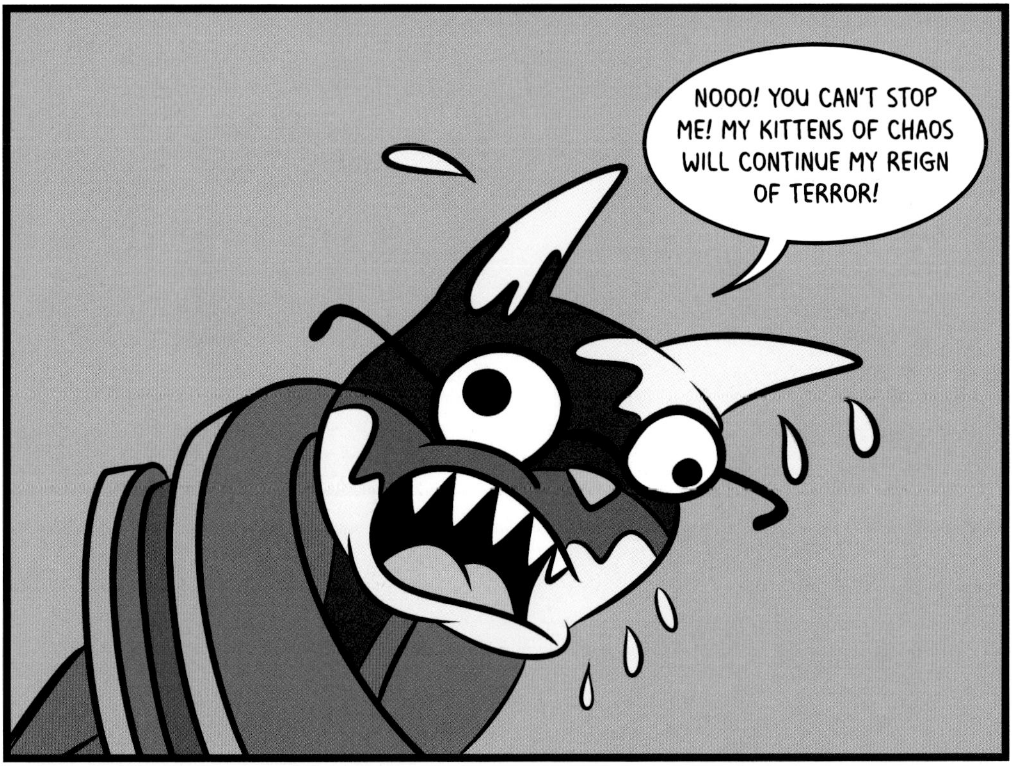
NOOO! YOU CAN'T STOP ME! MY KITTENS OF CHAOS WILL CONTINUE MY REIGN OF TERROR!

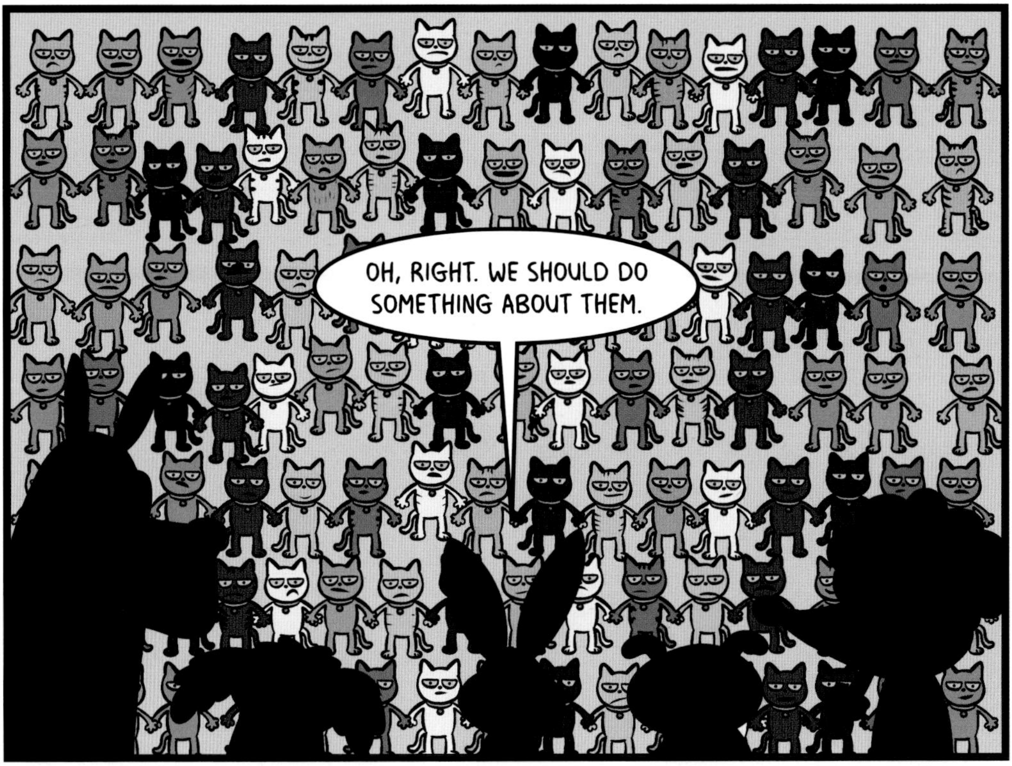
OH, RIGHT. WE SHOULD DO SOMETHING ABOUT THEM.

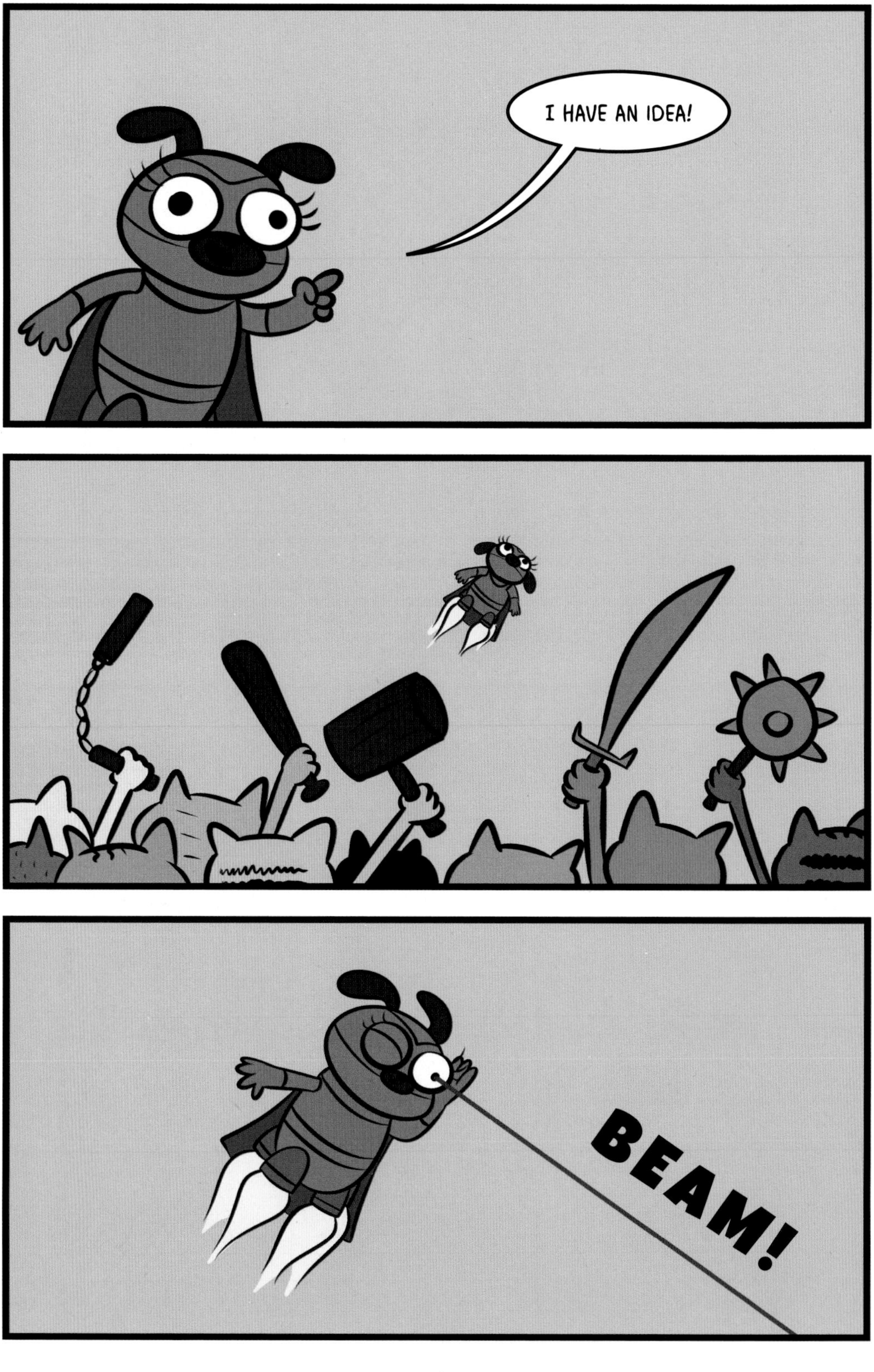
I HAVE AN IDEA!
BEAM!

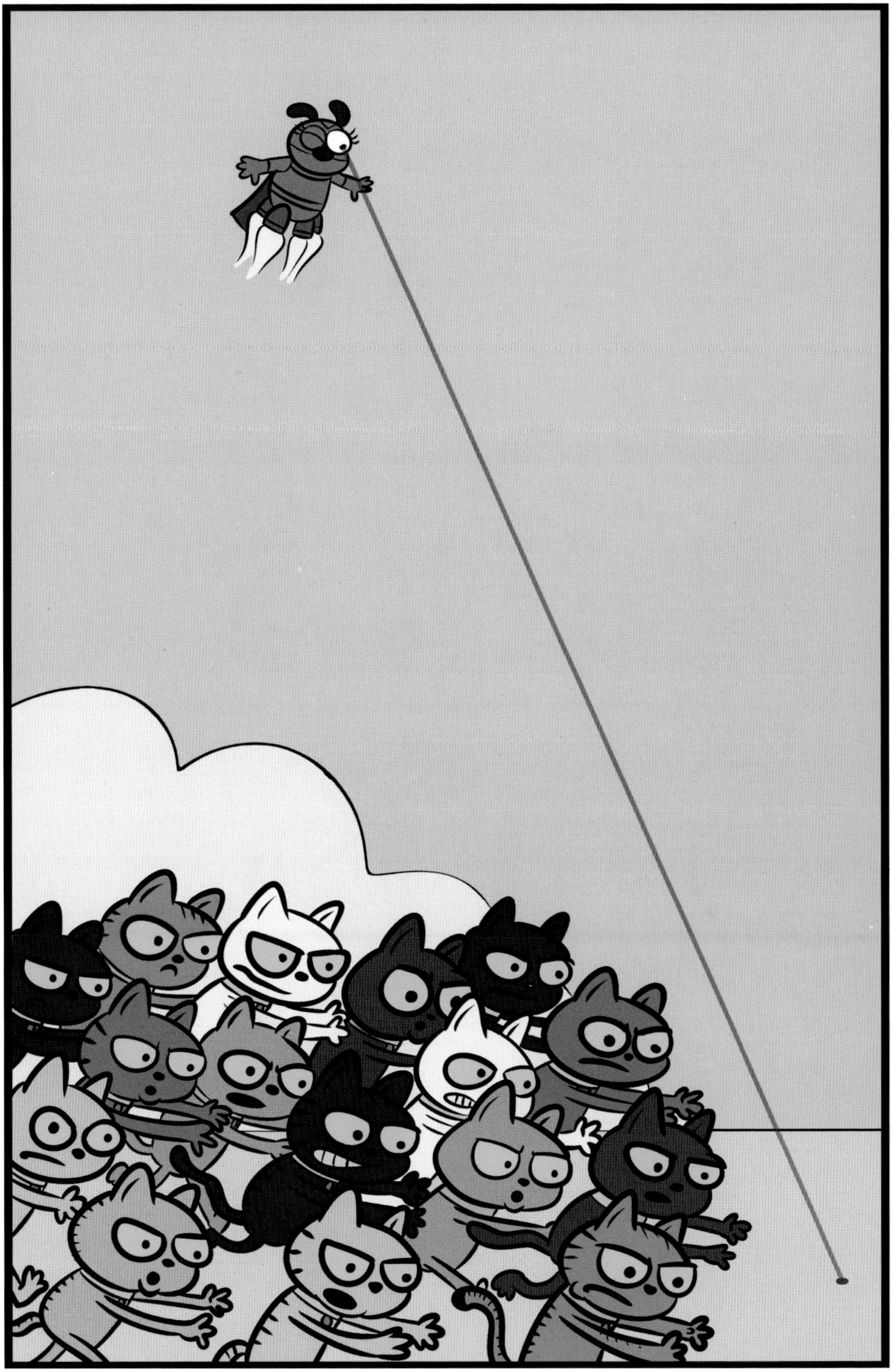

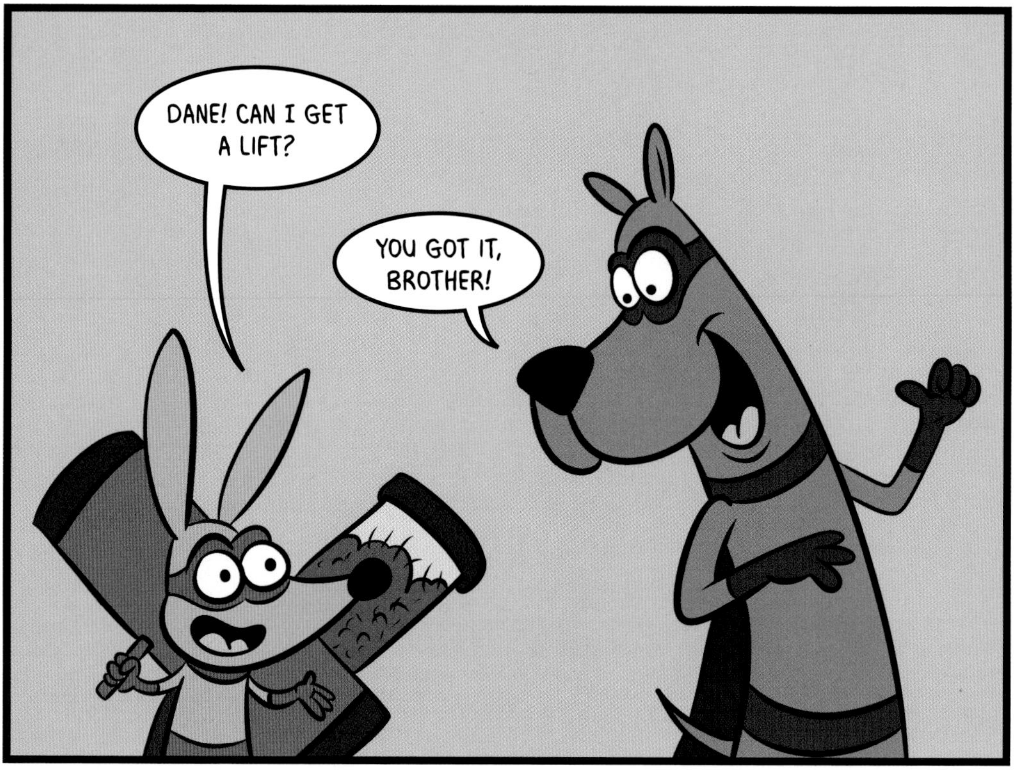
DANE! CAN I GET A LIFT?
YOU GOT IT, BROTHER!

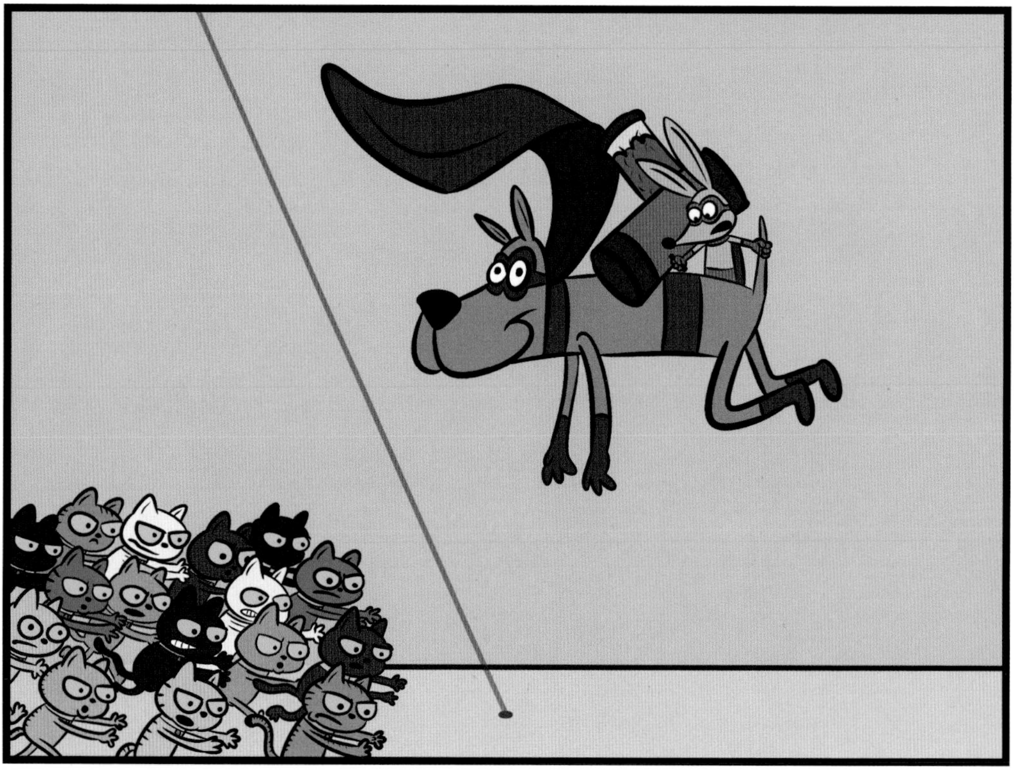

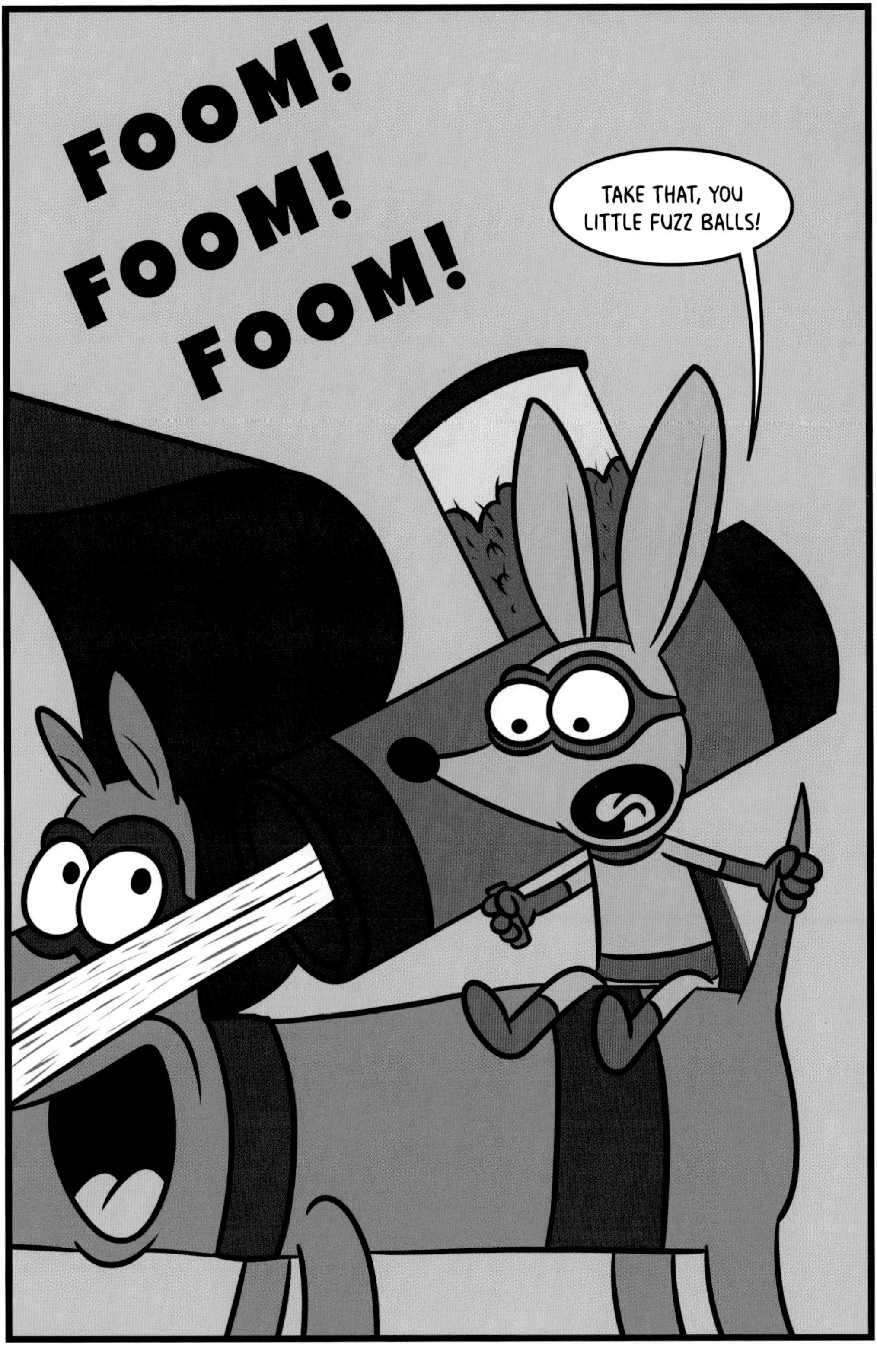
FOOM!
FOOM!
FOOM!
TAKE THAT, YOU LITTLE FUZZ BALLS!

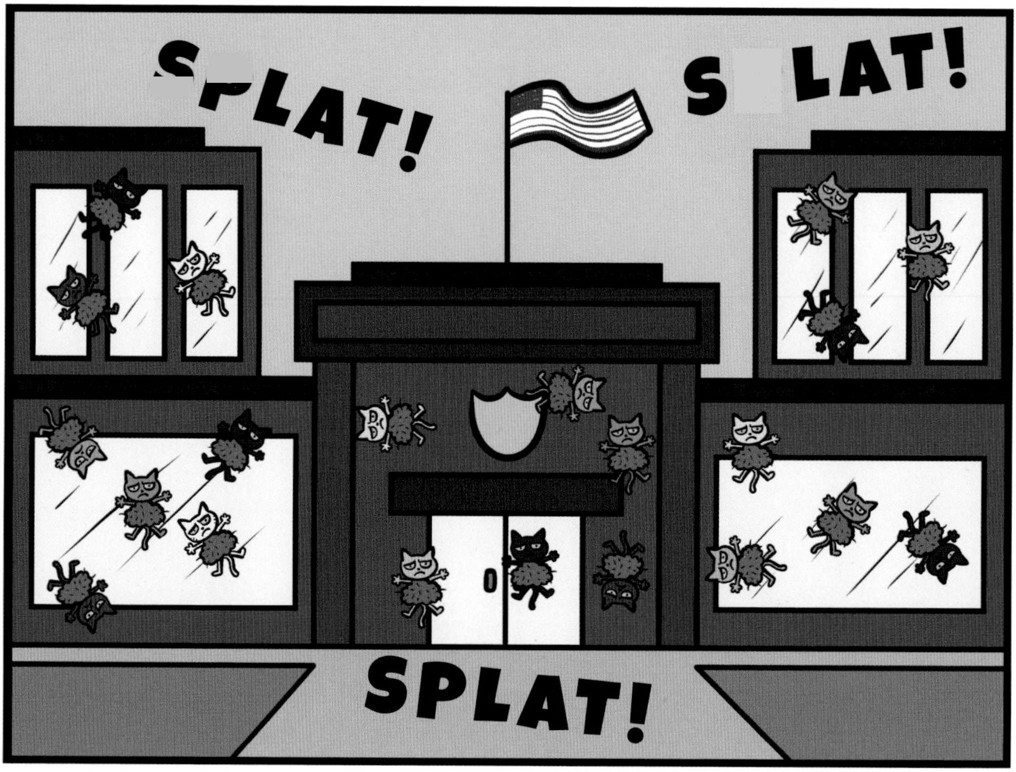
SPLAT!
SPLAT!
SPLAT!

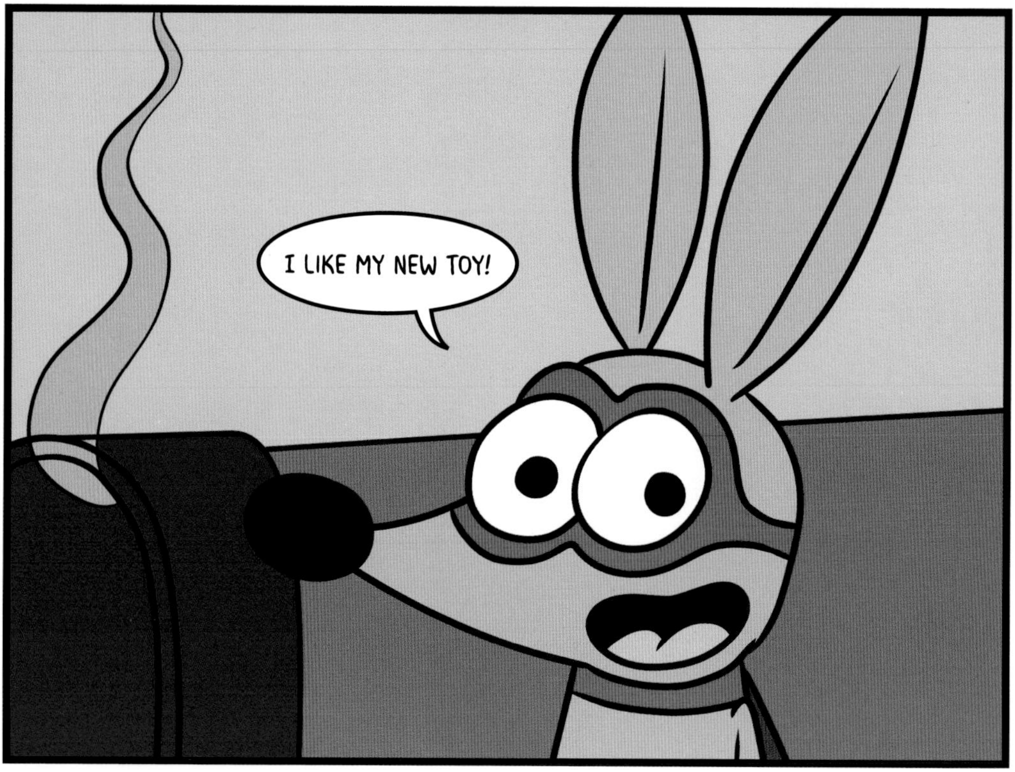
I LIKE MY NEW TOY!

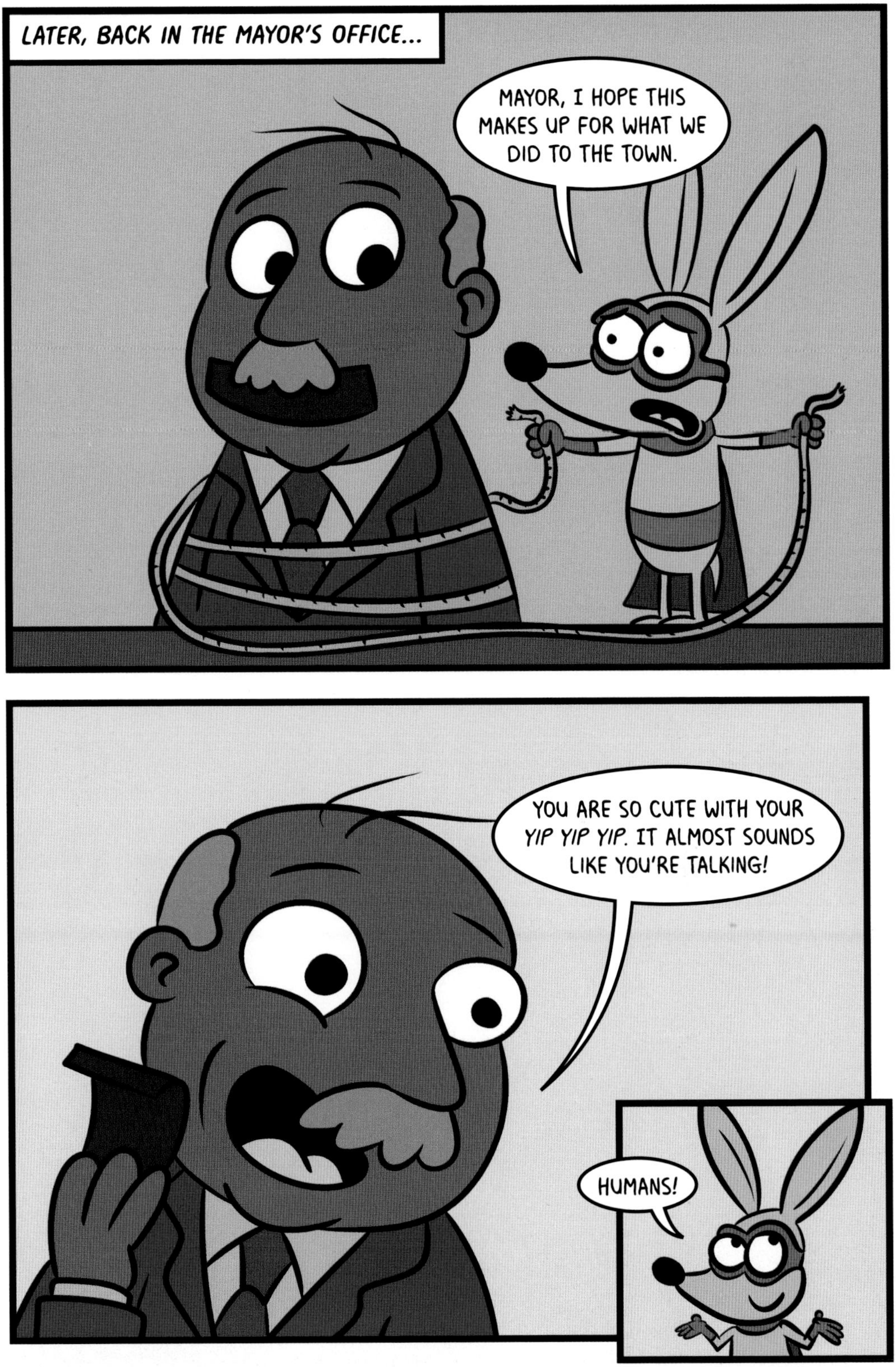
LATER, BACK IN THE MAYOR'S OFFICE...
MAYOR, I HOPE THIS MAKES UP FOR WHAT WE DID TO THE TOWN.
YOU ARE SO CUTE WITH YOUR *YIP YIP YIP*. IT ALMOST SOUNDS LIKE YOU'RE TALKING!
HUMANS!

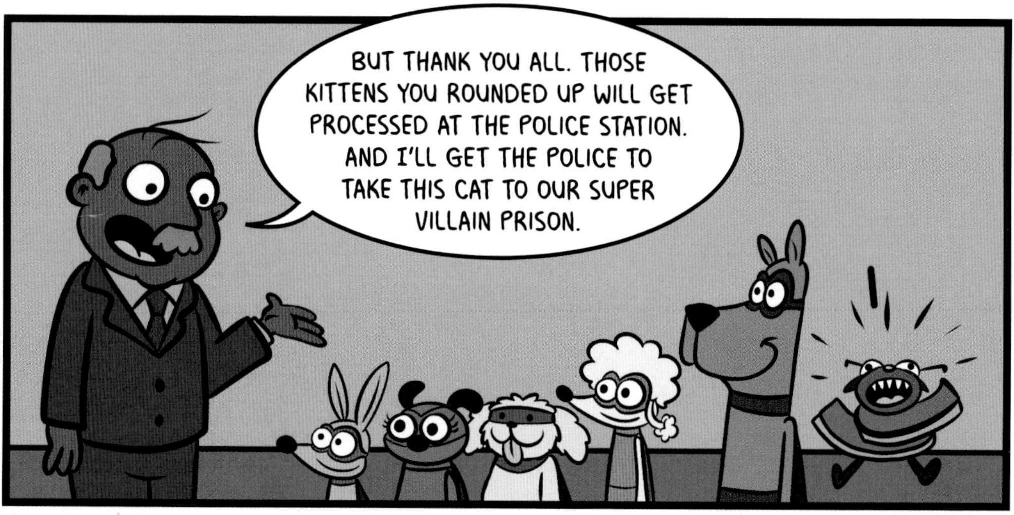
BUT THANK YOU ALL. THOSE KITTENS YOU ROUNDED UP WILL GET PROCESSED AT THE POLICE STATION. AND I'LL GET THE POLICE TO TAKE THIS CAT TO OUR SUPER VILLAIN PRISON.

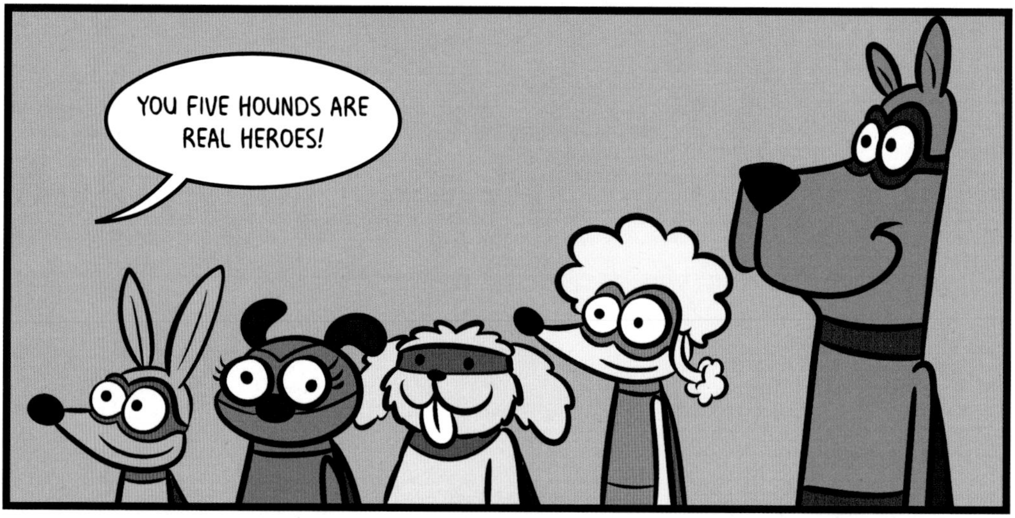
YOU FIVE HOUNDS ARE REAL HEROES!

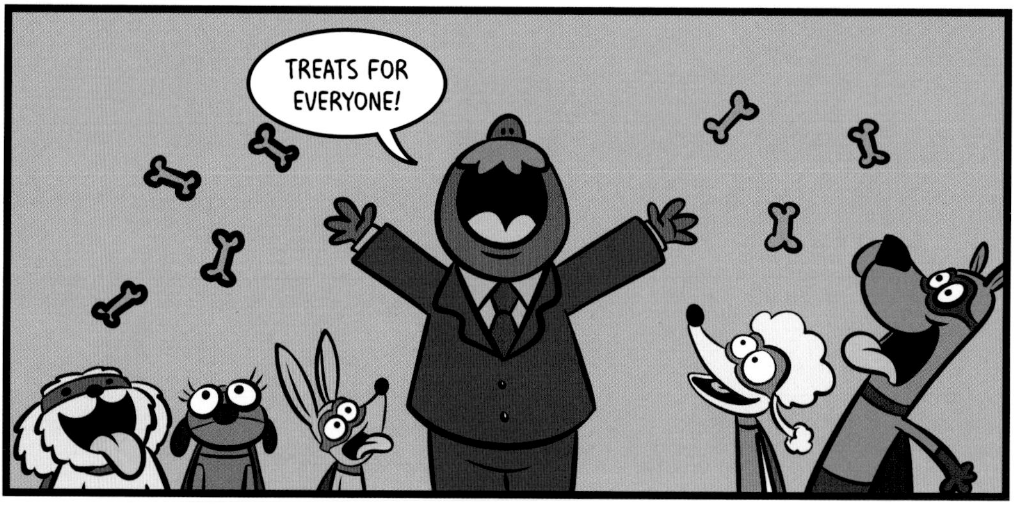
TREATS FOR EVERYONE!

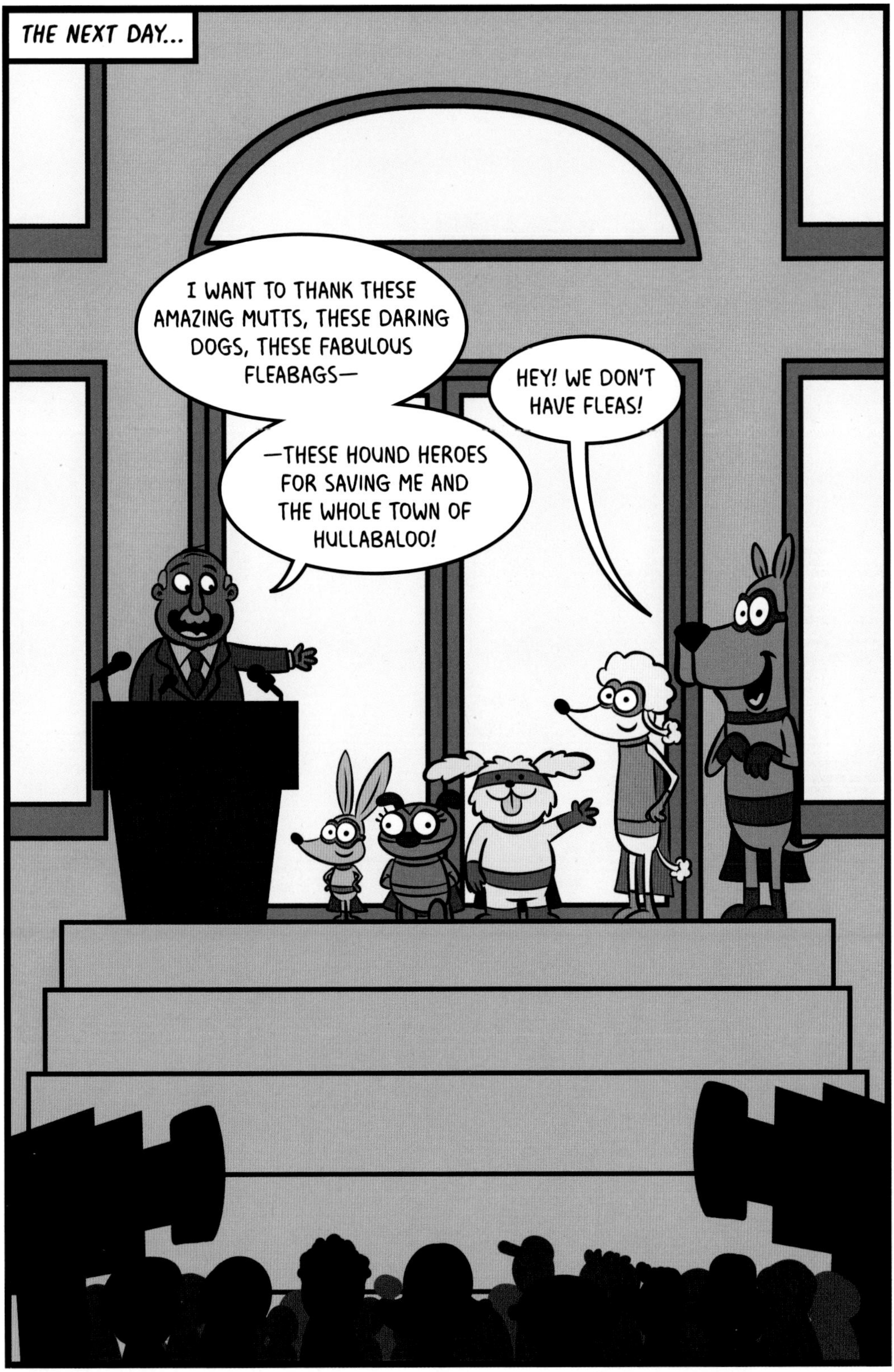
THE NEXT DAY...
I WANT TO THANK THESE AMAZING MUTTS, THESE DARING DOGS, THESE FABULOUS FLEABAGS—
—THESE HOUND HEROES FOR SAVING ME AND THE WHOLE TOWN OF HULLABALOO!
HEY! WE DON'T HAVE FLEAS!

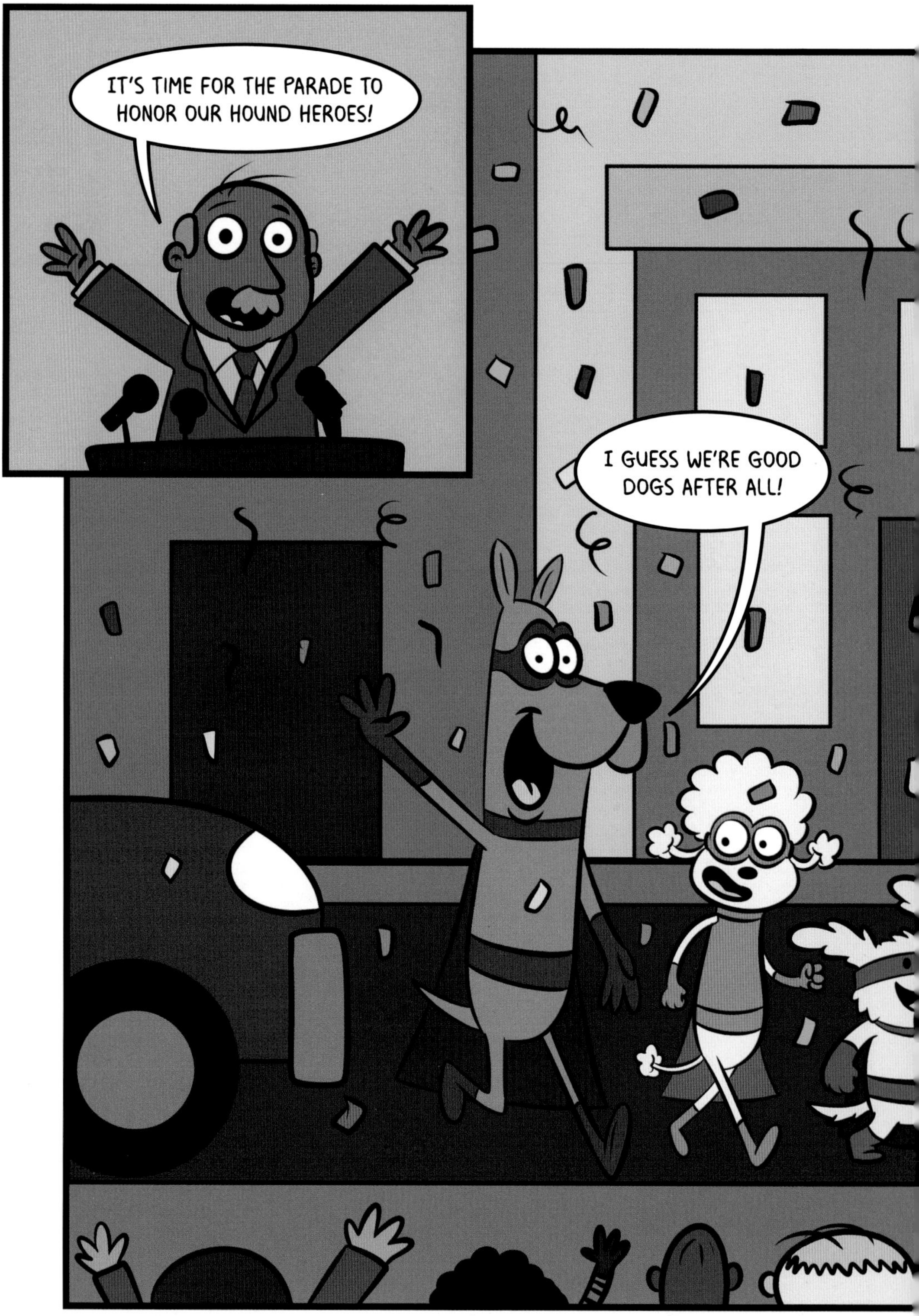
IT'S TIME FOR THE PARADE TO HONOR OUR HOUND HEROES!
I GUESS WE'RE GOOD DOGS AFTER ALL!

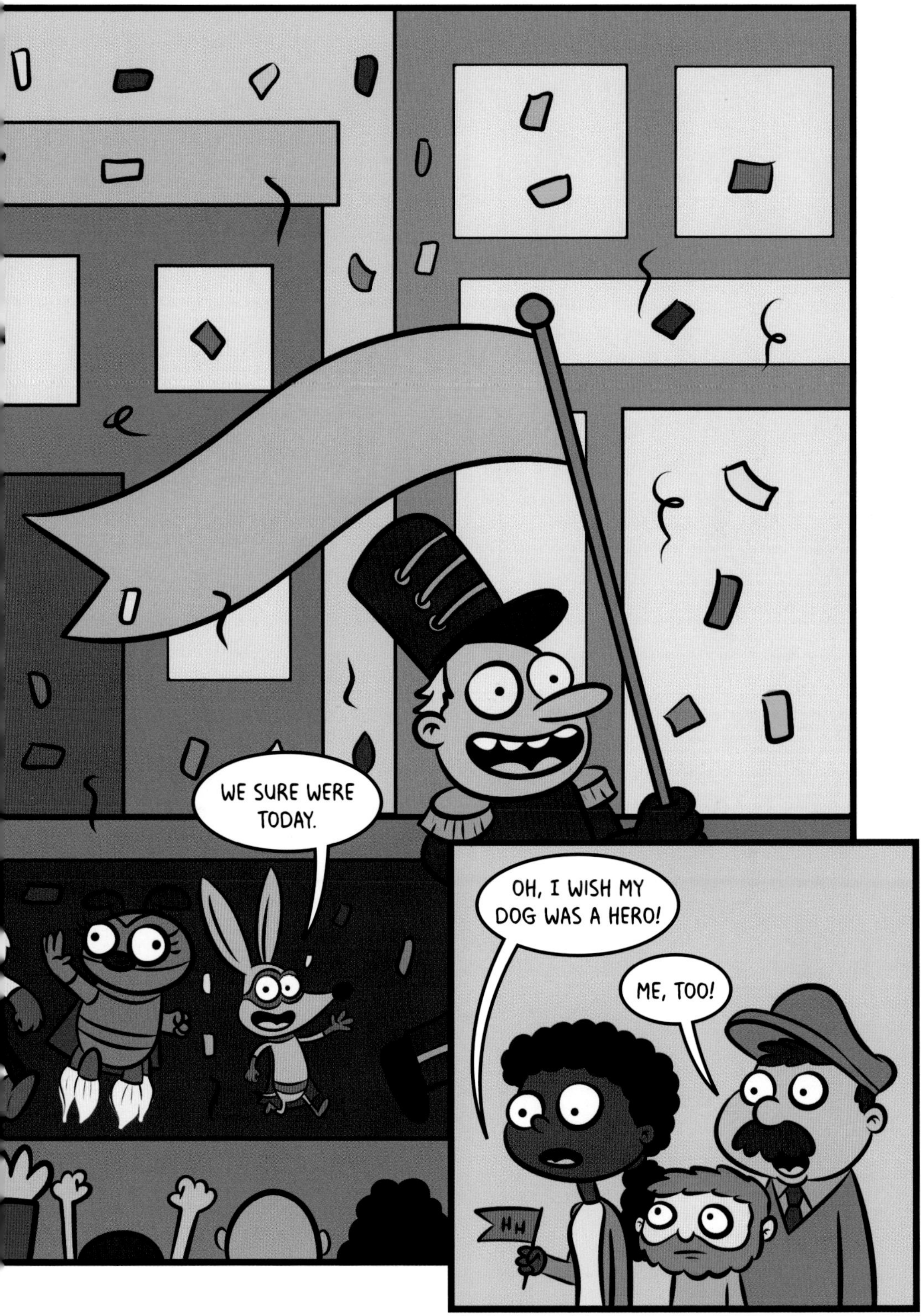

WE SURE WERE TODAY.
OH, I WISH MY DOG WAS A HERO!
ME, TOO!
HH

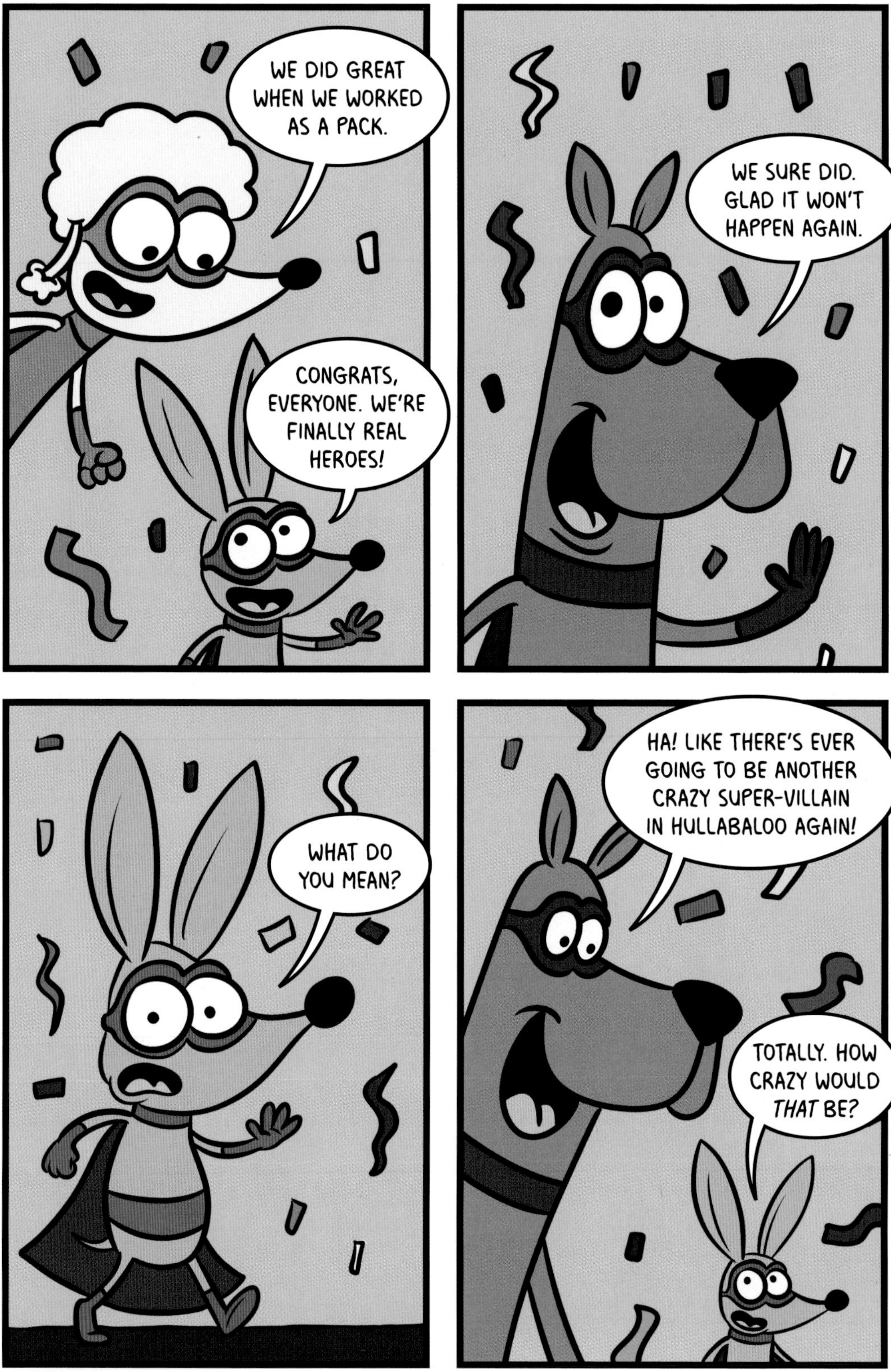
WE DID GREAT WHEN WE WORKED AS A PACK.
CONGRATS, EVERYONE. WE'RE FINALLY REAL HEROES!
WE SURE DID. GLAD IT WON'T HAPPEN AGAIN.
WHAT DO YOU MEAN?
HA! LIKE THERE'S EVER GOING TO BE ANOTHER CRAZY SUPER-VILLAIN IN HULLABALOO AGAIN!
TOTALLY. HOW CRAZY WOULD *THAT* BE?

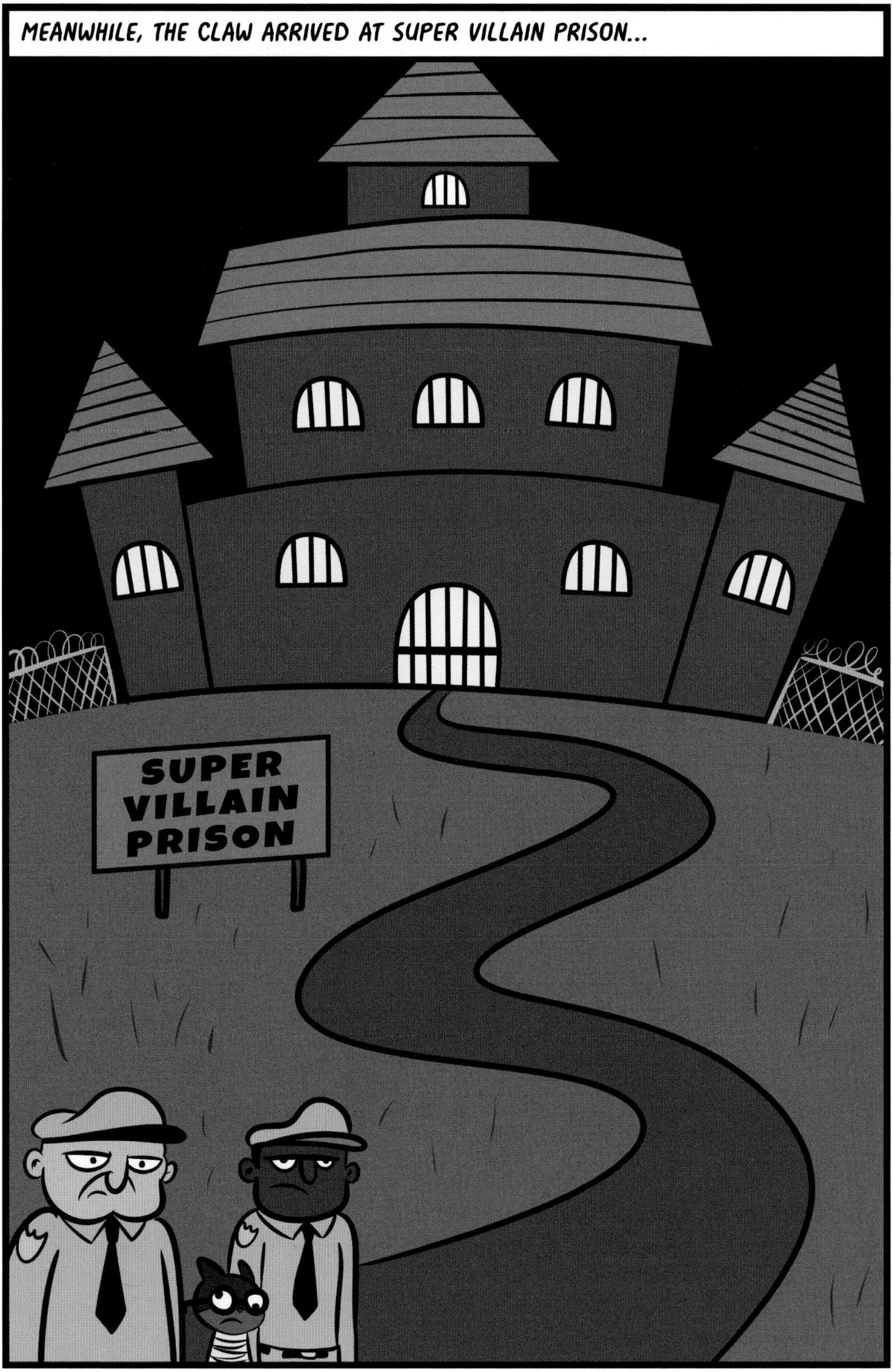
MEANWHILE, THE CLAW ARRIVED AT SUPER VILLAIN PRISON...
SUPER VILLAIN PRISON

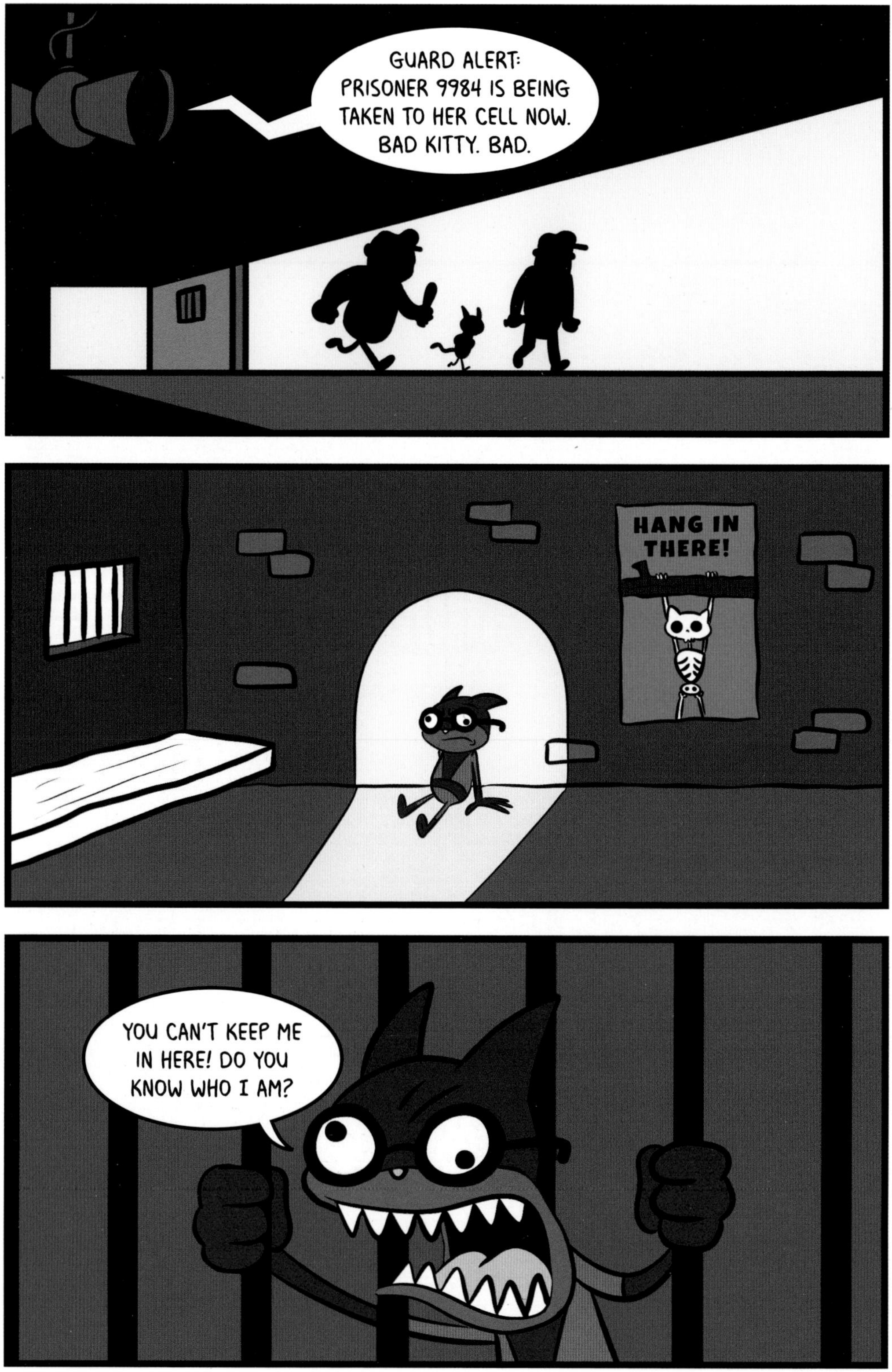
GUARD ALERT: PRISONER 9984 IS BEING TAKEN TO HER CELL NOW. BAD KITTY. BAD.
HANG IN THERE!
YOU CAN'T KEEP ME IN HERE! DO YOU KNOW WHO I AM?

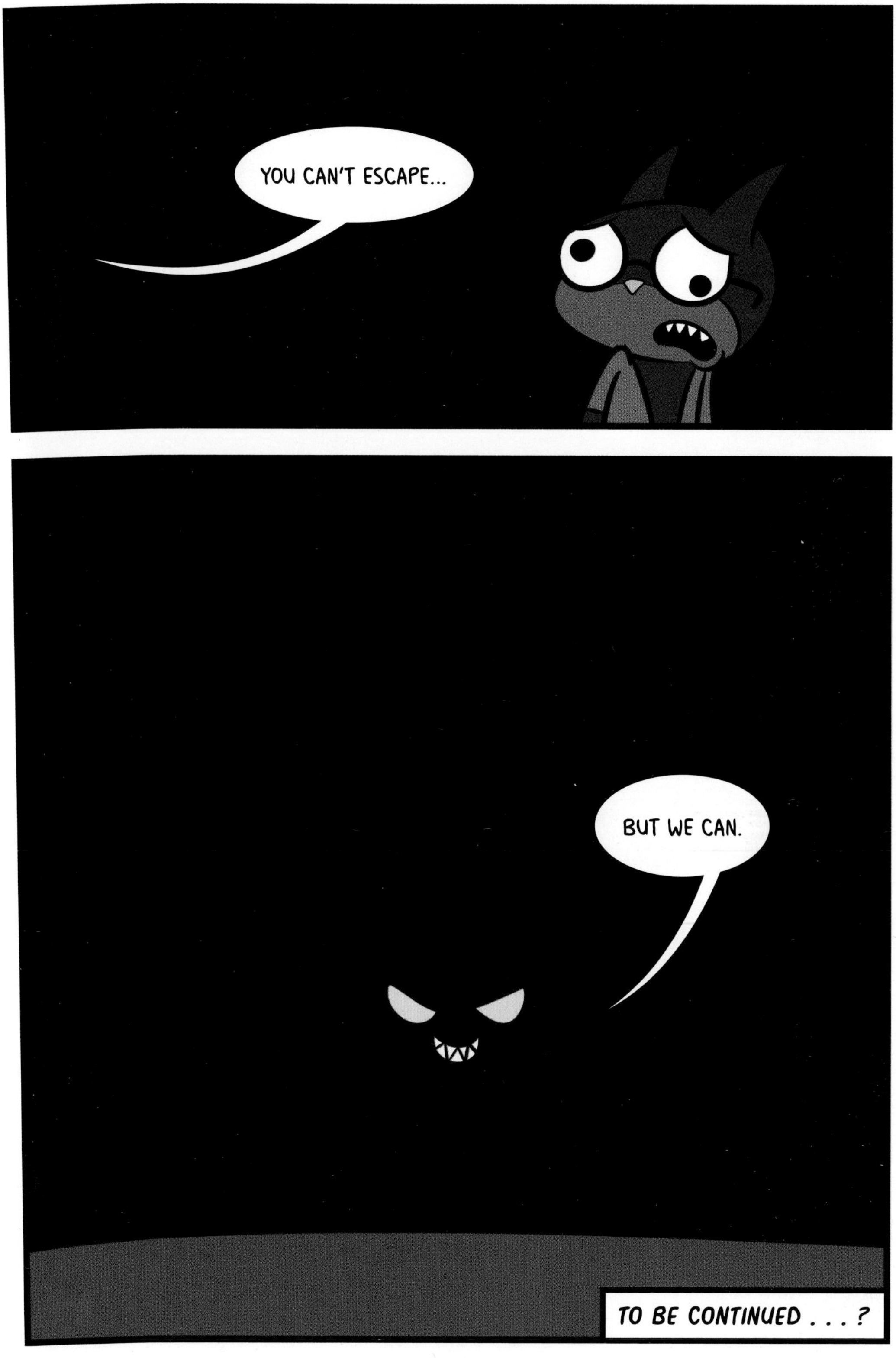
YOU CAN'T ESCAPE...
BUT WE CAN.
TO BE CONTINUED . . . ?

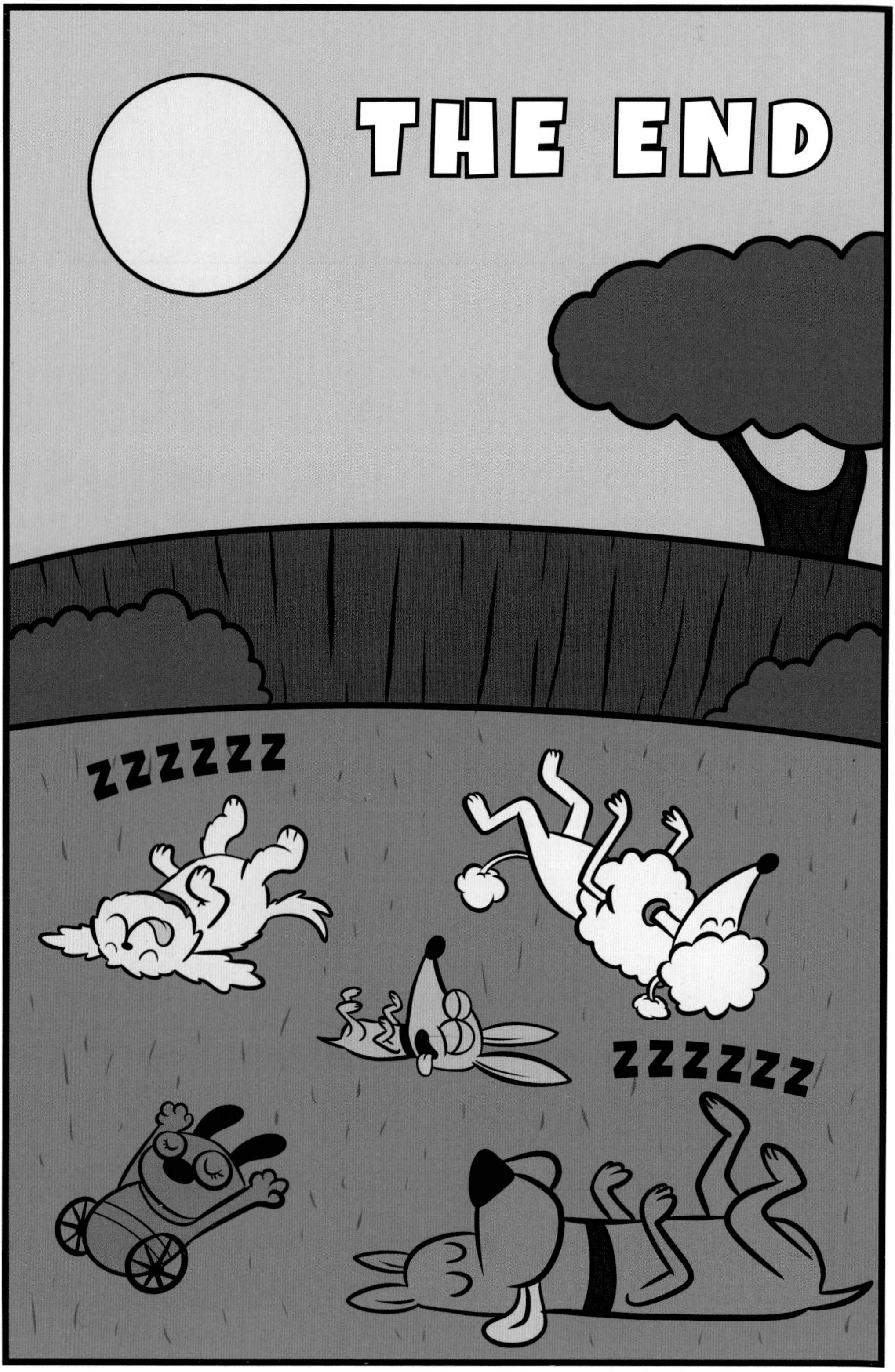
THE END
ZZZZZZ
ZZZZZZ